Acclaim for
The Genuine, Imitation, Plastic Kidnapping

"The most unrepentantly funny crime caper you'll ever find between the pages of a book. Elmore Leonard, eat your heart out!"
—Maegan Beaumont, author of
Carved in Darkness

"Les Edgerton serves up a gumbo of sexual deviants, small time hustlers, and serious criminals in a caper that reads like a deranged Damon Runyon tale relocated from Broadway to the French Quarter. *The Genuine, Imitation, Plastic Kidnapping* is not for the faint of heart, and that's just one of its selling points. If you like crime fiction that cracks wise while offering a peek into the darker recesses, this is the book for you."
—Bill Fitzhugh, author of
Pest Control and *The Exterminators*

"*The Genuine, Imitation, Plastic Kidnapping* is a dark crime comedy that will have you laughing from page one. It crackles with manic energy and mad thrills. If you're looking for a different kind of edgy crime novel, this is the one to grab."
—Bill Crider, author of
the Sheriff Dan Rhodes mysteries

"What makes this wild, wild tale so intriguing is the sense that it *must* be drawing on first-hand knowledge. Edgerton's sympathetic tough guy narrator gives you an authentic-feeling glimpse into the unique logic of small-time hustlers and born losers."
—Matthew Louis, author of
The Wrong Man and *Collision Cocktail*

"Masquerading as a novel, Les Edgerton's newest gem—*The Genuine, Imitation, Plastic Kidnapping*—is really a debauched weekend in steamy New Orleans, loaded with alcohol, drugs, whores, pistols, and a menacing bookie, all available for your personal and private entertainment between the covers. Narrator Pete Halliday—ex-con, gambler, boozer, ex-baseball pitcher and unwise wiseass—takes us places most don't really want to go, only to have the time of our lives when we get there."

—Jack Getze, author of
the Austin Carr mysteries

"There are two certainties when reading anything written by Les Edgerton. First, you'll get gritty, hard hitting noir straight out the top drawer that'll leave you punch drunk on the floor. Second is it'll be like nothing you've ever picked up before. *The Genuine, Imitation, Plastic Kidnapping* is no exception. Expect the unexpected. Read it, love it."

—Keith Nixon, author of *The Fix*

"There's nothing fake about *The Genuine, Imitation, Plastic Kidnapping*. Les Edgerton's latest book is the real deal, and has everything to keep you turning the pages. It's a caper, full of fun and high-jinx, but it's also bittersweet, engendering a full range of emotions. You'll smile, you'll wince, you'll laugh out loud, and sometimes you'll even cringe, but you'll come away from the read feeling thoroughly satisfied and entertained. A terrific read."

—Matt Hilton, author of
the best-selling Joe Hunter thrillers

"When it comes to writing crime stories, Les Edgerton can do pretty much it all, and *The Genuine, Imitation, Plastic Kidnapping* finds him in a mood to have fun. This book is like a raucous party for crime fiction lovers, complete with goons, guns, and schemes-within-schemes. Best of all, the comic voice of its ne'er-do-well narrator is a pleasure from start to finish."

—Jake Hinkson, author of
Hell on Church Street and *The Posthumous Man*

THE GENUINE, IMITATION, PLASTIC KIDNAPPING

ALSO BY LES EDGERTON

Memoir
Adrenaline Junkie

The Rapist
The Bitch
Just Like That
Bomb! (formerly *The Perfect Crime*)
Mirror, Mirror (*)
The Death of Tarpons

Short Story Collections
Monday's Meal
Lagniappe

Writer's How-to Craft Books
Finding Your Voice
Hooked

Sports Books
Surviving Little League (co-authored with son Mike when he was twelve)
Perfect Game USA and the Future of Baseball

Other books on business, hairstyling, etc.

(*) - forthcoming

LES EDGERTON

THE GENUINE, IMITATION, PLASTIC KIDNAPPING

Down & Out Books
3959 Van Dyke Rd, Ste. 265
Lutz, FL 33558
www.DownAndOutBooks.com

Cover design by JT Lindroos

ISBN: 1-937495-79-5
ISBN-13: 978-1-937495-79-4

For the loves of my life:
Mary, Britney, Sienna, Maria and Mike. Always.

For the only editor/publisher to ever stalk me.
Thanks, Eric Campbell!

And a big shout-out to the cover designer,
JT Lindroos who created the amazing cover.

And as always: for my readers. Without readers, writing is
like having sex with yourself. The feedback you get
for your performance is ultimately flawed.

And, lastly, for my best friend, Tom Rough, just because
he's the guy I want most to watch while he's reading this.
He has the best sense of humor in the universe and if
he laughs, I know it's funny. The pressure's on, Tom...

2003

A STREETCAR *NOT* NAMED DESIRE

The first glitch came up right away. In fine-tuning the kidnap plan, in which Tommy explained we'd go in dressed in three-piece suits like insurance salesmen in case any neighbors were up and about and noticed two guys dressed like shrimpers at this guy's house early in the morning. Well, I didn't have a three-piece suit and not even a two-piece suit, and upon further researching my memory, didn't even have a sports coat and after quizzing Tommy, discovered he didn't have one either. I figured we'd just go in like we were dressed, but Tommy wouldn't have none'a that.

"Jeez Louise, Pete. We can't do that. This is a big-money community where this guy lives. In-ground swimming pools, that gives you any idea. We show up looking like we usually dress, there's gonna be some dame across the street calling the cops for the two guys look like a home-invasion team."

Turns out he had a plan to get us a few bucks to get suits with. It was a strange-enough idea I thought it could work. I guess you had to be there when he was laying it down. Sounded righteous enough then…I mean, the guy was an Indian…

An hour later, Tommy and me are sitting on the St. Charles streetcar, at the stop by the zoo down by Club 4141, watching people get on in the front. The last two on are a young tourist couple in matching yellow Bermuda shorts.

"Cool," Tommy said. "Tourists. They'll have cash." He took a drag from his cigarette. He was sitting directly under the "No Smoking" sign, but held it outside the window.

I didn't disagree. There were maybe fifteen people on board, not counting us and the motorman. This was looking better and better. Might get as much as a couple of thousand out of this crew. Get us suits somewhere else than the bargain bins of the Men's Wearhouse.

"See that?" Tommy said. I followed his eyes which were locked on the buxom female member of the tourist couple. She was a looker.

"Yeah? So?"

"So this." He brought his forearm up, pretending to take a bite out of it.

"You wish," I said, grinning.

"Yeah, well I got something her boyfriend ain't."

I laughed out loud. "Right, Tommy. Ugliness. But I think she's maybe one of those weirdos goes for brains and looks. At least one of those."

Tommy turned and gave me a look. "I'm talking technique here," he said. "I got this technique."

"Technique?"

"Technique."

"What...you got a cute way of gettin' on and off?"

"Naw, man," he said, shaking his head like he can't believe how dumb I am. "That's like a big dick. Everybody's got that."

I snickered. "I don't recall you was so blessed in the big wang department, Tommy."

"Yeah, well I was cold that time. We just got out of the lake, for crissake. See, Pete, being a champion at sex is like being good at basketball. You got to be able to go strong to the hole."

There was a young gal behind us who I could see was trying to ignore what Tommy was saying. She squirmed in her seat and studied the scenery out the window, them mansions sliding by.

I was dying to know Tommy's "technique," and asked him.

"I piss in 'em," he said.

The gal behind us grabbed her purse and sniffed, loud, got up and moved three rows back to the last seat.

"Fuck you, lady," Tommy muttered. "You don't like the conversation, relocate."

I couldn't help smiling. "She did. What's this pissing thing?"

I saw the street sign flash by. Coming up was where we planned to do our thing. The corner where St. Charles turned onto Carrollton, by the Camellia Grill. Three blocks from where we'd stashed Tommy's Nova to make our getaway.

"Never mind," I said. "Here it comes. You ready?"

"I was born ready," Tommy said. He stood up and reached his hand into his waistband.

The gal who had relocated screamed out, "This man has a gun!"

Shit.

The streetcar went nuts. Pandemonium erupted—passengers screaming, brakes screeching as the conductor slammed the car to a half. Tommy lost his balance and recovered. The tourist woman in the front screamed one long banshee scream—*Ayyeeeaah!* She's just one long scream, punctuated only by the times she has to draw breath.

Eeeeeeeeeaaaaaayaaaaah! Ayaayaaya! Aaaaaayaeeee!

"Shut up!" Tommy screamed. "Shut the fuck up!"

He looked down at me where I was just kind of sitting, pretty much in shock.

"You on a break here, Pete?"

I just gawked at him. This wasn't what I'd envisioned. His eyes left mine and I followed his stare to the gal who'd blown the whistle on us in the rear seat. She had a gun out, trained on him with both hands, just like they do on TV. I couldn't move. My entire life didn't flash before my eyes, but about twenty-six years and three months of it did.

"I'm throwing up in my mouth, is what I'm doing," I said.

What had I got into?

"You'll wanna brush your teeth before you kiss any girls, then," he said.

Tommy brought his own gun up to bear on the woman in back, same two-handed grip she had. Mexican standoff.

He turned his head slightly down to me, still keeping his gaze on the woman. "Shoot her!" he said. This was just completely fucked.

"You got the gun, Captain Marvel," I said, finally. "*You* shoot her."

Instead of answering or shooting her, he began to back up toward the front door, his piece still trained on the woman. I got up to follow him. It got worse. Four people in the back pulled out weapons and pointed them our way.

"Shit! Shit, shit!" It was all Tommy could say. My sentiments exactly.

I had to hand it to him, though. He didn't lose it.

"Look, folks," he said. "We're gonna just get off now, leave all you good people be. Everybody just stay calm."

One of the male armed passengers near the back door stood up. He said, "Like hell. I'm taking you out, cowboy."

I felt like I was going to pass out.

The conductor opened the back door with his control and stood up. "Let 'em go," he said. "I don't want no blood in my car."

The guy with the gun didn't like what he was hearing. "Aw, man," he said in a whiney voice. "You can't just let criminals roam around. We got to take a stand. This is New Orleans, not Fucking-Pansy-Ass-New-York-City. We don't take no prisoners in this town."

"Listen, Dirty Harry," the conductor said. "This is *my* streetcar. *I* make the rules. Siddown and shut up and let these folks pass."

Tommy ran for the door and I was closer than his shadow behind him, leaping off a nanosecond after he did, scrambling as fast as we could across the street.

The mouthy man and the woman in back opened up with their pistolas. I didn't turn back to look, just kept running as hard as I could, but I heard glass shattering, people screaming, and the pop-pop-pop of handguns. Something whizzed just past my ear and I was pretty sure it wasn't a mosquito unless insects came in calibers. I ran smack into a braking car, bounced off the hood, got up and kept on running. My side was on fire. Any second now, I imagined a hot piece of lead finding my skull or some other tender part. The regrets were coming as fast as the bullets and I kept wondering like you do in such times of stress when it was exactly that God had dropped my case and went off to take a nap or something.

I knew when. Like all of my wrong turns, it had started with my gambling jones.

1993

Ten years before we had to jump off that streetcar, I'm in Scottsdale, Arizona at the Giants' park and sitting in the bullpen enjoying the crap out of the last game of spring training before we headed north. On my way to the Show. Better, I am about to win a shitload of money for the game we was currently engaged in against the fucking Dodgers. Well, at least get even with my bookie and that *was* a boatload. Plus, there was a hottie in the stands who kept showing me she'd forgot to wear her panties that day. Shining me two smiles: one horizontal and one vertical.

Two outs down and one more inning after this one and we'd would nail down the win over those assholes and I was feeling it. Only one man—catcher Mike Piazza—had reached base on a walk. Piazza had just stolen second and then third and that pissed all of us off. Catchers weren't supposed to steal.

The bullpen phone rang and it was Dusty. I could see him where he stood on the dugout steps and he was tapping his right arm. Dick Pole, our bullpen coach picked up the phone.

"Halliday!" he said. "Pete! Get warm."

Shit. I'd been nipping on a half-pint of Southern Comfort since the top of the second, knowing I wasn't going to play today. Why the fuck did Piazza have to steal third?

I knew why Baker wanted me.

See, I have a unique talent. As a relief pitcher, I'm so-so. I mean, I'm good enough to make a major league club. Got enough arm I can mop up, burn an inning or two with my junk, but what I really was was a one-out specialist.

My pick-off move. With variations. At one time, I had probably the best pick-off move in baseball. Well, in the National League. Well, to be more precise, in our division. Well, one of the best, anyway. On our club, for sure. Possibly.

I knew what Dusty wanted me to do. Get Piazza, get us out of the inning. He didn't even want me to pitch to the Dodger's second baseman Jody Reed who was standing there waiting on me. Just get Piazza. You gotta remember, nobody knew who Piazza was then. It was his rookie year, 1993. Nobody knew he'd end up being kind of good and winning the Rookie of the Year Award that year. He was just a dumb-fuck catcher then, and Dusty was pissed he'd stole a base. Two bases.

And, yeah, that was the plan. Instead of the pitching coach coming out to hand me the ball, it was Dusty.

"You been drinking, Halliday?" he said, sniffing the air and leaning in close to me when he handed me the ball.

Before I could lie, he said, "Ne'mind. Get Piazza. You got one pitch. I don't want you to throw to Reed. You throw even one pitch to Reed you'll be picking splinters out of your butt in Valdosta."

"Sure, Skip," I said, all teeth and outright joy. "Appreciate your confidence in me."

Kirt Manwaring, our catcher who hadn't said anything, just shook his head in disgust, spit a goober on the mound about where I usually set up and went back to the plate.

Reed stepped in, waggled his bat like he thought he was Henry Aaron, and Manwaring give me the sign. He showed the middle finger, which wasn't in our usual repertoire and I nodded. I went into the stretch—even though I didn't have to with nobody on first, except the stretch gave me a better line on what I intended to do than a full windup—whirled, and caught Piazza off the bag. He was only six-seven feet off—nobody in the park thought he'd even try to steal home. It was the perfect lead for what I wanted. He started to turn lazily to step back to the bag...and crumpled in the dirt.

I'd hit him in the nuts, a second before he'd turned.

Yelled, "Bam, sucka!" at the same instant I threw.

Plan A.

Never meant to throw to our third-sacker. Hit my target just like I'd drawn it up in my mind and like Dusty knew I would. Just another diamond accident.

Down he went on the ground, writhing like he'd been suddenly struck by the Holy Spirit and screeching in what mighta passed for those tongues which some churches favor. Our third baseman Matt Williams reached down, picked up the ball and tagged Piazza.

"Yer out!" screamed Blue, and then at me he yelled, "Watch your mouth, pitcher," and we all headed for the dugout, streaming around Tommy Lasorda who'd come out to argue the call, which got the same result as it usually does, allowing Tommy to get back to their hotel pool early, start working on his tan.

The crowd erupted the instant Blue's arm went up. Some old guy near our dugout fell over with a heart attack. After all, this was Scottsdale, one of God's primo waiting rooms, and if he hadn't keeled over then, he probably would have next day at the dog track, happen he was holding a winning two-dollar ticket.

The crowd wasn't done; came to its feet, roared "Charge" in a single voice. On my way in, I looked over at the hottie, who was waving with a cheerleader's practiced wave. Everyone in the stands were on their feet, I see, save one man two seats behind the dugout, attired in a blue suit. The only guy in the stands in formal attire. Weird. The organist struck up the William Tell Overture.

Inning over. One to go.

Everybody else sprinted to the dugout while I strode in with a king's mien. Kings don't run. I did take care to step over the first-base foul line. I didn't want any bad luck today.

The crowd still stood, yelling its lungs out. Everyone was

standing except the guy in the blue suit, I saw, when I popped out for a curtain call.

Just before I got to the dugout steps, I touched the bill of my cap, milking the crowd for another cheer and they obliged.

Dusty Baker was the first to meet me, putting his arm around me at the top of the dugout steps. "Man, Pete! That sure killed their rally! Perfect throw!"

We headed down the steps. Dusty grinned. "I only wish you had that kind of control on your pitches to the plate."

I grinned back. "Cap, you know you love me. I put butts in the seats."

Baker shook his head and went back up to the top of the dugout steps as Will Clark came up to lead off the last inning.

I wandered past the other players over to the dugout phone and dialed a number.

Dusty looked over. "Who you calling, Halliday? You got no business on that phone."

I started to hang up, then recovered. "Uh, my landlady, Cap. I think I left the windows open. It looks like rain." I turned sideways and spoke into the phone in a low voice. "Yo, Fat. It's me, Pete. I want a dime on Oakland. Same on the Red Sox. Clements goes tomorrow, right?" He said something. I paused. "Hey, man, I'm good. I'm winning this one, big-time. You know I'm—"

I held the phone away from him and saw Dusty mugging on me. I spoke back into the phone in a louder voice. "Yes. That's right. The bedroom window." I hung up, shined a grin at Dusty.

He just stared back, then did a funny thing. He looked straight up at the man in the blue suit sitting two rows up from the dugout. The man seemed intent on a device in his ear. A wire extended from the device to his pocket.

Just then, Will Clark, our first batter, smacked a ball that everyone in the park knew instantly was long gone. Out of the corner of my eye as I rushed to the front of the dugout with my teammates to cheer Will on, I saw Dusty watch his home run trot, then turn back to look at the man in the stands. The man nodded, removed the device from his ear and put it in his pocket. Dusty threw down his lineup card in disgust.

What the hell?

I hooked up with the girl in the stands as soon as the game was over and it turned out her name was Wendy. Big surprise. "With an 'i'," she said. "It was a 'y' when I was born, but I changed it." She squealed when I asked if she used a little heart instead of a dot over it. I think it convinced her I had extrasensory perception skills. "How 'bout we meet up at the Cowboy and Goat Roper's Saloon," I said. "Maybe around nine tonight?"

"Sure," she said, her chewing gum flying out and bouncing off my chest when she opened her mouth. She wasn't even embarrassed, which I took to be a good sign.

An hour after the game, I was still in my uniform, minus my jersey, shooting some stick with Salomon Torres. It wasn't the happy clubhouse it should have been. The Dodgers came back the last inning and put eight up and just like that, spring training was over. So was my plan to get square with my bookie, but hell, we were headed to S.F. in the morning. I was kind of sticking around in the clubhouse in case he'd decided to show up and ask for an installment. Or worse.

Torres broke and put one more ball in and then I ran the table. "Yes!" I said, and made the "cha-ching" guesture of triumph. Torres made a face and handed me a twenty-dollar bill, twisting his face further in disgust. Dusty stuck his head out of his office.

"Halliday! In here."

I glanced around at the few teammates still there. "Skip's gonna give me a bonus, I bet. Probably a new contract."

Over in the corner, Barry Bonds in his Barcolounger, looked up from staring at his own eight by ten glossy and smirked.

"Yeah, you the man, Pete." The other players laughed.

I breezed into Dusty's office, happy as a traded NY Yankee, kissed the twenty-dollar bill Torres had just handed me, and stuck it in my pocket.

"Siddown," Dusty said. He took the chair in front of the manager's desk.

Someone else was in the office. I hadn't seen him come in so he must have come in through the back. It was the Blue Suit from the stands.

"Sign this," Dusty said.

"What is it?" I said. I leaned forward to see the paper Dusty shoved at me.

"Your outright release."

I was floored. "What the fuck? I missed one lousy sign, Cap. Clark even misses signs. Bonds doesn't even look for 'em."

Dusty sighed, took off his glasses and rubbed his nose. "You ain't Clark, son, and you sure ain't Bonds. It ain't that, anyway. It's your gambling."

"Gambling? Who the fuck says I been gambling?" I looked over at the blue-suited man, gave him a good glare. Somehow, this guy was behind this.

"Me," the man said. "*I* say you've been gambling."

"Who the fuck are you?"

"Vernon Strassler. League office. You want to hear a phone tape?"

I couldn't help it. I groaned and slumped forward in my chair. Strassler placed a small tape recorder on the desk and punched a button.

A deep voice said, "You got the Fatman."

I heard my own voice reply. "Yo, Fat. Me, Pete. Gimme a dime on Oakland. Same on the Red Sox. Clements goes tomorrow, right?"

The deep voice said, "Pay what you owe, Halliday, and we'll talk. By Friday. That means all of it, hotshot."

I moaned again and louder as I listened to my own voice.

"Hey, man. I'm good. I'm winning this one, big-time. You know I'm…" A click sounded, followed by silence. Then: "Yes. That's right. The bedroom—"

Strassler turned off the machine.

Dusty shook his head sadly. "Sorry, son. Sign this for your severance pay."

I straightened up. "Dusty, I'll lay you five to one, if you give me another chance you'll never catch me gambling again. I—"

"The check's for ten thousand, Pete. You can thank me for the extra. The club was only going to give you five. We'll keep this out of the papers and expect you to do the same."

There wasn't anything left to do. I picked up the check and looked it over. I started to say something and ended up shaking my head and picking up the pen on the desk and signing the release form.

Dusty stood up and I followed his lead and took his offered hand for a last handshake.

"You know, kid," Dusty said, indicating the meeting was over. "It's none of my business, but you might want to look at your life. Gambling's cost you a wife and now baseball."

Bright and early the next morning, a woman teller counted out bills, put them in an envelope and handed it to me. I thanked her, stuck the envelope in my pocket and left.

I was walking down the bank steps when two men came up, one a beefy mountain of a man and the other slight and swarmy. They came up beside me, took me by the elbows and hustled me down the steps. All three of us walked to the alley beside the bank and went on back to a pair of dumpsters.

The big guy spun me around and pinned an armlock on me. The little guy snatched the envelop from his pocket, tore it open and counted the money. "Damn," he said, "Where's the other five?"

I frowned. "It's in the mail? You buy that?"

The little guy placed the wad of bills in his jacket pocket and nodded to his large partner who gripped me tighter. "Wise guy, huh?" the little guy said.

"Well, you wouldn't know it by my SATs. You know what? You look familiar. I got it! Your mom."

"My mom?" the little goon said.

"Yeah," I said. "Your mom. We been dating. Whenever I have an extra twenty. I just love it when she takes out her false teeth. You know…" I went on. "I might end up your stepfather. Think she'd grow a mustache for me?"

The little guy hauled off and socked me in the gut. I collapsed and struggled to right myself and get my breath back.

"Yeah," I said, wheezing my words out. "You hit about like your mom. I can see you're related. I suppose you wanna give me a blowjob now?"

"You fuck," the little guy screamed, and hit me again. As I folded in half like a WWII Japanese foot soldier unexpectedly finding himself in the same room as the Emperor, the little guy grabbed my hand and brought it around and secured it between his arm and chest. He bent four of my fingers back until they cracked. Audibly. Almost as loud as the scream I gave out, feeling like a complete bitch when I did, but couldn't help it.

When I woke up, I was lying in a hospital bed, my hand splinted and bandaged and feeling like I imagined those pennies we'd put on railroad tracks when we were kids might have if they had nerves running through Lincoln's face. Worse.

At least it wasn't my pitching hand. Not that it much mattered any more.

Two men were sitting there, staring at me. A white man and a black man.

My teammates. Rod "Shooter" Beck and Willie McGee.

Willie, said, "Dusty wanted to come, Pete, but the club had a fit."

"Loyal fuck, isn't he. At least you guys came."

Both men looked at each other. Rod said, "Some shit, huh, Pete? Almost make it to the Show and this is what you get. What're you gonna do now?"

Up to that minute, I hadn't thought much about it. I made my decision right then. "I'm going home to New Orleans." I worked up a grin. "This little setback is just a speed bump on my way to riches."

"You gonna keep on gambling, Pete?" Rod said. "Might want to reconsider that." Willie nodded in agreement.

"Nah," I said. "I'm done with that. It's time I used some of my mental dexterity."

"You're gonna keep feedin' that gamblin' jones, aren't you?" Willie said.

"No way, Jose. Gambling's a loser's game. I found that out the hard way. No, I bet you guys a hundred bucks each I'm back on my feet in a week. A month, tops. I'll be watching you guys in the World Series from my private box. Lighting Cubans with C-notes.

"I'm giving two to one odds," I said as they made their way out of the room. "No, *three* to one. Wait!"

They must not have heard me.

2003

BECAUSE SUPERMARKETS ARE WHERE THE MONEY IS...
(PARAPHRASING OF FAMOUS WILLIE SUTTON QUOTE)

That was all leading up to that close call I had with Tommy LeClerc down there in New Orleans, the time I succumbed to Tommy's numskull scheme to kidnap old man Deneuvé, and ransom him in a new, ingenious way...but then it isn't like it's the first time my brain waves have been snagged in the throes of an electrical brownout either, so maybe I ought to shoulder *some* of the blame for what went wrong if I was to be fair about it.

Except...I don't feel much like being fair about it. After all, it's not like I would have thought up such a lamebrain stunt on my own. No, the only man in town capable of an idiot plan of such magnitude was Tommy.

And the only man in town dumb enough to take part in it was...yours truly.

Old man Deneuvé. Otherwise and popularly known and referred to as "The Cajun Mafia King." Which, for anyone with the brains of a banana, should have been reason enough to never go within ten miles of the man, much less put the snatch on.

Not us geniuses. Not Tommy LeClerc and Pete Halliday.

If I'd only stayed with baseball, maybe none of this would have happened. I'm not saying I would've ended up in the Hall of Fame with Walter Johnson and Bob Feller and those other Legends of the Mound, but then again, who knows? I had some talent, no lie, and if the luck that came my way would have been good instead of terrible, maybe it'd be *my* glove you'd be gazing at on your vacation to Cooperstown, alongside Warren Spahn's. Well, my *hat* anyway. My cup?

The point is, I wasn't in the World Series where I should have been—I'm down in New Orleans, over in Fat City in Metry where the real non-tourist night life is, the pro's party playground, and things went on that were mostly out of my control, things that just sort of happened, and I'm knee-deep with the rest of the hogs before I realize we're bound for bacon, and isn't that a pretty accurate commentary on life itself!

It also got me hooked up with Cat. That's something for which on the one hand, I'll never forgive Tommy for—and on the other, I guess I can never thank him enough. I love her dearly and hardly ever throw it up to her about the loss of my former state of pure bachelor bliss and previous general abundant happiness which is now in abeyance and on hold. It probably wouldn't do much good to mention anyhow as, like as not, she'd come up with some smart-aleck remark about how I sound pretty sassy for someone whose life she helped to preserve and save. And isn't *that* just like a woman, too, to constantly keep bringing up and harping on every single little tiny favor they ever done for you, all the do-da day! But I love her, I surely do, and have bigger regrets in life than sharing the same bungalow and four-poster with her lovely self.

Maybe changing my name is really what started it all…

See, Pete's not my real name. Oh, it is, but it's my middle name, not the one I was referred to when I was a kid, or even when I was a six-foot, one-half-inch, one hundred-forty-three-pound nineteen-year-old baseball phenom throwing seeds over in Marietta in Single A, my eye still on the Bigs. My real name is Evan. When baseball throwed me out and I grasp the obvious fact I'm never going to be eligible for major endorsement bucks, I decided to head for the Big Easy to make my fortune. I suppose I could have settled down in San Fran and got a nine to five and a lunch pail, but it just wasn't in my nature at that time in my life. I had just missed out on the fame and glory a major leaguer gets as his due—I was *this* close—and I couldn't buy into the righteous scene. I needed excitement and I craved chances, mostly the chance to make a lot of money and have a lot of fun. Working in a factory or an office didn't seem to offer those kinds of opportunities. Hustling and being a criminal just seemed right.

Plus, I had a plan. A goal. Something I wanted in the worst way. Something no one in my family had ever had.

Independence. *True* independence. The kind you never get, working for somebody else. My pie in the sky was to become an entrepreneur, a businessman. Specifically, my dream was to get into the food business, own a po-boy restaurant. Nothing big or fancy, just po-boy sandwiches, shrimp, oyster po-boys and whatnot, and longneck beers, maybe whip up a little homemade boudin or andouille for the coonass trade. "Work for someone else, all you ever do is earn a paycheck; work for yourself and you may get rich," is what my old man always said, and he was right—he always worked for someone else and sure as hell never got rich. Half the time he got stiffed on the paycheck part, too, or at least that's the story he laid on Ma, but I suspect he just misplaced it on his way home, possibly somewhere near the race track.

"I'm sorry, darlin', Mr. Brown says he's a little cash poor this week so he won't be able to give me my pay until sometime after next Tuesday. It's been a tough year for farmers."

Probably some bookie found it and kept it. I figured working a square job would end me up in the same leaky boat as my dad had. No, the only way to achieve my dream wasn't through legal means—the kind of money I needed was only available to crooks, and that is mainly why I threw in with the outlaw element.

Besides, it was fun! Hustling was just downright enjoyable and a pleasure.

Only right away I see the name Evan has got to go, if I want some respect, although I have to admit, I always sorta liked my real name; it's got some pizzazz to it. Every day I'd be elbow to elbow at some bar with bozos with handles like "Billy" and "Bobby Joe" and the like, and I'd think, you'd figure a grown-up man that shaves twice a day would lose the damn "y" at the end of his name and take on the adult version, not keep on answering to some little kid's nickname that oughta be in a Big Mac commercial. And these were the clowns I was worried that would laugh at *my* name! I kept that opinion to myself as I was pretty sure the locals would miss the point.

"What? Your name is what? Evan? Ha! What kind of pansy name is that!"

When I was playing ball, it wasn't too bad; there was a bunch of college boys on the teams I was on with lots worse names than Evan, but the down and dirty crowd I fell in with when I came here to the Big Easy from my little mishap with the Giants didn't have a Rhodes scholar in the bunch, 'cept for Monk the Accountant, who was a principle loan shark, and who didn't come by his name by matriculating at Old Eli, but by the way he could compute compound interest in his head and right there on the spot and have the change right, too.

I could see straight out that a name like Evan was going to be nothing but a source of grief down here in the land of magnolias and Popeye's Spicy Fried Chicken. I'd already experienced some'a that in my halcyon years, guys up in the nickel seats in Scottsdale yelling, "Hey, Eh-vann, honey! What kinda name's that, Precious? No wonder yore ERA is triple yore sister's weight; yore skirts is interferin' with yore sissy fastball!" And other remarks in that vein that kept my social calendar full, busy duking it out with the local beer truck drivers under the stands.

And it wasn't so bad when I played up North, but then I wasn't in the North too much, once with Columbus and then a couple-three months with Rochester, and the whole rest of the time in tank towns like Waycross and Valdosta and Tarpon Springs, places not hardly big enough to support two whores with serious self-respect.

About the only place I played that my name wasn't a source of fun and amusement for the fans, was when I was up with the S.F. Giants for a cup of coffee which was more like a short decaf latte at the end of my final full season, the year before Dusty let me go in spring training. The bums in the suntan seats there didn't comment much on my handle as they were too busy climbing all over me for a few minor fielding misjudgments they thought I made. I'm not saying they were all wrong in their assessments, as perhaps one or two of those miscues were on rollers moving so slow my mom could of reached out and snagged 'em, sittin' in her rocker on the front porch while snapping green beans with her free hand and concentrating on a radio soap opera with the other. Out there, in San Francisco, where the pink flamingo is considered the national bird, the name Evan was kind of a hit. But then, you know, it was S.F. and them people are all named Darryl and Spencer and such.

And, hey, I was a pitcher, not no shortstop. 'Cept for Greg Maddux over in Atlanta, who cares if a pitcher misses a sharp grounder or two?

Anyway, here I was in the Town That Care Forgot, getting by, hustling a little pool, squiring a few older tourist ladies around to the hot spots in the Quarter, stuff like that. Waiting for my big break. When I came here, five years back, I fell in with the smart money boys and they took me under their wing, me being a kind of celebrity and all, having played the national pastime and even being drafted by the same club that Will Clark was on, Will Clark being a bigger name than God or even the sheriff of Jefferson Parish, Harry Lee himself, in these parts. We never hung out much, as we were on somewhat different career paths with different kinds of agents—he had one and I didn't— and were never on the big team at the same time for more than a couple of weeks, nor on any of the minor teams together. I don't believe Will did the minor league thing, come to think of it. I saw him play though. Man! He could just flat *crush* that pea! And look that look. Man! Killer glare is what Will had goin' for him. Scare that ball into the cheap seats.

So the locals adopted me, so to speak, account of my star status, and taught me all kinds of valuable skills, like how a crooked dice game's run, the slickest ways to brother-in-law a poker game, how to run a Ponzi and the Murphy and similar such money-making schemes, and I was playing my way up through the minors once again, you might say, learning the tricks of the scufflin' trade.

Things were pretty good. I was eating regular and only a month or two behind on the rent most of the time, and New Orleans was only the greatest place in the world to live, especially for a guy like me who's smart but mostly self-educated. I'd kind of been all over the map from the time I was a little mug, north, south, east and west. My pap was a pilot and mostly got jobs dusting crops and that meant we went where the work was, which was all over. Wheat in Kansas and citrus in Florida and celery in California. There wasn't a part of the country we hadn't been to at least six times, but the minute we hit New Orleans when I was in high school, I knew I'd come home and wouldn't ever want to live anywhere else. It had everything. Juicy, hot, gorgeous, sexy weather. Lots of folks, even native New Orleanians, hated the weather, but not me. I loved it, basked in it, fondled it, let it pour over me, soak me, drench me. It was like returning to the womb. My *insides* just plain *felt* good in the New Orleans heat. No muscle aches, no bones that creaked in *that* weather! Walk outside at midnight in New Orleans, your balls don't shrivel up in anticipation of Jack Frost like they do in Chicago or Des Moines. Your balls turn into *raisins* in Chicago at midnight, even in August. Not in New Orleans! In New Orleans, if you walk outside at midnight, your gonads expand and grow like they was on cojones steroids.

They become coconuts. They're twice as big as anywhere else on the planet as not only do they have a warm, moist climate to grow in, they get fed hot, spicy food all the time. They feel so good you just have to reach down and massage them every five minutes, in appreciation, let them know how fantastic the rest of your body feels in all that heat, all the parts and organs and limbs and juices, rejoicing, giving thanks and hosannas for their good fortune. That's some weather, brother!

And the chow! Louisiana's washday Monday's red beans and rice are so tangy and spicy you can't wait for Sunday to end! Is there any other place on earth has a meal like red beans and rice? So blistering fiery you can only slew down two, three, maybe four bites before you have to reach for and gulp down a whole, ice-cold longneck in one, long, bone-aching draught to cool the back of your throat, and can you imagine anything half as good as gazing across your plate at a black-haired, green-eyed Cajun sorceress with her round, white, quivering breasts falling plumb out of her red, red teddy as she leans toward you and smiles you her wicked, sparkling, white-toothed smile, and hands you the basket of for-real French bread, the evil, beautiful goddess who brewed up this exquisite feast, laced with spices that you can *feel* speeding toward your sex—can you imagine this!—and can you go away from this place at the bottom of the country once you've seen this and live in Boston or Fort Wayne or Kalamazoo or Salt Lake City, ever again?

I think not.

I couldn't.

New Orleans is a voo-doo spell.

New Orleans is a beautiful, enchanting, malignant, terrible mistress.

It'll suck you in, put a hex on you, make a slave of you.

It's wonderful.

* * *

Like I said, it all began with Tommy and his kidnapping scheme. This was before I found out that for sure, criminally, Tommy was a 15-watt bulb speckled with fly poop. At this point in our relationship, howsomever, he had this reputation of being a master outlaw and having a genius criminal mind. Everybody talked about what a great con Tommy was, what brilliant plans he could cook up with which to separate folks from their wealth. I thought I knew better since I'd already participated in one scheme a year or so before with him. A parking meter caper. That little job hadn't worked out so swell—I've had social diseases turned out better—but I guess I just thought it was one of those unlucky things, at the time. Little did I know that bad luck followed Tommy around, like three a.m. B.O. on a hooker working overtime. In the back of my mind, a kind of alarm went off, but I disregarded it and gave him the benefit of the doubt. I guess I figured his rep was probably well-deserved and our little disaster just one of those things.

Tommy claimed he was a criminal genius because of his Indian blood. Gave him people-reading skills the white-eyes didn't have, was his opinion. Who knows? Although he didn't much act like any Indians you see in the movies.

I was shooting pool in the Swamp Room down in Metry one afternoon, drinking a Barq's and putting the hustle on this off-shore rigger who was just about drunk enough to make me his sole heir, when Tommy walks in and gives me the sign. I didn't want to leave the game, 'specially as how this rhubarb can't lose his money quick enough and keeps springing for the drinks to boot, but since I'm under the mistaken impression that Tommy's one sharp con and I knowed he wouldn't interrupt an obvious business deal like he can see is cooking unless it was for something important, I have to check it out. I go over and whisper to him just in case he's missed the set-up, but he was onto it all right, and says, "Forget this huckleberry, Pete. I got something really big on and I need a pard."

Like I said, everyone knows Tommy's the real thing and never plays for chump change, so he gets my attention right away, even though the old common-sense alarm was buzzing in the background of my brain. I agreed to head over to a little joint in Fat City where we could talk in private, but before I left, I hadda get one more crack at Festus. I wander back over to the rigger and I go, "How about one more for a C-note? I'd stay longer, but that's my brother over there and he tells me Mom's in a bad way over to Charity Hospital and might not last out the night, so I got to go pretty soon."

He's got his money down on the table quicker than a sailor on his first date, and I have a sudden concern about who's tricking who, but no, I read Clem Kadiddlehopper right; he's a non-profit organization looking for ways to go in the red.

This is important money, so we lag for break, sighting down the long green felt, doing the size-up, and I get the honors, which was foreordained, at least in my estimation. He makes the rube mistake of a too-tight rack, and I capitalize, putting the eight ball in the left corner pocket, a done deal seven out of every ten times I get a rack that good, and he has to reach in his jeans for another hundred since the Marquis of Queensbury the world over says making the eight on the break pays double and likewise gets your knuckles broke in certain knowledgeable bars of which this is one, but I'm in a hurry and can't stand on ceremony, but go for the quick kill, and thank you very much young fella, it was mostly luck, I say, backing out and hoping he don't catch on until I'm in a different geographical location than he is.

Out we go, Tommy and me, walking kinda crisp-like, as I can sense ol' Festus is losing his grin and starting to add things up, which is bad news for me should I be dumb enough to stick around. I guess the Swamp Room is out of bounds for me for a spell, and I sure will remember what that rigger looks like for a lot longer, seeing as how he tops out at six-four, six-five and not carrying much of what you'd call a beer belly.

We make it out of the parking lot in good shape, spraying crushed oyster shells behind us as we are in a bit of a hurry, and hie ourselves on down to Fat City, stopping off for just a minute at one of those roadside Pascalé's Tamale Stands, which I can't pass by without getting one, and Tommy lays the deal on me in the backroom of The Speakeasy, while I ate the greasiest, most delicious Mexican foodstuff ever created. Man! Pascalé sure knows how to make a nasty, tasty tamale, kind can rip your stomach to shreds, give you helium in the midsection, make you want ten more just like it.

Tommy had the scam all written out already; formulas, figures, you name it, it was all there. Made sense, too, the way life insurance does when the guy with the polyester smile's sitting across the kitchen table from you. I had the same feeling that I got at those times, which should have been a tip-off, and sure enough, about ten minutes after I left him I couldn't remember much of any of the details of the plan except that I would be the guy to spend his nights in a six by eight room painted designer gray and featuring bars on the north wall, should things go hinky.

"What do folks usually rob when they after some fast cash?"

I didn't know what he was after, and he wouldn't just come out with it, only kept asking me the same thing. I hate it when a person asks you a question they already know the answer to but keep pestering you to come up with it so's they can show you what a dumb shit you are, compared to them.

"I dunno," I said, finally. "They hit a gas station? Liquor store?"

See, I knew that was the wrong answer. Obviously. But it was the answer Tommy wanted, to show how sharp he was and how thick my skull was, compared to his. I played along, made him feel superior. That was the part of Tommy's personality I could live without.

"Boy, Pete." He gave a deep sigh. "You the same as everybody else. It's no wonder you're hustling pool for chump change."

"A bank? A jewelry store?" He was kind of making me mad. "Why don't you just tell me the answer you're looking for, Tommy. Save us a lot of time here."

"A *bank*! I *knew* you'd say a bank! I *figured* you'd say a bank! If you *wouldn't'a* said a bank I'd'a had a heart attack and died right here!"

He was absolutely amazed at his remarkable insight into my predictability.

"Tommy, why don't you just come the fuck out and tell me what's on your mind?"

"Okay, Pete. Don't get sore, buddy. I just wanted to illustrate a point. That's exactly what most guys think of when they plan a score. They see gas stations, liquor stores, *banks*. Do you know what's wrong with that kind of thinking?"

I dummied up. This game needed two to play and I decided not to be his straight man. He stared at me a long minute and I outwaited him, staring back. I won. He let out a long, drawn-out sigh, like I was just about too dimwitted to live and he was sad he had to be this close to that much ignorance. Sometimes I wished Tommy'd been raised by a pack of mimes. Our conversations would be better if he didn't talk.

"There ain't no money in liquor stores, Pete. There ain't no money at gas stations and there ain't no money in jewelry stores. There ain't even any money in banks. Not *real* money. The real money's kept in the vault with a time-lock on it, don't open until night-time when the bank's closed or there's forty-eleven guards standing around, something like that. The most you get in a bank is five, ten grand. Twenty, maybe, you get lucky. Chicken feed!"

I would have been okay with half a twenty-thousand-dollar score, but I knew what he was saying and it was true. Not only wasn't there any money at all in gas stations and liquor stores, there wasn't much more in banks and not only that, there's a kazillion secret alarms going off the whole time the robbers is hitting the place, which is why they never get away with it. Electronic wonderlands are what banks are.

"You know where the serious money is?" He got to it, finally, giving me time to digest things.

"Armored cars?"

"Pete, you keep thinking the same way all losers think. Armored cars are exactly like banks. They're guarded like...like armored cars. I'm just going to tell you, because it's pretty obvious you are never going to guess the right answer here.

"Supermarkets."

"*Supermarkets?*"

"Is there an echo in here? Yeah, Pete, supermarkets. Supermarkets have all the money in the world. They do a hundred thousand an hour, on slow days. Busy days, well, forget it! And at least half of its cash. That's the beauty part."

"You want to rob a supermarket?"

"In a way."

"What the fuck does 'in a way' mean, Tommy? Either you hold up a supermarket or you don't. Or was you thinking of burglary? They got those huge safes, don't they? You ever cracked a safe? I sure haven't and I bet you ain't, neither. What we gonna do? Just lift that baby up and tote it out on our backs? There's a couple hernias happening before we get it off the ground, one for you and one for me. Been a while since I hit the ol' weight room, bench-pressed six hundred kilos. You, too, I bet. Tommy, we are con-men, not hold-up guys, not B and E guys. We use our wits, not our muscle, least one of us does, and I had thought you did, too."

I stood up.

"Tommy, let me give you a piece of friendly advice. Get yourself down to Charity Hospital and get yourself one of them cat scans. The damage might be neurological and not mental after all. See, maybe this isn't all because of your old man working over your mom on Saturday nights all the time that did this to you, and maybe it wasn't the time somebody stole your trike when you was two did this neither. Maybe, just maybe, your condition is due to a nasty fall you had, out of some tree when you was pretending to be Superman. There's maybe some operation that can help. They can do wondrous things nowadays with these kinds of things. I'll be seeing you and good luck. I really mean that sincerely."

I turned to go and he grabbed my arm.

"Siddown, chump. Let me lay this out for you."

I should've kept on going, but I didn't. I sat back down again. Mistake-a-mundo.

"We're not going to burglarize a store and we're not going to hold it up, either. At least, not exactly."

He got my curiosity. I cracked wise.

"I know. Don't tell me, Tommy. We're gonna call up this store and tell them we'd like some money on account of we're a couple of pretty nice fellers, but down on our luck, and would they please put a couple hundred thou in a bag and we'll be by to pick it up in an hour or so, thank you very much. Oh, and please don't go calling the police as that would be a major inconvenience for us and may lead to major restrictions of our daily movements and freedom in general. Is that the plan, Tommy? I had heard you were a wondrous master criminal with a mad, genius bent for schemes and such, but I gotta confess that I am having serious doubts about such a reputation as you enjoy in these parts; that perhaps it may not be altogether deserved. And I am not even thinking about that parking meter scam you roped me into last year. Honest. That could have just been a mistake. I am giving you the benefit of the doubt on that one. This, however, is a genuine, certifiable, lunatic idea, the product of a bad childhood with lots of trips to the woodshed. Isn't that your pappy I heard about, ain't allowed within two hundred yards of a grade school and Chuckie Cheese has revoked his Chuckie E-Z-Pay credit card? Your childhood may be at fault here."

"Just shaddup, Pete. The more you open your trap, the more inclined I am to seek out another partner, perhaps one with something more than oxygen preventing his ears from collaps-ing inwards. My plan is nothing like you imagine. We will get every quarter, nickel, dime and penny in the store I have in mind—at least the large bills, down to the ones—and we will accomplish this by a means you would not be able to come up with on your own in a million or so years.

"We are going to perform a kidnapping.

"The manager.

"We are going to kidnap the wife of the manager of the SaveMore in Kenner, and because of his great love for his woman, he is going to go down to the store, open the safe, remove the money and bring it to us to keep us from doing bodily harm to her person."

As he talked, I began to see the beauty of his scheme. I also began to see the shortcomings. Like, if we got caught, how a couple of fortune tellers would be proved right that had said I had a short life line on my left hand and one about the same length on my right.

"How come you can't just do this yourself?" I asked him, and his answer was that his plan took two participants, one to stay with the wife and one to go with the manager and pick up the money.

"Wouldn't that be sweet! Turn on a brain cell, Pete! One of us has to stay and guard the wife and one has to go with him to make sure he doesn't do something funny like call the cops and set a trap for us. They could be waiting up the street for when we leave. Someone has to go with him to be sure he doesn't do something cute like that."

I saw his point.

I was elected to stay with the wife.

I bought the whole deal.

It sounded like it couldn't miss.

Ha.

* * *

That stuff I told you about in the beginning of all this—financing the suits we were going to wear to our kidnap—was our first bad move. The first of a long series of even worse moves…

For five years, I did all right.

Then…

Ten seconds from our failed streetcar heist and bullets still whizzing randomly, I followed Tommy as he ran around a house, heard the shots cease.

"Fuck this!" I said to Tommy, who'd slowed down to a trot once we were out of sight.

"No shit," he said. "Who woulda figured the Marines would be on that streetcar?"

We kept jogging until we were three blocks away and saw Tommy's car up the street where we'd left it. We got to the car which was a good thing. I couldn't go another step. I leaned over, put my hands on my knees, panted like I'd just run the kickoff back a hundred yards for a touchdown. At least what I imagined that to feel like. Getting my wind back, I twisted my head up to look at Tommy. "You kidding me? A motherfucker without a gun in this town is about as rare as a rabbi in a Santa Claus suit."

We heard the faint sound of sirens up on St. Charles. Getting louder. Sounded like they were starting to sweep the neighborhood.

We headed out to Veterans' Highway and the second we turned onto it, a siren sounded at a distance, coming closer. Tommy looked at me and slowed down and my heart speeded up.

The cruiser passed us and the second he did, Tommy tipped the beer can he'd been drinking out of, drained it, and tossed it in his back seat, which was already littered with about two cases worth of aluminum cans. He speeded back up.

"Some Indian," I said. "This car oughta be reported to Pollution Control."

"You don't like it?"

Before I could say anything, he braked for the light we'd come up on. He got out, opened the back door and swept a mass of debris onto the street with his arm. It made a pile of at least two feet high. He jumped back behind the wheel…and ran the still-red light. Cars honked.

What an asshole. "I gotta believe you're outta the redskin union," I said. "Chief Sitting-Bull…Bull-*shit*, that's you."

He flashed me a shit-eating grin.

"Screw you," I said. "That's the last job I pull with you."

"Oh, yeah? What about Sam the Bam."

He was referring to the debt I owed my bookie. It was a nut-crusher.

"I'll get it somehow," I said.

"Right," he said. "Your favorite aunt's gonna leave you her Coke-Cola stocks, right?"

"What I'm gonna do is quit betting the fucking Saints and their lousy-ass quarterback."

He was quiet for a minute, then said, "Pete, you know I got the plan to get us right."

"Oh, yeah. That genius plan with the supermarket guy? That's your much-better-than-robbing-a-streetcar plan, right?"

He didn't have an answer for that.

There was no way in hell I was going to do his supermarket kidnap piece of shit plan. I'd figure out a way to keep Sam the Bam off my ass until I could come up with what I owed. I just had to figure out an angle.

We ended up going to this hole-in-the-wall bar Tommy could run a tab in. He was going to talk and I said I'd listen, but I knew I wouldn't. I could use a beer, though.

We're sitting in this dump, knocking back longnecks, staring at the TV where a Giants-Mets game is going on.

"Oh, man," I said. "They're walking Bonds again."

"You ever play with Bonds?" Tommy asked.

"Some," I said. "I got let go just before we went up north. He'd just got traded to us."

A good-looking hooker with a serious hard body got up from the bar and passed us on her way out. Her ass was flat-out bouncing.

"Now, there's one I could definitely piss in," Tommy said. "You just know she'd freak. Probably wanna get married."

"What the fuck's up with this pissing thing?"

"You piss in 'em. In their...whaddya-callit...their vagina. Their honeyspot. While you're doin' it."

"You *what*?"

"Yeah," he said. Said it serious as a heart attack. "Nothing to it, really, but you know how many guys do that?"

"My guess would be zero," I said. "Why would you want to?"

He looked at me and the look he gave me was that he was sitting across from the dumbest son-of-a-bitch he'd ever known. "It drives bitches crazy. It's like the biggest nut they ever felt. You ain't been around much, have you, Pete?"

"Jesus, Tommy! It can't be done, dude."

"Says who? I done it lots of times."

"I'm telling you it's impossible."

"And why's that, Mr. Encyclopedia Britannica?"

"Pressure."

"Pressure?"

"Yeah, moron. Squeeze your cock sometime when you're pissin'. Use the tips'a your thumb and forefinger. That should be enough."

Tommy sighed, like the burden of talking to such a dumbass was wearing him out. "A woman's pussy ain't that tight," he said.

I had to laugh. "Yeah, well, I guess you got an edge there most of us don't, Penrod." I shook my head. "You know, your brain waves is in a perpetual brown-out, Tommy."

"Crack all you want," he said. Then: "Forget that shit. What're we gonna do about Sam the Bam, buddy? I'm into him, too, you know."

Jesus. Sam the Bam. I stared off into the distance. "All I ever wanted to do was open me a lousy po-boy shop. Maybe win fifty grand on the Series. Giants losing…"

The side door of the bar where I was facing, opened and the devil walked in. Sam the Bam Capelli himself. Dressed as usual in expensive flash-trash, the Sicilian with the Godfather wardrobe.

I started to get up, but realized there was no way out. I groaned and slumped back down in my chair. Sam came up.

"Well, well. If it ain't my two favorite chumps."

Tommy got on his perky smile. "Hey, Sam. We was just saying we ought to go over and pay you a visit." He looked at me as if he wanted me to nod my head in agreement or something. I just shook my head and looked away.

Sam smirked and grabbed the chair between us. He twirled it around and plopped his fat ass in it.

"That so?" he said. "That mean you got my money?"

"Well…" Tommy began. "Not exactly. We got a firm line on it, though."

"Is that right, Tommy? Now, that puts my mind at ease."

He smiled broadly, then reached over and grabbed Tommy's earlobe and twisted it savagely and yanked Tommy across the table to him.

"Ow! Ow! Jesus!" Tommy yelped.

A man a couple of tables over got up and moved to the far end of the bar. I wished we could trade places.

"Listen, dickhead," Sam said to Tommy, then looked sideways at me. "You, too, Dickhead Number Two. You two numbnuts come up with what you owe or you're gonna know what swamp water tastes like. Get my implication?"

He shoved Tommy back in his chair. Tommy's hand flew to his ear. He groaned and doubled over in pain. Sam got up, turned the chair back around.

I couldn't believe what happened next. Especially since I was the one did it.

I looked up at Sam, turned on my best "innocent" face, and said, "Does this mean you and me are off for the prom, Sam?"

Tommy moaned and I'm pretty sure it wasn't pain that caused it. Sam just blinked like he couldn't believe his ears.

"I'm gonna enjoy this, Halliday. You, I'm gonna take a personal interest in."

Fuck this fat slob, I thought. I felt downright suicidal and went with it. "Oh, goody. For a minute there, I thought you didn't like me, Sam. That would ruin my day. I'm usually friends with all the morons in town."

I just didn't care. It hadn't been a very good day and my mood reflected it, I guess. Fuck it. I was this close to having been in the major leagues and I was tired of catching crap from pieces of shit like this.

Sam took a step back toward the table. His hand went inside his jacket pocket. Out of the corner of my eye I saw the guy who'd moved to the bar get up and exit quickly through the front door. Smart man.

The bartender moved to the far end, picked up the paper and pretended to be interested in it, except I could see him peering over the top of it.

Fuck it. In for a penny, in for a buck thirty-five.

"You gonna whack me, Sam? Here? You didn't invent night baseball, I guess. Are you really that dumb?"

"Who you think you're talking to?" he growled. His face was contorted.

I was going to die, but this actually felt kind of fun. I think I heard Tommy peeing his pants, sounded like water trickling from his chair, but I could have mistaken. It could have just been sweat running off his balls.

"You know what you remind me of, Sam? The kind of guy that sucks in his gut when his daughter walks in the room."

Sam stared at me like he was trying to decide something. Finally, he spoke, and with a small, quiet voice that I knew was serious. "Monday, asshole," he said. "You got till Monday. Then I wanna hear your mouth."

He turned and walked back out the door. I saw the bartender's head reappear above the bar. I hadn't realized he'd ducked down. There was absolute silence in the bar for long seconds. I realized I'd been holding my breath and let it out. Then Tommy spoke, his voice low and hushed. "Are you *insane?* Are you fucking *insane?*"

"No," I said, my legs turning to jelly. "Just full of it."

"You know much about Sam, Pete?"

"Fuck Sam."

"Yeah, fuck Sam. Right. You ever hear about how Sam laid an ax up alongside his own mom's head when he was ten? She tried to take away his squares. Jesus Christ, Pete. Jesus H. Christ!"

It kind of hit me then and if I'd been able to see myself in a mirror at that moment, I have no doubt my kisser was white as a KKKer's sheet.

"I fucked up, didn't I?"

"No shit. You for sure got the big dog mad. Now what you gonna do?"

I thought about his question. "I'm all out of ideas," I told him.

"You ain't never had an idea all your own in your whole entire life, Pete. You're the original-diginal second banana. C'mon. I don't wanna talk here."

I shrugged, got up and followed him into the bathroom. We stood, side by side, peeing into the pair of urinals, when Tommy, with his one hand holding his johnson, put his other hand on my shoulder and opened his mouth to say something. At that exact moment, a guy walked in, saw us and walked back out, shaking his head and muttering to himself. I shook Tommy's hand off about as violently as I could and gave him my best "don't fuck with me or I'll kill you" look.

"Fuck'm," Tommy said. I just shook my own head, zipped up, and walked over to the sink. Tommy followed me over, washed his own hands, then wet his hair and began combing it back, admiring himself in the mirror.

"The deal is," he began, "you babysit this guy's wife while me and him go and get the money out of his safe. This guy what runs the SaveMore in Kenner."

I really must look stupid to Tommy.

"I'm a hustler, not no fucking kidnapper," I said.

"What you are is a dead man if you don't get Sam his money. He's gonna smoke you even if you do get him his money. Man! I can't believe you did that back there. I'm gonna get killed just because I know you."

He slipped his comb into his back pocket and headed for the door while I was drying my hands.

"Hey!" I said to his disappearing back. "Hold on. I didn't say I'm in."

We went in like insurance salesmen just like Tommy'd laid it out. Three-piece suits, briefcases, the whole bit. At six-thirty in the morning. Seems Tommy had a friend who was an assistant manager at the Men's Wearhouse who could be talked into letting us have some threads on credit. We'd just have to pay double the price on the stickers. Seemed reasonable usury, the credit place we were in.

Standing there, waiting for someone to answer the doorbell, I kept saying over and over, "I'm having a dream here. I'm having a dumb-ass attack in this dream…"

Nothing suspicious about us at all, just two hustling estate-planner types, out hitting the whole life/double indemnity trail early, hustling to beat the competition. We walked up to the mark's house dressed that way in case any of the neighbors were out watering their lawns and also so the victims would open the door. Who would suspect guys who looked like Chamber of Commerce types?

A woman in a pink bathrobe and matching pink hair curlers opened the door.

"We don't want any," she said and tried to close the door. Tommy put his foot in the door just like the vacuum cleaner salesman in all the jokes, at the same time trying to get his .45 out from the coat pocket where he stuck it. He fumbled it, almost dropped it, then got his mitt around it.

"I ain't said what we got yet, lady," he said.

The woman was looking at the glass in her hand and it didn't look like she saw what Tommy had in his hand. She coughed a whiskey cough and began hacking and wheezing until she got it under control. When she looked back up at Tommy, it looked like she still didn't grasp that he had a gun in his hand.

"You don't look like Ed McMahon, honey," she said. "And he's the only guy that's got what I want this time of day." She started to close the door again and Tommy blocked it with his knee. That's when she saw the gun. Her mouth made a silent O.

"Well, now, why didn't you say that was what you're selling?" she said. She let the door swing open behind her and walked back into the kitchen. "By all means. Come in, boys."

Tommy and I gave each other a look and went into the house. I closed the door behind me.

The woman was standing by the counter. It looked like she was waiting for a blender that was making a racket to be done.

"Is this a rape or a robbery?" she said. "Not that it makes much difference. I'll need a cup of coffee before you begin. I hate getting raped before I've had my coffee."

This wasn't going exactly as I'd envisioned it.

"Tommy," I whispered. "We got us a Hostess Ding-Dong here, brudda..." We just stood there, looking at her. I was waiting for Tommy to do something. Damned if I knew what to do.

The woman went to the kitchen cabinet over the stove and

began pulling out cups. She started screeching. "Honey! Honey, we got company. Avon calling." She lighted up a long cigarette she took from a pack of Benson & Hedges on the counter.

A smallish man, in brown dress pants and a white shirt, poked his head around the corner from the hallway. He had a blue bow tie in his hand. He saw the gun in Tommy's hand and blanched. I figured this was Fred, the manager, Tommy'd talked about. I couldn't remember his wife's name or if Tommy'd even told me.

"Oh, hi, pumpkin," she said. "Guess who's here?" She shined us a weak smile. "A couple of low-lifes." She paused. "And so early in the morning. You ready for your coffee, dear?"

Tommy finally seemed to come awake. He motioned with his gun for Fred to come into the kitchen. He came in, brow furrowed. He looked first at his wife, then at us, then back at his wife. "What's this, LaVerne? Who are these men and what do they want?"

Tommy said, "Hey, Fred. We're having a little coffee. Sit the fuck down and join us."

Fred didn't act like a supermarket manager, at least he didn't act the way I thought supermarket managers acted. He seemed more irritated than scared.

He eyed Tommy and said, "Have we met?"

Tommy raised his .45 at him. "Meet Mister Smith and his brother Mister Wesson."

I didn't point out that he was holding a Glock Model 21, sister of the same one I had stuck in my own pocket.

The man sat down on one of the tall counter chairs.

This was just plain nuts. I went over and looked through the little window in the front door. The neighborhood looked okay. Nobody stirring.

No cops with red lights anyway.

The wife—LaVerne?—putzed around making coffee. She dumped a big dollop of vodka into a cup and poured the other half full of coffee. She pretty much ignored us.

"Surprised I know your name, Fred? I got some more surprises for you."

I caught Tommy's eye. "'Scuse me. I need to talk to you a minute."

He acted pained, but he strolled over to me where I was standing by the front door.

I whispered to him, my face close to his. "This is fucked, Tommy. Look around. I don't think there's any great love affair going on here. Did you see what the missus just put in her coffee cup? It's half vodka! She's a lush and I bet ol' Fred there hopes we ice her, once you run the deal down to him. We need to leave."

Tommy just gave me that smirk I was getting tired of seeing. "Naw, Pete," he said, talking as if he was explaining fractions to a six-year-old. "You're reading this all wrong. He loves her. You'll see."

He walked back to the kitchen table and held his gun up for effect.

"Listen up, folks, my partner and I need to talk. Don't try anything weird, Fred. You either, lady. I've got my eye on you."

LaVerne batted her eyes at him. "And me without my makeup on!"

He strolled back to me.

"Look, Pete. I'm going to lay something on you that will set your mind at ease. Pete, I am half Indian. Half Pawnee, half Cherokee, and half French. Ten percent German. Being Indian, I have unique skills. For instance, I can read human nature like a deer trail. This man loves this woman deeply. The eyes, Pete. It's in his eyes. The eyes are like lie detectors to the red man. Trust me."

I looked at him and pictured him in the same gray cell I was picturing for myself.

"Half Pawnee, plus half Cherokee, plus half French, and your little toe's German, huh? That equals *all* asshole..."

He just doesn't get it. He walked back to the table where

LaVerne was just setting down the coffee carafe and a couple of new cups.

"Here it is, gents," she said. "Drink hearty. I know I am." She sloshed more Stoli into her own cup and swished it around and then tipped it back and took a healthy glug.

Tommy ignored her. He addressed Fred. "Now, Freddie," he began. "You want to be clear on all this. You and me are going to go down to your store and…"

I could feel a tiny bead of sweat roll down my nose. I wiped it off and caught LaVerne's eye. She smiled at me.

Tommy was still going on, explaining to the both of them that we were professional cold-blooded kidnappers and unless Fred followed his instructions exactly, he and his lovely missus were both going to be items on the obits page in the *Times-Picayune*. My take on LaVerne was that she wasn't focusing all that well. I'm not sure she was capable at that point.

Just before Tommy left with Fred, I got him over in the corner for one last plea to his sanity. "I am getting bad, bad vibes about this, Tommy. I would seriously question whether ol' Fred here would really go to the wall for the lovely LaVerne at this point in their relationship." I tried my best to get through to him, but I could see it was a losing proposition. I tried, anyway. "In fact, Tommy, I have a suspicion that he may even relish the prospect that she might achieve a state of room temperature as per our threats should he not comply with our stated wishes and get in touch with the authorities, against our explicit instructions. What say you?"

"Naw," he said. "He loves her. You'll see. Besides, it's not *his* money he'll be giving us; it's the company's. And don't forget—I'll be with him every step of the way. There's no way he could call the cops, even if he wanted to. Your fears are groundless."

I didn't know what else to say, so I didn't.

I was still trying to figure out how I might be yet able to dissolve our partnership, when he went back to the table and explained to Fred and LaVerne how the kidnapping and payoff was going to go down once more to be sure they got it right. I, the Mad Dog Killer—he called me that—would stay with LaVerne here in the house while he would go with Fred to the store where he would open the safe and get the money. In case any of his loyal employees wanted to know what they were doing, Fred was to tell the assistant manager or head cashier or whoever got nosy that Tommy was a detective and that the police had received a tip there was going to be a robbery and he was there to provide security in getting the money out. Fred was also to explain that in a few minutes, other detectives, male and female, would be along to take the regular clerk's places and thwart the robbery.

It was an ingenuous plan, I had to admit, and the more I thought about it, the more I thought just maybe Tommy knew what he was doing.

That's what I thought.

I guess you had to be there. Little did I know that if I had been in China at that moment that it was about to be Chinese New Year's and the start of the Year of the Baboon.

"You're a fool."

"What?" It was the lovely LaVerne. We were sitting at the kitchen table. Tommy and Fred had been gone a long time. A *long* time. Enough of a long time that she had killed the first bottle of vodka and was halfway toward the bottom of a second.

"What's that supposed to mean?"

She had her head up now and was really working on the Stoli, not bothering with the coffee mixer any more, just tipping the bottle up and letting 'er rip. I had to admire her—she could drink that stuff like there was an AA meeting coming up in ten minutes and she had to make hay.

"You don't think Fred's going to give you guys any money, do you? I mean, seriously?"

I didn't like the way she said that and I especially didn't like the little laugh she gave.

"What's he care? It's not like it's his money. Hell, he'll probably make out like a bandit. Say we stole twice as much as we did. Insurance company'll pitch a bitch, but they'll come through, sure as rain."

She stopped in the middle of a major swallow and gave me a funny look.

"You really don't know, do you?"

"Know what? What the fuck don't I know?"

"Shit." She looked down at the table. "I'm being kidnapped by a couple of amateurs who are going to get their dicks shot off. I'll probably end up getting shot myself by some stupid cop with a hangover and a burning desire to have his name in headlines."

"You think Fred'll call the man?"

She snorted. "I'm amazed that they're not here already. Although I don't think it's the cops he'll call. You should only wish."

I was getting a sinking feeling in my gut and I didn't think it was the remains of Pascale's tamale from the night before.

"What—" Before I could get the next word out, one hell of a commotion broke out just down the street. I watched, stunned, as at least half dozen police cars roared past the house and tore right up into the yard of a house halfway down the block, about the same number coming from the other direction, and then heard a bullhorn thundering out: "INSIDE THE HOUSE! COME OUT WITH YOUR HANDS UP AND NO ONE WILL GET HURT!"

The chances of two kidnappings taking place so close together at the same time was fairly remote, I figured. I doubted Vegas would even give odds on something like that, no matter how much you wanted to lay down. It also occurred to me that it would be in my best interests to leave the lovely Mrs. LaVerne Frehaun and her house and get as far from this address as my legs could carry me in the shortest period of time.

LaVerne hadn't even seemed to notice either the action down the street, which we could plainly see out of the kitchen window, as she had sort of passed out, her head flopped down on the table, and I was just getting up to make my way out the back door, when she raised up, fixed a bleary eye on me and said, "You interested in the real money?"

Knock me down. Talk about a cool customer.

"Ma'am?"

"Don't you want the serious money he keeps?"

"I heard you. Are you aware there's an F.O.P. convention going on at your neighbors over there? I think I will take my French leave now, thank you. I have grown to like you, LaVerne—an awful lot—and hate to do this, but I am going to go now and I will have to smack you over the head so's you won't be tempted to go screaming out the door once I leave. This is nothing personal, you know."

"Wait a minute, Charlie," she said, a weary tone to her voice. All that lifting of the bottle must have about wore her out. "We've got a little time before they figure out they got the wrong place and dope out which is the right one. Come on. I'll make you a rich man."

I was wrong about that "Year of the Baboon" thing. It was the Year of the Seriously Challenged Nutcase.

I saw she wasn't near as drunk as she had seemed. She seemed suddenly as sober as a turkey at six a.m. on Thanksgiving morning. I was a bit nervous with all the action down the street, but she had definitely got my attention with talk about "serious" money.

She pulled herself to her feet, steadied herself and then walked over to the counter and picked up the phone receiver on the wall. I started to get up and do what I didn't have a clue.

"What the fuck?" I said.

She looked at me and smiled. "Don't piss your pants, junior." She dialed a number and I took another step toward her and she held up her hand like a traffic cop. I obeyed. "Hello?" she said. "Bill there?" She listened a second. "Good. Send his cab over to LaVerne's house. The street behind. He'll know where." She listened again. "Just tell him the eagle has landed. Ten minutes. Don't be late. Tell him that. He'll understand." She paused again, held the phone away from her for a brief second, then said into it, "Just do it, schmo."

She hung up, stood there with her hands on her hips, staring at me like she was trying to decide something. It was plain to both of us that I wasn't in control of the situation.

She turned and walked past me and down the hall. "I'll get you out of here and with a bundle besides, Gilligan," she said. I followed, after a second. What else was I to do? I could hear the police outside talking over that bullhorn. *Come out,* I think they were saying, and they weren't saying "please" unless please sounds like "motherfucker" from a distance.

I went into a room I seen was the master bedroom and watched LaVerne go over to the closet, open the door, step inside, and take down a large suitcase that was up high on a shelf, behind some odds and ends. I could tell it was a load by the way she grunted and almost fell over as she jerked it down. She lugged it over and threw it up on the bed.

"Open it," she ordered, and of course I did as she said.

Damn.

It was money. A suitcase full of money, just like you see a million times in the movies. But this wasn't any movie. This was real. More money than I ever imagined I would be standing in a room next to.

"That's...money," I said. Quite the genius.

LaVerne gave me a look. "My, you're the brainy one, aintcha?"

I guess it was unanimous.

"Do you know why those cops are out there now?" she said.

I shook my head up and down.

"No you don't," she said. "You haven't thought it through.

All you think is that you're busted. You think you better get the fuck out of here because in a few minutes they're going to find out they've got the wrong house surrounded and pretty soon they'll be outside the right one. Even the dumbest donut-gobbling cop out there is going to figure that out eventually and find out which is the right house. This one. The one with you and me in it. That's what you think, right?

She was a good guesser, I had to give her that. That was exactly what I thought.

She shook her head in a disgusted way and shut the suitcase. She walked over to the closet again and reached up on the shelf again and came out with a small blue case, one of those that women like to put cosmetics and junk like that in. She opened it up and looked inside and seemed satisfied, closing it. I couldn't see what was in it.

This was just all too much for my brain to handle.

LaVerne strode over to the dresser and began yanking out clothes and throwing them on the bed. She undid the belt on her robe and let it fall. She was buck naked. The whole time I just stood there, staring.

"Man!" I said, before I thought. She gave me a smile. I couldn't take my eyes off her mammaries. They were museum-quality.

"Humongous, aren't they?" she said. "Fred's big idea of a birthday present. I'd rather had a trip to Bermuda."

I kind of nodded, but mostly just stood there opening and closing my mouth without saying anything.

She went back to the closet, reached in and grabbed a black cocktail dress and pulled it over her head. The dress really showed off her assets. Both of them. There was a pair of black pumps sitting on the floor beside the bed. She slipped them on and walked over to the dresser, pulling rollers out of her hair as she walked, dropping them to the floor, one by one. She ran her fingers through her hair and picked up a brush on the dresser and bent over at the waist and brushed vigorously and then straightened up and shook her head and ran her fingers through it away from her face and smiled at me.

"My darlin' husband Freddie blew the whistle on you and your friend. And me. You didn't really think he was going to give you any money, did you? For *me*?" She laughed. "You ain't never been married, have you? Only reason he called the cops is he hoped maybe there'd be a shootout and maybe I'd end up in a body bag along with you. Otherwise, he would have called...someone else."

Her smile vanished. "Come on," she said. "Grab the suitcase and let's go. I think we'd better hurry."

I didn't argue. It looked like one of us had a plan. I sure didn't. I guessed I'd use hers until I came up with my own.

I hoisted the suitcase and about dropped it on my foot. Damn! Money weighed more than I could have imagined. LaVerne grabbed her makeup case off the dresser top and said, "Let's boogie, Austin Powers."

Out the back door we went, me following her. She cut through the neighbor's yard in back to the next street over, me right on her heels. No way I was going to lose her. Not with every cop in New Orleans a block over.

We came out to the street in the middle of it and she looked up and down both ways. A taxi turned the corner on our left and she began waving like a Norfolk sailor's wife when the fleet pulls in. The cab pulled up and we piled in, LaVerne in front and me in back with the suitcase. For a second, I had the thought that maybe I could just boogie on down the road with the money, but I didn't have the cojones, I guess. Where would I go? Sirens were going on everywhere, coming from every direction.

We all heard the bullhorn, even though all the windows in the cab were up and the A/C was pounding on high.

"YOU IN THERE! THIS IS YOUR LAST CHANCE!"

Slowly, we left all that behind us as we pulled away.

I realized I was sweating like a priest in a roomful of choir boys.

I took in my surroundings. LaVerne was talking to the driver and it was plain they knew each other. My first clue was when she locked lips with him and the second was when she called him Bill Baby. He didn't look like much—just a balding, average-looking guy of indeterminate middle age.

She was saying something to him.

"I hate the name LaVerne," she said to him. She turned around to include me in the conversation. "I think I've always hated my name. I've never felt like a LaVerne. What do you think I should change it to?"

Even though she was looking at me, I wasn't sure who she was asking her question of.

She shrugged and turned back to the driver.

"Uptown, honey. They'll be all over the airport. I've got an idea."

Bill spoke for the first time. "This is it, then, pumpkin?"

Pumpkin?

LaVerne said, "You got it, sugar. Time to rock and roll." She leaned over and planted a kiss on Bill Baby's cheek, who made a fist and exclaimed, "Yes!"

Must have been his scintillating conversational skills, I figured, was the attraction.

We came up on Carrollton Avenue where Bill took a left and then a couple of blocks after that ran into the levee and St. Charles where he took another left. Heading downtown. He kept looking back at me in his mirror.

"You look familiar," he said. Then: "I got it! You're on TV! You're one'a them guys tried to rob that streetcar!"

What do you say to that? My heart sank. Our pictures were on TV? We were fucked.

When we drove past the 4141 Club, LaVerne looked over at Bill. They must have had some kind of silent communication going on, because he nodded, even though she hadn't said a word, and pulled over to the curb. She told me to open up the suitcase. She reached back and took one of the packets and held it up for me to see. They all had thick rubber bands around them. She rifled through it and it was all hundreds. She took off the band and peeled off five one hundred-dollar bills and thrust them at me. "Here," she said. "Here's some walking-around money." She shined me a big smile. I smiled back. I was starting to come to my senses again, the shock of the past few minutes beginning to wear off. If she thought she was going to buy me off with this she was mistaken. I guess she'd forgotten I had a gun.

At least that's what I was thinking then.

It didn't turn out quite that way.

"Close the suitcase," she said, and I did.

As I was deliberating on the best way to get rid of her and Bill and take the suitcase and digging around in my pocket to reach my gun to put this plan into action, LaVerne popped open the makeup case she'd brought with her and pulled out a gun. A really big shiny gun. Pointed at me.

"Say goodbye, Harvard Law."

She turned to her monosyllabic squeeze while I fumbled with the door. "Mr. Mad Dog Killer has decided to get out and walk. He gets carsick. Don't you, Mr. Killer?"

IF IT WASN'T FOR BAD LUCK...

My luck wasn't all bad, not really. There was a bright side. I was five hundred bucks richer than when I'd started the day and another cab came by not ten minutes after LaVerne and Bill had rode off into the sunset. Another ten minutes later, I was walking into the lobby at the Fairmont Hotel in the CBD and over to the bank of pay phones.

I slipped a quarter into the slot and dialed Tommy's home number. It rang four times and then Tommy's voice came on. A recording.

"If you're a good-looking lady, leave your number. If you're a bill-collector, I died." This scintillating message was followed by a brief pause and then a "heh-heh" and then the beep.

I went ballistic. "You cockroach! Fucking *Mafia*, Tommy! Are you insane?" I paused a second, getting myself under some kind of control. "Fuck it. If you made it, meet me where we said. You seen the TV? We're all over the place. They must have had some kind of surveillance camera on that streetcar. Everybody in town wants our ass." I paused again, then said, "And when was the last time a good-looking lady called *this* number, you jackoff!"

I hung up.

* * *

I was easing onto a barstool in a joint in East New Orleans, the bar Tommy had said to meet him at to celebrate the success of our caper and split up the loot. I don't know why I went there. I knew that if Fred had blown the whistle on him, Tommy was no doubt sitting in a chair at the crossbar hotel, answering a bunch of questions guys in bad suits were throwing at him.

This wasn't your average bar Tommy'd picked; all the barmaids had plastic boobs, so you could tell it was high-class. You couldn't even get a longneck in the place. They brought out the beer in those little jars my mom used to put green beans up in. The price they charged for a beer, you'da thought they'd serve it to you in solid crystal or something, but no, we get our suds in a fruit jar. I forget the name. Chez, something. All the cars in the parking lot was made in Germany and Italy, nary a one in the good old U.S. of A. or Japan, and I don't believe I seen one single pickup truck. This was some class joint, all right. You don't see a cowboy hat or a red headband in a New Orleans bar, you're in sirloin steak country.

Fucking Kenny G playing in the background. Kenny-fucking-G! In New Orleans! I could feel pimples popping out on my cheeks. If the Beach Boys or Chuck Mangione followed, I was going to leave. Go out the back door and ralph.

Had the A/C up too high, too. One thing I like about bars over in the Quarters or out in Fat City, they don't go nuts with the air conditioning. Keep the doors open, have a big fan going, let the sights, sounds, and smells of the city drift in. It adds to the flavor. New Orleans has a smell that's all its own. I can't explain it, except that it's a good smell; it's got jambalaya in it, and Mississippi River water, and oyster po-boys and the rank odor of spilled beer and old piss on the floor, and some kind of flowers, those purple ones you see everywhere, and garlic. You don't get a smell like that anywhere else in the world, and I love it. I'm an absolute freak for it. If I was a blind man, New Orleans is where I'd make my home, provided I had any sense. You could live a rich, full life, just through your nose. Except in places like this, where they took all the character out of it. Might as well been in New Jersey at some chrome and fern bar with a bunch of pansies in pony tails. Only good thing about this dump was the waitress' boobs. They were positively works of art. I wished I could of been the personnel director of this joint, do the hiring interviews.

Imagine my surprise when, halfway through the fourth shot of Jack Daniels, in he strolled, not exactly all agrin, but not wearing handcuffs, either. He plopped down on the stool beside me.

"Hi, Chief," I said, by way of greeting. "Tracked me down, did you, you sly redskin, you. You injuns can sure read sign, can't you? Almost as good as you can read people. It's the eyes, I hear. The eyes never lie."

I wanted to stay mad at Tommy, or even *get* mad, but I couldn't. I was really glad he'd escaped. For a couple of reasons, not the least of which I figured that if he had gotten busted, he would have rolled over on me in a nano-second. And it really wasn't his fault the plan had gone south, even though I'd tried to warn him that Fred and LaVerne didn't appear to have the hottest romance in town going. Who would'a knowed, *really*? I mean, even if the guy hated his old lady, you'd figure he'd still do the right thing by her, especially since it wasn't even his money.

"What happened?"

"It was horrible," he said. He threw back the shot of Wild Turkey I'd bought him and I signaled the bartender who came down and poured another.

"Pete, it was nuts. We walked in the store, just like I planned. We go up to the cage, the little office where the safe is, and all the way the little cocksucker's smiling and nodding at people, customers, the help, everybody, just like I told him to do. It was perfect. He goes right to the safe and opens it in two seconds flat."

"What went wrong?"

"It was horrible. What didn't?"

"You said that, Tommy. You already said that. What the fuck went wrong? He's doing everything you told him."

"Yeah. Up to then. He reaches into the safe and he comes out with this pistol. The biggest, fucking gun I ever saw. The barrel was three feet long, looked like a .357 on steroids."

He looked sideways at me and shook his head.

"He says, 'Stick 'em up.' 'Stick 'em up!' Like *he* was the goddamned criminal."

"So what'd you do?"

"So what the fuck you *think* I did, asshole? I stuck 'em up! He had a fuckin' bazooka, for crissake!"

"Then how'd you get away? How'd you get here?"

"Well, he gets to yelling and screeching at all these other motherfuckers to call the cops, get the cops over here to the store, over to his house cause his old lady's being held at gunpoint, and he tells me to lay down on the floor. I was going to do like he said, when something distracted him, some chippie screaming or something and he looked away for a second and I just took off, running."

"And you got away, just like that?"

"Sure. Just like that. What the fuck are you, *stupid*? No, not just like that. The bastard starts shootin' at me, bullets flyin' all over the place, sounded like World War Three. I thought I was gonna pee my pants, tell you the truth. Maybe I *did* pee my pants—I don't know. I was runnin' so fast, I think I did piss my pants and they air-dried." He glanced down at his crotch.

"There was bullets whizzin' everywhere. I think an old lady got hit. Me? I was lucky. I got the fuck away. Plus, the guy can't hit the broad side of nothin'. So yeah, stupid. I got away, 'just like that!' Piece of cake. So what's your story, sweetheart?"

I filled him in, told him about LaVerne and Bill and the suit-case full of money.

Neither of us said anything for a while. Just sat there and nursed our drinks. After a while, I said, "I think we're in deep shit here, Tommy."

He gave me a dirty look. "No kidding, Pete. Right now, every cop in town's looking for us. We'd best be getting out of town for a while, let things cool down."

"Tommy, I don't think it's the cops we have to worry about so much. Think about it. If there was as much money in that suitcase as there was, where do you think it came from?"

"I dunno. He stole it himself from the store?"

"What, skimming on the canned peas? Use your head, Tommy. I don't know where a guy like that would get that kind of dough, but I know it ain't from kickbacks from the dairy suppliers. I got a funny feeling about this. I got a feeling we stumbled onto something we oughtn't've. I got a real funny feeling about this whole deal. It's wacky. It don't smell right, not one bit right. I think we need to check this out and quick. I think we may be involved in something over our heads, here."

"Pete, you're scarin' me."

"I think you should be scared, Tommy. I think the smart thing to do right now is to be good and scared."

He sat there a minute, chewing on everything. Then he said, "I am going to make a quick phone call and see if I can find out anything about this. I know a guy should know if what you suspect is true or not."

"I ain't 'suspecting' anything," I said. "Make your call."

When he came back, I knew we were in trouble. It was all over his kisser like date night acne on a sixteen-year-old.

"Pete, we are dead men."

I looked at him. "That's the headline. What's the article say?"

"My friend says the word is already being put out on the street. Find the two guys what robbed Fred and bring them in."

"That doesn't make any sense, Tommy. We didn't rob him. Remember? He called the cops and shot at you. You didn't get the money."

"But *you* did."

"*I* did? What the hell are you talking about?"

"You walked out of his house with his wife and a suitcase with five hundred G's in it."

"Well, yeah…but *I* didn't get it. *LaVerne* got it. You know that. I told you. You think I lied? You think I got a suitcase full of money sitting under my stool? Take a look, chump."

"They don't know that, Pete. They think you got the money and iced his old lady. Correction. They think *we* got the money."

"Wow. There was five hundred thousand in that suitcase? Damn! Who the hell's this 'they' you're talking about? The cops?"

"Worse."

"Who can be worse than the cops, Tommy?"

Shit. I knew the answer to that already. I just needed to hear it, officially.

"Not…"

"Yeah."

"Oh, shit."

"You're right, 'oh shit.'"

"What the fuck is ol' bow-tie Fred doing with mob money?"

"Because, Pete, ol' bow-tie Fred *is* the goddamn Mafia. At least, he works for them. The SaveMore he manages is one of their businesses. They use it for a lot of things, mostly to launder drug money. That was drug money his old lady snatched. They want it back. That's why they are very anxious to find the two guys they think took it. Which is you and me. Which is why, I repeat: We are dead men."

I drained my glass.

"What are we gonna do, Tommy? Why the hell did I ever let you get me into this? Go off your meds for twenty seconds, this is the shit that happens." I was talking more to myself than him.

"I need to think," he said. "I'll figure something out, don't worry. Don't forget: There's Indian blood flowing through these veins. Indians are good at getting out of white man's traps. I'll get us out of this one.”

I groaned. All I could think of was about a thousand John Wayne movies, each of which ended about the same way for the genius Indians.

“We have both got to get off the street for a while, until I get this doped out,” he was saying. “Have you got any place safe to go? You for sure can’t go to your crib. They may not know who we are right now, but these guys are good. It won’t be long before they figure out who we are.”

I shook my head, trying to keep the tears down, retain the semblance of a manliness I sure didn’t feel.

“Okay. That’s okay. I’m going to send you to a friend of mine who’ll take you in. She knows how to keep her mouth shut. You lay low at her place until I get in touch with you, tell you our next step.”

He must have seen how depressed I was.

“Cheer up, goombah. You’re going to like this lady. Her name’s Cat and she’s a firecracker. Cajun babe. Good people. She’s a working girl.”

Working girl?

CAT

Tommy made a phone call and fixed it up. She said, sure send him around to Polly's Western Tap, she'd be in sometime that evening, pick me up and it was fine, I could bunk in with her for a few days. He didn't tell her what was happening, only that I was his pard on a deal that went kind of sour and it wasn't a good idea for me to be at my old address right now.

Normally, I don't get drunk. Not since Wichita Falls. When I was on the best damned pitching streak of my life, six games straight with no losses and four outright wins and not just wins but a one-hitter and a three-hitter, pitches coming off my hand so perfect they were within an eighth of an inch where I aimed 'em, and then I had to go out and get clobbered by a bottle of Old Remember. Went and messed my timing up all to hell. Screwed it up to the extent that my E.R.A. fell off near four points and I got sent down to some bohunk team in the Ozarks that didn't even own a bus, but mostly hitch-hiked to the away contests. Demon Rum had nary passed my lips since that tragic time, except in moderate amounts and never the day before a big game.

So what did I do, knowing my past track record while under the influence and that spirits and liquor is what gets me in most of life's little jams? I got bombed. Stinking. Sitting in the dive Tommy sent me to, out in Kenner, this joint called Polly's out on Airline Highway. One of those places the TV evangelists used to like to come to and find dates before the publicity got too fierce.

Leaning on the bar, head propped up on my elbow so it wouldn't fall down and kill the two cockroaches doing their mating dance, I was trying to concentrate on the country-western band that was winging along in a different key than their lead singer was fracturing notes in. There was a bleached blonde of indeterminate age, sitting by herself at a little table directly in front of the band, and after a while it became obvious she had some kind of connection to the singer, an angular, grizzled cowboy who kept coming over to her table and sitting with her between sets. She reminded me of those women you see in the newsreels on the anniversary of Elvis Presley's death, in line at Gracie Mansion to pay their respects. My guess was she was the singer's wife or girlfriend or just maybe his number one fan.

A little drama began to unfold as I sucked on my Dixie. Various females kept sashaying up to the singer and speaking to him or waving at him as they Texas two-stepped by, and the blonde gave each of them this homicidal glare, even saying something to one or two of them. After about an hour of this interplay, one of the women, this redhead with seriously big hair, just stepped right up on the stage and wrapped her arms around the singer and planted a lip-lock on him.

This bit of familiarity sent the blonde into instant and frenzied action. Up from her table, she shot on a line for the other woman, and in a heartbeat they were down on the floor before the bandstand, scratching and clawing and screaming and kicking each other, and the joint just generally came alive. The band played on, slipping into what must have been their hillbilly brawl number, while the center of all this attention, the featured singer, just kept on wailing, even though it was his lady that was down on the floor, making the fur fly. He was some consummate professional. The fingernails were flying and then the redhead digs a digit into the other gal's eye socket and extracts her eyeball, which goes rolling across the floor right toward me, and right up under my stool. Her *eyeball*! My stomach did a three-sixty and it was all I could do to hold the contents down and all I wanted to do is depart the premises and forget what I just seen—I give all my attention and energy on getting my heebie jeebie shakes under control, but I didn't dare step off the stool on account of I was scared I might accidentally step on the poor lady's baby blue and squash it. I ain't never seen nobody gouge out an entire eyeball before this instance, though I seen plenty try.

I was trying to dope out my next move, puke or leave, when the bartender and another guy came running out, yanked the women apart, grabbed one apiece and threw them over their shoulders, and hustled them outside, kicking and yammering, the redhead screeching about how she was gonna get her other eye as well and then work on extracting her tongue and lungs and various other organs, and the other one squawking something about a sorry bitch that was gonna end up inhaling bayou water time her and her friends got done with her.

I couldn't get over how the band never missed a sour note, nor how the singer just kept on like nothing had happened, like there wasn't a human being's eyeball lying just under my barstool, and I'm in complete awe of their professionalism. I'm also thinking I've been in some tough hillbilly bars but this one has to be number one on the leader board, when I felt some-one's hand on the back of my neck and this voice, not two inches from my ear said, "Some fun, huh? She got RuthAnn's eye again. She always does. That Lucy!"

"Lucy?" I turned sharply, and there was this diminutive, green-eyed, black-haired girl, flashing the whitest teeth I had ever seen.

"Oh, sure, I guess you wouldn't know Lucy, would you? You haven't been here before, have you?"

I started to say something, what I have absolutely no idea, but the girl didn't give me a chance. She reached down, under my stool and picked it up. *She picked up the eyeball.* My guts did a gainer and a half and started moving uphill at a dead run, and then I seen it wasn't a real eyeball after all. Well, it was, but it wasn't a *human* eyeball, it was a *glass* eyeball!

"It isn't real."

The girl gave me a puzzled look and then her face cleared.

"Oh. No, it's not. I guess you wouldn't have known that, would you?"

She started to laugh.

"I'm Cat. Cathy Hebert. People call me Cat. You're Pete, aren't you? Tommy gave a good description." (She pronounced her last name *A-Bear* and it wasn't until later I found out it was spelled like it was.) "You must be in absolute shock," she said, her words interspersed with giggles. "See, this is a regular deal here at Polly's. Slim, that's Lucy's old man, sings here every Friday and Saturday night and Lucy, she sits right up front so she can keep an eye on him. Then the women start after him. It's the same thing, every week. Lucy doesn't do much until RuthAnn comes in and starts flirting with Slim and then she goes berserk. This is Lucy's eye. Every week, like church, this happens. RuthAnn gouges out Lucy's eyeball and they get kicked out. Slim keeps on playing and pretty soon some other gal will flirt with him and he'll end up with her time the night's over. It's better than *Days of Our Lives*.

She turned and caught the bartender's eye and flipped him the eyeball with an underhand toss. She had a pretty good arm. Could have taught a few pitchers how to make the throw to home plate on the suicide squeeze.

"Tell Lucy that Cat was the one turned her eye in, Frank," she said to the bartender. He was the same one who'd carried one of the tag-team lady wrestlers out. He nodded and put the orb into a shot glass and set it on the backbar, next to a bottle of Old Crow.

She winked and said, "Whoever turns in her eye, she buys them a drink next time she sees them, sometimes gives them a ten-dollar bill for a reward. You wouldn't believe how much those things are worth!"

The thing I noticed about Cat the most—other than the obvious, that she had a set of cabachis that wouldn't quit—was her...colors. The colors of her hair, her teeth, her eyes, her skin. Vivid. Technicolors. They were so intense, they could only be described in terms of clichés. The black of her hair was that blue-black raven kind of black. The green of her eyes the most Irish of greens. And so on. You get the picture. I figured her to be Irish, but within an hour I had heard the main outline of her life's story—or so I thought at the time—and some of what I learned was that she was a Cajun—or coonass as she said—and was a full-time waitress and a part-time prostitute and she liked white wine and Willie Nelson and wasn't it lucky—this was her night off and I would certainly be welcome to come on over to her place in Fat City and stay as long as I wanted, being as I was Tommy's friend.

We danced and drank some and had an all-around good time as you will in New Orleans where the girls are somewhat different than girls in other geographical parts and will let you know what is on their mind, which is generally the same as a man's, which to say is S-E-X, spelled with a capital F.

First, we had to go to a mall, get her a blouse for work. It was kind of nice, walking around, looking at stuff, dresses and things with her. We sat down on a bench on the upper level and looked at the activity below on the main floor. They had this big tank with water set up in it and people were racing boats by remote control. I bought Cat an order of beignets and we both had a cup of cafe au lait.

"Those look like fun," I said.

"I knew a guy had those," she said. "It was his hobby. Had one as big as the real thing, I swear, could pull a skier."

We laughed and talked and got to know each other a little, and by the time we left I knew I was going to like staying with her. She was easy to be around.

I guess she liked me, too. "Let's get biological," she said, the minute we walked into her apartment, and for a second I didn't get what she was saying, but she started walking toward what I figured was her bedroom and shucking a different article of clothing with each step, so I figured out her drift pretty quick.

We hit it off, which is what I am attempting to get down here, and later, when I got my lower jaw back up off my chest where it had fallen to after a gander at the Taj Mahal she called her bedroom, well, the sex was only the best I'd ever had, the Coup de Ville of fucking, and I believe the same for her, too, although I didn't take a poll, 'specially seeing as how she was a pro and had maybe seen some that was better between the sheets than I was and I didn't really care to hear that. But I believe it was pretty fantastic for her as well, judging by the sound effects and manner in which she just generally lost her mind and senses when the love train came up over that rise and started on down that hill, as they say.

"Come here," she said, after we got our breathing back down to a slow panting, after doing the dirty the first time. She stood up and extended her hand. She was calling the shots in this movie for sure. Whatever she said to do, I just did. She took me by the hand and led me into the bathroom. She stepped into the tub and laid down on her back and looked up at me, beaming. "Go ahead," she said. "Do me."

"Shouldn't we have some water in there? You could get a nasty porcelain burn." I said. "Also, you might give me a couple more minutes to recoup. I'm not fifteen anymore."

"You silly," was her answer. "I don't want to screw. I want a shower. You know. *Golden* shower. Is that a problem?"

Turns out, that part of my sex education was not up-to-date, as she explained when I went to turn on the hot water spigot. When she laid out the game rules for the kind of shower she was after, my eyebrows did the McDonald's arches thing, but then, when in Rome as they say, get Italian, so I did, and believe it or not, it was kind of a turn-on, and I got into the spirit of the moment and got real creative, of course doing the usual writing in the snow method to begin with, but once I got going and began to see the possibilities, the artist in me came out. There must be some element of the psychological to the golden shower thing, but what it is I don't know as this was my first experience with the procedure, but whatever the mind twist, I knew right then that while this was something that I couldn't get behind with the same degree of eagerness as Cat could, it wasn't all that terrible, and I also knew that never again would I hear that old put-down "Piss on you" without having a different frame of reference than I'd had previously.

There was some more things about that night that was a little off my usual routine with a lady, besides the water sport we indulged in; some complicated games with vibrators, for instance, one gizmo that was a *serious* piece of equipment, looked like you could bust up sidewalks with it provided you was man enough to handle it, and when she first asked me to smack her around in the heat of passion it was maybe more than a bit awkward, but once I got the hang of it and seen how much fun she was having, I found out I could really put the wood to it and say, it wasn't half-bad and give me the material for one of the best war stories I could ever pass on to the boys. The redder you made her bottom the hotter she got and the more she screamed and moaned and thrashed about, the more it made for a better time for yours truly; for a while there, she was as hot as a South American shooting war and we were both cooking.

She was a squealer. Her squeal wasn't a cute squeal, either. It was one of those numbers that go right through you, sounded like somebody shoving ice down Dolly Parton's dress. Her regular voice wasn't too hot, neither, being one of those high-pitched jobs that sound like she's sniffing helium or maybe somebody's got a thumb up her Hershey highway, and when she got real excited, over stuff you wouldn't believe, like when they played her favorite Bee Gees tune on the oldies station, which is what happened when we're in the midst of our first sexual encounter, she goes up and down, waving her arms and sucking her words in instead of exhaling out the way most folks do. It was a treat, watching her get worked up over something. Jumping all around, squealing, waving her arms and those words coming out, going up at the end, something like, "Oh, Jesus! Oh, Lordy! That's my goddamn favorite song of all time! Don't you just die when they play that! What's the name of that, anyway? Saturday something, isn't it?"

The first time her voice was cute, especially when you've just made fantastic love and she's hit all the high notes, but then the next morning you wake up with an elephant tramping around in your skull and this high-pitched noise bouncing off the bedroom walls and you realize she hasn't shut up yet. You begin to think she's never gonna shut up unless somebody takes a two-by-four to her, and pretty soon you're looking around for a suitable hunk of wood or start to try and guess where she keeps the big knives.

It turned out she had another flaw. She liked dope, specifically coke, and was highly disappointed I wasn't holding, making it plain that if I wanted to enjoy an extended visit, I would get a warmer welcome if I could make it snow.

Except for that, we had a roaring good time and when I finally conked out in the early a.m. I have to admit I was about as in love as I'd ever been with one of the fairer and opposite gender at this stage of the game, disregarding the register her voice was in, the one dogs is familiar with. Truth, I was knocked out, just plain, honest goofy nuts over her. If she'd been a pimp instead of a trick, she could have turned *me* out, after *that* night! Man! I'd met some girls in my life, but she was the best in the sack I've ever been with before or since. Well…as it turns out, there hasn't been any "since." And my experience is probably a lot more than the average Joe's, being a ballplayer and manly jock figure and a sex idol to lots of girls in towns we played ball in.

We talked some, too, in between the sex. At the time it seemed like we never stopped screwing, but we must've, once in a while, cause, looking back later, I seen she'd told me quite a bit about herself.

"How'd you get to be a whore?" I asked, always the inquisitive, and regretting the question almost as soon as I'd asked it, thinking maybe I was being a bit indelicate. Turned out she didn't mind. One thing about Cat; she had no false impressions of herself. What you saw was what you got, like it or not.

"My ma sold me. When I was ten."

"*Sold* you?"

"Yeah. To this rich guy. He was in the rackets."

"What do you mean, 'sold you?'"

"Just that." She laughed, but I could tell there wasn't a lot of joy in it. "This guy liked young girls. Young boys, too. He bought me from my ma. We were kind of poor. Ma was a user. I don't think she'd done it if she hadn't been sick, strung out."

"User?" This was all a bit too much for a boy from the Midwest. I had known some rough trade before, but this was all a first for me.

"Yeah. Smack. Heroin was her choice of drug. She liked it more than she liked me, I guess." She laughed again and this time there was no hiding the bitterness in her voice and in her eyes. Her eyes were lasers, seeing beyond me to somewhere in her past, somewhere no one but her had ever been to. And then, just as quickly, the look disappeared and she visibly softened.

"Look, Pete, don't go feeling sorry for me or any crap like that. I'm okay. It hurt for a while, her doing that, but it wasn't like it was her fault, not really. You ever been strung out?"

When I shook my head no, she went on.

"When you got a jones, you got a jones. Ain't nothing more important. That was my mama. She just had a jones that crushed her Cajun ass. And it wasn't all that bad, with that guy. He wasn't that big, in the pecker department, although at that age I thought he was, and he had other things to do, he was a busy guy, so it wasn't like he was messin' with me every five minutes. Once or twice a week was it, three minutes, in and out. An easy money trick is what we call it, on the street. Sometimes, I wouldn't see him for a month at a time. Mostly, he treated me nice. Gave me ice cream any time I wanted it. Dolls. He'd buy me any doll I ever wanted. You shoulda seen my Barbie collection. I had 'em all, and two of some of them."

I thought I had heard everything, but this was new territory. She told me more, lots more, more than I really wanted to hear. I wanted to kill this old geezer for what he'd done to her, and I hardly knew her.

She knew where her mother lived, but she had never talked to her since the day she traded her for a hundred dollars and a needlefull.

"A hundred dollars?"

"Yeah." She laughed, but it was a bitter laugh.

"I guess he offered fifty and she jacked him up to a C-note. I can't figure out if she was just desperate for more money or if she just honestly felt I was worth more. I like to think she thought I was worth more than he was offering." Again, she snorted, but the chuckle was without mirth.

"I see Granny, sometimes. She talks to me about Mom. She's still a junkie. Once a junkie, always a junkie. You can lick it for a while, but the monkey's always there, just waiting. The monkey knows. The monkey knows you're not going far."

"Granny" was her grandmother and her only other living blood relative that she knew of. An old and feeble lady, whose mind was kind of gone but whose love for Cat was whole; it seems she was much more a mother to Cat than Cat's mom had been. Cat went over to visit her once or twice a year and to check on her mother, vicariously, through her. She didn't say that, but she didn't have to. I could read between the lines and what I read made me feel sadder than the last pup at the dog pound when the choosing's all done.

And madder than a cheerleader with a broken mirror.

She wouldn't tell me who the asshole who had purchased her from her mother was, only that he was still around, still in New Orleans, and that no, she didn't see him anymore, but she read about him in the papers, from time to time, he was still big in the rackets and a prominent citizen. He'd thrown her out in the streets when she was thirteen.

"I made a big mistake," was how she put it. "I got older. He doesn't like his women too old. Actually, thirteen was pushing it. I lasted longer than most. He usually dumps 'em by the time they're eleven, twelve at the most. He must have thought I was one red hot mama!"

She ended up in the French Quarter, whoring to the sailors and tourists, selling drugs, rolling drunks, just about anything to turn a buck, keep alive. She was the true hustler's apprentice, unlike me who had come into it as a second career and who could never be in her league not having started young enough.

Something happened. She was smarter than most. She began to notice things. There were others like her, had the same experience.

"They're all dead now. All of them. I don't know even one that's still alive."

Packs of young girls, young boys, were out there on the streets, right now, for whatever reason, she said. Look around, next time you're partying, having a good time. Check out the working class.

Most died, she said. Got stabbed, shot, overdosed.

"I had a friend, I guess we were best friends," she said. "One day we're down in the Quarter, hustling, and we meet these Russian sailors, took 'em in this doorway, did a number on them. Both these guys are jabbering in Russian the whole time and we started giggling. I don't know why, we just did." A look came over her face I couldn't describe. The saddest thing I ever saw, that look. A look of just pure misery, that's the only way I could describe it. She went on with her story.

"The guy she was with didn't like it, I guess. Danielle's giggling. Probly thought she was laughing at his little wee-wee. He started hitting her. That wasn't so unusual. Usually, lots of guys like to hit a girl a little bit. Makes 'em feel good, manly. Then his buddy started smacking her, too. We were both screaming and the guys were yelling in Russian and then one of them hit her really hard and she fell down and I knew right then, I just *knew*, she was dead."

A little tear ran down her cheek and I reached over to pat her, but she pushed my hand away.

"She was dead, all right. That last blow just scrambled her brains. There was blood and goo coming out of her nose and her ears and her head was bent funny. She was just sitting there, on the sidewalk, her head down on her chest like there was no neck-bone. I started screaming and I just screamed and screamed and screamed and the Russian guys, well, they just hit the bricks, and pretty soon, here come a cop and I was still screaming and he smacked me across the mouth and I quit. I guess that stuff works. Hitting a screamer, I mean. It did for me, anyway."

She stopped and reached for her cigarettes and lit one.

"Well? Then, what happened?"

"Huh? Oh, nothing. I told the cop what happened and then some other cops he called, a couple of detectives, and then I went over to the station with them and they got on the phone and after a while they said I could go. 'What about Danielle?' I said. 'What about those Russians? Are you going to arrest them?'

"'It would be taken care of,' they said. 'It would be taken care of.'"

She snorted.

"Well? What happened? Did they arrest the Russians?"

"No. I didn't hear what happened until a few weeks later. A cop, sort of a friend of mine, a guy I gave freebies to once in a while and who did favors in return, like not arresting me every five minutes, told me they called the State Department, or something like that, and some guys in suits came down and they had a big pow-wow and decided to let them and their ship leave, not make a big deal about it, cause an international incident or anything."

"They let the guys go?" I was incredulous.

"Yeah. It was just some black whore down in the Quarters. Wasn't nobody important."

She smiled and her eyes were focused on something far away. Her smile had no mirth in it.

"Danielle and me were both the same age. I was a little older. She'd just had her birthday the day before. She was thirteen, she thought. She wasn't sure. She was born at home and then her mom gave her to her sister. She had too many already. Her mom's sister raised her until her uncle started banging her and then she kicked her out on the street. She was twelve when that happened. At least she thought she was. They never had birthday parties, so she wasn't sure. She looked thirteen, though. I think she was."

Cat's eyes were shiny.

"Hell, she looked *thirty*," she said after a second or two.

She said she observed this and thought about it and thought about it and kept thinking about it. She said she saw what her future held if she didn't do something about it. She had no education, no home to go back to. But she was smart. She was different from the other street people. She snuck off to libraries whenever she got a chance, read books, magazines. She loved to read about rich folks, to learn. She'd read the movie magazines, *People*, *Architectural Digest*. She found out there was a world beyond the narrow streets of the French Quarters. She also figured out what would happen if she stayed on her present course. She did the best thing she could do, took the only avenue she could see was open to her, the only path that would allow her to escape the streets and survive. She became a waitress. And she graduated from the streets. She was a call girl now, at the top of her game. She got anywhere from a hundred on up. A thousand, she said. I charged a thousand for a weekend once, and got it, she said.

"I am hoping you are not planning on sending me a bill," I joked; as I am fairly well broke although I have hopes of latching onto some real dough in the very near future, and first she gave me a dirty look, but then she laughed, a merrier sound this time, and said, "No, Pete, this was a freebie, our biological date. This was for fun, not business," she said, and when she said that, of course I wished there were a few of my buddies around to hear her, as it makes any guy feel tremendous to have a professional in the business of sex say he is good in the sack.

"Besides," she said. "I have ESP and I have the strangest feeling about you and me. We are going to have some fun in the future. I can see your aura and when it mixes with mine, there is a different color than I have ever seen. I don't know what that means, yet, but I have a good feeling about it."

The color of our combined aura was a kind of mint green with a red outline. That's what Cat said, but I couldn't see any-thing green in the room except her curtains, but they were closer to a blue in my opinion. Who knows? That ESP stuff gives me the willies anyway. I always wonder if people who claim they have all those special powers can read your mind or figure out what you're thinking. That's the last thing I need! A chick going around reading your mind! Can you imagine? You'd be dead in two days. She'd kill you. Women are always getting bent out of shape over what they think you said anyway, just think how screwed up it would get if they actually knew what you were thinking. Like when you're playing hide the boner and you're singing out her name and cussing like you just can't help your-self, you're having such a great time, and really all you're thinking about is did I fill up the car like I was going to, and I sure wish she'd get her nut so I could catch David Letterman's monologue.

No, ESP is not a quality I would like to see in someone I was boinking. I had better watch my step with her if I was smart, before I got in over my head.

I told her some about myself as that only seemed fair, and she said she wished she had seen me play ball and she said she liked my plan to open a po-boy joint.

"I never heard of one of them going under, did you?" she said. "They're always busy. Maybe I could help you get it started. I'm a very good waitress, you know. If you're new to food service, I could help you out there, show you some of the tricks of the trade. There's more to it than meets the eye, you know."

I told her I appreciated her offer and would take her up on it when the time came. Of course, at that time I didn't know if she was as good a waitress as she claimed, but even if she wasn't, it was decent of her to offer her help.

She may or may not be a good waitress, but one thing was for sure. She was some fine lay in the hay.

Some lay indeed.

That was Cat and that was our beginning.

TRICKIN' WITH THE GALS

Cat was gone when I woke up. I guessed she'd gone to her waitressing gig. I remembered how she'd made it clear it would be a good idea if I came up with some toot for her if I wanted to keep on being the star guest at her hotel. I tried to think of the closest place I could score some coke. I didn't think it would be a good idea to show my face all over town. Go someplace close by, cut a quick deal and be back in the apartment. I left her apartment, taking care that I left the door unlocked as I didn't have a key and hiked over to Veteran's Highway and flagged down a cab. I looked inside to see if it was Bill. No such luck.

"Fat City," I told the hack. "The Speakeasy."

The first person I seen when I walked in was Arnie Beld. The biggest donut gobbler in New Orleans and possibly in all of Louisiana. Arnie was the cop that had busted Tommy and me on the parking meter thing. I hated him. I looked around but didn't see anybody else I recognized. I didn't have much time, and I knew something about Beld. Arnie was a crime-fighter by day, but since he'd busted Tommy and me, I'd found out he dabbled a bit on the other side of the law, as well, and we'd developed something of a professional relationship. He was the money behind a pawn shop over in Algiers that specialized in goods that had somehow lost their original bills of sales. I'd sold him a few TV's and other items from time to time.

"Arnie," I went, slapping him on the back and sliding onto the barstool next to him. I hated having to be nice to the creep. No self-respecting con in town would have anything to do with him, other than to do business. Word was, he'd do anything, and I mean *anything*, to turn a buck. Most of the cops on the NOPD were straight shooters, hard guys you didn't want to mess with. They might be on the opposite side that we were, but there was a kind of grudging respect most of us had for each other. Arnie was just one of the bad apples that nobody respected, cop *or* crook.

Seeing him again, brought back the memory of when he busted Tommy and me for breaking into parking meters. A bad memory.

Tommy'd talked me into it, said there was serious money in parking meters, at least ten bucks a meter. Hundred bucks or more a block, he said. Go all the way around the block, there's four hundred bucks. Think of all the blocks in New Orleans, he said. Hundreds. Thousands, even. We'll be rich, he said. Best of all, it's a renewable resource. We can set up a regular route.

We got eighty-five cents. Got busted breaking into the first meter. They didn't come apart exactly like Tommy said they would. Six seconds, he said. Six seconds per meter. Ten bucks per meter. It would be a breeze.

"The Parking Meter Bandits" is what the *Times-Picayune* called us.

The thing was, I didn't want to bust into that particular meter. There was a drunk leaning up against a building half a block away. Let's go, I said. There's a guy down there.

Oh, him, says Tommy. He's just a hick from Indiana, can't hold his liquor. C'mon, let's go. Don't be such a chickenshit. Hand me the screwdriver.

The drunk turned out to be an off-duty cop. Lieutenant Arnie Beld. He was drunk, all right, but somehow sober enough to make a bust.

"Arnie, it's great seeing you. How you been?"

"Pete!" He turned and gave me this oily grin and gave me the fist to the shoulder thing, acted like I was his best friend. That was sad. I found I couldn't keep up the friendship thing. He made me nauseous.

"Arnie, keep your paws off me. I need a favor and you owe me one. Your guy in Algiers chumped me on a Zenith I brought in two weeks ago. Matter of fact, you owe me more than one favor, but one is all I need, right now. I need a gram of coke. I know you got one or you can get it. I need it right away. Whaddya say? Can you help me or do I need to look under another rock?"

He couldn't recognize a direct insult if it was spelled out. Probably everybody he knew talked like that to him. He was still smiling, like he thought I was joshing him like we was old buds.

"Pete, you are one lucky pisan. It just so happens I have got some of the finest product you have ever seen. This stuff is all rocks. I am surprised, however, Pete. I am surprised that you are buying coke. I had thought you were a non-user."

"Just give me the stuff, Arnie. And this better be good shit. If this shit has been stepped on too much, I'll be back."

He gave me a pained look. "Would I stiff you, Pete? One of my best suppliers of fine electronic merchandise? My best friend? Pete, this stuff is so pure, the price should be double."

We went in the bathroom and cut the deal. I could tell from looking it was some weak shit, probably trampled to death, give whoever used it a serious case of the runs. There just wasn't enough time to locate something better, and I figured Cat maybe wouldn't know the difference anyway. Besides, it would be better for her, snorting vitamins or baby laxative instead of drugs.

Just before I left, he said, "I saw you and your pal Tommy."

I didn't get what he was saying.

"On TV. You the guys tried to rob the streetcar."

"You gonna bust me?"

"Naw. You didn't get nothin'—no harm, no foul—besides

you're one of my best suppliers. Who wants to kill the golden goose? Not me, brudda."

I paid him and laid an extra twenty on him for not arresting me and went back out to the cab.

Jesus! I needed to get the hell out of town and soon.

There was just something about Arnie that made my skin crawl. It wasn't just the parking meter bust, either. A bust's a bust, no matter what, but there was something about Arnie himself I didn't like. He was *greasy*, that was it. No morals, no code of ethics, no honor. That's why I was so surprised he hadn't nailed me, got himself a collar. I did take him a lot of merchandise, so I guess he was speaking truth about why he didn't run me in.

He was like some pitchers I'd known. There's hardly a thrower I'd ever been around who wouldn't wet down a pitch once in a while, heave the old spitter. It's all part of the game. Get in a tight spot, two on base, up by one run, bottom of the inning, toughest out in the league in front of you, your career hanging by a thread, who can blame a guy for juicing up the pill a little?

But there were some who would rather throw the wet one than a legit pitch, even when the legit one was the better choice. They just plain liked breaking the rules, so to speak.

That was Arnie. He liked to do things simply because they were evil or wrong. No other reason. He was an oil can. A pure creep.

I wasn't crazy about buying drugs, from Arnie or anyone else for that matter. Drugs were something else I'd given up a while back, couldn't see the point in them anymore, but sometimes you just got to grease the deal. I wasn't too ecstatic about parting with a hundred and twenty of my hard-earned stash either, but that was the cost of doing business, getting Cat to let me crash at her place. It might have been cheaper to go to a motel, but motels would be the first place the mob guys would look for me at.

* * *

"They got guys out everywhere looking for us."

The air conditioning was turned up to its frostiest, but as soon as I heard Tommy say those words, the sweat started to roll.

He was sitting across from me at Cat's kitchen table and we were sharing the bottle of Wild Turkey he'd brought with him. It was late morning for everybody else in New Orleans; sundown for Tommy and me.

"I saw Arnie Beld earlier this morning, Tommy. Remember Arnie?"

"You went out? Are you nuts? What if they already figured out who it was snatched Fred's old lady?"

"Don't worry. I was careful. Besides, if they had, I'd be dead already. You, too, I imagine." I didn't tell him what Arnie had said about seeing us on TV.

"The word is, Sam's the one's gonna get the contract for the kidnappers."

"Sam?"

"Sam The Bam."

"*Capelli?*"

"Yeah. Sam Capelli. Sam The Bam."

"Jeez-Louise," I said.

"Double that," Tommy said.

"How long you think we got before they figure out it was us?"

"Not long. They got ways. Remember, Fred saw us. These guys probly got a better sketch artist than the NOPD. It ain't like we're unknowns. We're on TV, too. You got those ears, remember?"

"Fuck you, Tommy. There ain't nothing wrong with my ears."

"No, not much. They only stick out like car doors. You look like an ugly Clark Gable, Pete. Love child of Clark Gable and Bette Midler. Face it. I might be able to fade into a crowd, but not you. Not with that kisser."

I decided to forget it. We had more important things to do

than argue about my good looks.

"What are we gonna do?"

"The word I got from my source, is that the word's been put out that if whoever took it pays back the dough, they might forget what was done. They figure the kidnappers probly aren't stupid—they wouldn't'a hit a mob business if they'd known what it was. My guy says they're gonna give the 'nappers a chance to give it back. How long, I don't know. A week or two, maybe. Unless they figure out who done it first. So see, it's maybe not so bad as we thought it was."

"Tommy, are you insane or what? We don't *have* the money! Freddie's *wife* has the money! The lovely LaVerne has the money and is probably got it stashed under her bed in her hotel room in Rio while she's out laying on the beach, working on her tan and thinking up what her new name is going to be and how many diamonds a gal can put around her neck before she's considered gauche. Her pal Bill's probably riding around in a Cadillac cab, trying to learn espanol and figure out the currency so's he don't get stiffed on tips."

"Yeah. You're right. That *is* a problem, isn't it?"

"Tommy, you ought to be President. I believe I'll nominate you, next election. You have got a way of looking at serious matters like they are not all that weighty after all. I imagine you'll want to appoint a blue-ribbon commission to study our problem. I feel very good about this now. I'll admit, Tommy—I'll admit, that for a minute there, I honestly thought we had a major situation here, but I can see you have things under control and that all of my worries were nothing but foolishness, the wild, delirious thoughts of a paranoid lunatic."

He got up and walked over to the refrigerator and opened it.

"More ice?"

I shook my head.

Seated again, he said, "Pete, I understand where you're coming from. I really do. But, Pete, I am going to lay something on you that will bring a smile back to your mug and a spring in your step. I am an Indian, Pete; I believe I have mentioned that fact, and it is clear you do not know what that truly means. It means that I, like my forebears, have faced overwhelming odds against large numbers of the palefaces before and my, our, cunning has brought us out of tight spots in the past, as it will here.

"I have an ace in the hole, Pete.

"I have a plan that will not only enable us to write off this debt to the Mafia; it will make us rich men as well."

I couldn't wait to hear this.

"What's this wonderful scheme, Tommy? Tell me this—does it involve parking meters? Please tell me it doesn't."

"No, Pete, it doesn't involve parking meters. Can't you ever let that rest? I still say that idea would have worked. We just caught a little bad luck. No. This idea I got is big. Really big. This deal will make us rich. We can pay back the supermarket money and still have more money than we can ever spend. And the beauty of it is, we already have experience."

"We do?"

"Absolutely. What I have in mind is another kidnapping. A *better* kidnapping. This time we'll do it right. What I have come up with here—" he tapped his head, "—is ingenuous; it's a stroke of genius. I came up with it thinking about our little experience with Freddie. Can you believe that! Out of a disaster comes a miracle. I told you Indians could outfox the white man. Didn't I tell you that?"

I looked at him. He was a complete hamburger short of a Happy Meal. Plus a couple of fries and the dill pickle. Maybe the soft drink, too.

"Tommy, are you insane? I can see stuff leaking out of the soft spot on your head from here."

"Pete, I see you are not in the right mood to discuss this right now. Tell you what: I am going to give you a little time to think it over. There's some things I got to check on. Meet me out at Bennigan's tomorrow afternoon. I'll have all the details ironed out then."

I started to say something and he waved his hand.

"Don't say any more right now, Pete. Just hear me out. When I lay this plan on you you're gonna jump up and down with joy, it's so perfect. Just keep an open mind. I'll see you tomorrow."

He left. Just got up and walked out the door.

Kidnap.

Gawd a'mighty.

It was just starting to dawn on me what could have happened on the first kidnap. Not that enough hadn't already happened. The thing was, it had all happened so fast, Tommy's pitch and then bam! we're out there doing it. I was just coming to the realization that if everything *had* gone okay, if we'd ended up with the money, we could still have got caught and gone to jail. Didn't kidnapping carry the same penalty as murder? I seemed to remember hearing that it did.

Kidnap.

Damn.

I was still studying on my options laying out at the pool when Cat came home, snapping her fingers, her radio strapped to her waist and a wire going to her ear. I'd killed a gallon of Dago red, and the sun was in a different part of the sky, and I wondered did she want to go out and pick up some mud bugs out to Deannie's and eat them out by the pool.

"We'll get a six-pack, too," I said. "My treat. Oh, here." I handed her the gram I'd scored from Arnie and she grinned and put her arms around me and planted a big wet one on my lips. She stuck it in her purse.

"That sounds good," she said, us heading up to her apartment and me watching the way her butt moved up the stairs. "We could do that, but later, I got a job. I got a part for you, too, make you fifty bucks."

That kind of talk made me skittish, being as how I know how Cat makes her serious money, laying down with rich guys, but I ask her what it is and she says, "It's this wealthy old fart, rich as the President, likes three people in the room with him when he's got a stiff one on."

Already, I don't like the tone of this. There's a lot of hustles that aren't the kind you want to write your momma about in your Christmas letter, but having sex with someone of the same biological persuasion never was on my list, not even down there near the bottom. I know some guys who did things like that, but I have never been that hungry or poor I could see the attraction in such acts, and I wasn't even close to being that bottomed out, even now, so I said, "No thanks, Cat, I'll pass on this one, but you can be sure I'll be waiting up for you to rub your back when you get back home from your job tonight, honey."

She laughs in that voice of hers and I look around to see did any dogs notice, and she says, "It's not like that, Pete. He doesn't want to get it on with a dude—he just likes one in the room. Hell, *we* don't even get it on with him, not the regular way." We, meaning her and another girl as it turned out. She has Jackie, a black friend of hers in mind for the third starring role, she says. Jackie's an old pro, has done this number with the trick before.

"See, he rents us all a room at a hotel, and then shucks all his clothes off and lays down on the floor."

So far the layout looked pretty simple, but I was anxious for her to tell me where I'm at during the proceedings and what I'm doing.

"Me and Jackie, we get naked too, 'cept for these special high heels he likes us to wear," and she goes into the bedroom closet and brings out these Bally weapons that are all gold and sparkly and have heels that're longer than my willie and dangerous-looking at the tips.

"The deal is, me and Jackie wear these and walk up and down on his back while he's crying out with pleasure, and we cuss him out. Like, you know, 'yore Mama knows you been a bad boy and now you need chastised. Yore a scum-suckin' piece a' shit and need this t'get right.' Things like that. Plus, all the time, we're whipping on him with this," and she shows me this blacksnake that comes from the property room of RKO pictures or whoever made the old Lash LaRue films.

"The trick is to draw blood, but not cut deep. It takes a sensitive touch to do it right, the way he likes it. He says I'm the best at it." She beams, full of pride at her professionalism. She still hasn't got to what I'm doing while this madcap revelry is taking place.

"Don't worry, baby-face. You don't have to do none of those things. You don't even have to take off your clothes. You just sit on a stool behind the wetbar and call him names. It adds effect, helps him get off. You make the drinks, too."

"That's it?" I say, skeptical. I'm looking for the twist in the game, something she's not telling me yet.

"Yep. That's it. For that, you get fifty bucks, me and Jackie get two hundred fifty each, and usually he takes us out after for etouffée. It's fun; you'll see."

Yes, indeedy. I'm pretty excited about the upcoming events, I can tell you! Won't this be something to tell the boys on poker night! The time I played the Cussing Bartender in the Menage a Trois.

I go anyway, after I make Cat promise she's not withholding important information about the gig. She swears she's not, the whole thing's duller than the last day at an Odd Fellows convention, and the restaurant he takes them to is always first-rate.

One surprise though, at the beginning. He sends his personal limo, with a black driver that could of been the twin of The Hulk, size-wise, that is; this slab of beef bigger'n any lineman the Saints has got, to pick us up. I'm expecting a cab ride, and hoping we draw my friend from the kidnap and get a lead on LaVerne, and here cruises up this block-long hotel on wheels, bar, TV, the works.

"Hell, you could save the price of the room," I cracked, climbing in behind Cat, who's decked out in a little number wasn't picked up at any Discount City close-out sale. She'd made me put on the only suit I had packed, after she passed over it with an iron. The suit I'd used in our supermarket kidnap caper.

"We could all stomp around in here pretty good and still have room for a few of the Saints' cheerleaders, should he desire a bigger and more professional rooting section."

Cat doesn't smile at me, so I know she's in her career mode now, no messing or funning around, this is serious stuff, like the African country in the front is gonna tell the boss we're poking fun at his Kennedy bus.

We pick up her friend Jackie; she's standing out in the yard in the Ninth Ward neighborhood she lives in, all decked out in a purple outfit and about forty-eleven people all gathered around to give her a send-off and see the cruise ship she's departing in. That mob of black people made me kinda nervous, but then I remember the block of granite sitting in the front and I guess he's packing an Uzi, which would be in character by the looks of him, and I relax. Then I get another thought makes me sweaty. I'm wondering if Alonzo the Mountain—our driver— knows any mob guys, and has maybe heard our description.

We get to the hotel, which I won't name as it's one of those on Canal that charges a month's salary for eight hours sleep, and I don't want no lawsuits, I was to let out what kind of hijinks are going on in some of the high roller rooms, but it was one Mr. George Bush favors, when he's down seeing the local color. I think we even get the room he stays in, it's big enough for about eleven hundred Secret Service types, plus the old lady and a couple of kids, with a pet or two thrown in, keep the kiddies happy.

"This isn't a *room*," Cat whispers, when I remark on the layout. "This's a *suite*," and I say, "It sure is *sweet*; I had the dough it cost to lease this baby for a night, I could get my mom a *good* iron lung, one that don't need to be run with a foot pedal. Do some traveling on the change, too, see the Grand Canyon, Disneyland, get some good seats at the Grand Ol' Opry on our swing through."

Cat, she ain't laughing at none of my quips, so I drop the act and pretend to be serious, too.

Just then, in walks this guy looks like more of a movie star than Caesar Romero, same silver hair you know he don't get cut down at Benny's No-Waiting Haircuts, and he shakes hands all around, the girls, too, like he was the ambassador to Finland and we're all up for the hounds and the fox hunt, got tired of floating around on our yacht, nibbling caviar and such. He's Robert something or other. I don't know if he even said his last name, I think not. It's just two whores and a hustler what's out of work and on the run, but he treats us like we see each other every day in our adjoining boxes at the racetrack.

Alonzo the driver has made himself scarce, although I got a sneaky feeling he's around somewheres close, just in case things get out of hand with the frolicking about to come down and he has to nip in and help out the boss, and it's just us four party animals standing around in a wing of the hotel, drinking cocktails and exchanging small talk chit-chat about the stock market and what-not.

After a spot of this, the host excuses himself and goes into another room and comes out in a minute and this mother ain't got a stitch on, not even his saddle oxfords, and I try and look like this is what I'm usually doing on a lazy Sunday afternoon, but I ain't quite sure where I'm supposed to be in this scene. Cat takes care of that.

"Over there," she points, and I climb up on the barstool that's indicated. "You can mix yourself a drink if you want. When we're ready, I'll tell you what to do and when." She and Jackie leave the room and I'm alone with Robert the nude guy. This was some fun, I'll tell you. He is saying something about the upcoming elections and I'm trying hard not to sneak a peek at his equipment. Not that I'm curious, but it's a known fact that when a guy is naked in front of another guy, like in a public bathroom, we got to check each other out, see how we stack up, but we got to do it on the q.t. so's the other party doesn't get the wrong idea, think we're swishy or something. From what I can tell, the girls is gonna be disappointed, which makes me feel a little better, but not much.

I for sure took up her suggestion of a drink, making myself up a concoction that 7-Eleven would be proud to market along with its Giant Slurpee. I figured I needed every ounce of alcohol I could get inside my body for the ensuing events as this was not my normal hustle and I wasn't altogether crystal clear on the particulars as to what might be expected of me. If Cat thought she was going to lay a new wrinkle in the game on me once I was there, and I'd be intimidated enough to go along with it, I wanted the courage to just say no. I got a brief mental picture of Alonzo blocking my way should I decide to take French leave, should unexpected developments occur, and it wasn't a comforting image.

Turned out there wasn't anything to worry about. Things commenced to transpire pretty much the way Cat had said they would. Her and Jackie had both dropped their designer originals in the other room and put on the stilts they'd brought and took turns prancing up and down on Robert's back, while I called him a few names and he acted the surprised and captured tourist. It took a while to get into the spirit of it, especially since he'd been so nice and polite and all, but by and by it started to come to me, and before I know it, I'm whoopin' and hollerin' like the two gals, and calling him names I hadn't heard of or used since my own pappy nailed me for sneaking nips outta his private stock of Old Rotgut. All the time, the subject of our little drama, is laying there, squirming and moaning like it's not his idea originally, and he's been captured by whacko Amazon man-haters and their native guide, and then he slips it into high gear, squirming like a nightcrawler dropped on an August sidewalk, and Cat comes over for a sip of my Manhattan-slash-boiler-maker, taking a break while Jackie trips the light fantastic for a spell, and wipes the sweat off her forehead with one of the monogrammed hotel towels. She's been working, that girl has!

She gives me a grin, and says, "It's almost over now, Pete. He's about to come."

I just nod and take a good slug myself, this is all just a bit too weird, even for someone of my accumulated experience, and the old guy's really going to town, now.

"Ooooohhhhh," he gives out in a voice that raises the hackles on the back of my neck, but I keep up with my part, being the pro I am.

"Filthy cocksucker," I sing out and take a swig.

"I'm bad, so-oooo bad," he comes in with.

"Scum-lickin' pussy," says one of the girls, and we're all shouting and yelling out names you wouldn't hear at a revival meeting, and the whip's going good now, and both girls drop down to their knees alongside the old geezer slapping him on the back with their open hands, and I'm singing out some good zingers and slugging down the vodka and other assorted spirits as fast as I can, and the choir's in full voice, we're all wailing like one of those old time funerals in the Quarters, and the girls are spanking him all over his back and butt, which, incidentally, looks like prime grade chuck at this point, but isn't so bad as it appears as the wounds is all just below the surface and apt to clear up in a week or so with the proper salves and medications and skilled nursing and stuff. He starts singing out real good himself now, like he was in one of them churches that speaks in tongues and handles live rattlesnakes for fun, and the whole operation just takes off into high gear, and I'm drinking straight out of the bottle, never mind the mix, fuck the mix, and just when I'm wondering why the SWAT team isn't busting down the door, he whips up and down like Flipper would if he got tossed up from the high seas onto shore, and then just as quick goes all limp and lays there shuddering and moaning like some little puppy that just got kicked up against the door for peeing on the rug. That's it, game's over with the winning field goal I see, and none too soon. I'm seeing double on account of the strong drink and excitement, and then the girls back off and go into one of the other rooms, to shower and change is my guess, but who knows as this has all happened so fast and is new, uncharted territory for yours truly.

Here I am, sitting out there, all alone with the trick, and I see he hasn't moved; I mean he hasn't *moved*, isn't moving at all now, doesn't even appear to be breathing, and I get this sinking feeling that the girls have worked him over a bit more than he paid for, and how are we going to explain his demise to ol' Alonzo, who I figure is pretty attached to the old guy, and who I'm also pretty sure is sitting close by in one of the front rooms, perusing last year's *Reader's Digest* or the hotel Gideon, and just waiting to ferry us all around for the meal part of the evening's activities.

Just when I'm calculating the chances of surviving a jump to the street from the third floor we happen to be on, he makes this grunting noise which like to scares me to death, not expecting it, and pushes himself up from the floor. He gives me a big wink.

"Pete," he says, striking up a conversation like I hadn't just got done watching him participate in the weirdo willie sex walkathon but were just two traveling salesmen found ourselves sitting at some hotel bar, "you are an all right guy. I can see you are wise in the ways of the world and are a lad who knows how to keep things to himself. I could use a young man like you in my organization. If you ever need a job, look me up." He was talking to me in the friendliest way, but I have to admit, sitting around chewing the fat with a naked man who I had just witnessed getting stomped on and crop-whipped to the finish in the Pervert Sweepstakes by two hookers made me just a tad nervous.

Not wanting to seem disrespectful, I said, "Yes, sir. I appreciate that, sir. I'll keep that in mind, sir," but I couldn't look him in the eye, only just kind of kept my head down like I was checking out my French manicure.

"Good," he said, and reached over and squeezed my shoulder, which, I have to be totally honest; gave me the heebie jeebies, as he was buck naked and scratching his nuts with his other hand at the same time he's kneading my shoulder. "You ever decide you might like to work for me, you can find me down at the Fairmont Hotel, in the main bar, most afternoons. I have a lot of enterprises, both here and in Texas, and I'll just bet we can find a suitable spot for a smart fella like you seem to be."

"I'll sure keep that in mind, sir," I said, wishing he'd just leave or at least go put some shorts or something on. It's not that I haven't been around naked guys before—I played baseball for Christ sake—but we were *all* naked. It's a lot different when one of you has got clothes on and the other hasn't. It's unnatural, somehow. That must have been all that was on his mind, cause he shines me this big grin and offers me his hand, which I take and we shake like we just agreed to something, and he turns away and takes his naked ass into the room where the girls have gone, a spring in his step like he's just won the Camptown Races, and then here come the girls, all squeaky-clean and redressed in their outfits, and am I glad to see them.

"Robert'll be along in a minute," says Cat. "He has to take a shower, and then we can go."

The oddest thought pushed its way into my head. *This is some whore.* She has taken the profession and pushed it to new artistic levels. I figured most people were like me, thought being a hooker was a piece of cake. Just lay on your back and take it easy and don't forget the money on the dresser. Maybe that was true, for most, but not this lady. I found myself looking at her with newfound esteem. This was a hooker in the high minors, if not the big leagues. She was as much an all-star in her field as Ty Cobb had been between the baselines.

I said, "Where'd you learn to do stuff like that to guys? You know, you're really something. You, too," I added quickly, to Jackie, smiling. Cat gave me a look I couldn't figure out, and the slightest hint of a smile came to her eyes, which vanished almost as soon as it appeared. Her serious, "work" face appeared, and her eyes, which had softened briefly, hardened again.

"C'mon, let's go," she said, walking past me. I stood there

and Jackie went by, brushing my arm as if on purpose and catching my eye for an instant, and raised her eyebrows in an exaggerated gesture. I thought I saw the slightest wink but I wasn't sure. That was the most communicating Jackie had done since I'd met her, hours before. I hadn't been too sure of her before, mostly figured she didn't have much use for white boys like myself, but now I got the feeling we might become friends.

And then it was like I didn't exist, Cat and Jackie began to argue over where they want Robert to take us for dinner, and I ask can't we just get some Chinese take-out—all of a sudden I don't feel so good as the action and the booze has wore me out to the point where a nap sounds like just the ticket—and the girls just laugh so I guess we're going out and nobody cares what *I* want or how *I'm* feeling.

He takes us to Arnaud's and when I see where we're going, I start to get the pep back in my step. I'd seen Arnaud's a million times, but never did I think I'd be inside, but here we go and he says to order anything we want. I check out what costs the most and it's a close one between the figures on the right side of the menu and the Brazilian national debt, so it don't matter what I pick, I'm getting full value, so I get what I like, which is a nice, juicy steak and I figure to round out the shipment with appetizers, most of which appears to be made of stuff that don't come from our own native shores. The truffles sound delightful, so I place a double order for those, and there was some other things with French names I had 'em send around, and all in all it was a delightful dining and gastronomic experience I won't forget tomorrow and probably not even next year.

The girls went for the crawfish etoufee, some bisque and drinks that were pastel colors and had umbrellas to shade them from the intense heat of the table candles, and Robert had the boys in the kitchen whip up the baked salmon for him, which is one of the things I had considered, but it's not like you can't get a can of tuna or salmon any day of the week down at Schweggman's, so I stayed with good old American beef, charbroiled on the outside, well-done in the interior, and slathered with plenty of catsup and a good brand of steak sauce which the waiter pretended they didn't have until Robert tells him to fetch it and he does.

We had a nice conversation, me and Robert and the girls, except I didn't hardly catch the drift of any of it. They was going on about books and movies and stuff I'd never heard of, and that Cat! She was turning out to be full of one surprise after the next, gabbing with this guy like they were classmates in Senior Philosophy 101 or something. Jackie's hanging in there, too, with the ten-dollar words, and none of the subjects that was brought up was on books or movies I ever seen, not even any of the classics featuring John Rambo, of which I knew plenty about, if I had only been quizzed, which I wasn't. What they was talking about was interesting I guess, but too much work to gab about on a regular basis; you'd have to memorize a lot more names than I had time for, but, all in all, we had a swell time with His Nibs, and then he had us sent home in the limo, we'd have to excuse him, he said, he wanted to take a turn in the Quarter, get some air, and there was a blue envelop with the letters "R.D." in fancy script on the outside he passed out to each of us and then he excused himself to go to the john, shaking hands all around before he left. We're supposed to go now, Cat said, Alonzo will be waiting outside. I opened mine up right away and inside is two twenties and a ten, and I knew already that Cat and Jackie were supposed to get two and a half bills for their main starring role.

Cat did the funniest thing, on the way to the door. We were all in a line, Jackie leading, then Cat and then me, and Cat reached over and stuck her envelop in Jackie's purse which was one of those big suitcases some gals carry, and open. I started to say something, but she put her finger to her lips when she saw I'd seen her, and I kept my lip zipped.

There was one part about the restaurant thing that was disturbing. When we were going out, a guy I had before known only by sight was standing outside. He was waiting on us. On me, actually. It was Sam "The Bam" Capelli. We had a conversation. He talked; I listened. And tried to keep my sudden attack of diarrhea from erupting.

"Hi, Pete," he goes. I had a sick feeling about this. This was no chance encounter. I didn't think he'd ice me right there on the main drag, but then you never know, these crazy mob types. I look over at Alonzo, over at the car, helping the girls climb into the limo, but it don't look like he's who I should figure on for assistance, happen trouble should commence. It was pretty clear we'd been made. The only thing I could think of was that he thought we still had the money and was under orders to get it back before he terminated us.

"Hi, Sam," I say, and giggle before I can help it. I hate it when that happens, but in tense situations I been known to do that. I shine a monkey grin and Sam smiles back and that's when I got really scared and had to fight like crazy to keep from squeezing one out. Sam don't never smile.

"I'm close to getting your money," I said. That even sounded lame to me.

"Sorry to hear about your hooking up with Tommy," he goes on, and that spot in my stomach begins to kick up and throb. He wasn't talking about the money I owed him.

"I just want you to know we know you are the guys. Fred gave us a good description. Seen your TV appearance, too."

He paused and brought out a pack of Luckies and tapped one out.

"Here's the good news. The boss says I should give you a chance to give the money back. We figure you were just out for a score, didn't know who you were messing with. That about right?" He squinted through the cigarette smoke that was curling around his eyes.

I thought about denying everything, then had a moment of lucidity, and nixed that brainstorm. "Yes, sir. That's it exactly. But, Mr. Capelli, we don't have the money. We never did.

LaVerne, that's Fred's wife, she took it."

He looked at me and I hope I never see eyes like that again in this lifetime.

"You don't say. You know, Pete, I might tend to not believe that, but fact is, we're aware of the situation between Fred and his lovely spouse. This leaves me in a bit of a quandary though, Pete. On the one hand, I know the boss wants his money. He's waiting for me to bring it to him right now. On the other, it's only half a mil, not really all that much. He might want to make an example out of you guys more than he wants the money. I just don't know, partner."

Just then I heard Cat yell at me from the car.

"Come on, Pete. We don't have all night." I waved at her to just give me a minute. Sam was standing in the shadows where I don't think they could see who it was from the car.

"I'll tell you what, Pete. I'm just the hired hand here. I'll tell the boss your sad story and see what he says. He may be in a generous mood, give you a little time to find LaVerne. I seen him like that before. I *think* I have. We'll be looking right along with you, give you a helping hand, so to speak. I think I'll let you go with your little friends for now. I think the boss would approve of that."

I turned to go, needing to go to the bathroom in the worst way.

"Oh…and Pete?"

My head turned and I half expected to see a gun in his hand.

"Pete, I know I don't have to tell you. Don't leave town." He gave me what I think was a grin. "I always wanted to use that line."

Oh, shit, I'm thinking. I need to get me to a church and log some time on my knees, tell the Man about the Titanic I'm on and the iceberg coming up, and could He see His way to saving me a place on a lifeboat. One day and already these guys have figured out who we were. I started to say something, but Sam waved his hand.

"Shut up, Pete." He spoke in a soft voice and his lips smiled, slightly, but his eyes were a flat black latex, with no life in them.

"Shut up, and listen up. One more thing: You try anything funny before I get back to you, it'll be worse. I got the hit, you know. You mess up, it won't just be a hit. It'll be *painful*. Remember that."

The hit? The hit? Oh, fuck, oh, fuck, oh, fuck, I'm dead; is all that kept running through my brain. The Cosa Nostra has put a contract out on us and we are going to be laying down somewhere with pennies on our eyes, soon. My knees kinda went and I thought I would faint, right there on Bourbon Street, faint dead away with the tourists and hayseeds passing by, looking down at the drunk laying on the sidewalk, Cat and Jackie and Alonzo peeking out of the limo thinking I had a heart attack. I *knew* I only had seconds left before I would begin to achieve room temperature.

Things kind of went blank for a minute and I must have started to slip, cause next thing I know Sam has got his knuckles dug into my arm and is hoisting me up. He put his face close to mine, and said, "You want to listen real good, Pete. This is your lucky day. The hit's off, temporarily. Unless you don't pay up. I'm talking about the money you took from Fred and I'm talking about the money you owe me. You and Tommy. I haven't forgot that. This other don't trump that. It just puts it in second place for a bit. I don't care who pays me. I don't get paid, you both are in some serious trouble. *Terminal* trouble, if you catch my meaning. If the boss gives you any time, there's gonna be interest on the dough. That just goes without saying. The interest is two G's a week. That is, if the boss is in a generous mood and gives you some time."

Two G's a week? It might as well be two *million*, least as far as I was concerned. I looked toward the car. Alonzo was just standing there, no expression on his face, holding the door, waiting for me. Everything that had just happened had only taken a brief moment or two, but it seemed like forever.

"Don't try and skip on me, Pete," Sam was saying. "I can find you anytime I want. I did just now, didn't I? That might tell you something." He still had hold of my arm, the tingle just starting in the extremities where the blood flow had ceased. "I'm going to let you go with your little friends. This is just a friendly warning. I'm in a charitable mood, Pete, which makes you lucky. It also helps I'm a baseball fan. If I wasn't a baseball fan, and if I didn't think you were telling the truth about Fred's wife, me and you wouldn't be having this conversation. I don't think you'd be talking to anyone. I've got faith in you, son. You're going to find LaVerne and that money, aren't you? And that other you owe me."

I almost didn't realize he had let go of my arm and was walking away. I stood there for a minute, concentrating on keeping on my feet, and then I did the only thing I could. I walked over to the car where Alonzo and the girls were waiting, climbed in, smiled at Cat, and then threw up all over everything.

Nobody was in a party mood when Alonzo left us off.

TOMMY IS NO HELP

The next morning I wake up, Cat's gone, I've got a major revolution going on in my head and I'm not in the bed, but on the couch, along with my suitcase, which is on my stomach and which I'm holding with both arms.

There's a note.

It says something to the effect that I better be out of town by sundown, partner, and I gather from the tone that Cat's not happy with me after last night and wishes me to relocate for the duration of my vacation.

I imagine she's not real happy about my tossing my cookies up all over the limo and her party dress. All the indications point to that conclusion, at least from the language in her note. Even her penmanship looks angry, even if the actual words weren't a pretty accurate clue. Maybe it was the way the pen had ripped through the paper when she crossed her t's.

I look at the clock and figure I've got about six hours until she hits home and I can talk some sense into her, for which purpose I'll need at least one gram of coke and probably two. In the meantime, it's time to take inventory, make some plans, find out what the deal is on Tommy.

The alternative is not healthy.

* * *

I can't fucking believe it. There is no justice in this world, none of it for me, anyway. Tommy doesn't make our appointment. I'm out at Bennigan's in Metry, slopping suds with the accountant and car salesmen bunch, and after the nineteenth flattop asked me what my portfolio was in and I tell him I ain't got that tendency, it starts to dawn on me that I've been stiffed by my kidnapping pard.

Mexico. That's the ticket. I'll catch the first Greyhound smoking west.

The more I thought about Mexico, the better I began to feel. Warm weather, spicy chili, and brown-skinned senioritas. I always had a way with the Spanish sisters.

I remembered the time I played winter ball in Caracas, Venezuela, when I was in Double A ball and taking my winters south so's I could maybe make the jump quicker to the Bigs, and this little espanol honey I'd been romancing wiggled her little jumping bean butt up to me on the street, shining on the teeth like she was gonna throw me a hug and some sugar and I saw the razor flash in her hand about one kazillioneth of a second before I set the new world's speed record for crossing avenues with all of my assorted molecules and atoms intact and as previously arranged. At the time, I didn't have a good handle on the local culture is what happened. Seems that down in Bananaland, you're supposed to *personally* tell a gal you're broken up, not let her learn about such unilateral decisions from her best friend. See, it's not the split-up they get nasty about; it's the manner in which they receive the message. Especially if the messenger happens to be her best friend and it's her you've been out flamencoing till dawn with. They've got a limited sense of humor about such situations in their society, and what got me is that we weren't even married or anything permanent like that. I hate to think what would happen if we'd been hitched up and I got surprised with some tootsie.

But that was a long time ago when I was just a raw youth. Now, I had the benefit of vast experience and wouldn't be making the kind of gaffes I had before.

That was the ticket. Lay out in Juarez for a while, soak up the sun, let things cool down over here. Maybe I'd just live down there with our southern neighbors, learn the lingo, see what kinda pool players they were.

Maybe I'd get even farther away, go on down to Central America, hire on as one of those mercenaries, get some CIA bucks, get on the government payroll.

First, I give Tommy the charity of the doubt, figure, hell, maybe his alarm didn't go off, but I got a stronger feeling that he just did what I was considering, only sooner. Asshole took a powder, left me high and dry, and here I sit with a buncha Yuppie twinks who're snickering behind their hands at the dude drinking domestic, which is me.

I slug down my long-neck and order another and wonder what's my next brilliant move, only nothing pops into the old computer bank. I don't have a clue where my feet are gonna take me next, except I hope it's to a place Sam has never heard of. So I do the only thing comes to mind: I order another Pearl and start transferring it to my inner self, my best idea to stick around a while longer and see if Tommy suddenly remembers he's got a pressing appointment with me and walks in the door.

Sure.

This gets the results as pretty much expected, about the same payoff as my usual trifecta bet on the Derby, with the long shot holding down the middle position, and the trifecta odds look a lot shorter than the odds of ol' Tom strolling in anytime in the next five months. It *could* happen, but it's not a breath-holding moment. Just when I'm ready to move left of center, grab a go-cup and depart the C.P.A. convention, in he walks, Mr. Tommy LeClerc and am I a happy hombre.

I can see the news is not good by the way he is smiling.

"Hi, Pete," he calls out, bird-dogging straight for my table.

"Tommy," I say, and he plops down in the seat opposite, and orders two Pearls from the former Miss Sugar Cane who's our friendly server and whom I previously had to practically light myself on fire to get a beer from. She's there so fast, this time, I figure she's under the misimpression Tommy's somebody important that can help her chosen career, somebody like Mr. Bert Parks.

I can't for the life of me figure why Tommy gets such good service everywhere he goes but he does. It can't be because of how he dresses, leisure suits with the stitching showing, and he has this greasy hairdo which he only combs on the occasion of his birthday. Anybody else can sit there an hour and the waiters and waitresses are practically falling over you and never see your hand waving for a drink; you're in their blind spot, but Tommy walks in the joint and they're there in a New York second, whipping out lighters for his cigar and he doesn't even smoke. And he always wears long-sleeved shirts, even when it's the hottest. I always wondered about that.

"Tommy, are you a drug addict?"

He looked at me as if I was crazy.

"I mean, you always wear those long-sleeved shirts. I even seen you wearing a jacket when it's eighty-five out."

"I can't stand the cold, Pete. It's something in my blood. You'll think this is funny: I even have to have a blanket on my bed at night. Air conditioning kills me."

I laughed.

"You for sure aren't an Eskimo Indian, are you! I thought all Indians were supposed to be outdoorsy, walk around in a little towel or something, sleep under the stars on a bed of pine needles. You're the damndest Indian I ever saw!"

"You ever hear of stereotypes, Pete? You might want to get into the twentieth century sometime, learn something about sociology."

"Sam says hey," I gave him the needle, all cheery-like and grinning like one of those Benzedrine addicts up in the Drooling Academy that's got the inside of their skulls reamed out.

"Sam who?" he plays back, like he's Ollie and I'm Stan.

"You seen Sam?"

"No," I say. "Just trying to make you laugh. Yeah, I saw Sam. We had quite a little chat. Wish you could of been there reminding you of what he said. You mighta thought up some bon mots I couldn't come up with at the time, what with my knees banging together so hard I couldn't hear myself think. We coulda used you at this little meet, let Sam know we're clued in and no Gomers, but sharp dudes that knows what to do with corner combination shots."

I said, "You remember us talking about Sam, Tommy? He give me a message to pass on to my *partner*. He says we got to come up with the money. Well, maybe we do. He was gonna ask the main man if he would cut us a break, give us some time to track the lovely and elusive LaVerne down, come up with the money that is rightfully his. Plus interest. Plus the juice. Plus your left nut. Plus what we owe him personally. He's gonna get back to us. Have his people call our people."

I kept talking. I couldn't shut up. Nerves. "Sam's gonna kill us, Tommy. What are we gonna do? We're dead men. Any minute now, we are going to start getting phone calls and brochures in the mail from funeral homes offering us fabulous savings if we act immediately."

He was quiet for a minute and went several times for his glass of beer but kept putting his hand back in his lap.

"You know, Pete, you're right. That's something to think on."

He was silent again, staring down at his glass. It was about empty, as was mine, but our eager beaver waitress was nowhere to be seen. The service had dropped off considerably. It might have had something to do with how Tommy'd stiffed her on the tip, giving her a quarter and a nickel. He lifted his head in a minute and looked at me. He was grinning. I wondered how he'd react to *good* news.

"I told you I got an idea, Pete, something I been working on since our little misfortunate adventure with Fred and LaVerne. Something I come up with for this little emergency such as we find ourselves with. Listen to this." He leaned over and whispered in my ear.

I should have got up and left right then and there. Not me, though. I'm the kind has to go down in the coal mine *after* the shaft collapses.

He had an idea all right. The craziest idea I'd ever heard of. It was a way for both of us to make some real money, not only pay off our debts, but come out rich as ex-Vice Presidents. At least according to Tommy's view. All he whispered was a couple of sentences, but that was enough to make me move.

I stood up. "Tommy, I'm leaving. I shoulda left when I seen you coming in, but no, I had to stay. You know why? Because I'm unlucky. No, I'm not unlucky, not as much as I'm plain stupid. I've heard some wild scams from you before, but this is just plain wacko. You think I've forgotten the parking meter thing, don't you? You think I've got Alzheimer's and have even forgotten the caper we just pulled. I haven't forgotten, Tommy. I'll *never* forget, Tommy. I'll never forget in a million years, not that I'll live that long. I won't live that long just because I've stood this close to you and I know that pisses God off, Tommy. Anybody that comes within five feet of you, God curses, Tommy. Did you know that? It's true. I'm damned, just for having a conversation with you. I'm double cursed for having participated in these jobs with you."

I got my breath.

"Tommy, just tell Sam to come and put one in my brainpan, after he gets done doing you. At least, that way, it'll be painless. I get mixed up with you in this caper you have dreamed up, if I'm not taken out in a slow, lingering, *painful* manner, I'll be buried so far up in Angola Prison I won't even receive mail. There's no zip code where they'll bury us. There's longevity in my family, but so far nobody's lived to be two hundred and eleven years old, and that's about what I'd be, time I'd get out. Unless, of course, they elect to fry us instead. Tommy, this last little deal was just a simple kidnapping and look what happened.

You're talking about something that could turn into a death which the state would look at as murder, no matter we maybe didn't mean to kill the guy. They have a peculiar way of looking at such things. No, Tommy, include me out on this one. You're a crazy man. Insane, too."

I turned and walked away, out the door, what he'd just proposed the only thing in my head. I couldn't get rid of it. It was on a billboard that took up the whole space behind my eyes.

Amputation. That was the operative word. That was his ace plan, the cabal that was going to make us richer than the sheriff of Metry. The color in Tommy's shorts must have seeped into his blood stream, got into his brain, caused extensive chemical damage, more than was there already.

I had to think. I had to come up with a plan to either find LaVerne and get the money back or get out of town for a spell. A spell of about fifty years, I figured.

On the walk back to Cat's, I racked my brain, but nothing came up that made sense. It looked like it was down to making a run for it. But where? And how? I wasn't exactly rolling in traveler's checks and I'd misplaced my CD's.

I tried, I really tried, but Tommy's word kept popping up in my skull.

Amputation.

As in to snatch somebody, whack off and hold one of his appendages for ransom. As in FBI and guys in three-piece suits that all looked like Efrem Zimbalist, Junior, and couldn't wait to put holes in you, prove their sharpshooter medals were no fluke.

Amputation.

As in a judge that looks over the top of the bench and says I'm gonna send you away to jail for so long that when you get out, everybody'll be speaking Japanese in the streets and using chopsticks to eat Popeye's extra-spicy. I started feeling light-headed and dizzy as I walked, because Tommy's great idea scared me so much, I knew I was gonna do it.

I walked by a gas station and went inside, picked up a map, figured I'd pick out a spot to run to. When I got to Cat's, I spread it out on the kitchen table and discovered I'd gotten the wrong map. It only showed the U.S. of A, Canada, Mexico, and parts of Central America. It didn't cover enough territory, show a place where I'd feel safe enough.

Amputation.

I turned the A/C up higher. It was sure hot and muggy in here, the way I was sweating. Cat ought to get the maintenance guy up here to fix her thermostat, thing reading sixty-two when the perspiration's pouring off a guy, must be broke.

I took another gander at the map. Maybe Alaska. Skagway looked interesting. Would I need a passport?

I did the only thing I could, under the circumstances.

I got roaring, stinking drunk.

Amputation.

Shit.

THE PHONE RINGS—BUT IT'S NOT ED MCMAHON

Just when the word "suicide" starts to become an integral part of my thinking vocabulary and I'm wondering how long it takes on the down stroke when you step off the Greater New Orleans bridge, something comes over me and I slip into some kind of a Zen state where I just don't give a rat's behind what happens next. I dope out a half-assed plan to get hold of some bucks and just light out of town. If I make it, fine, if not, then it's been an interesting life only it would have turned out better if I had been able to learn to wait on the hanging curve.

The hell with this jive, I thought. I'm not walking around with my dick shriveled up and my hands sweaty. I'll just do my best to lose this town. Once I decided that, I felt better. I took a shower and changed my T-shirt and jeans and walked down to Fat City. There wasn't anybody in the Speakeasy when I went in, so I had a Pearl and chinned with the bartender for a while. She was pretty stoned, going to the bathroom every eighty-five seconds or so to powder her nose, but she said, yeah, there's usually some out-of-towners, tourists, stop in most afternoons to shoot pool and take in the local flavor, so I stuck around to see if I could maybe add to my bankroll before I lit out. Nothing like swatting mosquitoes and sweating malaria when an elephant's bearing down on your ass.

I figured if I could run my wad up to seven, eight hundred bucks, I could catch a Trailways smoking somewhere—Idaho or something—and keep on the lam long enough that Sam gets tired of chasing after me. I started having this daydream about moving from town to town, ending up in Montana where I'd get me a mountain babe what didn't shave under her arms nor her legs, called me Sugarbunch, made piles of chocolate chip cookies, and wore a blue gingham apron and not much else. I was going pretty good with this scene when who walks in but Tommy, and right up to me like he had earlier over to Bennigan's, and right away, I knew fate was rolling me nothing but straight boxcars and snake-eyes.

I sighed and pointed at the bottle of Jack behind the bar, and the girl poured a glass half full and slapped water over it with her little gasoline pump. Beer wasn't going to be strong enough for the next few minutes. I could have ordered one for Tommy and he would have drunk it, but I thought, what the hell, let him buy his own, he's the salesman with the pitch, and why pay for a bad time which I know is about to commence. Whatever he lays on me has got to be sorry news in the long run, but I see no way out at the present. The Montana thing looked good while I was staring at the bottom of a beer bottle, but reality was checking in. I knew I'd never get out of the city limits, 'less it was in the trunk of a car and I was leaving to be an alligator's lunch.

"Turkey and Coke," he says, waiting until she poured the drink and named the price before he came up with the required exact change. He reached back into his pocket like he was look-ing for the map to the lost Comstock lode and pulled out a quarter, which he laid with great ceremony on the bar. "For you," he said, to the bartender, and she snorted, causing her nose to begin bleeding so that she had to make another bath-room rendezvous for first aid, leaving us all alone.

"First, to restate our position: Sam's gonna erase us, 'less we come up with some money, quick-like," he said, as if we hadn't already had this conversation and I had just flown in from my weekly business meeting in Dallas.

"Tommy," I said. "You ever think you might piss me off and there wouldn't be enough left of you for Sam to shoot?" He ignored that.

"I'm just bringing this up so that you are fully aware of the situation. *Our* situation."

"Fuck you, Tommy. Every one of your stupid ideas gets me closer to a state of extreme rigor mortis. I think I'll live longer if I relocate far enough away from you. I hate your stupid face, Tommy, for getting me into this mess. All I ever wanted was not that much. Just enough to open me a po-boy joint. Is that too much to wish for?" I was talking out loud to myself, at this point.

He said, "That's the point, Pete. I don't see where we got any choice, but to be partners. We're both in the same boat, so to speak. And I've got a feeling the only plan you got is to catch a plane. Seems to me you need me. I represent the only chance you got."

I hated to admit it, but he was right. The idea of being partners again, with anybody, not to mention a no-brainer like Tommy, made me grind my molars, but I was fantasizing I could fix up whatever lame plan he had and maybe make it work. Sure I could. As soon as that thought flashed through my brainpan, a second thought followed hot on its heels that suggested this might be a good time to have my CAT scan updated.

But, hell, I had to confess that Tommy's idea, no matter how bad it might be, represented something a thousand percent better than anything I had been able to come up with. If this didn't work, whatever it was he had up his sleeve, I probably wouldn't be any worse off than I was now, provided we didn't get caught. Dead is dead. I could still always try and make a run for it. Like to China, maybe, learn to plant rice, wear one of them funny hats, make believe noodles was turkey and dressing come the Christmas holidays.

"So what's this great kidnap plan, Tommy?" I asked. "How's it work, exactly? You said something about amputating a hand.

That's when you lost me. I'm not sure I really want to hear this. What? We're gonna snatch the mayor or the governor and hold his meathook for ransom? You know how many people'd pay us to just keep either of those turkeys? They ain't exactly the most popular citizens we got here in this part of the country. They for sure ain't never won an election on the popular vote. Not the *live* popular vote, that is. I hear they are pretty popular in certain cemeteries."

He snickered. "Naw, Pete. Not the mayor. Somebody better. And my idea has got a wrinkle you won't believe. This is an Indian idea: cunning and slick. My idea makes this kidnapping absolutely foolproof. Listen, what's the most common thing goes wrong in a kidnap?"

I pondered that a minute. "Well, let's see...there's the FBI, for starters. Then you got the local cops and then you got the state militia, case you snatch one that's too young; all them mothers get blurry-eyed and phone the governor and quick as the Saints can lose a coin toss, you got every uniform in the state including Boy Scouts, looking for you. Hell, they even get the KKK out for the right kidnap victim."

"No, Pete, really think about it. I mean, what's the thing that usually gets the kidnappers caught? The one thing more than any other thing?"

That was easy.

"Tommy, the first thing that gets kidnappers nailed is for them to sit in some bar in Fat City discussing the arrangements. Just the fact that I'm across from you, listening to this pipe dream is probably enough to convict me. I can tell you right now, I got a powerful feeling we're gonna both of us be sitting up in Angola eating red beans and wondering why our girlfriends insist on keeping those damned mustaches and beards, before this year's up."

"No, Pete, you keep missin' the question. There's one thing that always gets the bad guys caught." You could tell Tommy liked the phrase "bad guys" the way he said it, like he really thought he *was* bad. Made him feel like a no-filter cigarette kind of hombre. He'd seen too many movies, was my guess. A lot of hours spent in the dark at the Bijou, whacking off and role-playing the Clint Eastwood parts.

Neither of us said anything for a minute, and I realized he was still waiting for me to answer his stupid question, but I was sick and tired of the game. If he wanted me to come up with some kind of answer I hadn't already, he'd wait until the Saints were two touchdown favorites in the Super Bowl.

Finally, he says, obviously disappointed I hadn't come up with the answer he was after, "Pete, the bad guys always get caught 'cause the person payin' the ransom calls in the cops."

This was his great revelation? Of course they call the cops! You ever meet anyone who's worth a cool million outta your pocket? I mean a wife or a husband? Kids, yeah, maybe, at least ones that ain't yet teenagers, but your spouse? I mean a *for-real* million, that's sitting there on the kitchen table, not some *abstract* million that's a figure on their bank statement. Who's worth that?

Most human beings, they might start out with all the best of good intentions, figure to do their utmost to get poor old hubby George or dear old honey-bell Alice out of the clutches of the terrible 'nappers, but let them draw the dough out of the bank and sit and watch it all piled up there on the kitchen table for five minutes, let it sink in that this is really a *million fucking dollars*, and I'll bet most folks can't wait to get their finger to dialing 911. They keep looking at that stack of greenbacks, they'll be breaking their necks to get to a phone! Hell, they'll be sticking their heads out the window, screaming for a cop.

I relay this bit of knowledge about human psychology to Tommy, but it turns out he's had this insight and that's the whole basis for his plan. Not only that, he's got a new twist on a regular job of kidnap that makes my toes curl when he lays it on me.

"That's right, Pete, it's darn near impossible to do a decent job of kidnappin' 'cause the paying party always has to go run and drag the cops into it. That means you got to kill the victim and you mess up, leave the bottom half of your left thumbprint on the doorknob or something, and bingo, you're looking up at a guy in black robes and a case of chronic constipation and he's discussing your sad ass future over which he has the deciding vote. Next thing you know, you're chained to some antisocial dude that's flirting with you on the bus ride to Angola, and you know if you break his heart he's gonna break your head.

"I got a way around that.

"The cop part, I mean. I guarantee, with my plan, the cops will not be a factor."

I was sure curious how he was going to accomplish this.

"By eliminating the middle man. We're gonna make the kidnapped party give us the ransom money hisself. Plus, we're gonna make the stakes too high for him to not want to call the cops till *after* he pays us."

Sure we were. We'd just put the guy on his honor; say, look pal, do us a favor, will you? Run down to the bank and withdraw a million bucks. Or just write us a check. Don't say anything to the authorities until we're in Buenos Aires. We'll call you from there to give you the all-clear. I wondered if Tommy wanted to get his own CAT scan checked out while I was getting mine done. I mentioned that. "Wasn't that the idea with Fred and LaVerne?" I said. "He was gonna give us money so his sweetie didn't get whacked?"

He just laughed. An evil laugh, a laugh that sent chills down my neck.

"*Amputation*," he said, cryptically, and he looked around like he thought the CIA was in town. Just the one word I'd been hearing since he first said it, and then he says it again. "Amputation." Then, "Just think about that, Pete. That's the element was missing with Fred."

Think about what? I thought of the wino who hangs around uptown, has no legs, scoots around on a little pallet on wheels.

He wasn't making any sense. I just didn't get it. Then he explained a little bit of what he had in mind. *That* was the part that curled my toes. And got me interested. And got me scared. Sweaty-hands scared.

Before I could chime in with my valuable opinion of Tommy's grand scheme, he said, "Come on. Let's blow this joint, Pete. Don't answer me now—just think on it. When you're ready to do the smart thing, let me know and I'll fill you in on the details. Let's go have us some fun. I got an idea how we can pick up a few bucks. Not as much as the kidnap, but some pocket money. You decide what you want to do is make a run for it, you're gonna need some loot, aren't you? Let's not talk about my idea for a while, just think about it, and lets you and me go out and pick up a few bucks, pull a nice easy scam, quit all this worrying for a while."

Turns out his idea, when he explained it, appealed to me and now I was really spooked. I was finding that being on the same wave length as Tommy was not a comforting thought, when you realize he is what you might call the "criminally stupid."

It occurred to me that I was getting sucked into what could only be called "The Vortex of Tommy LeClerc's Insanity." I could feel it happening, but was powerless to stop it. It was like being caught in the undertow out in the Gulf. I hadn't agreed to participate in his kidnapping scheme yet, but I knew I would. It was only a matter of time. It was a weakness of mine, a character flaw; being easily dissuaded and sold bogus goods that anybody else could see was bogus a mile away. I could drop a hundred bucks faster than Democrats raise taxes and drop girlfriends, on a street corner shell game…and I *know how it works*! It's not under *any* of the cups. It's palmed in the con's hand until he chooses a cup, *not* the one you picked. I *know* that… and I still bet money it's under one of the cups! There's just something about larceny that proves irresistible to me. It's kind of like heroin to a junkie or graves registration lists to a Chicago alderman.

What Tommy had in mind was to go over to Algiers, take in this cock fight that goes every Friday night, and make some money off the rubes that attend such sporting events. Be like a busman's holiday, for us master criminals, give us a break and time to relax and think about Tommy's great scheme. And make a few bucks. No matter what, both of us needed some dough, if for nothing else for getaway bread. There's always a truckload of betting money floating around a cock fight. Why else hold one?

I'm still not decided about the kidnap scheme, even though I got this sinking feeling that when it goes down, I'll be right there in the front row, but I could use some change in my jeans for when I make my break if I do, and this is a hustle I've got some experience in and can see how it will work.

Tommy has this angle, turns out. He knows one of the guys who's got roosters fighting and this guy's got him a for-sure ringer, a champion cock that looks like any sissy bluebird could whup him, feathers all dirty and bedraggled, cross-eyed and limping and all twisted-up looking. That's the way Tommy described this bird, and he said, there ain't a sharpie in coveralls in the place what wouldn't jump on a chance to bet against this turkey, 'specially to two young know-nothing city slickers such as we were gonna look like.

I liked it.

If he was telling the truth about this bird, this might be the easiest money I'd made in a month.

"This is the real low-down, Pete," he says. "My pal's cock is the legit thing, an honest-to-God ringer. This is money in the bank. My friend Jim-Bob just bought this rooster from a hillbilly over in Alabama what give him up on account of he'd done whipped all the birds in that neck of the woods and he couldn't get him no more fights with the locals, on account of they're all tapped out, puttin' their pokes on Slant-Eyed Joe. That's what Jim-Bob calls him, 'Slant-Eyed Joe.' Beautiful bird! Money machine! The guy sells him to Jim-Bob for the mortgage on his shack, and it's a good deal for both of 'em seein' as how Jim's gonna earn *three* houses with this bird, and all the Alabama guy's been doin' lately is puttin' out money on chicken lunches for ol' Slant-Eye."

Even though I know Tommy's about one-half bullshit and the other half some unidentifiable material that smelled funny, I get a good feeling about this one. For one thing, I know this ain't the first time a scam like this has been pulled, in the cockfighting game; these old pros do it all the time, go to some other state where the sport of clodhoppers is king, find some scrufty-looking killer rooster that's whipped everything in feathers and either trade for a similar specimen they own that's in the same no-betting syndrome, or else buy him outright, take him home and make some easy money. So that part of his story rung true, and I just had a feeling about the way he laid it out that Tommy was telling the truth.

I was party to a setup something like this one time down in the winter leagues, when we got this grudge game set up with the locals in Sonora who claimed they could whip our bunch which was mostly boys from north of the border. We bet the ranch, knowing we could dust their butts, bunch of old men and young kids thought they could beat us pros, and then the day of the game come, and they trot out this pitcher who looks a lot like the picture on my Juan Marichal rookie card, and we go, oh, for twenty-seven and lose our lunch money for the next three months. We wasn't gonna pay up for a while, but when we seen their knife collection, we felt it was the only sporting thing to do.

It felt nice to be on the money-*making* side of a ringer scam for a change.

We go in Tommy's car.

"Look like you ain't got many brains," says Tommy, as we walk back this lane. We came down this dirt road outside Algiers that the Romans woulda paved, and parked away from the hundred and fifty pickup trucks in this field, just in case we had to depart the premises suddenly. "Look dumb," he says, again.

"Can I use your name?" I said. "Or is it enough to just try and match your facial expressions?" This goes right over Tommy, who says "huh?" and we walk about a day's march and we're there. There's this huge tent you can see probably doubles for all the big Klan rallies and there's lots of yelling and hooraying going on, about six cock fights being held all at once and a dice game or two taking place on the fringes plus some hookers working the Port A Johns. A host of entrepreneurs going at the American Dream. We were the only foreigners didn't have on bib overhauls, so that part of the plan was working— we looked like a couple of slickers didn't know the end of the chicken the food went in from the end it come out.

"Let's find the real money," Tommy says, and that takes about a minute and a half. We just searched out the biggest crowd. There was cockfights going on all over the place. Later, when the amateurs got played out, there'd be just one and that's when the serious money'd come out.

We both spotted our mark at the same time, not like he was hiding out or anything. Big, fat guy, wearing a Saints baseball hat, bibs like everyone else, and a big ol' Navy Colt .45 sticking right out of his front pocket, like some outlaw in the Old West. He was holding a wad of bills that would of choked a porno movie queen. We eyeballed his action for a while and sure enough, he was the heavy hitter we was looking for. He had three-four stooges making bets for him, too. They kept coming up to him, handing him bills, sometimes taking some which he gave up with a frown, but mostly they was sticking money in his fist, making his wad even bigger. He was handling the heavy action himself.

"He's the one," whispered Tommy, hand over his mouth. "Let's get established with Barney there. Try and lose a few, make him think what we know about cock-fightin' ain't diddly-squat, set him up for when Jim-Bob fights ol' Slant-Eyed Joe.

This injun'll show you how the redman takes off palefaces."

Where had I heard this philosophy before? I got a funny feeling, a sense of déjà vu, but shook it off. Tommy was right— this was the right way to run the game. We had to establish ourselves as chumps so he wouldn't hesitate to take a big bet and give up good odds.

Turned out, it wasn't that hard to lose money. The way we did it was to bet the ones we thought were gonna win. It's hard to lose on purpose, no matter how smart it was, and we both kept betting the best-looking birds and watching them get whipped. There must of been a bus-load of ringers at this event. It was a good thing we had inside information or else we'd gambled away the family farm. It appeared as if good looks was a detriment to a chicken in this game. The winners was all ugly as ex-wives.

Tommy grins at me after we paid off two-three bets, like, *See? It's workin'*, but I knew he wasn't really trying to lose any more than I was.

Then something happened, we both got lucky and won a couple and all of a sudden we're both up a few hundred bucks and wondering what's going wrong. The next bet pays off, too, and the big guy is scowling like the pup that's on the hind-tit, and the way he snaps the bills off is hard-core evidence he's displeased with how life is currently slapping him around, and now we're starting to look like sharpies, which is not a good prescription for continued good health in parts like these. Since we both doubled up on the last bet, trying to get back to even money and take on our desired persona as stupid but rich, we now have almost five hundred bucks in our jeans and are coming across as cock-fighting Nick the Greek's, which was not the plan we started out with before the first pitch was thrown. This is in line with most of my life and a situation I'm familiar with, although not comfortable with; no, not at all.

Our timing on the scam remains impeccable as just then Tommy points out this little runt making for our ring, and says,

"That's Jim-Bob," and it's time to get the real money down. We name a figure of a thousand each and the guy nods at us, but he forgot to wear his smile and lets us know he'll take the bet, but we are going to have to lay odds, which is a development that wasn't in the original prospectus, but one we will have to live with. I give Tommy the eye, the very *nervous* eye, and he winks, so I go ahead and bet under the prevailing conditions but my heart ain't in it and the main part of my brain is occupied with wondering how we're gonna get out of here with our money, once we collect. The other, more negative part of my brain, is wondering how we're going to get out of here if we lose, being as the sum we have just wagered is not within the purview of either of us, individually or collectively. Tommy has doubled his bet, at the last minute. Looking around, I notice most of the guys seem to be related, probably all cousins on their mother's sides or something, and the gene pool they have come out of is not Olympic size, and my antiperspirant is definitely on the fritz with the thought of what might be in the cards, but the die was cast.

It was weird—every man Jack here *did* look alike. I thought of the comedian I saw once down at Storyville one time that did a bit on Algiers, when he said, the most burning question most folks had over there was "If a man and woman get a divorce in Algiers, are they still legally considered brother and sister?" Looking over this bunch, that was a question I bet more than one of them had asked themselves.

Boy, oh boy. All the money I had in the world, plus some I didn't have, was tied up in a chicken named Slant-Eyed Joe, and when ol' Jim brought ol' Slant-Eyed out from under his arm and set him down in that ring, all I could think was, that was the most pitiful chicken ever walked a barnyard. He sure as shit *had* to be a fighter, he was too butt-ugly to be a lover. He was the ugliest chicken I ever seen in my life. Hell, he was the ugliest *anything* I ever seen. I seen revenue agents look prettier than this bird.

He looked even worse than what Tommy'd described, and all of a sudden, I went from feeling sick to feeling terminal. This buzzard looked sick, too, on top of it, like maybe he'd got the chicken pox or something, could barely hold his head up, and looked to me like he was in the middle of a major, change-of-life molt. Had a bad limp as well, and I was just getting ready to suggest to Tommy that maybe we shouldn't wait around for the grand finale and other festivities, but take our French leave right now whilst everyone was occupied, when two things happened at once. There's one hell of a commotion over by where you come into the tent; somebody is blaring something out on one of them electronic bullhorns, and I see guns and knives and all sorts of things hit the ground. It dawns on me that we've been busted, and I am so happy at this turn of events as it is clear we are about to lose a bundle of money we don't presently own. I want to find me a deputy sheriff and make sure I don't get over-looked in the arrest procedures. Slant-Eyed Joe takes this opportunity to reach over and peck his opponent in the eye, thereby killing him dead, in one peck, and my joy takes a one-eighty as I sense we are never going to see our winnings.

Sure enough, the commotion was the law. Algiers sheriffs, about a thousand of them, walking in with riot guns pointed upward and bracelets for all.

Not only was it humiliating to be handcuffed with my hands behind my back, they add insult to injury by making the whole crowd walk up to the highway. They'd parked the police vans up there so's not to attract attention until they were ready to raid the party. The blisters I'd got hiking down to the tent earlier were getting stepbrother and stepsister blisters to keep 'em company, and my back was getting sore where this clown kept poking me with his nightstick. Least I kept pretending it was his nightstick and not the barrel of a .12 gauge. I didn't peek, as we were all stumbling around in the dark, and if it was a shotgun I'd just as soon not be aware of it. In my mind, it was a nightstick. Nightsticks don't go off when you trip and ventilate a person.

We spent a lovely night in the Algiers lockup, in the bullpen, and I didn't speak to Tommy. Not a word. He came up to me, grinning, and I didn't say a word, but I guess he saw something in my face because he backed off and went clear across the room and stayed over there all night.

They took our money as evidence. That was the bad part. We had to face the judge in the morning. That was the worse part. I was sure there was gonna be a fine involved somewhere before we were done, and since the state had seized most all the money I owned in the world, it didn't look likely I was going to be able to pay any such levy, nor make bail. I wasn't a chipper camper, thinking about all of this. Tommy better bail me out if he gets out, I was thinking, but that prospect didn't cheer me up too much, once I got to computing the odds of that occurring.

"I was there merely as an observer," I tell the judge next morning, "studying human behavior."

"I don't give a damn if you're Margaret Mead," fires back His Eminence, peeping down over his wire-frames. "Thirty days or five hundred dollars."

It wasn't fair. I even brought up my college education, my full semester at Delgado Junior College and the Berlitz course in espanol I'd took when I was playing winter ball, but did that carry any weight? Ha!

So much for the value of an education these days.

And then they had the unmitigated effrontery to put me in the same cell as the "Dream Flyer."

The Dream Flyer.

That's what I called him from the very start—it was *me* that named him, give him the name all the newspapers and TV reporters used—people read about him in the paper and probably thought some reporter give him that name, but it was me that pinned his moniker on him, all right.

I was right about Tommy. He made his own bail somehow,

must have had a friend or relative on the outside, but he didn't come through for his buddy and rap partner, mainly me. Didn't even stop by on his way out to say good-bye and good luck. That was no surprise.

The state kept my money, claimed it was gambling money and therefore theirs. They had the best game in town, seems like. I couldn't understand their logic, but it was their ballgame, all I was doing was financing it. I'd made a serious tactical mistake, one a real outlaw should never make. I'd forgot it was an election year. That kinda oversight will ruin you as a big-time crook, and it wasn't like I didn't know better. I'd just been so busy lately with Sam and all that business I'd got behind in my editorial page reading. Hell, they *never* bust cock fights—leastways I never heard of it before—Christ, half the spectators and participants is usually cops—but here I was in the Algiers parish jail, and here I would be another twenty-nine days. Time I got out, Sam would have time to build a really good mad. That was a comforting thought, let me sleep easy at night knowing who the welcoming committee was apt to be day I got out.

Even without that knowledge pressing down on my brain, it would have been hard catching any zees, what with my roomie being the infamous Dream Flyer. Like I mentioned, I'm the one that named him, not no reporter. One of the other inmates let it out that's what I called him, and that's how he got to be famous. His real name, which I never saw in the papers much, was Karol Bloch, with a K, not a C, the way the papers had it at first but which don't matter anyhow since nobody remembers his real name anyway.

I bet I know more about him than his real mother, whom he didn't much like to begin with and so never did any serious confiding in, like he did with me. In fact, he'd whacked his mom when he was twelve, he said, caved her head in with his official Boy Scout hatchet and got away with it; she was always after him to eat his vegetables and other terrible stuff like that, he said, and the law pinned it on some poor hobo that was passing through as they never figured it was her cute little boy, so it seems they wasn't close like regular families. Him and Sam The Bam could trade some childhood stories, I bet. Being cell-mates makes you tighter than twins, and what I don't know about Karol wouldn't take three sentences to tell nor half the time it takes to chug a Pearl.

"I'm gonna beat the rap," he goes, first day I seen him, and I only half-listened cause everybody in stir's gonna beat the rap; it's not like that's a front-page item. He'd killed somebody else, a girl, and got caught this time. He was a lot smarter about erasing people and not getting caught when he was younger, it appears.

"I raped her, sure, but I didn't kill her. I wasn't even close to her. She killed herself."

I shook my head in sympathy mostly because that's what you do in such situations in jail, you agree like a politician, especially if you're in the same cell as a stone-cold killer. Not agreeing with folks like that makes them upset, and a six by eight cell is no place to get on someone's wrong side, especially a mad-dog crazed killer with a chromosome mix-up like Karol. You can't just walk away from a dispute and hop on a Trailways bus, happen they take exception to something you say that offends them. So I agreed with him most of the time, maybe arguing once in a while on some minor point just to show him I was no pushover but a tough customer, same as him.

"I got me a plan," he says, and proceeds to let me in on the details. It seems laying around in jail with lots of idle time on his hands gets him to reminiscing about when he was a kid and he comes up with this idea that when he was just a tadpole, he could fly. The story he gives me is that he could slip right out of his body, like you get out of a wetsuit, and float around and go into other rooms like to see if his parents was doing the nasty or what-not, and one thing leads to another, and pretty soon he figures out how to fly while still in his body, by holding his breath and suspending his molecules, or something. First time, he finds this out by accident, when he was jumping off a little hill, and finds out he can stay in the air longer than he usually can, and then, aware of his supernatural ability and with a lot of diligent practice, he gets to where he can take off from a flat spot and go clear up into the clouds and even higher. Kind of a seven-year-old Superman, 'cept he didn't have any x-ray vision or incredible strength. He could just fly. Then he claims he got older and interested in girls and lost the art. You shoulda kept flying, I said to him—girls is what got you into this mess—but when he doesn't laugh, I drop the subject pretty quick.

I asked for another cell-mate about then, but they said no, they was overcrowded, besides he'll be gone soon, he's just down here in Algiers to testify in some other trial or other, and then he's going back up to Angola where they're gonna fry his sorry, crazy ass.

After giving me this look that makes my blood turn to the ketchup that lost the race, he tells me that he remembers all this flying business again, under the duress and stress of the situation he's in, and not only that, he's been practicing every night and has regained his powers. He's been up in our cell six weeks before I arrive as it's been a long trial that he's a witness in, some inmate whacking out another inmate, and he's been busy working out the aeronautics, so he's up to the point of loop-de-loops and such, or so he claims. Since I only been here a few days, I can't attest to this, but I think one night I seen him raise up off the floor a couple of inches, but then it might just have been a dream, since I seen one of my old girlfriends, Princess, sitting over in the corner on the toilet, doing her nails, that same night. I had just drunk a half-pint of applejack I got for a pack of tailor-mades, maybe an hour before I dozed off, so maybe my eyes were deceiving me.

He said he liked me and if I wanted to, some morning when they let us out for chow, we could join hands and soar away to freedom together. Since we were three flights up, on the third tier, I passed on the offer, and to tell the truth had more than one anxious moment when they'd let us out each morning, thinking he might just get the thought in his head to grab my hand and save me in spite of myself. I kept my hands jammed in my pockets when the door opened, each time, and tried to let him go out first, and thankfully, he never tried to get me to go hang-gliding or trick soaring with him.

Dying don't bother him none, he says, but getting exterminated for a crime he didn't commit, that gets his dander up. He's got this philosophy that there's this God that has this big ant farm to play with, which is Earth and earthlings, and all of these rules we're supposed to go by while we're here, just to keep the ant farm humming along smooth-like, and when we die, we just get sent to another kind of ant farm where God plays with us in a different way and we dress different, all in white clothes and singing hymns and stuff, only other difference is that there gravity's not such a big deal and we get to have lunch with the Big Kahuna, or, if we get sent to the alternative place on account of breaking too many rules at the first ant farm, there's another guy in charge who's some kind of Darth Vader type. Karol says he refuses to play by the established rules and doesn't care when or even if he croaks since he has no control over it anyway. What makes him get tight jaws though, is when other earthlings *think* it matters to him that he's gonna die, when it really doesn't.

Weird, huh? Seems like I never make friends with any ordinary Joes, insurance salesmen or whatnot.

I *really* wanted out of that cell.

So his big plan was to wait until his big day up at Angola State Prison, when they took him to the little room that's Total Electric; he's gonna just up and fly away from 'em. Then he'll come back and allow them to fricassee his earthly unit. This will prove his innocence, he says, and also make a statement to the world that dyin' don't mean squat in his eye, and then he can die justified and peaceful-like.

He shoulda been on a total acorn diet, he's that big a squirrel.

There is always nut cases in jail, and I've met a couple of

them, but the Dream Flyer, he is for sure a sandwich without the bread.

Least he *was*. The day they was scheduled to barbecue him, they let me go up to a conference room and listen to the radio for when it happened. All the radio stations had remotes there since it was such a big deal, and slow news day otherwise—the governor hadn't been indicted for anything in over a month—and I guess the turnkey thought we was bosom buddies since we celled together awhile, and so I got to go up and listen. Since anything beats laying around in your cell staring at your trouser worm, I figured why not, and went up to listen to how it was going for ol' Karol.

Believe it or not, he never made it to the electric chair. Of course you know that unless you've been residing in Lower Slobovia, because that's all that was on the news for days.

He fell and broke his neck, is what it said in the papers, but they weren't real clear about what went on, only that he fell thirty-some feet and squashed himself like a ripe honeydew. Neck-breaking was the official cause of death, but the way I heard it from one of the guards that was there, there wasn't a bone left in one piece, let alone the neck bone. He went from Dream Flyer to Dream Whip.

I was sure glad that I hadn't let him talk me into ascending to freedom via the aerial escape route whilst we were cellmates.

Cat called.

It was the damnedest thing.

She had been on my mind, too. That was normal. A guy goes to jail, practically every time there's a slow moment, the first thing he thinks about is the last piece of tail he had. It was more than that, though. She was starting to get to me and I didn't like it. I mean, she's a *whore*. It's not like she's the girl next door and I mooned over her in high school or anything, usta write her name in my algebra book.

I'd think things like that and then I'd remember I was a crook. Your basic criminal type, destined for a short rope and a long fall, and I was ashamed of my sorry self for looking down on *her*. I wasn't any better a person than she was. In fact, I was worse. I had never hit the big time in anything, been the best in anything, but Cat had. She was the best whore I ever knew.

I knew what my problem with her was. I was like those cracker types who pick on blacks because they just have to feel there is someone lower than they were. To make themselves feel like something by pretending there is worse slobs than they are.

I was a real dirtball. The more I thought about it, the more I knew that was an apt description. All Cat had done was take me in off the street, make beautiful love to me, and let me wipe out her wine stash, eat her food, sleep in her bed. I couldn't think of any two other people who would have done the same for me, in any situation.

"You got a call, Halliday. Down in the day room. Let's go."

"Hi, baby, how ya doin'?" It was Cat.

"I saw in the paper you were busted. Do you need anything? Toothpaste? Cigarettes? Oh, that's right, you don't smoke, do you? 'Cept in bed!" She laughed.

"Cat! It's great to hear your voice! I don't suppose you'd want to go my bail, would you sweetheart, get me outta here? And yeah, I smoke."

"Pete, you're a nice guy, but I don't go bail for guys. Don't do the crime if you can't do the time, is what I always say. You only got thirty days anyway, is what they said when I called. Give you time to rest up, sweetie, work on your tan, catch up on your letter writing."

"You're funny, Cat. Seriously, how about getting me out? It's no fun in here. Besides, there's another reason I'd like to get out of here ahead of schedule."

"I know. He came by looking for you."

I got a chill.

"Who came by?"

"Sam The Bam."

"You know *Sam?*"

"Honey, I'm a prostie. I know everybody that's in the rackets, or wishes they were. I know all the preachers, too. Preachers and gangsters, that's the bulk of my clientele. You're in some deep shit, sweetie. I wish I could help you out, but I think you're on your own on this one. You get out of your troubles, come on by. I need a shower. Oh, and don't worry about your suitcase. I'll take care of it. I sent your suit to the cleaners. Hey, babe, I gotta go. Call waiting's kicking in. Must be a john. Luck."

"Wait!"

"What?"

"I gotta ask you something. Why did you stick your money in Jackie's purse at Arnaud's?"

"None of your business."

"No, c'mon. Why? Are you stupid, or what? You just worked your ass off and you go and give up your hard-earned cash to some whore."

"Fuck you, Pete. You forget I'm a whore, too? If you have to know, I stuck it in her purse 'cause I knew she wouldn't take it if I just handed it to her. Jackie's got a lot of pride. Fact is, she called me up and wanted to give it back. The reason I gave it to her is that Jackie's got two kids she's tryin' t'raise by herself and has been through some hard times lately. She had pneumonia for almost a month and couldn't work. She'd do the same for me, if I was in a fix. Not that it's any of your business. Listen, my call-waiting's having a hemorrhage. Stay cool, chum."

And she hung up.

Her call depressed me, left me thinking about the few times we'd shared. Chances were good Cat would prove to be the last woman I'd've made love to, time Sam got through rearranging body parts and burning them in different parts of the state. I didn't think he'd just break a few bones for this one, not as much money was involved. No, he'd have to make an example out of me, show the other loan sharks he wasn't weak. I'd have to be whacked and it would have to be a particularly brutal, nasty whacking, make a statement. A designer whacking.

I wish I'd met Cat sooner.

Imagine, giving your hard-earned bucks to a chippie. She was something, that girl. I couldn't get over that. I never knew any crook that would do such a thing. She could do a thing like that, but she wouldn't bail me out. I couldn't figure her out. Hard *and* soft, that's what she was, couldn't make up her mind.

Women!

I wish I was still playing baseball.

I wish I had me a po-boy joint.

I wish I could fly out of here.

All this gets me to putting my thinking cap on. The desperate thinking cap. Laying on my bunk all day gets me to figuring maybe there's an outside chance that the Dream Flyer might have been onto something after all. I'm thinking I can even remember something way back when I was a youngster, just learning how to take a ground ball in the nuts, keep the runner from advancing, that I used to be able to get out of my own body and float around the room. The thing is, I can't tell at this point if I really do remember something like that, or if my chats with the Dream Flyer have made me only imagine such a memory. The more I study on it, the more I'm almost positive I do remember it.

I'd been practicing for over a week before Karol took his header. Just to see if maybe I can get out of my body a little bit for a few minutes or so, maybe fly over to the chow hall and get a bite to eat, a glass of OJ, maybe some of those delicious beans I loved so well. If that were to work, then I guess it's possible for me to actually fly. I remembered everything the Dream Flyer told me about suspending the molecules and such, and if it's possible, I guess I can do it as good as he could.

Actually, *better*, I hope.

If it can be done, then I'm saved. I mean, not only is there not a jail built that could ever hold me, I wouldn't have to worry about my little business with Sam The Bam.

I could get me a whole new career. Think of it! Pull a bank job, money bag in each hand, I run out into the street and then go straight up in the air and head south to Acapulco, flying low to keep clear of the radar, maybe fly over and pick up Cat, take her with me, under one arm. Man! You can bet for sure that if I dope out how to do this flying business I won't be making any more chickenfeed bets on cockfights.

So far, I'm not having much luck, though. It better come soon. Tomorrow's my last day in here. I'll bet I won't be surprised at the welcoming committee when I walk out. Sims and Sam and their workout squad. I'm sure hoping I'm airborne, have mastered the Dream Flyer Flying Technique, time they unlock that front door and hand me my walking papers. Maybe I could do something get my stay at the Crossbar Hotel extended. Hit one of the guards, maybe. That ought to be good for a longer bit. And even though I complained about the constant smell of old urine, it's not like I couldn't get used to it.

No, I couldn't.

Let's see now, he said you suspend your molecules and do something with your breath...

HERE'S THE DEAL

Sure enough, there's a welcoming committee waiting for me when they cut me loose from the Algiers jail. Only it's not Sam The Bam with a designated hit man, but Tommy, of all people. I figured Sam not to be far off, probably had Tommy followed so he could whack us both together. I was surprised Tommy hadn't tried to disappear, gone underground or at least tried. The molecule thing hadn't worked for me any better than it had for the Dream Flyer. At least, I'd only fallen off my bunk when I tried to solo, not three tiers like he had.

Tommy had his car there, waiting. I could have walked off, but what was the use? It was only a matter of time before I'd be face to face with Sam. Might as well get it over with. Besides, there was just the spark of hope that we might still be able to work something out. The same spark of hope the cow holds onto during the train ride to Kansas City. But a spark, nonetheless.

Yeah.

There wasn't much said when he came up to me outside the Algiers jail.

"Hi, Pete."

"Yeah."

"Car's over here. C'mon."

"Yeah."

We were in the car and rolling before the heavy conversation commenced. Tommy drove to the Algiers' ferry where we sat in a long line. I had no idea where he was taking me.

"Tommy, I might, I *might* be interested. I have to tell you I think you are a wonderful human being, Tommy," I said. "And a faithful partner. I am going to kill you at some point. You know that, don't you?"

Just then, the line began to move. He put the car in drive and we rolled onto the ferry. He killed the engine and jumped out of the car and I did the same. We went over to stand by the railing, look down at the oil slick they called the Mighty Mississippi. I looked to see if there were any bodies floating around. I noticed mine wasn't there. Yet.

"Sam thinks you get sprung tomorrow," he said. I was lighting the first cigarette I'd had since I'd walked out of jail. The wind kept putting out the match flame.

"Those'll give you cancer," Tommy said.

"You know, you're right, Ace," I said. "I'd hate like hell to catch cancer before Sam gets a chance to tear out my larynx. Think he'll be mad if I ruin his fun? Tommy, I don't need a mother. I need money. Tell me how I'm gonna get some. And this kidnapping deal better be better than the cockfight deal. Why does Sam think I'm getting out tomorrow?"

"'Cause that's what I told him," he said.

"Well, aren't you the sport," I said. "That gives me twenty-four hours to lose this burg."

"If you don't help me out on this kidnappin', I'll have to call Sam and tell him you got out early. That would not be a good thing for you. I got a place I can hide at. Do you?"

He was right, there. It would be a perfectly awful thing for me. And no, I didn't have a hideout I felt real comfortable with. Not since Sam knew about Cat.

"Tommy, I ought to drop kick you into the river here, and I might just do it yet. Don't threaten me. All right, let's hear it. Lay it out for me. This better make some kind of sense. You said something before about an amputation. What's that all about? Why did I ask that?" The last question was more to myself than to Tommy.

"Pete, you flap your lip a lot. First of all, you couldn't drop-kick your *mother* into the river, and second, I got some good news for you I shouldn't give you. Fact is, I'd be crazy to give you this news, if I want your help in this kidnapping which *is going to work*, but I'm a straight-shootin' Indian, Pete, and I'm going to tell you anyway, even though you don't deserve for me to."

What the hell was he babbling about?

"Here." He thrust something at me. It was a bankbook. "Savings Passport Account" it said, on the front. My name was inside. The balance was a thousand dollars.

"What's this?"

"It's money, dummy."

"I can see it's money. Why are you giving it to me?"

"Because I'm nuts, Pete. I'm an absolute raving nutcase." He shook his head. "I really am."

I didn't understand. It was a *lot* of money. Getting-away money.

"It's the money from the cockfight."

"Huh?"

"I went over to Algiers, looked up that fat farmer, got us our winnings."

"How the hell…"

"Listen, do you think that bust wasn't rigged? I saw Porky being escorted by one of them sheriffs, only he was going in a different direction than the rest of us were. I tried to tell you that in jail but you wouldn't even talk to me."

I remembered. He was right.

"I did some checking when I got out. I found out the judge is this guy's brother-in-law. Plus, I talked to Jim-Bob. All them guys over there are related. He got his money, he said, and he told me how to get mine."

"How?"

"I went to his house and persuaded him to do the honorable

thing, pay off his debt."

"How'd you do that?"

"With my persuader." He lifted his shirt and I saw the pistol handle sticking out of his trousers.

"I'll be damned."

Then, "Thanks, man. You didn't have to do that. I appreciate it." I *did* appreciate it. It was a righteous thing to do.

"So get off my case, Pete. We made some money there, just like I said we would, and I got it for us. Yours is there. A thousand bucks. I set up an account for you, make you some interest on it. You got enough there to get out of town, if you want. You don't have to throw in with me. Of course, how far do you think you'll get on a thousand dollars? Florida, maybe? I wouldn't bet on much farther. I think you should consider my proposition a little more carefully, weigh the pros and cons. All you can buy with what you got there is a ticket out of town and a little time. Sooner or later, Sam is gonna find you and whack you. You need serious money if you want to go on living. You need to pay Sam back, not try and hide out. He'll find you, sooner or later. You know he will."

We were halfway across the river by now. Coming in to New Orleans, you could smell it. First day out of jail after thirty days, you could *really* smell it. Hot and sexy, a couple hundred thousand red hot little mamas, stepping out of steamy baths and showers, their skin sticky from the heat, getting ready for Saturday night, and guys spraying cologne on, anticipating the women. The smell was the smell of foreplay, of musky, dusky sex. An image of Cat rose in my mind, slipping on a black satin number, same color as her hair, all shiny and glossy, breasts and hips and pelvis and legs, ripe and pulsing. I could almost pick her own individual scent out of all the smells floating out over the river. Every night is Saturday night in the Big Easy, but Saturday night is killer night. I was wondering if I'd ever have another one of those kinda nights again.

I had to admit Tommy was standing in a different light in my eyes, now. He'd turned out to be a stand-up guy and not only that, his last scam had worked even though it had taken a bit longer to collect than we'd figured. He sure hadn't had to tell me what he'd done and he sure as hell hadn't had to give me the money, especially when he was taking a big chance I'd just pack it in and take off with my new stake. I decided the least I could do was listen to his whole plan.

He started talking and I'll be damned if his idea didn't make a twisted kind of sense. It also made every sweat pore in my body go into overdrive.

"Remember that question I asked you? Before? What's the most common thing goes wrong with a kidnap?"

"Yeah," I said. "The cops get called in. The FBI. So? We already been over that. How's the amputation bit come into this?"

"You'll see," he said. "Just listen." He went back to the car, opened the door and reached under the front seat and extracted a paper bag and brought it back over to where I was alongside the railing. It was a bottle. He offered and I took a slug, knowing it was Wild Turkey and wishing it was Mr. Daniels. Some tourists, kids in their twenties, all slobbery and lovesick, came on back and stood near us, mooning over the "beautiful Mississippi," and I looked to see what they were jabbering about, but all I could see was a bunch of beer cans floating along. For a second, I thought I spotted an arm just below the surface, but no, it was just the branch of a log sailing out to the Gulf.

"The big mistake most kidnappers make, is they bring in a middleman to deliver the payoff. This gives the cops a chance to tail 'em and make the bust. Follow?"

I was with him so far. Following Tommy was like tailing a bicycle with a Harley. You never had to get out of second gear. And you was always in danger of falling asleep. But he was turning out to not be such a bad guy, and all his ideas weren't dogshit, maybe.

"I figured out a way to eliminate the middleman. We get the kidnap victim himself to pick up the money and deliver it."

"Tommy, you told me that already. How you gonna do that? Find some benevolent soul, tell him to hike on down to his friendly bank, pick up the money, bring it back? Tell him we'll send out for ribs while we're waiting, get ready for the party that's gonna follow? How's an amputation work into all this—you gonna threaten to cut off his foot he don't come back?"

"I'm gonna show you, Pete. Once you see the set-up, everything will be clear. Just remember the key word: Amputation. Now, I bet you got the picture." He stood staring at me with this dumb little smile like he had just give out the secret of the Sphinx or how One-Hour Martinizing is accomplished. I didn't get it.

The only picture I had was one of me sitting in the electric chair which hadn't hardly yet cooled off from the Dream Flyer meltdown, Tommy sitting on my lap in a state energy conservation move. The amputation part hadn't come crystal clear, and the early prognosis was that it wasn't going to be without more charts and diagrams. I started using my brain to think up a speech for Sam that would keep him from injuring me once he figured out I had headed for Miami.

"I already kidnapped the mark, Pete. That's where we're heading now."

My legs like to give out on me, going all rubbery and quivery, and I began to seriously regret I'd never been able to wait on the slow curve more than ever before.

"That's why I told Sam you get out tomorrow and we'd have the bread. This caper goes down today. By tomorrow, this time, we'll have more cash than you ever seen in one place. Sam will no longer be a problem. What do we owe? Twenty plus the juice and Sam's interest, something like that? Thirty G's, maybe? We're gonna have a hundred times that. The guy I snatched has got to have two, three million just layin' around the house in cookie jars. I ain't sayin' any more. You'll see the whole deal in just a few minutes."

The ferry bumped into the end of the dock, and in a daze, I

walked back to the car. This was going down too, too fast. I needed time to think. I needed a drink. I needed at least twenty drinks. And I'd prefer to have them served in another time zone, one in which I'd have to make sign language to the bartender on account of the language barrier.

I was in it now. There was no way out. I was partners with Tommy LeClerc in a lunatic kidnapping scheme. I was either gonna be wearing some gorilla in Angola's friendship ring, or fertilizing rice in some field in Slidell, this time next year. The third possibility, the one we was shooting for, just didn't seem attainable. The one where we're sitting on a beach in Cannes, sipping Stingers and having the pool girl massage our backs. That possibility just wasn't viable. Not with Tommy as a partner. It was too much to expect another successful caper. Not two in a row.

I grabbed the paper bag out of Tommy's hand and inhaled about half the bottle. It didn't help.

He took the bottle out of my hand and tossed down the rest. Then he threw the bottle, bag and all into the Mississippi.

"Tommy, you are the damndest so-called Indian I ever seen. All that shit about reading eyes was a bunch of crap from where I sit. And now. You just tossed trash into the river. Aren't you guys supposed to get all teary-eyed over pollution? What the hell kind of Indian are you anyways? I bet you don't worship the Great Spirit neither." I snorted.

"Fuck a buncha Great Spirits," is all he said. "Great Spirits! Lotta good any Great Spirits ever did for me or my red brethren." He looked up at the sky. "I didn't mean that," he said, softly. "Not entirely."

Twenty minutes later, we're walking into this house somewhere in the Ninth Ward, in a part cops are shy about cruising after dark, and it was just like Tommy described. Only worse.

"Holy Mother of God!" I said. "Holy fucking Christ!"

There he was, just like Tommy said, all tied up in a chair in the living room, a gag stuck in his mouth. Tommy was ear to ear smiles, looked like he just signed a long-term contract as a stunt man in porno movies.

"I told ya." Tommy was beaming like somebody had just told him he was Howard Hughes long-lost son.

"I'm leaving. Tommy, you're insane. I want no part of this. They electrocute you for this in this state. They don't let go of the switch until your brain looks like an over-easy Camellia Grill omelet." I turned to go and he grabbed my arm.

"We ain't gonna kill him, man," he said, in a whiney voice not befitting a master criminal such as he was pretending to be. "We're just gonna whack his hand off, then let 'im go. That way, worst happens we get busted for aggravated assault."

See what I mean about Tommy? Swiss cheese brains with extra-large holes.

I was trying to calculate how far I'd get in this neighborhood on foot before my honky throat would be slit. I liked my chances out there better than I did in here with this Loony Tune. I tried to reason with Tommy, knowing it was a bad use of oxygen.

"Tommy, it don't matter if you was to ransom his legs, his balls, or his whole, entire self—it's still kidnap any way you cut it. You think this'll get us a five-hundred-dollar fine and sixty days in stir? Who's your legal counsel—Peppermint Patty?" I turn to go, and he jumps up in my face, eyes pleading.

"Just listen a minute, Pete. We *got* to do this. Sam's gonna tie us both together and drop us into Lake Ponchartrain. I know it and you know it. You even pointed that out to me. We got no choice. It's do this or let Sam's boys make a wish with our legs right before they use us for up-close target practice. Hell, the whole town knows what we're into him for. You think he's gonna forgive that kind of money? I'm not talking about Fred's half a mil, even. You got a better way to raise the kinda dough we need? You think that lousy thousand bucks you got can get you where you need to be? In Tibet?"

He put his hands on my shoulders and leaned in close to me, spraying me with vaporized Wild Turkey.

"Just listen to my plan. This is the most foolproof idea anybody ever had. They'll be copyin' this idea for the next three centuries. The Sicilians will be green they didn't think of it first. We'll be in the Kidnap Hall of Fame!"

He was insane. Certifiable.

"Tommy, you have somehow got it in your head that you are some kind of master criminal. I don't know how that has happened, but it has. You even had me believing it myself at one time and I am a reasonably smart dude, so I can see how you, being the total lamebrain that you are, could have conned yourself into thinking you are some sharp gangster. You know what you remind me of? Those guys on the shopping channel, selling Ginsu knives and Genuine, Imitation Plastic Elvis Presley TV Trays to idiots. That's what you have come up with here, Tommy. A Genuine, Imitation Plastic Kidnap Scheme. You are a fruit loop and I will now take my leave of you and go have Sam kill me. It will be a relief to be dead and not have to share air space with such a fruit loop as you."

At least he was right about the dough. I recognized the man all trussed up in the chair. He had the kind of money Tommy kept talking about, all right. He wasn't hard to recognize. His mug was in the paper more than Charlie Brown's. The victim was none other than Charles Lacy Deneuvé.

Charles Lacy Deneuvé. The Cajun Mafia King. Murder, prostitution, drugs, loan-sharking, you name it, Deneuvé was probably behind it, especially if it was big money. He was also a socialite, heir, and any other damned adjective you could tie to money. Old money and new money, he had it both, more greenbacks than ten Republicans. And that wasn't all. He'd turned out to be the black sheep of the Deneuvé family, got all mixed up with the mob, got himself connected, years ago. Now, in addition to the family fortune, which was considerable by most reports, all by itself, he had a river of money flowing in from everything from dog tracks in Alabama to cocoa farms in Bolivia. His Cajun mob was connected to the Italian mob—and he was connected to the government, as far as Washington, it was rumored.

I started considering all his connections and who he was and had to sit down. With Sam The Bam, I only had to get to, say, Argentina, to escape his clutches. To get far enough away from Deneuvé, I'd have to get a seat on the next space shuttle. And on one that wasn't just going to the moon. No, one of those really faraway places, like Xanabu 12.

This was not just your average rich guy Tommy'd snatched. This was the *worse* rich guy in the world. My heart was fibrillating at warp speed.

Then…there *was* the money. Tommy had definitely picked the right guy for that. Old man Deneuvé probably had ten million just laying around the house in small bills, from last weekend's drug action.

There was a story going around that illustrated just how rich he was. It seems Deneuvé had this big yacht he kept tied up off-shore on account of it drew too much water for Lake Ponchartrain. He used to give all these big to-dos on it, and one time he had this fancy dinner party on board, with the featured guests including such as the mayor, the governor, visiting other Cajun Mafia big cheeses, even the Metry sheriff—*that's* how big the party was, and it commences to sprinkle. Well, the head maître d heads all the hob nobs downstairs where they see the exact same spread laid out below and another whole crew down there, throwing away courses in tune with what's being eaten by the upstairs crowd as they finished.

It turns out, it was set up just so's in the event of a rain like what we get in New Orleans, the honored guests wouldn't have to miss a bite of their Oysters Bienville.

Somebody told me once that Aristotle Onassis did something like that himself, only the word was, Onassis got the idea from

Deneuvé. The thing was, there's probably lots of guys who could afford to do a stunt like that, only it turns out Deneuvé's been doing the same thing for years, on the off-chance it might sprinkle and cause his guests to get annoyed, and *he never told anybody about it.* That's *real* money. Me, I'd be down in some bar, first time I thought it up, telling the cutest girl I could find, just to impress her. Not Deneuvé. He was the real article.

He was always pulling high-brow stunts like that, that showed he was the genuine money boy.

How Tommy'd got him here, tied up like Jack the Ripper's best girl, spit dribbling from the corner of his mouth where a white rag protruded, I could only guess. Some said Deneuvé was an old queen, part-time, so that must have been it. Tommy had been known to do some part-time sex hustling, just as he had been known to bust into parking meters for the change. There wasn't a whole lot Tommy drew the line at, for a buck. Or less.

I wiped about a gallon of salt water off my forehead, and said, "Tommy, I'm gonna tell you the truth. This is some serious bad shit here, man. You're gonna get fried and I'll get my nose melted off, just standing this close to you. I pass, Tommy. I'll take my chances with Sam. Most he's likely to do is break all my major bones, put a bullet in my brain. This guy here is *serious* shit."

I look again at the old man tied up in the chair, eyes bugged out like a poodle giving birth of a litter of Great Danes, and I decide to depart. Fast.

"Hold on, pal." Tommy grabbed my arm as I stood up. "You're in this now, all the way. You're an accessory." He planted his body in my way and I saw the way it was. Only way out was to clock him. That wasn't any concern; I could deck Tommy with *your* punch, but the noise might bring company. If someone saw me here with Tommy and Deneuvé, I was going to be on a free bus ride to Angola, sure as birds fly south to Brazil and mechanics bus north to Detroit. That would be the easy part. The hard part would be dodging all the boys what wanted to collect the trillion-dollar bounty Deneuvé or his people would have on our heads. I remembered an article in the *Times-Picayune* a while back, said the world community was shrinking. Was it ever! For some of us more than others. Right now, it was about the size of a ping pong ball. A fucking B-B!

Even if by some amazing miracle we pulled this off, then there'd be Tommy himself to worry about. This whole thing was nothing but an ulcer event. Tommy could keep a secret about as good as *The National Enquirer*; his street name shoulda been Hurricane Tommy, the way he flapped his lip all the time. First time he had two-three swallows of Turkey, he'd be bragging to some bimbo about what a great, all-time kidnapper he was, and both of us would end up sitting on a prison blanket complaining that the other one never shaved their legs anymore.

I sighed, thinking that my mother certainly never figured this for her bouncing baby boy. It's funny, how you can just be minding your business, staying out of trouble, and it just comes and looks you up, no matter where you are.

Timbuktu. I could be in friggin' Timbuktu and just having a nice little cup of rice wine, shooting a little nine-ball, and in would come some jerk named Tommy Won Ton and get me mixed up in some fix. I attracted losers like Cat attracted horny men. I thought of her as the "cock-magnet" sometimes; just call me the "bozo-magnet."

I considered all the alternatives once again, and knew I had to go along with it. It was the bottom of the ninth, score tied, two out, bases loaded, me at bat, and a full count, and the umpire standing behind me is the opposing pitcher's brother-in-law, so a walk is probably out of the question. The next pitch would have to bounce at least three-four times on the way to the plate before it would be called a ball.

Throwing in with Tommy in this kidnap was the only one of my choices that had a possible reward to it, and a way out. I had to swing at the ball, even if the odds against us were so high the smart money in Vegas would catch a hernia laughing at our chances.

"Okay, Tommy. When and what you gonna whack and what do I hafta do?"

I walked over and sat down on a sofa with brown flowers on it, across from Deneuvé. Hell, he'd seen me already, I was already a dead man. The sofa smelled like urine, but what the heck, I was already in the shit, what was a little piss? Tommy saw that I wasn't going to make a break for it and came over and sat next to me. Nearer the door. I guess he didn't trust me completely. Deneuvé gave out some kind of little moan, but I kept my head averted, not making eye contact. I had the weird thought that if I didn't make eye contact, maybe I wasn't really here. That's the kind of reasoning my stressed-out brain was undergoing.

"Tonight. We'll do it tonight. Don't worry. I'll do all the hard stuff. Lookit this."

He got up and went over in the far corner of the room where a large grocery bag sat on the floor. He brought it over and dumped the contents out on the sofa next to me.

"Everything. I got everything we need right here."

He wasn't stretching the truth about everything. He could of had a nice garage sale with what was there, opened a booth in a flea market.

Hacksaw, kite twine, pliers; there was a soldering iron, a box of baggies like you use to put dope in, a bottle of some kinda clear stuff, rags that looked like old diapers, and a brand-new fifth of Wild Turkey. Some other odds and ends and that was it.

"What's all this for?"

"I told you. Amputation."

That's right, he had said that. The picture was still a bit fuzzy. No need to be concerned, Tommy was about to clear all that up. Those were my thoughts.

"Remember I kept askin' you why the kidnappers always get caught? You had part of the answer when you said, 'cause the cops get called in.' And I said I had the answer to that. I said we're gonna eliminate the middle man, the guy what's supposed to bring the money."

"You're gonna let old man Deneuvé walk outta here, go home and fetch us back a suitcase fulla money? Tommy, I truly hate to say this to you, on account of I don't want to upset the delicate balance of nuts and raisins of such an obviously completely deranged fruitcake as you appear to be, but you are a truly dangerous man, walking around with that much air in your skull. You're dangerous to yourself, but that's your lookout, but you are also dangerous to me, and that's *my* lookout, and I just changed my mind about this caper. I'll be going, now. Have a nice day, helium-head."

I tried to stand up and he pointed the soldering iron at me like it was some pistol, and silly me, I sat down again. My brain wasn't hitting on all eight cylinders yet, being fagged out by all the recent events. I swear, I thought that iron was a gun. Maybe I was just tired out.

"You still don't get it, do you? You're part right. We *are* gonna let Deneuvé go on home by himself and get us the money. Only difference is, he's gonna be without his right hand. And one of us will drive him home."

"Tommy, where'd you ever get an idea like this? What comic book are you reading?" It was an intellectual question. I wanted to see how his dingbat mind worked.

"Pete, just listen. I read this story in the *Times-Picayune*. Some guy over in East New Orleans got his hand caught in a conveyor belt or somethin'. Everybody else was gone t'lunch so he grabs his mitt and trots over four blocks to the hospital and they sew it back on. It's as good as new, now, the story said, and the guy goes back to work in six weeks, arm-wrasslin' his co-workers and everything.

"This got me to thinking. If you was to kidnap some rich dude and cut off his hand and hold the hand for ransom, it'd be better than the old-fashioned way. The way we done it before. I bet if ol' Fred was minus an appendage he wouldn't't'a pulled a gun on me. This twist makes a kidnap fool-proof, with the new advantages.

"First off, a guy what's got his hand detached ain't gonna go to the cops. He's gonna arrange his priorities different. He's gonna come up with the money, get his hand back, and *then* go to the cops. Or, in Deneuvé's case, to his standing army. *And* the cops, probly. Anyway, this gets rid of the dangerous part of putting the snatch on someone."

"What part's that?"

"Boy and howdy, Pete. You just don't listen, do you? What have we been talkin' about? What was the question I keep asking you?"

I dummied up. He was making me mad.

"The part where the middle man calls in the FBI. See, when you kidnap a kid or a wife or something, they always call the cops and the bad guys always get caught. Pretty much what happened with Fred. Watch TV, Pete, learn something! See, you'd call the cops if they had your wife and wanted a couple of million dollars—I mean, a *couple of million-fucking dollars*! But if it was your right hand they was in possession of, the hand you diddle your old lady and your girlfriend with, the hand you pick your nose with, the hand you spank the monkey with; *that* makes it a whole new ballgame. No way you're gonna dick around with that hand, take a chance of not gettin' it back, not like you might with the little darlin' better half. No, sir. You're gonna get that money gathered up and hustle it down to the kidnappers as quick as you can, before it rots and they can't sew it back on."

He was grinning like he'd just successfully explained the fine art of the blow job to a gorgeous blind girl. He was proud as a teenager with fresh-tongued ear wax, and a wet spot on his jeans. He was right, too, damn it.

For once, I had to admit Tommy was onto something. That was a shocker, for Tommy to have an insight into human psychology. I didn't even have to think about what he said much. I bet he was right; a person *would* be a lot less likely to take chances with their prime meathook than they would with their lovin' spouse. There was still a few details I wasn't too clear on yet, but I could start to see the beauty of this. However, there was still one detail in particular I wanted to know about. I picked up the bottle of Wild Turkey.

"This how you're gonna knock him out when you remove his appendage?" A lot depended on his answer. If he answered yes, I was going, really going. No fooling around this time. I'd come back when he had little details like that worked out better.

"Yeah. What's wrong with that?"

I got up, excused myself.

"Sorry, Tommy. I got to be leaving, now. You had me there for a minute. Look, call me up when you get the kinks in this plan ironed out. I'm just gonna go out that door and walk down to the river and drown myself. Tie a cement block around my neck and jump in. Save Sam the trouble. It's been grand, knowing you. You wouldn't happen to know where I can pick up a good, stout piece of rope and a concrete block, would you? Oh, never mind. I'll just improvise. Listen, Tommy, you have a nice day, y'hear?"

Only I didn't move right away. I stood there a second. I should have left like I'd said I was, gone out that door. 'Specially when he got to giggling like a teenager filling up his first condom with water.

WE ARE NOT SKILLED SURGEONS

I stood there a second, thinking I'm just gonna hafta knock out ol' Tommy, get out of this bad dream, when he calms down, chokes down his last giggle, and says, "Pete, I'm just kiddin'. Of course, that's not what we're gonna use t'knock Deneuvé out with." He was referring to the bottle of Turkey.

"*This* is what I got for that." He held up the bottle of clear stuff. "This stuff. It's chloroform. The Turkey's for *us*, man."

I sat back down.

"Well, then, what's the pliers for? I thought you was gonna cut his hand off. You gonna twist it like a piece of copper pipe?"

He laughed. Scary-like.

"You're a riot, man. Naw, I don't know why I got that. Thought it might come in handy. I ain't never done this before, y'know. Hard tellin' what all we'll need. Might as well be prepared. Boy Scouts, that's us."

I had a thought.

"He's gonna bleed t'death, Tommy."

"No, man; no way. That's what the solder iron's for. To cauterize him. I read this story once that big-time wrasslers, like in the Olympics, use a hair curling iron to cauterize their nose if it gets broken, so's they can go on wrasslin'. See, they got a twenty-second time limit or something like that, t'get back inta the ring and keep on wrasslin'. So they just stick a curling iron up their snot-lockers. Their teammates hold 'em down, jam it up their nose. I figured you needed more heat for a cut-off hand, so we're gonna use the solder iron."

I was becoming more and more delighted that I wasn't some wealthy person of Tommy's acquaintance. If I was going to be part of this, I was at least happy I was sitting on the sofa with Tommy, and not *across* the room, facing us, all tied up in a chair. I heard a kind of animal noise, from Deneuvé, through his nose, and even though I don't look, I am pretty sure he has passed out. All that talk about cauterizing must have upset him. He didn't do a thing different than what I would have, our seating position being reversed.

"Lookit this."

Tommy shoved several sheets of paper at me. They had drawings and a lot of words I ain't never had my eye on before. He'd mimeographed them from someplace. *Campbell's Operative Orthopaedics* is what it said in the corner of one of the pages.

"You read all this?" What I meant was: Did he *understand* all this.

"Sure. Don't make much sense, though. They use a lotta college-boy words and stuff. No problem. I pretty well doped it out. Copied this outta the library over at East Jeff Hospital. Told 'em I was a free-lance writer, doing an article on amputations. That's some of the stuff I was doing when you were in the can. Research."

I was wondering how Tommy could carry that off, when I remembered Mr. Moneybags sitting not six feet away. If he could get a smart dude like that up to this room in the Ninth Ward, he could sell bacon bits to a pig farmer. That was something else I was curious about.

"How'd you get him up here, anyway," I asked.

"I don't want to talk about that," he said. "I got him here, that's the main thing."

"Promised t'suck his love muscle, didn't ya?" I said, but he ignored me. I picked up one of the pages.

"Ex-ten-sor dig-i-tor-um com...communis muscle," I read,

tripping over the words, but glad I had learned phonics.

"Ah, don't worry about that stuff. We don't have t'know what veins and things are called. All that's important is to know how to whack it off and how much it's worth to him."

"He'll go into shock."

"Naw. Well, probly not. The guy in the paper didn't. He hiked four blocks to the hospital, stepped up to the doc, and said, 'Shake, partner.'"

"Tommy."

"Well, maybe he didn't say 'shake'—I just made that part up. But he did walk four blocks—that *was* in the paper. 'Sides, look at ol' Deneuvé. He's strong as a horse, especially for an old geezer. You wouldn't believe what he had in mind when we got here. I bet *your* heart wouldn't take it!"

I was burning to know what Deneuvé had in mind, but Tommy dummied up again. I said, "Okay, smart-ass, you got this all doped out. But there's one thing you didn't figure."

"What?"

"How long's he got before it can't be sewn back on? I bet it's not very long."

He had been waiting for that question. I hated the smug way he answered.

"Eight hours. That's max. That's what the librarian at East Jeff said. I figure an hour after we lop off his hand, we're on the road to Miami, the back seat full of money. Get us a plane out of there for parts south. Besides, what's it matter if he does die or his hand turns black like an avocado? It's not like we was Marcus Welby or somethin', Pete. You think I'm worried about losin' my operating privileges over to Charity Hospital? You are one weird criminal, Pete. I bet if you was fixin' t'break into a house and they had padlocks on the doors, it'd never cross your brain t'just knock a hole in the side of the house! You are some rule-followin' square! How'd you get into this line of work?"

There wasn't much I could say to that.

We woke up Deneuvé. Tommy wanted to explain to him

what was going to go down, so there would be no mistakes. He read him the article he'd clipped out of the paper, and I'm damned if he wasn't telling the truth. I read it myself, soon as he was done using it for the Kidnap Story Hour for Deneuvé's benefit. It was the damnedest thing, this guy really did get his hand cut off and sewed back on again. The article said incidents like that happened all the time.

Deneuvé took this all in, the whites of his eyes bulging and little snorting sounds coming from his nose. He couldn't comment too much as he had a handkerchief stuffed into his mouth, but he got the drift of what was to go down, you could tell. Once or twice, he seemed to be going out again, but he got it under control and stayed with us.

Then Tommy showed him the pages from the Campbell's thing, waved 'em under his nose, and told him not to worry, that while we maybe weren't exactly skilled surgeons, any reasonably handy fellas such as we was could take care of this procedure fairly easily. I could see this set Deneuvé at ease, as he relaxed so much right then he went to sleep.

"We gotta let him know the score," Tommy says, while we wait for Deneuvé to wake up from his nap. "I think he's got the overall picture, don't you? He wants his hand back he's gonna have t'play ball with us, our way." I started to make a joke about how's he gonna play ball with his throwing arm minus an essential part, but I let it go.

"There's another side to this particular kidnappin' that's good, too," he said. "In fact, it's why I thought of Deneuvé here to begin with. If I do say so, this was a stroke of genius, my pickin' him." He didn't think too much of himself, but was he ever the minority party.

"Two things, actually," he went on, anxious to let me in on his brilliance. "One, the fact that it's Deneuvé and not some other rich cat who keeps his stash in the bank. Deneuvé always has a big stash around the house, on account of the business dealings he's involved with and two, all we're asking for is a couple of million, which is pin money to a guy like him. He makes that much at lunch, most days. It's not like it's his entire fortune. There ain't no doubt he'll bring out the money, knowing we got his hand."

Tommy was dead right on both counts. As much as I hated to admit it, I would have to admit he had finally hit upon something that might work. Actually, the second thing. The cockfight scam had turned out okay, too. This scheme was starting to feel and smell right. I wasn't too ecstatic over the hand-removing operation that was to come, but I forced my mind off that. Maybe Tommy would just do that part by himself, not need my assistance.

"So when we gonna begin the festivities?" I asked, not that I was all that eager to get cranking.

"Tonight. We want it to be dark. It'll be harder for someone to notice an old geezer going into his house with a bloody stump."

That's what he said, but I think the real reason he wanted to wait was the delicate state of his stomach. He wanted time to get plastered before he started working out with that hacksaw. I still wasn't clear exactly what my part in the operation was to be.

Deneuvé started making coming-to noises again, funny sounds from his nose, and we waited until his eyes were open and focused, and then Tommy ran down the rest to him, so's he'd know what was expected of him.

We'd whack his hand—at this part of the pep talk Deneuvé almost went under again—and the deal was that we'd release him in front of his house and wait fifteen minutes to come out with the ransom. Or rather, it was yours truly what would escort him to his home, just in case he decided to get cute and have his boys grab us and torture us, make us tell him where the hand could be found. Tommy would take the hand to another location and wait for my call telling him I was clear with the money, and then we'd phone Deneuvé and tell him where to find his appendage. Even I wouldn't know where I was calling to, just in case Deneuvé got the bright idea to have me tortured to reveal where Tommy was.

The plan was a gem. Unlike the other cons I'd hooked up with Tommy on, this one was a beaut. He'd really put the old thinking log on. I began to let myself think about what a million dollars might look like, all spread out on the floor, and some of the different ways there was to spend it.

Something occurred to me.

"Tommy, whose house is this?"

"Nobody's. Why?"

"Whaddya mean, *nobody's*? It's got to be *somebody's*. Is it yours?"

"No. I rented it."

"Oh. Aren't you afraid they can trace you?"

"Naw. We'll be long gone by the time they figure that out. Besides, you don't think I rented it in *my* name do you? C'mon, Pete, do I look that stupid?"

I had the weirdest feeling like I already knew the answer to the question I asked next.

"What name did you use?"

My feeling was right on the money. He'd used *my* name.

I almost hit him. I came *this* close to hitting him, but I thought, what the hell, he's right. We'll either be long gone by the time they find out whose name is on the lease, or...we'll be dead, which, in either case, wouldn't matter whose name the damned house was rented in.

It was now about two in the afternoon. Tommy said he thought he'd just lay around and knock a few shots back, and I allowed as how I was getting a little bit of cabin fever and thought I'd take off for a while. What I had in mind was see if Cat was home, maybe grab a quickie. Tommy read my mind.

"Wanna go get some poontang, huh? Cat, I bet. I knew you'd like her," he said. "Tell you what. Let's you and me go down to Claude's, have us a couple of brews, fine-tune this plan a little, and you can call her, see if she wants to join us."

Cat, Tommy and me isn't what I had in mind, but I seen a way around it. "Yeah, I said. "But maybe Cat and I will want to get out, take a drive, maybe go to a movie until it's time."

"Sure," he said. "Or get you some poontang. That what you had in mind?"

Claude's was the best place we could go, if we were gonna go out in public, Tommy explained, on the way over. "No honkies go in there hardly ever. Anybody recognizes us from the TV ain't gonna give us up. They got that black code. Plus, we all look alike to the brothers."

I wasn't too sure about any black code, but what the hell.

When we went in, sure enough—there's about twenty-five black brothers and the noise level went down appreciably the second we walked in. Tommy fetched us a couple of brewskies from the bartender while I used the coin phone in the back to call Cat and tell her where we were and invite her to join us, which she said she might, and we went on back to a booth. After a couple of minutes and some looks from the brothers I wasn't crazy about, things seemed to go back to normal. Somebody played the juke box and B.B. King began to sing.

"Tommy," I said. "I guess I'm with you on this deal—way I see it, I got no choice. But I have to wonder if you've covered all the bases here. If you've told me everything, for instance."

"What else would there be?" he said. "Have I ever held anything out on you in our partnership, Pete?"

"Well," I said. "I wasn't aware we had a partnership, but yeah, you have held stuff out on me before." I leaned forward until my face was a foot from his. "Why the fuck didn't you tell me ol' Fred ran a Mafia laundering operation?"

"You think I knew that? I look stupid?"

I leaned back, turned my head like I was talking to the imaginary person sitting to my right. "This is too easy," I said. "I'll leave this one for an amateur."

Tommy looked contrite. "Look," he said. "I know I fucked up. But now I got the solution: Deneuvé."

I was having second thoughts about that. No, make that third and fourth thoughts.

"Oh, that's swell, Tommy. Now my mind is at ease. For a minute there, I thought I was a dead man."

He flashed me a smile. "Only one thing is gonna get us out of this alive. My plan."

"Yeah," I said. "Or the Second Coming."

We had us a second beer each—Tommy had to go up to the bar as it looked like the waitress was on break—and he laid out some of the other details. He was just finishing up with all that and the door opened and in sashayed Cat, hips swinging.

That got a reaction from the crowd. There was a hitch in the noise level and I could see the brothers stare and the sisters dig elbows into their dates. Looked like we were really on the radar now.

"Hey, Cat," Tommy said.

"Hey, Tommy. Hey, Pete." She slid in beside Tommy. So that's the way it was going to be.

"What's your pleasure, Miss?" It was the bartender. Come to wait on us.

She shined him all of her teeth. "You wouldn't have Parfait Amore, would you, sugar?" she said. The only thing left off of her Scarlett O'Hara impression was batting her eyelashes. Pulling down her top a couple extra inches to show off her twins probably made up for that.

"Ah," the barkeep said. "The Drink of Love. I'm sorry, no."

"That's all right," Cat said. "I'll have Black and White, neat, water back."

"From my bottle to your glass," said the bartender and whirled around like a matador and quickstepped back to behind the bar and began pouring.

I looked down at mine and Pete's beers, both empty.

The bartender returned with Cat's two glasses.

Tommy looked up at him and tried to match Cat's smile. "Uh," he said. "You suppose my friend and I could get a refill?"

The best way I could describe how the bartender looked at him was "frosty." "I'm a bartender, not a waiter, Jack," he said, and stalked away.

Tommy shot me a "fuck me" look and shook it off. "Look," he said to me. "I've got some more stuff to do before tonight—" here he narrowed his eyes and furrowed his brow at me like I was supposed to pay special attention to what he was saying, "—and I'll see you back at 'the place' at six, Pete. Six. O'clock. Got it?"

He stood there waiting until I repeated his instructions.

"Yeah, Tommy. Six o'clock. I'll set my alarm."

He nodded, gave Cat a little salute, and walked to the door and out.

Cat smiled. "When Tommy told me about you, he said you used to play baseball, Pete. Did you ever meet Mickey Mantle or Babe Ruth?"

I guess this was her version of chit-chat and socializing.

I leaned forward, put my head in my hands. "Mantle and Ruth? Oh, yeah. We was all teammates. Back when baseball was fun." With Tommy gone, I was starting to have buyer's remorse about this kidnap. "Right now," I went on, more to me than to her, "I'm in a rundown between third and home. You got any idea what Tommy's brilliant scheme is that we're supposed to do?"

She gave me a coy little smile and stirred her drink. "I think so," she said. "He's grabbed some rich dude. Tommy's a smart guy. We're all gonna be rich."

We? Tommy had neglected to fill me in on the part where Cat was involved in his plan. I was just about to quiz her on that, in a particularly witty and cutting way, when the front door of the bar opened, letting in a shaft of brilliant New Orleans' afternoon sun.

And Sam Capelli.

At first, I didn't realize it was him, not paying strict attention like I shoulda been. He was halfway back before it dawned on me who it was. I flopped down below the table, like I had dropped my change, going down quicker'n vanilla ice cream off a sugar cone in August.

"What?" said Cat, and I yanked on her Capris, and whispered, "It's Sam. Capelli. You know him, you said. He sees me, the only thing left to do is make the funeral arrangements. What the hell's he doin' here? They don't serve no pasta here. God! Let me know what he does."

What he does is plunk his large ass in the booth right next to ours. Cat don't hafta tell me. When he plopped his butt on the seat, he did it with such force the edge of my seat smacked me on the head so hard I saw stars. I almost yelped, but kept it in by biting my lip in half. I sat there with blood running down my chin and tears in my eyes from the pain.

Now I was in it but good. I'm sitting on the floor under the table in a booth in a black bar with a hooker the only thing between me and Doctor Death. There was other places I would rather be at, just then. I couldn't stay down there for the rest of my life; somebody was sure to take note of the honky on the floor, that is, if Cat didn't blow the whistle first to save her own ass.

Just then, she leaned over with an evil leer and whisper, "I shouldn't do this, asswipe, but I feel sorry for you. I'll get you out of here."

"How?" I whispered back. If she had an idea could spring me out of this jam, I'd go pick out the ring tomorrow, order the tux.

"I'll create a diversion. When I do, you slip out the back, get my car and park up the block. I'll be along presently." She reached into her purse and took something out and handed it to me. Car keys. "It's the red Buick convertible."

What was she going to do, I wondered. Take her clothes off? I couldn't think of much else she could do to not only get Sam but the other twenty-five black guys not to notice me go out the back.

What she did do, I wouldn't have guessed in a thousand years.

She didn't take her clothes off.

She stood up and she threw a fit.

I mean, *she threw a fit.*

She starts yelling and screeching and wandering around the bar, and screaming out all kinds of derogatory things about our black brethren. Like she said the N word. A bunch of times. "Cocksucker!" she yelled. "Mufucker! N-nigger! F-Fuck. Mutha, mutha, mutha…fuck! Nigger! Whoop!"

You coulda drove a fork lift into my mouth, it was that far open.

"Pussy, pussy, pussy! Whoop! Whoop, whoop, whoop! N-nigger! Shit! Fuck!

She was in high gear now. All I could see from the floor was black guys moving toward her from all corners.

She kind of staggers up toward the front door, giving out with the insults, and it ain't two seconds before she's drawn a major crowd around her. From under the booth I see a dozen or more black dudes, most of whom have things flashing in their hands, like razors and knives and other sharp and dangerous objects. It appears as if we're about to have a honky woman massacre. The booth shoots back again as Sam gets up and catches me up alongside the head again, and I chomp half my tongue off this time, but keep the sound effects down, just barely. It probably don't matter; there is so much noise and babble up at the front of the bar by now nobody woulda heard me anyway, everybody present with the same fierce desire to be the first to smack Cat, separate her from her gizzard.

Then I caught on, almost too late. This was the diversion she was talking about, giving me a chance to slip away out the back door. I couldn't figure out how she planned to walk away from this, being as how she was using every racial epithet any cracker had ever thought up. I hoped she knew what she was doing, but it sure looked like a suicide mission from where I was. Might as well one of us get out alive, I thought, and crawled out fast. Nobody paid me any attention, they was all up front, trying t'get at Cat and rip her apart, I figured, and I silently wished her luck and made for the back door. As I was going out, I heard her voice above the murmur of the men, and she was screeching, "Tourette's; I got Tourette's. It's a disease." I shoulda split soon as I was clear of that door, but I hung around a minute and listened.

"Man, I hearda that," a man's voice said. "It was on TV," said another. "Oprah, I think." "Yeah, poor bitch can't help herself," said still another, and another voice, I could swear it was Sam, said, "My brother-in-law has that, always yelling cusswords and stuff when he gets an attack," and then I was gone, whipping out through the back parking lot, knocking over a couple of garbage cans I didn't stay around to pick up. I ran the whole way till I got to the car, grabbed the keys out of my pocket, jumped in, and started it up.

I did like she said, pulled past the bar and parked about half a block up.

The door of Claude's burst open and a wave of black humanity poured out. Black except for the white hooker and Sam The Bam, who were way in the back taking up the rear of the mob.

Then the damnedest thing happened. Three or four black dudes were around Cat, and it looked like they were slapping her on the back and hugging her. No, they must be stabbing her. No, by golly, they were patting her on the back and hugging her! I put the car in reverse and rolled toward her. When I got close, I leaned over and opened her door and pushed it out, trying to keep the car in the middle of the street, and just as I came abreast of her, I honked the horn and yelled, "Hit it, Cat! Jump in!"

She waved at me and took a bottle of beer a smiling brother handed her and just sauntered over to me. She climbed in the car and just as she gets in, I hear a voice I don't wanna never hear again in my life, yelling. It was Sam. He was trying to knock guys down and they were turning when he elbowed them but then got polite and got out of his way when they saw his gun.

"Better kick it, slick," Cat said.

I was half a beat ahead of her, the car already leaving rubber and fishtailing as I floored it.

Bam! Bam! Bam!

I look in the rearview mirror and see Sam standing in the street, a two-handed grip on his piece just like Dirty Harry.

A slug hit the rear window and it shattered just before I turned the corner on two wheels. I flew through a stop sign and we almost got broadsided by a huge, oncoming garbage truck, but I drove around him and got clear.

"How…how the hell…" I couldn't get the words together.

Cat was laughing so hard she started to choke. She wiped tears from her eyes. "I always wanted to try that!" she said.

"Try what?" I said. "What in holy hell was all that back there?"

I went up Terpsichore, went under the Ponchartrain Express and turned left on Thalia, taking that on up to Magazine. I turned left onto the Street of Dreams.

I looked over at Cat, trying to spot bruises, contusions, slash marks, but she's clean as a newborn, not a scratch on her.

"What happened, Cat?" I said, and she starts laughing so hard I thought she'd bust her bra.

"I saw Digger O'Henry do that one time in a bar over on Camp Street," she said. "He bet a bunch of other hillbillies he could go into this black bar and call 'em all niggers and they'd end up buying him a drink. He done just what I did; went in this joint and starts yelling out all kinda names that black folks don't normally go for, and then goes into this 'Tourette's' thing. I'll be damned if don't everybody believe him and they end up buying him drinks and wanting to know where they can send money for the Tourette's fund."

"I'll be damned," I said. "They went for that lame shit?"

"Well…not really," she said. "I think they was just playing

along with a good-looking woman. I figure they just played along 'cause I showed some balls."

"Fuck me," I said. "Just, fuck me. I am a dead man no matter what I do."

"You're the 'glass is half-empty' type, aren't you?" she said, her smile fading. "Your song is already getting old. Turn left here."

We got to her crib, we did it in the bed, on the floor, sitting on the stool—me—in the bathroom, and on the wicker chair in the living room—her. We were two active love-making machines going at it in such a frenzy that anyone watching would think we were in danger of throwing a rod.

"Boy!" said Cat, when we finally lay back and I lit one up, "I'd like to see you after about a three-year stretch in Angola, you're this jacked up after only thirty days. Let me give you my phone number for your wallet, case you ever find yourself doing serious jail time, and find yourself at loose ends, day you get out."

"You know," she said after a minute of silence, in a quiet voice, "I never gave away this much free pussy in the last ten years. Makes me feel like I'm turning into a straight woman. That's funny—that's what I've always wanted to do. Pete, I want to quit whoring. There's something better out there for me. I know there is. I want to go to school, learn a trade, something. Maybe even go to college. Maybe help you out with your po-boy joint, go in partners. Whaddya think?"

I looked over at her laying on my arm, her smell a smell of warmth and sweat and faint perfume and her breath and who knows what else, there was the smell of woman coming up and filling my nostrils, and she gave me this look like I had never seen anyone give me before, and I knew she had done it in a moment of weakness, her guard down, and she regretted it, I knew, from the funny look that followed right after, and I knew also, right then, just as sure as earthworms hate lakes and cane fishing poles and boat rides, that I was in for it now. I had just acquired my first love jones, and I was pretty sure she had, too, the way she was talking about careers and futures and things. I was scared silly. This was big, grown-up, *serious* stuff. This was that stuff they wrote all those damned books about. I had to get my head back on straight. I swear, I had never met a girl like this. This was dangerous ground. A guy could get his balls crushed, by a girl like this.

I swear, just like in that song, my heart skipped a beat.

I did the only thing I could under the circumstances.

"Come on," I said, jumping up and grabbing my shirt. "Let's go watch us some TV, have us a drink."

She stood up and looked at me with the saddest eyes I ever seen on a human being, eyes like some poor, dumb animal you're about to plug between the eyes, like some deer or something, and she said, "You're a bastard, Pete. You're a worthless, useless, no-good motherfucker."

"What?" I said.

"You know what. I saw your eyes. You felt something, too."

"What?" I repeated. She was backing me into some kind of corner. I felt like a coon up a tree, the black and tan hounds all around, a flashlight shining my eyes.

"All right, asshole. I'll say it first. We got the start of something here, Pete. I don't know what it is, but it scares me. You're the wrong kind of guy for me. I'm probably the wrong kind of girl for you. I don't know. I don't know anything, right now. This is crazy. I can't believe I'm falling for somebody like you. I can't fucking believe this shit. I'm going to find some guy owns a factory, somebody wants to buy me diamonds. I can't afford to like a loser like you. Nothing personal, Pete. You just don't fit my long-range plans. You aren't ever going to have that po-boy restaurant. You're a dreamer, and the worst kind of dreamer, the kind whose dreams don't ever come true."

She was talking more to herself than to me, now.

"This is insane. This is suicide. This is a man who makes his living robbing parking meters. This is not a man Cat Herbert should fall in love with."

Goddamn it! Did everybody in New Orleans know about that?

"How the fuck do you know about that? That wasn't my fault, by the way. That was Tommy LeClerc's fault. I didn't even want to do it."

She laughed, and I couldn't tell if it was a laugh of joy or something else. It seemed to me that there was a note of hysteria in it.

"Pete, have you ever read a story called *Alibi Ike*? You should, you know. It's your life story. Hell."

She came over and put her arms around me and put her face up to be kissed. I didn't know what to do so I kissed her. I could hear the hounds and the hunters coming. I was one treed coon.

"Pete, you like me too, don't you? I know you do. What are we going to do?"

I stood there the longest time, staring at her, not saying a word—what could I say? I thought about her giving her hard-earned money to Jackie and I knew she had something special, something different than most girls, and that it was a fool that would screw it up with her. I couldn't get that out of my mind—her slipping Jackie her envelop. But, man, my palms were sure sweating and my throat was sure dryer than a broke alcoholic's. Sure, I had felt something the same time she had, and maybe it was love, who knows, but now what I was feeling was scared and it must have showed because she pushed me away, something passed over her eyes and she shined me a weak grin and said, "Okay, pal. You win. I'm being silly. We're just a biological date, aren't we," and the moment was gone. She said, "Forget what I said. It's just the silly female in me coming out. I like you like I like my dog. Which I don't have any more, by the way. You're cute, but not that cute. I sure hope you didn't think I was serious, 'cause I wasn't. Not at all. Are you kidding me?

Serious about a penny-ante hustler? Ha! I'm *Cat*, buster. I don't get serious. Especially over some loser like you. Come on. Let's get out of here. I'll take you to get your car. You can tell me all about jail. Did you get raped?"

That was a close one. It felt like being in a rundown between third and home. If I'd told her what I really felt, who knows what would have happened? Ever since she'd told me why she'd given her money to Jackie, I'd started feeling different about her. Soft, mushy feelings. Weird feelings. I guess I'd won, somehow, only I didn't feel like I had. I didn't feel trapped any more, but I felt worse. I felt like I had thrown something away I didn't want thrown away. It was like when there are runners on first and third and the batter hits one at you and you throw to second and as soon as the ball leaves your hand you know you done the wrong thing. You shoulda thrown to home. The little third-base coach in my head was telling me I'd thrown to the wrong base. In the car, we were like a couple of pallbearers on the way to the cemetery. I wanted to say I was sorry; I didn't mean it, Cat; there's something happening inside me, too, but I just couldn't. I thought about saying something, but the longer I thought about it, the harder it was and then the time was past.

COMPLICATIONS

"Bye, Pete," she said, when I got out. She leaned out her window and smiled and she looked like she was about ten years old. It almost looked like she was going to cry. "Give me a call sometime when you got a hundred bucks, sailor. I'll show you a real good time." She tore out, squealing the tires.

I sat in my car the longest time, thinking. I'd really blown it. Of all the girls I'd known, not a one was like Cat. Good-looking, smart, and she had a heart. Hell, she was a hooker and she had a bigger heart than any of those rich gals that always have their names in the paper for headin' up the Charity of the Month could ever have. Like to see them give practically their last dollar to help out someone. Collect other people's money, give away some of their own money they don't need anyway, but I'd like to see any of them ladies give away dough that they really needed. And to somebody like Jackie? A hooker? No way.

There wasn't anybody like her I'd ever run across, no way. And I'd thrown her away.

For a minute, I considered going back to her apartment, ringing her bell and telling her what I was feeling, but it was too late for that. She'd just think I was weak.

"Dammit," I said, out loud, turning the ignition key. "T'hell with women. T'hell with *all* women. They just make your life miserable tryin' t'figure out what they want, and then you give it to them, and in the end they just crush your ass anyway. I need *that*?"

The damn car wouldn't start.

Dead battery.

I got lucky, caught a cab only a block away.

I had a bit of a panic, going back to the Ninth Ward, couldn't remember what street the house Tommy and Deneuvé were waiting in, and I had the cabbie drive back and forth past several streets that looked halfway familiar until I found it, just as it was getting dark, which would have made it impossible to find.

I open the door which ain't locked, go inside and Deneuvé's still there, wide-awake, his eyes screaming, and those little noises coming out of his nose, and I see he's particularly agitated. I see what the matter is right off; he's got the hugest cockroach doing the fandango on his forehead, so I do him a favor and go over and brush it off. Tommy is laying on the floor on his back, the bottle of Wild Turkey half-empty and sitting upright beside him, and you could tell he has got serious sinus problems by the sounds he is making in his sleep.

I go over and collapse on the sofa, figuring I'd grab a quick nap before we went to work. It's just early evening, so we got plenty of time, no need to wake Tommy up just yet. A half hour of Z's will make things look a lot brighter.

I couldn't help dreaming about Cat, this really weird dream where we are screwing to beat the band in her waterbed and there's this bloody stump of a hand that keeps smacking her on the ass.

I slept, but I didn't get a lot of rest. It was a wonder I could still keep up ol' willie with that bloody hand all over Cat's rear end. Half the time, I kept shaking it, like we was closing some kind of deal or something. It was some dream that was more like a French movie minus the subtitles.

Half-awake and half into a fitful sleep, the realization that

I'd lost Cat hit home. I hadn't even known I liked her, and all at once I was realizing I felt about her the same as she said she had about me, earlier. I had about as bad a case of the lovesick jones as you could get, the kind of down and dirty blues Tammy Wynette can get her dulcet pipes around. I groaned aloud as the blackbird of sadness flew over and sat on my head and took a big dump all over me. This felt almost as bad as the day when I was given my unconditional release from baseball, when I hung up my cleats for the last time. *It's your own fault,* a little voice kept saying, but I paid it no mind. Least, I tried not to. *Hell,* I remember thinking, just before I drifted off. *She'd just end up screwing over me anyway, sometime or other.* It still felt bad, like the day I got my baseball walking papers.

No, this felt even worse.

I had thought that to be the blackest day of my existence.

I had thought that.

KIDNAPPIN'S EASY, *SURGERY'S* HARD

I must have caught one whale of a nap, 'cause when I looked up, I was lying on the floor, and Tommy was lugging Deneuvé over to the sofa where I'd started out, dreaming about me and Cat. The old man was making a kind of high-pitched whining noise, sort of the sound a jet plane makes when it's warming up, getting ready to take off. I sat up and rubbed my eyes.

"Whatcha doin'?"

Sweat was running off both their faces: Tommy's from exertion and Deneuvé's from concern.

"What's it look like I'm doing, dummy? I'm putting him on the operating table. Your arm broke, you can't help?" His words had that Wild Turkey mush to them.

I got up, a little wavy, but he already had him up on the couch, legs and arms both trussed up, arms in front.

Tommy wiped his face with his sleeve and reached over for the bottle of chloroform, keeping his knee on Deneuvé's chest. Deneuvé hummed louder and in a higher register.

"He wants to tell us something," I said.

Tommy gave me a drop-dead look, no matter he'd just waked me out of a serious coma and heartbreak dream, and said, "No shit he wants t'tell us something. He wants t'tell us not to cut his hand off for which favor he'll be so appreciative he'll just run right home and fetch the money for us and we won't have to bother ourselves with all this trouble. He wants t'tell us he'll throw in another million or two, free of charge, just for us bein' so kind and benevolent." He snorted. "You sure you're not a Sunday school teacher or somethin'? I swear t'God, Pete, sometimes I think you just got your first pair of long pants." He turned back to his work, and I stepped over to see if I could be of help, not that I really wanted to.

I didn't much like this side of Tommy, the smart-ass side. That was supposed to be my role, but I figured he was just nervous. Like I was solid bedrock my own self!

I wondered why he'd gone ahead and started the proceedings on his own and guessed he just wanted to get it over with, figured I'd come around when the action begun. There didn't seem to be much I could do right then, so I just stood around and watched him work, and hoped I wouldn't pass out, embarrass myself.

He got the lid to the bottle off, soaked the rag in chloroform and slapped it to Deneuvé's face. You could see Deneuvé struggling like a girl on her first date, and then quicker than I would have thought, his body just sort of went whoosh, like the air'd been let out, and he was under.

"This is some good shit," Tommy said. *Good* shit, it was great! I was feeling a little less edgy seeing Deneuvé out cold, like somehow he wasn't the most dangerous man in New Orleans when he was in Dreamland. And, besides, I hate to see any man suffer, even a drug dealer like him.

The chloroform stunk something terrible. I stepped over and grabbed the rag where Tommy had dropped it and threw it as far across the room as I could. Unfortunately, when I tossed it, I also accidentally knocked over the bottle of chloroform which Tommy had neglected to close. In a second, it smelled like General Hospital at rush hour and I was getting hazy.

"Jesus Christ!" Tommy yelled. "We'll all be out!"

He had a point. My peepers were already dragging, Mr. Sandman was shoveling sand to beat the band. The fumes filled the room. Tommy was screechin' something about grabbing the bottle and some rags and his voice and the room were going in slow motion from where I stood. It was getting hard to concentrate.

"Just shut up," I said, murder on my mind. Murder must have been in my voice as well. Tommy glared at me and I could see his bad eye drooping and I wondered which one of us was gonna fade out first. He tried to say something else, but he must of forgot what it was he wanted to say, 'cause nothing came out. At least I don't think it did. I was wading through what felt like swamp mud but what I could see was only thick air and fumbled through the things Tommy'd shoved on the floor. I got hold of one of the diapers and soaked up as much of the spill as I could. I left the rag there to soak some more out of the carpet and got the lid back on the bottle, but it was more than half gone. I was really getting woozy. I threw the diaper over in the far corner with the first rag and the air seemed to clear a little. Then I remembered Tommy and he wasn't there. He was gone.

I have to admit it. I panicked. There was Deneuvé over there, lying on the sofa, out like Ali's sparring partner, and here was I, chloroform was filling the air and the host of this goddamned party was nowhere to be seen. I did the only thing I could think of.

I screamed.

"Tommeeeeee!"

"What?" he said, in this normal voice that made me jump about as high as the ceiling, and there he was, only about six feet away, over at the door, inhaling the oxygen from the outside.

He just shook his head at me and closed the door and went back over to Deneuvé on the sofa. I worried for an instant about somebody hearing my yell and calling the cops and decided that wasn't highly likely, not in this neighborhood. Screams were just a normal part of the audio background, your average night of mayhem on this block.

Tommy was busy with the task at hand. He sat down next to Deneuvé who was still nodding out on the couch and cut the bonds from his arms. He grabbed one arm and slung it over the arm of the couch and reached for the hacksaw.

"Wait a minute, Tommy," I said. "Does it matter which hand you cut off?"

That made him stop.

"Yeah," he decided, after a second. "The right hand. I think. He might hardly never use his left." He flung the first hand back which was the left and grabbed the other one, bringing the saw to Deneuvé's wrist.

"How do you know he's right-handed?"

This stopped the action again. Tommy looked at the hand he held, glared at me, then glared at the hand.

"You're a son-of-a-bitch, Pete," he said. He put the saw to the wrist, took it away, put it back again, and withdrew it once more. I could see the fury in his eyes. He let go the hand.

"You're a bastard, Pete. Why'd you have to bring up something like that for, anyway? How the hell should I know if he's right or left-handed? I fucking sure ain't gonna wait for him to wake up and tell me." He picked up the saw once more and placed the blade to the wrist. "Sometimes you got to take chances in life, Pete. This is one of those times. I'm cuttin' this one, no matter which one it is."

It was the left.

I pointed that out.

This really set him off. He stood up, thrust Deneuvé's hand from him like he'd seen all of it he wanted to, and stomped out of the room, into the kitchen. I could hear him rummaging around in the cupboard, shoving things here and there, something fell on the floor and broke, and then he came back out, a water glass in his hand.

"Where's that bottle?" he said, but I don't think he was talking to me, more to himself. I wasn't going to answer him, at any rate. Conversation between us wasn't going so hot, at the present.

He found the bottle where he'd left it on the floor and jerked it up and stormed back into the kitchen. It got real quiet in there.

After a few minutes, I went on in, thinking he'd had enough time to cool off. He had. He had his head in his hands, just staring at the half-full glass of Wild Turkey in front of him. I sat down and took a pull out of the bottle. We just sat there for about five minutes, him staring at the glass which he hadn't touched and me taking a nip every now and then out of the bottle.

At last, he spoke, and you could tell he was at the end of his rope. It was in his voice. The mental stress and strain had got him by the short hairs. He kept on staring at his glass and his voice was low, beat.

"Pete, I'm not mad at you anymore. I just don't think I can go on with this. You try and figure every angle, rack your noodle sideways to cover every single little thing that can screw up, and then something like this happens."

I tried to console him.

"Tommy, maybe it ain't important which hand you whack. Do the right one. Odds are, that's the important one."

He sighed. "Pete, you don't understand. These old geezers, especially the ones like Deneuvé there, they got more pride than Elvis. We don't get the right hand; I mean the *correct* hand, his *main* hand, he might just decide not to pay us. Hell, we get the wrong one, his secondary hand, he might see it as no big thing, just a badge of honor. Show he's got serious beans in his jeans, that kind of thing."

He could be right. These old boys, they were hard. The more I thought about it, the more I was convinced he was right. We'd be better off not to take either hand less we could figure out which was the main one for him.

"We could feel for calluses," I suggested. "Wouldn't the prime hand be more callused?"

"You think he's got a ditch-digger's hands from countin' thousand-dollar bills? 'Sides, even if he did manual labor, which he ain't never done in his entire life, both hands'd be the same.

That ain't gonna tell us diddly-squat."

We were back to square one. I had yet another bright idea.

"Why don't we call somebody? His mom or somebody, tell them we're his buds, want to buy him a birthday present, something that will tell us if he's right or left-handed, something…" I tried to think what kind of gift would have to be decided knowing that.

"I know! We'll call up his ma and tell her we were all in Little League together and we want to give him this joke gift for his birthday. We want to give him a catcher's mitt, bring back the old ball-playing memories!" I thought it was a stroke of genius.

Tommy didn't. He didn't even say anything, but his look did. I thought about my idea some more. Tommy's look was right. My idea sucked.

All of a sudden, Tommy stood up and picked up the glass of Turkey and chugged the whole thing, pretty near half a glass full.

"Dammit," he said, wiping off his mouth with the back of his hand. "I didn't come this far to up and quit now. We'll take off the right one and fuck it if we guessed wrong."

It occurred to me that I was supposed to be the one designated to deliver Deneuvé back to his house, minus his hand, and wait for him to bring me out the money. That got me a little more concerned about slicing off the wrong accessory.

"Uh, Tommy," I said. "Let's talk about this some more. We don't want to make any major tactical mistakes at this late hour, do we?"

I got still another brainstorm only this time it was a winner.

"Hey, what if we whack off a foot, instead? Or," inspiration suddenly struck me, "why don't we just nip off *both* hands? That way, we'd be right either way."

Tommy had already gotten up and started for the other room where Deneuvé was, but that brought him up short. You could see the wheels turning by the look on his kisser.

"You know, that might not be such a bad idea, Pete. That might not be a bad idea at all."

He was going to say something else, but just then we heard a thumping noise in the other room, like the front door banging. Our eyes met and the same thought struck both of us at the same time. Deneuvé? We'd forgot about him completely! We ran into the room.

"My God," said Tommy. "OhGodohGodohGodohGodohGod!" Over and over. I sprinted to the door and there he was, halfway down the walk, on his stomach pulling himself along with his hands. He must have still been too groggy to have thought about untying his feet.

"Tommy! Here he is!"

We flew out the door and grabbed him. For someone half dopey from chloroform, he sure put up one hell of a struggle. We lost him again, he twisted completely away wiggling like a nightcrawler allergic to fishhooks, and then we just picked him up like a sack of potatoes, uncooperative, *writhing* potatoes, and hauled his ass back inside, looking every which way while we're doing it, checking to see if any of the neighbors were out.

We were in luck. There didn't seem to be anybody out on the street except a couple of star-crossed kidnappers and their unwilling victim. We hustled him back inside and threw him onto the sofa and Tommy tied his hands back up while I closed and locked the door and got my heartbeat back down to about a thousand beats a second. Tommy hadda bust him in the chops to quiet him down a little. Worked about as good as the chloroform, except for being more messy, what with the blood trickling out of his nose.

"Jesus, Tommy," I said, standing by the door and peeking out to see if the cops were coming. "Can you believe it! Is this just not our night, or what?"

All you could hear was the rasping of our breath, Tommy's and mine, and Deneuvé wheezing through his nose. He hadn't thought to take the handkerchief out of his mouth when he made his break, which was good for us. One good yell and it wouldn't have mattered what neighborhood we were in, someone would have called the cops. The blood running from his nose had saturated the gag until it looked like a six-year-old girl after her first go-around with her mom's rouge.

"Hell, I hope he don't bleed to death from his nose before he does his hand," I cracked, trying to inject a little levity into the situation. Tommy didn't laugh, so I dropped the humor.

Deneuvé started making movements like he was coming to again, so Tommy went over to where I'd thrown the rags and brought one back and put it over his nose and he relaxed right away. This stuff was great! I was starting to think of other possibilities, like if you could sneak it along on dates, use it on the girl if she turned out to be the resistant type.

"Let's do it, Pete," Tommy said, standing up and rubbing his hands together. He went out into the kitchen and brought back the bottle of Turkey and took a huge pull and handed it to me. I took one about as big. I looked at the bottle and figured we'd better go ahead and do it, all right. The bottle was seven-eighths gone. Once we started sobering up, it might be a bit harder to go on with the operating. For Tommy, that is. There was no way I was capable of cross-cutting that hand even if I drank enough to have the blind staggers. That was Tommy's department, all the way.

Tommy gave Deneuvé another hit with the chloroform and cut the cord around his hands. He picked up the hacksaw and tested the sharpness of the blade on his thumb. He reached over and took another swig of the Turkey and then announced he was ready to commence. He was going through some emotional changes, I could see that, now that it was nitty-gritty time. He began talking out loud to himself, but I could see it was for my benefit.

"Asshole don't understand how hard this is to do. Had to psyche myself up for six hours to be able to do this. Think know-it-all assholes'd have the guts to do this? No way, José. This is a very delicate operation and takes the courage of a lion." He paused, peeked over to see if I was listening and was properly ashamed and chastised, took a deep breath and clenched his teeth, the words hissing as he continued talking to himself.

"Fuck the play-by-play, Tommy. I know you're a great guy to do the hard work and I'm a zero for not, but remember this was your idea, not mine. Just do it, why don'tcha? I thought injuns were good at stuff like this, separatin' people from parts of their bodies. You know, like scalps?"

He drew the saw in a backstroke to get the teeth started, the same way you do when you saw the barrel off a .12 gauge. I had stepped over and was standing right in front, not a foot away, and at first there was nothing, not even a line. I wondered if he'd broke the skin. Then a white line appeared and quickly turned pink, and then, man the blood began to seep like water over a little kid's wading pool when they forgot to watch the hose. The Wild Turkey I'd drunk began a slow boil in the pit of my stomach, felt like a belly dancer workshop going on in there, and I began to rub my own wrist which had developed sympathy pains. I had to look twice to be sure it was all right.

"Harder. Got to do it harder," Tommy hissed, and put more wood into it on the downstroke. That's when the juice really started to come, not spurting but flowing. Heavy-duty flowing.

"Shit!" Tommy yelled. "I forgot to plug in the solder iron. Where the hell is it?"

I found it on the coffee table and ran to plug it in. The cord wouldn't reach to the couch—I seen that right away. I left it plugged in, dropping the iron to the floor, and ran around looking for a closer plug. There wasn't any. Tommy had dropped the saw and was holding Deneuvé's wrist in both hands, applying pressure. His face was whiter than the sheet of the head Klansman at the elections meeting, and beads of sweat were popping out all over his face. He wasn't smiling. The blood continued to run, but not as much as before, and just then Deneuvé moaned and tried to sit up.

"Holy Christ!" Tommy screeched. "He's comin' to! Get the fuckin' chloroform!"

"Which you want, the chloroform or the iron?" I said. "Make up your mind." This was not the tightly organized caper I'd hoped for.

"*The fucking chloroform!*"

I bit my tongue, rather than say what was on my mind, and ran across the room, looking for the rags I'd tossed. I found it in a jiffy and ran back with it. Tommy was trying to hold Deneuvé's bleeding arm with one hand and punching him in the face with the other. Droplets of blood were flying everywhere. I stuck the rag over Deneuvé's nose and mouth. He opened his eyes wide, not six inches from mine, and then they slammed shut. At the same time, he tensed like he'd been hit with a cattle prod and then just slumped back into the sofa. Tommy's face was soaking wet and there was gore everywhere. It looked like an explosion on boiler number nine at the ketchup factory.

"Get the iron," Tommy said, his words high and reedy. "Where's that goddamned iron? We got to cauterize him as we go."

I stepped over to where I'd left the iron and both of us noticed a new problem at the same time. You couldn't actually make out the iron itself. It was hidden in the smoke. The carpet was on fire. Not actual flames, but sort of a smolder.

"Holy fuck," was all Tommy could say. "Holy fuck."

I must not have given Deneuvé as good a dose of the chloroform as I thought, 'cause just as we were noticing the smoke, he shot straight up, eyes as big as cantaloupe halves. Tommy just smacked him, sucker-punched him, and he went as limp as the gay caballero's handshake. I ran over and grabbed the soldering iron cord and snatched it from where it was plugged in, stomping on the area where it had lain. There was a red glow in the brown carpet, but now was not the time to put it out. I gave it a fast stomp with my foot, mistake, and that sent sparks flying, but I couldn't stay around and play fire department. Tommy was shrieking and acting generally like Sybil with all the personalities turned loose at once. I ran the iron over to him. It seemed to be what he wanted most, though it was hard to tell. He was yelling about everything, me, Deneuvé, the fire, his ex-wife, *everything*.

I thrust the iron at him and he grabbed the wrong end.

"Fu-uuuuck!" He was in some kinda pain, seemed to me.

"You stupid shit!"

Me! He was yelling at me! Like *I* was the blind idiot what had latched onto the business end, instead of his own dumb self!

"Listen, Tommy," I said. "There's no sense in getting testy with me. Open your eyes, watch what you're grabbin'." I was getting more than tired of his screeching and his orders and especially, his constant panics.

"And listen to this, Tommy," I went on, while he's massaging his paw and shooting death ray looks at me. "If you remember, I didn't want to do this in the first goddamned place. If you can't calm down and act like a human being, I'm just gonna go. I got better things to do than stand around and watch you act insane or like a little kid. You could of planned this better, you know. Kidnapper, heal thyself."

"No!" he howled, his voice hysterical. "Don't go! Don't go! It'll be all right. I know how to do it now. We'll hit his wrist a lick with the iron and then you run back and plug it in again. Do that two, three times, we got the bleeding stopped. Get me one of those diapers for my hand. I think all the meat's cooked."

I threw him one of the rags on the table and he wrapped it around his hand.

"Go in the kitchen and find a plate," he ordered, back in his Hitler mode. I didn't argue, just did what he said. He seemed to have gotten hold of himself.

"Put the iron on the plate when you heat it up," he said, when I came back out. "Now, plug the iron in again. All the heat's gone. It's in my hand. I could cauterize him with my fingers if it wouldn't hurt so much."

I caught his little sarcasm but ignored it, figuring he deserved to get off a little shot like that.

Smoke was really filling up the room, making it harder to see, but there were no flames. While I was waiting for the iron to heat back up, I ran back into the kitchen and found a pan and filled it with water and came out and threw it on the rug where it was glowing. That put most of the fire out, but made it smolder worse. Plus there was something in the rug that released its odor when the water hit it. Tommy must have noticed it, too. "What's that smell?" he said.

"Cats, is my guess," I said.

I sneak a peek over at Tommy, and he's holding onto Deneuvé's wrist with a death grip, but the blood's still flowing. It was hard to tell if it was flowing a lot or not, since a little blood can go a long way, but if it had been *my* blood, I'da said it was flowing a lot. The iron glowed red, so I picked it up. Tommy took a long hard look this time before he picked an end.

He took the iron, but with the rag on his hand it must've been hard to handle, 'cause it slipped and fell into his lap. There was some screeching and goings-on there, I'll tell you, him going one way and the iron another, but after he patted himself and made sure all his personal business was intact and not scorched, he threw the rag off his hand, and picked up the iron again. There's a new problem as now the rug's ignited in a new spot, where the iron had fallen, but that's a minor glitch in Tommy's mind, I guess. He looked really mad, and I guess he was getting kinda beat up and burned and all. He was starting to look in worse shape than Deneuvé and he didn't have the benefit Deneuvé did, of being out cold. I guess he took it all fairly well, considering.

He took hold of Deneuvé's wrist again, the blood still coming, and socked the soldering iron to it. It made a sizzling sound and an image of fast food steak houses flashed through my mind. Then the smell hit me and it must have hit Tommy about the same time since regurgitated Wild Turkey hit the deck in two different places at almost the same second. We couldn't have been more precise if we was the Rockettes or the Saints' cheerleaders. Just then, Deneuvé decides to crap his pants, being as how he'd missed his morning constitutional, and things were getting spicy. There was a regular smorgasbord of smells floating around in the room, but a few of 'em I was missing what with puke up my nose. This was not the way I'd envisioned proceedings in the planning stages.

I was halfway down the block by the time Tommy caught up to me.

"Where the hell you goin'?" He was yanking at my arm, and I pulled away from him.

"Come on back, Pete. We're not done. We're almost done. You're kissin' away a million bucks."

I just stared at him and then went on walking. I didn't have a clue where I was going to walk to and I didn't much care. Let Sam eradicate me. If Deneuvé's people didn't beat him to it. It was all just too much trouble. I was fresh out of ambition and energy. Tommy clutched at my arm again and I just turned and gave him the frostiest look I was capable of.

"Touch me again, Tommy, and I'll kill you. I'll hit you so hard I'll wipe out half your family. Just get the fuck out of my face. In fact, move off the fucking planet. Get on one of your own. There's not enough room on this one for both of us."

He didn't say a word, just turned and walked back toward the house. I watched him for a minute. I could tell which one he was making for. It was the one with all the smoke coming out. He began to trot and then run in earnest, the last few feet. I waited until I saw him go inside and then I began walking in the opposite direction.

I walked another block. And a half. And then, I turned around and walked the whole way back. The smoke was really rolling out now.

When I walked back in I could see things had changed. Tommy had pulled the sofa with Deneuvé on it closer to the wall by the plug-in. He was getting ready to take another crack at sawing. The smells had changed, intensified.

And it looked like virgin night at the cathouse. Blood was everywhere. Tommy musta heard me coming in the door and didn't know who it was at first. His head snapped back like the center did when the quarterback grabbed the wrong ball, and then he seen it was just me and he went back to laying the hacksaw up against Deneuvé's wrist.

He laid the wood to it, this time. It was surprising how quick a hand can get detached when a body puts a mind to it, wants to get the job over and done with. It was over half cut through, and it was the weirdest thing. It kept moving the whole time, trying to make a fist, it looked like. I was fascinated, watching it. Gave me the creeps. Must've bothered Tommy, too—he kept slapping at it with his other hand every now and then, like he was trying to make it stop, but that hand had a mind of its own, kept twitching and stuff. Tommy's nerves must have been getting kind of jangled, 'cause he laid the hacksaw down on the floor and wiped his brow. I seen he'd worked up quite a lather.

"Let's check it, when we're done," I said, cracking wise. "Count the rings, see how old this redwood is."

That didn't fetch a laugh, so I guessed Tommy was deep into his serious mode. He has the chloroform rag all ready beside him, takes it and slaps a little more from the bottle on it and holds it on Deneuvé's mouth hole for a couple of seconds.

"So," he said, not looking my way. "Decided not to run out on me, eh? Thought about all that money, huh?"

I came over and stood beside him. "What can I do?"

"Nothin'," he said. "Not just yet. I'm almost done. You can get a baggie. Throw some more water on the rug. Clean the place up a little. It won't be long now."

Clean the place up! Was he hoping to get his deposit back from the landlord after we vacated?

I did what he said anyway, and came back over to where he and Deneuvé were when I was done. Tommy was right. He *was* almost done. The hand was hanging half off his wrist, just making little jumping moves and twitches every now and then, but acting pretty docile now, compared to earlier. It was only hanging on by a little meat and part of the bone. I made a mental note to never order steak tartare again. I noticed there wasn't much blood coming from the severed part and then I saw why. Tommy'd tied it off with kite twine.

"Whyn't you think of that before?" I asked, pointing, and he followed my finger and grinned.

"Woulda been easier, wouldn't it?" he said, and I nodded and then smiled myself, and all of a sudden the tension was lifted and we both knew this was going to work.

He lit a cigarette and sat there smoking for a while. After the activities of the past hour, this seemed almost peaceful, just three guys sitting around a living room, having a smoke break. I broke out a Camel myself.

"Didja hear the one about the woman golfer what got stung by a bee?" Tommy says. I didn't believe I had.

"She goes screechin' inta the clubhouse, yellin' at the top of her lungs, 'I been stung! I been stung by a bee!' The club pro comes running over and says t'her, 'Just calm down, get it together. Now, just exactly where did this bee sting you?' The lady says, 'Between the first and second holes! and the golf pro says, 'Well, lady, I know what your problem is,' and she says, 'What?' and he says, 'Your stance is too wide.'"

It took a minute and then it sunk in and we're both howling like two Boy Scouts on our first group jerkoff, and I'd say the atmosphere had considerably lightened.

Tommy stood up and dropped his cigarette to the floor and stubbed it out with his toe, messing up the carpet I'd just cleaned, but it didn't matter. Two more pulls with the hacksaw and it was done, the hand was off.

"Here," he said, smirking like a guy with a fat wife who'd just heard about no-fault divorces. He tossed the hand to me like it was a softball and I was too surprised to do anything but catch it, which gave my stomach a little lurch, but I kept it down. I shoved the hand into a baggie.

"Put a twistie on it and throw it in the fridge." Tommy said, beaming. "We done it, partner. By golly, we done it!"

And we had. We'd really gone and done it. Now, all that was left to do was drop Deneuvé off at his house, smoke a butt and wait for him to come out with the loot, and we'd be on our merry Jamaican way. He'd have his hand back, we'd have a suitcase full of greenbacks, heading for an airport somewhere, and everybody in Robin's merry band would be bunch of happy green-clad fellas.

I started for the kitchen, my stomach settling down, the grin on my puss about as big and wide as the one I see on Tommy's. The only one of this madcap trio that wasn't in hog heaven was Deneuvé, but then he was still napping and maybe couldn't appreciate the beauty of the moment anyway, from his vantage point.

It was a great moment in an outlaw career.

It was too brief, however.

The sound of doom reached our ears. From no more'n three blocks away from the house, maybe two. I looked at Tommy and he looked at me and we both read the same thing in each other's eyes.

It was sirens. Coming fast.

"Fire trucks," he said, as if perhaps I was deaf.

"Somebody saw the smoke," I said, as if he'd just come in off the porch.

"We're fucked," he said, and this time I didn't say a word. There was nothing to add to what had just been said.

WE ARE IN SOME DEEP, DEEP SHIT...
AND THE TOILET PAPER ROLL'S EMPTY

"We got to be goin'," Tommy said, and I had to agree with that.

"Where?" I said, my mind blank as a blonde with peroxide poisoning.

"Out back," he said. "They won't get what's goin' on for a few minutes. That'll give us enough time to get to the car and get the fuck out of here. We'll have to leave Deneuvé. Not enough time to lug him with us."

"Great idea," I said. It was, too. Anything that suggested scramming and had a workable flight plan to go with it was appealing.

"Let's boogie," I said.

We could hear the fire trucks turning the corner. We hit the back door full tilt and were halfway across the back yard, when Tommy snatches me from behind by my shirt and almost gives me a heart attack when I'm yanked back.

"Did you get it?" he yelled.

"Get what?" My heart is lumbering along at only about two thousand pops per second, a mere fraction of the rate it had been bumping along at only a second before.

"The *hand*. Did you get the *hand*?" He was shouting. No... he was *screaming*.

Damn. It had slipped my mind, what with all the excitement. He read my face. "Go back."

"Huh?" This was one crazy motherfucker. I shouldn't stand so close to him, is what I was thinking. There might be radiation, alpha waves, something.

"You heard me. That's a two million dollar fucking hand. Go back and get it."

I was gonna debate with him but the gun that suddenly materialized in his hand and was aimed in the direction of my body unit gave me pause. This was a development I didn't care for at all. None of this.

Any second, about twenty burly firemen were going to be crashing into the house, and I sure wasn't keen about being found keeping company with a recent amputee, who was all tied up and dopey from chloroform, and not too likely to put in a good word for me. I sighed, trying to decide which was the worse fate, wondering if Tommy would really shoot me, and then I remembered something. The baggie. It was still in my hand. With Deneuvé's fist. I had never put it in the fridge after all.

I held it up.

"It's here, Tommy. I got it."

He stuck the gun in his belt.

"Let's book then, mate. We're under control."

We ran like watermelon thieves.

We made the car all right and it was good he'd parked down the street, else it might have been awkward asking the firemen to move their trucks and let us out.

Tommy was in a bit of a hurry to leave, which don't do the tire warranty much good, but we made the corner on two wheels saving the rubber on half of them, and we screamed down the street until I mentioned it might look less suspicious if we was traveling closer to the legal speed limit instead of the LeMans pace we seemed to be on. Tommy seen the logic in that and applied the brakes, a little too quick for my comfort as my head cracked the windshield. That's two things I got against him, just in the last ten minutes. I ain't forgot the gun he had pointed at the same space I was occupying. Somewhere down the line he was gonna pay for that.

He made the first decision, which was to head for his crib. We're talking and making up this movie as we tool along. We'll get to his house, he said, catch our breath, think it out, and get some Bactine on his hand, which he starts to remember, and becomes the only topic on his pinhead mind.

Look at this hand on my lap, is what goes through my own mind, you think *you* got problems; but I keep it to myself as I see his nerves are kinda raggedy. You'd thought he never got a little burn before on his little candy ass.

That paw in the baggie was starting to bug me. I swear it was still moving. I put it in the seat beside me, closer to Tommy, and kept an eye on it, checking to see if it was crawling over toward me or was it just my active imagination. That was a hand I was anxious to trade, PDQ.

We pulled into the drive at Tommy's place, a cracker box shotgun house in the low-rent district, a lotta little kids playing in the dirt in their yards and throwing rocks at the passing cars, and go in and his girlfriend's there, which information he hadn't seen fit to pass on to me beforehand. She's quite the ace house-keeper from the looks of things, place looked like a good spot to hold a sanitation engineer's convention—make everybody feel like they're on the job.

Her first words were charming. "Who's this bozo, another one a' yore lousy criminal friends?"

Well, honey, I think, you expect ol' Tommy here to be bringing home the president of the chamber of commerce or the king of Norway?

"Ever cross your mind to empty one of these?" is what I say to her, pointing to an ashtray, least I think that's what's under the pile of butts on the coffee table, though that could of been just a lucky guess. That gets me a dirty look. I'm wondering if it's safe to put out my cigarette in it, what with all the combustibles in it and besides she needed to be put down a peg and it was obvious Tommy wasn't the man for the job.

She ignores me pretty much from then on, seeing as I'll give it back better than she gives it out, and turns on Tommy, niggling about naggely things like, "Where you been? You promised t'go with me to Mom's."

Now *that* was a scary image—that there were *two* of them.

I had a manager in Single A had a wife that was kind of like this tomato, always harping on her old man, giving him grief. He used to pray for road trips, he told me once. I saw him in a hotel downtown one time during a long home stand and asked what he was doing there and he said he'd rented a room. His wife thought we was still on a swing down through Georgia, he said.

"Shut up," said Tommy to her, too late—I already seen he's PW'd. He gave me the sign and I follow him out through the kitchen, which ain't gonna make many *House Beautiful* covers, on out into the garage, and he takes the hand from me, which I've been forced to carry, and he tucks it into the deep freeze, under some veal cutlets, and I make a mental note to decline any dining invitations he decides to offer, especially if the main course is a beef product don't look familiar or I ain't seen him buy, personally. I was certainly glad to be rid of that hand. I'd had it hid inside my shirt so's the neighbors wouldn't see what we was transporting and I swear the fingers were trying to tickle my stomach.

We go back into the house—I'm feeling like Tommy's cocker spaniel that hasta follow him around the house—and Wanda, that's her name, is slamming cupboards and drawers, but she doesn't fool me—it's not housecleaning she's up to, just giving Tommy a message he ain't gonna get any first-grade sex in the next decade or so. And I figure she's on a hunt for the big bottle of industrial strength Midol. A big chunk of raw meat would calm her down better, I bet myself.

An image of Cat and me sitting around the house acting like Tommy and Wanda popped into my head and I got the shivers. Maybe it was a good thing she'd kissed me off, saved me from all this ecstasy Tommy was enjoying.

"Get me some salve," Tommy said to her. "I burnt my hand bad working on the car."

"Gonna be hard t'beat yore meat then, ain't it," she said, but got it for him, and me and him go on into the bedroom. Tommy locked the door. We could hear a symphony of doors and drawers slamming and a lot of creative cussing. I could see why Tommy would want to make a lot of money and leave town. She was some prize. I could see where a lot of guys might envy him, having a knockout old lady like that. All I know is, if she was a magazine I wouldn't be buying it for the photo spread.

"Get that smile off your puss," he said. "You don't know the whole story. She's a firecracker in bed." Then, "What're we gonna do now? Now we got to bring the middleman in, what I was trying to avoid."

"Tommy, I'm tired of your orders. Who died and made you Pope? The next time you decide to pull a gun on me, I'm gonna shove it up your butt and pull the trigger three times before your hemorrhoids have a chance to twitch. I'm tired of being nice to you. You're the kind what don't appreciate it. Now you got me in this sad and sorry mess I didn't wanna be in in the first place, but don't you worry. I'm gonna get us out of it."

He started to say something, but musta seen the look in my eyes, 'cause he didn't get anything out, only gets this pouty look on his mug and starts slathering salve on his wounded paw.

"Better hope that don't get infected," I said, giving him a little more of the needle. "It could end up in the freezer with the other one."

I laughed at something that occurred to me.

"Wouldn't that be a hoot," I said. "Your hand and his in the freezer, and we get 'em mixed up, send the wrong hand to Deneuvé. Think he'd be upset, get a hand that only wants to play with his willie all day and pick his nose?"

You could tell he didn't think that was funny, though he didn't come right out and say so. I didn't much care. He had an attitude about as sweet as his old lady's. I'd bet a dime it was a fun time sitting around *that* house most evenings, watching the tube and popping corn.

"This is what we're gonna do, Tommy," I began. "First, we need some stuff. I got an idea will save us. You can thank Cat partially for it. I remembered something we saw at a mall first time we met."

I outlined my stroke of genius to him and he laps it up. I knew he would, soon as I thought of it. For a guy who's only come up with one original idea in his whole career, and that one turns to buffalo diarrhea, he's gotta like anything that keeps his spindly ass afloat, and this was one zinger of an idea, if I did say so myself. Even *his* mind, which operated at about thirty strokes over par most days, could see the beauty of this.

THE PLAN

"First off," I said, "the good part of this kidnap's over with. We got to bring the middleman in now, like you say, looks like. Deneuvé is back home by now, or in a hospital, and you can bet he's got his guys out looking for us."

"Yeah," Tommy said, and there is dead silence. He is looking at me for the words that are gonna save the day.

"He has also got his phone at home covered by somebody works for him. He knows the score, knows we got his hand, and figures we got to call him if we want the money. He wants his hand back, you can bet on that. What we got to do, is figure out a way to get the money without getting caught. And I don't mean the FBI. I mean by his boys.

"What we do, Tommy, is we get one of them remote control boats, a big one, and we go plant it on one of those steamboats the tourists are always riding on, that go up the Mighty Oil-Slick. We get one big enough and powerful enough it can pull a raft. The raft will be the two million. We call 'em, we call Deneuvé or his boys or whoever's handling the arrangements on his end, and we give 'em our instructions, where to bring the money, what to look for. We tell them to wrap the money in something waterproof, something that will float. I saw these kind of boats, the time me and Cat met. We was at a mall and they was racin' 'em, in a big, ol' tank. Neatest thing you ever saw. Cat said she knew a guy had one big as a yacht, could tow tugs, so I know they got the horsepower for this, we get one big enough.

"We call up Deneuvé, his people, whoever, tell them what to do, go down to the Natchez. Bring the money in this waterproof bale that can float, find the boat where we've hidden it, attach it to the remote-control boat and throw the whole works in the river."

"How do *we* get it?" he said.

This was one dense outlaw. If brains were hamburger the only place his would be a whole patty would be MacDonald's.

"*Remote* control, Tommy. Read my lips, listen up. Didn't you hear me say we were gonna get us a *remote*-control boat?"

You could see the dawn break over the horizon. He was tragic, needed a map to find his own bathroom.

"Oh!" he said when the light bulb went on, like he'd just figured out electricity.

I decided to just go ahead and explain the rest of it, ignore his comments and hope he got the principle points.

"Meanwhile, we're upstream at a place only we know where we're gonna be, and when the Natchez comes by where we're hiding, we wave a flag at them and they drop the boat and the money in the water. We sail it right up to us."

"How will they know it's us wavin' this flag? Won't we be too far away to recognize?"

MacDonald's wouldn't serve his brains either, they was worse than hamburger.

"Tommy, we tell them to watch for a flag, when we give them the payoff instructions. We just got to take a chance there's nobody else out waving flags same time we are. I think we'll be all right there. This has been an off-year for flag-waving along the river, I believe. I am sure that I read something to that effect only last week in the *Times-Picayune*. It was on the idiot page. I am surprised that you missed it."

It was dangerous, leaving the house, not knowing how close Deneuvé might be to finding us, but then it was more dangerous staying there, with *two* mental defectives.

"You just got here," Wanda wailed when she saw we're leaving. "I haven't seen you in a week and you're here five minutes and now you're going out already. Is this what it's gonna be like when we get married?"

"You go pick out your drapes, honey," I told her, as we headed out the door. "Me'n Tommy are going down to get fitted for our tuxes. Call the caterer, too. Only thing I ask, is that you get plenty of mudbugs and shrimp." Tommy didn't say a word.

In the car, all I said was, "You told her you were gonna *marry* her?"

First, we went to a hobby store to try to find a boat. We got the biggest thing they had in the store, a thing that looked like it could have done some damage in The Big One: W.W. Two. This was a *serious* hobby, it looked like, to some folks. Four or five of these things, you could start your own navy, lick some of the smaller banana republics, maybe even give our own fleet a decent tussle way they keep lowering the defense outlay. We get the warship model, and I figure they're going to have to widen the door for us to get it out, but it just makes it, by the barnacles. We don't have the exact measurements or weight of what two million bucks is gonna total out to, but I describe to the clerk, the size I estimate it's going to be, and he said, sure; this baby will haul *you* around.

The clerk, a kid with nine million zits, said we shouldn't have no trouble steering either. It's a piece of cake, he said. Little kids do it. You'll pick up the knack in no time. Time was running short, so we don't ask for a shakedown cruise or a tryout. Deneuvé's hand was already turning a funny kind of black the last time we looked at it, right before we left the house, so we had to make this deal go or we were out of time, and he'd have to get used to having the wife cut up his porterhouse for him, rest of his life.

Tommy didn't have enough jack to pay for the boat, as Wanda had cleaned his poke, and the tag had a number on it which was a bit more than I'd figured, closer to the price I would of thought a real boat would go for, so he talks the kid into taking a check. I had a thousand bucks, which he mentioned, but I pointed out it was in a savings account—thanks to him—and the banks was closed at that particular time of day, so he comes up with the idea of passing a check. I could see it was something he *wanted* to do. See if he had the ol' touch. I was interested to see how this would go, and I had to give Tommy credit—he was slick. I noticed he signed his name Mark something or other, I don't know what the last name was, but it didn't have none of the letters LeClerc had, except maybe the "E" at the beginning. The kid took it, never even asked for a driver's license, nothing, almost even let Tommy make it out for more than the boat cost, as he gave the kid the fairy tale that we were short on cash and needed a hundred dollars for gas money. Sorry, said the kid, store policy says checks accepted only for amount of purchase, proud that he'd followed the store rules so good. There'd be a new kid behind that counter come next week, I thought, unless his dad owned the store in which case the family might be in the papers on account of the murder, but I didn't mention it to the youngster.

The kid put it in a cardboard box that I figure a refrigerator had come in and taped it up good and we were gone.

We drove down to Canal Street and parked Tommy's car. I ended up lugging the boat. It must have been a hundred degrees in the shade tree area. I was pure water by the time Tommy paid for our tickets and we got on board the Natchez. We picked up a schedule so's we could check the next scheduled voyage, for Deneuvé's people, and then we poked around hunting for a good place to stash it.

We ended up looking that boat over from front to back and there wasn't one single blessed place to hide it. My great idea was a bust. We'd have to come up with something else.

Maybe we could climb on the remote-control boat and sail

out into the Gulf, catch the trade winds to Mexico.

For once, Tommy earned his keep.

"I got it!" he said, just when it looked like we were permanently snagged. He whipped a pen out of his pocket and scribbled something on the box in big letters. It was Deneuvé's name, address, and phone number. He got all the information he needed out of a little book he had in his back pocket.

"I get it," I said. "We drop it in a mailbox and as soon as he gets it, in three weeks, we get on with the deal. Better send it express mail," I advised. "He'll get it in less than two weeks, that way."

He gave me a superior look and I guess I deserved it.

"No, dummy. We don't mail it. We turn it in to lost and found, up on the dock, at the Natchez' office, tell 'em we found it on the ship. *They* notify Deneuvé they got it. Probably call him right up."

Two original ideas in a lifetime. It was almost too much to believe. I didn't mention how that would leave his heirs, as frankly, it *was* a great idea and one we could use.

Soon as the boat hit the dock, we jumped off and took the package up to the little shack where they sell the tickets and turned it in.

"Will you see whoever lost this gets it back?" Tommy said, in his best good citizen voice, and the girl said, "Of course. We'll notify them right away."

"We'd better call Deneuvé right off," said Tommy, as we walked away. "He won't know what's goin' on if that girl gets hold of him first."

We shagged into the Jackson Brewery Shopping Center and found a pay phone and Tommy made the call.

We both figured Deneuvé himself wouldn't be available. We kind of thought he'd be taking a nap by now or be down at some hospital. He was at home though, answered the phone himself, and said he was anxious to see us. Sorry, said Tommy, we got a different notion, and he laid it on him. Deneuvé can't hardly come himself, he said, being as he's in a poorly way, so would it be all right he send some of his trusted associates with the two million we asked for?

"Send the mayor, I don't care," said Tommy, and I could hear every word between them as I had my face right up to the receiver with Tommy's and catching some funny looks from the boys and girls going up and down the mall, like they never before saw what went on down on Bourbon Street.

"Just so's your associates play it the way I tell you, everything will be jake."

"He's gonna do it," said Tommy, when he hangs the phone up, like I haven't been right there wondering where the closest place to purchase breath mints for him might be.

An hour later, we're at the spot we want to be. As we are shooting from the hip now, we just picked the first place along the River Road that looked isolated. We just stayed in the car, popped some of the beers we stopped and got with what Tommy claimed was his last dollar, and took in the view.

"About forty-five minutes," Tommy estimated, looking at his watch and shaking it, probably making Mickey dizzy. We'd timed it earlier, on our maiden voyage.

Three beers later, here she came, the Natchez, and our two million. We could hear her horn before she rounded the bend. I wondered how people slept around here when she came through at midnight. Must make for a lot of loosey-goosey situations. I started imagining some poor slob, about to get it on with this babe he's wined and dined and tricked up to his place, and just when he's about to plant the old joystick, here comes the Natchez, tootin' Gabriel's horn, sounding like it's in the room with them. Drives her off the bed slats, ruins a blossoming relationship. Not to mention what such a driving poke might do to your love muscle. Make it your love pretzel.

I got a chuckle out of the picture, and Tommy stared at me like I was nuts and shakes his head.

"Let's do it," he said, and I was with him all the way on this one. We clambered out of the car and I grabbed the flag we'd picked up at a store at the Jackson Brewery and we tracked on down to the edge of the river and unfurled Old Glory, and I never felt more patriotic. A lump came up in my throat and my eyes got misty. Not a word was said, but I could tell Tommy was as moved as I was. Also, a bit nervous. This was a great plan, but then so had been the original scheme, and look at how good that had come off. All the sweating wasn't done, I figured.

The Natchez hove into view just then, and we hiked the flag up as high as we could, so Deneuvé's people could see it. At first, nothing happened. We could see the people now, walking around on the different decks, gawking at the sights, the dead trees, beer cans, oil spills, all the wonderful attractions tourists go bananas over, and then there was a commotion down near the rear end of the boat, and a big splash, and we could see it in the water, bright canary yellow, and we know it's the boat we bought and this thing is cooking, for real.

"All right!" Tommy yelled. "We're home free! We're gonna be rich!"

Only there was a hitch. It wasn't as easy to control as the kid from the store claimed. In fact, it went exactly opposite the way it was supposed to, didn't drive at all like a Buick with power steering. When I pulled left, it went right. Before I could figure the stupid thing out, it had turned and headed back toward the Natchez. A major panic set in. Tommy screamed like somebody had thumped him in the soft parts, and I'm doing figure eights with the goddamned control thingamabob, while at the same time trying to keep it out of Tommy's clutches, as he's got the bright idea he can do better and is trying to get it away from me. It was like teaching synchronized aerobics at an epileptic rehab center. The boat, which we're both trying to watch, just keeps on heading toward the Natchez, no matter what I do, totally ignoring what electronic commands are being sent.

And then, it disappeared.

It just flat-out disappeared.

IT AIN'T OVER TILL IT'S OVER... AND SOMETIMES NOT EVEN THEN

"Oh, man," said Tommy. "You stupid shit." He said this right after a brief pause, in which we died. At least I did, and I guessed Tommy was doing the same. I can't even say anything. He's right. I am a stupid shit. I shoulda had a trial run with the boat. I felt just like I did when I threw to the wrong base and the winning run scored, in the playoffs back in Double A.

"In a minute," he went on, "there's gonna be twenty-dollar bills all over the Mississip and folks are gonna be divin' offa that tub and we're not even gonna have cab fare to the Quarter. I'm about on empty," he said, meaning the car. "I'd planned to buy some gas with part of my share. I wonder how far we can get on foot before Deneuvé's goons get us?"

That was a thought I was trying to keep away from active brain cells.

While Tommy was committing mental hara-kiri on the river bank, and I've already done mine, I didn't even know I was doing it, but my hands were still working the remote-control doohickey and my teary eyes were still watching the Natchez sail along on her merry way. It got twenty yards farther along and I saw a flash of yellow on the other side where it had passed, and I started up the vocal chords at scream level.

"We still got it, Tommy!" I let out. "There it is!"

And it was. It must have gone underneath the boat. It was

making a beeline for Algiers. I started fiddling with the knob in a serious fashion and still nothing happened, and a terrible thought burst my bubble of elation. What if we were out of range?

Just when I was convinced that was the situation, the yellow blob began turning. It was moving like an early morning wino, lurching here and there, but so was I, on the controls. And then I got it, figured out how it worked, and here came that beauty home to Papa, heading directly at us, getting bigger and more gorgeous every inch it came closer. There was no doubt, now. I had control and it was coming to us.

The rest was a snap. Once Tommy got calmed down from the whooping and celebrating and my ears quit ringing, we went down to the edge of the river and scooped it up. There was the package, tied to it just like we'd requested, water-proofed paper like we'd said to put it in, and it looked big enough to be the payoff for six ransoms. That was one huge bundle. That was all that saved it from being sunk by the steamboat, was my guess. It rode so low in the water that when it bumped into the Natchez it must have driven it down almost clear to the bottom and then it bobbed up, safe and sound, on the other side.

I tore the corner of the package open. They hadn't stiffed us. There was nothing but Presidents. Twenty, fifty- and hundred-dollar bills.

We'd done it.

I sneaked a peek at Tommy, to see if he was getting a hard on like I was. He musta been—he had that goofy look on his face like people do when the girl starts shucking her skivvies and taking her uppers out.

"Let's get the fuck out of here," he said. "Fast." We left the boat and just grabbed the bale and threw it in the back seat.

The first thing we had to do was get to a pay phone, honor our part of the bargain. The second thing we had to do was lose this part of the planet.

"We don't have passports," Tommy mentioned, rolling up

River Road. I hoped we made a gas station before he ran out. That bale looked awful heavy to be toting in this heat. Not to mention how it would make us stand out.

Passports was a detail I hadn't thought of either.

"We'll just go someplace we don't need them, first," I said. Man! Money made you smarter. I always knew it did. The ideas were flowing out of the top of my head, coming out of my ears.

"With the kinda loot we're holding, we can buy passports. We'll just hie on down to Mexico. We've got a few days before Deneuvé's bloodhounds can track us down, and by then we'll be history, gone someplace they ain't even mapped yet. Mexico. That's the place. You can buy anything in Mexico, you got money. And by God, we got money! I played baseball there, Tommy. You're gonna love the senioritas!" My brains were churning with the ideas, all genius stuff. Having real money must raise your I.Q. a hundred points.

The first convenience store we passed, Tommy turned into.

"Here's the phone number," he said, handing me a scrap of paper. "I'll wait out here and watch the money."

"You got a quarter?" I said. "I seem to be without any silver." We both laughed.

"Sure," said Tommy. "Just get change for this." He pried loose a twenty from the bale in back. "Get a receipt, Pete," he joked, as I got out. "We can put it down on our 1040's. We got to show some expenses or the IRS will eat us alive." We both hooted. I was even starting to like Tommy. Money changed your whole perspective on everything in life, even toward cruds like Tommy.

I walked on air into the 7-Eleven and made change, flirting with the girl behind the counter, winking at her. She didn't wink back. Must get a lot of millionaires in here, I thought. If she only knew. I went on back and picked up the phone. It was answered on the first ring and it was old man Deneuvé his own self. He sounded kind of antsy, like he'd been biting his nails. On the hand he had left.

"Where is it?" he said, not bothering with social amenities.

I told him. He'd been square with us.

"There's a girl there, don't know nothing about this. It's my partner's girlfriend. You'll notice her outstanding housekeeping and should it happen you hold a conversation with her, she'll jazz your nerves. You'll feel like hurting her but it ain't worth it. Even if you was to waste her, it wouldn't be no skin off Tommy's ass. I just want you to know that, sure, she's a pig, but she's not any part of this, doesn't have a clue. And Mr. Deneuvé? Your hand's in the freezer out in the garage. My partner says to help yourself to the veal cutlets it's under. He doesn't think he'll be needing them anymore and if you don't take them, they'll just go to waste."

There was some heavy breathing on the other end, so I guessed he was still listening.

"No hard feelings, I hope, sir," I added. "You'll be happy to hear your hand's in tip-top shape, should be easy to reattach. Hell, you'll probably take ten strokes off your golf game, soon's the stitches come out. That is, if it doesn't fly off first time you tee off." I couldn't help that last remark. Money makes you witty, as well as smart it, seemed.

"We had a little more time, we might get you a nice French manicure before we send it back, but I don't think time allows. You understand. Have a nice day, sir," I said, once I stuffed back a snicker, but I was speaking into a dead phone. Probably in a rush to get somewhere was my guess. People are just in too big a hurry nowadays in today's hustle-bustle world. I'd tell that to my ol' partner Tommy and he'd get a snort.

I hung up the phone. I could see Tommy through the window. I held up my hand, made an O with my finger and thumb. Tommy waved.

And took off.

With two million in twenty- and fifty-dollar bills.

Minus the twenty I had.

Which was minus a quarter for the phone call.

Minus all the good-will he'd built up between us.

I had a bank book, but it was sitting in a closed bank.

I ran out the door, but it was too late. I could hear him laying rubber in two gears. I guess he wasn't quite as low on gas as he'd claimed.

I was papaya pulp.

I was not as smart as I was a few minutes back when I was a millionaire.

Definitely not as smart.

Without money, I was just plain dumb.

There went my dream. No chain of po-boy restaurants. Not even a Kool-Aid stand. No chance with Cat. No more birthdays.

The kind of luck I was blessed with, I'da been the guy who would've invested his entire fortune in a billfold factory just before the Great Depression hit...

WISHT I'D LEARNED TO THROW THE SLOW CURVE

This just tore it. This was absolutely the last, final, amen, termi-nal, fucking straw that put a big, fat period on the whole deal. I did the only thing left to do. I sat down on the curb outside the 7-Eleven and bawled. Big crocodile tears, big as quail's eggs. I was material for a country-western song. Throw in something about a pickup truck and we're talking platinum album, world-wide tour, six girls at a time in the motel room.

Here I sat, the co-perpetuator of the slickest kidnap scam to ever go down in the annals of professional snatchers, and I'm soaking up driveway dust with nineteen dollars and seventy-five cents in my Levi's, and a bank account that was basically worth-less. I had to get out of town *now*, not next Monday when the banks opened again. A thought struck me and I groaned aloud. The banks wouldn't be open Monday neither. It was Columbus Day. Outsmarted by a second-rate hustler is what I was, down and out and a sitting duck for Sam Capelli or Deneuvé's boys, whichever was the first to find me. It wouldn't be hard. We're not two miles from where we picked up the money and I'd bet Deneuvé's executives were already burning up the roads looking for us.

I don't even know where I am for sure, except that I'm not far enough away from Deneuvé's beagles. I've been dumped along River Road somewhere, out along the way to Destin. Wherever it is, there sure wasn't any streetcar to catch, not that

I had any place to take it to. My mind scrambled around for a way out of the pickle I was in, but nothing that would work came up. I was the biggest turkey on the farm, the day before Thanksgiving. I could smell the cranberries.

I needed a nineteen-dollar-and-seventy-five-cent escape plan and there didn't appear to be a large number of those rattling around in the old brain cavity. Cat's face passed in front of my gray matter, but I scratched that idea pronto. Odds were excellent that Deneuvé already had a line on who I was, and if he didn't just yet, it was only a matter of time, especially when they got done interviewing Tommy's girl Wanda, and once she told them who he hung out with. She would probably view that disclosure with a great deal of pleasure. One thing would lead to another, and soon enough Sam The Bam would be involved in the manhunt, and then they'd find out about Cat, so calling her was out of the question, not to mention the fact that she had pretty much told me we were ancient history as far as any mutual future went.

I stood up, without a clue as to what my next move was gonna be, only that I wasn't gonna make it sitting there, and a car pulls up. Not a car, a limo, and damned if it don't occur to me that this particular limo looked familiar, which doesn't make a lot of sense as limos aren't a big part of my life. The party animals I hang around with don't travel in that mode of transportation as a rule, not unless one of them finds one with the keys in the ignition. Then it hit me. It looked like the limo that silver-haired trick sent for Cat and Jackie and me on that job where they used the whips and high heels. What was his name? Oh yeah, Robert.

Robert.

I seemed to remember something and it was something important, something I needed to remember.

A job. That was it. Robert had offered me a job. He'd said something about Texas. Texas! A huge state, one a guy on the lam could get lost in easy. I was saved. It was Robert's limo, all right. Now, I recognized it for sure. I went over and banged on the passenger window.

There was no response.

I banged again, harder, and tried the door. It was locked.

I rapped again and the door shot open, knocking me almost off my feet.

It wasn't Robert.

It was some old lady, white hair and glasses hung on a chain around her neck and she started shrieking at me to get the fuck away from her car!

I couldn't believe the language. She looked like Aunt Bea on the old Mayberry RFD show on TV.

"Get the fuck away from my car, you bum! I'll call a cop! Perry, call the police!"

I backed away.

"Lady, I'm sorry. I thought you were someone else. I didn't mean anything."

She got back in the car and this little guy got out of the front.

"Buddy, take a hike," he said, and struck a karate pose.

I started walking down the road.

At least, I had a half-assed plan now, when five minutes ago no hope at all existed. All I had to do was get to the Fairmont Hotel, look up Robert, and take that job he had promised. Get my butt out of town, over to Texas.

I could see a cab coming up River Road, headed back to town and I ran out in the middle of the road and hailed it. I told him where I wanted to go and that I only had five bucks, could he get me downtown for that, and he said, sure, why not, I was gonna have to deadhead back anyway, we'll just keep the meter off and won't call this one in, and we were off. No sense in paying full fare if you don't have to, is my motto, and I needed to keep as much of the nineteen bucks and change as I could to buy a drink or two at the Fairmont bar just in case Robert wasn't there right away, and I had to wait for him.

I climb out of the cab on Canal in front of the Fairmont and hike on inside, head straight to the main bar where Robert says he hangs out, most days. There was maybe three-four millionaires sitting around, nursing ethyl alcohol, keep their engines running, but that's it.

No Robert.

I've got fourteen bucks exactly in my jeans, as I had got weak and give the cabbie the silver for a tip. You'd think he'd be grateful, but he lays one of those injured sniffs on me and lays rubber leaving, without so much as a gracias in any language.

By the looks of this dump, fourteen bucks won't last long in here. Order the wrong drink and my stash would be history.

"Run a tab," I say, sliding up on a stool, "and it'll be Jack and water each time. I'm waiting for a guy named Robert, hangs here. Guy with silver hair, has a chauffeur goes by the handle of Alonzo. Know him?"

The barkeep nods and says he stops by every day, should be in presently, and I must have dropped the right name as he doesn't ask for the money up front like bartenders do in most places I frequent, and I am not dressed the best at present being a little mussed due to the activities of the near past.

Third round and he still hasn't showed and it's an hour I been here and now it's getting tense. The bartender is getting slower and slower to come down for the refills and I can sense there is a question in his mind whether he is going to be able to collect for the drinks he has poured from someone dressed such as I was, and not in designer jeans such as the rest of the clientele was. But he has too much class to say anything, at least just yet, and he comes down and pours another.

I can tell this is a class place and he is a class act barkeep, because he asks if I want the old ice or new, and of course I tell him the old, just add some to it. Guys that schlep drinks nowadays are punks, mostly; they think they're doing you a favor by throwing out your ice and giving you new. I suspect they're not drinkers, don't know the value of old ice that's been seasoned.

It's going on an hour and a half by now, and he is sneaking looks down my way. I don't know how much longer I can nurse this drink, as it is mostly lost the yellow and looks more like 7-Up, so I call him down and whip out my ten-spot and ask him for change for the cigarette machine. I figure he sees I got money, he'll rest easy, thinking there's plenty more where that came from. If you call the ten-spot I laid out plenty, then we're all right, but I don't tell him my balance because I have a feeling I'm into him for way more than what is on my person at present.

"How 'bout some change, partner," I say. "For the cigarette machine. And where is it? Lobby?"

He takes the ten and tells me he will be glad to fetch it for me, what brand, and in a couple of minutes he comes back with the Camels and my change. I know he must have made a mistake in accounting as all he give back was a fiver and two quarters, and I know they been talking about raising the tax but this is a little much, even considering there's Democrats loose with the vote.

"Uh, friend, I only wanted one pack," I say when I roll the five over and see there's no bills stuck to it under. "How much are cigarettes goin' for these days? I musta been out of town for a while. Did the opposition party get in?"

I just about fell out when he told me and I see I got the correct change, after all. I see now that the real money is to be made in cigarettes, not drugs, and now I see also that it is going to be difficult leaving here happen Robert is a no-show, as if butts are this much, there is no way I can pay this bar tab which is probably in triple figures by now.

The sweat was starting to roll. I ordered one more drink and it became clear from my friendly bartender's manner that I better roll out some bucks and catch up my bill before the next one, and on top of that, when I need my wits the most, I am copping a major buzz as this is a different color label of Jack than what I usually imbibe and I was pretty much drunk is what I was. Just when I think it's time to go to the john and sneak on out, in came his nibs, and I offered up a quick hosanna, as my bony butt is saved. I hope. If there is no job forthcoming and if he doesn't spring for my drinks, I am cooked, as I am pretty sure that if I can't come up with the gelt, I am headed for the slammer and won't be too hard for Sam to find.

Robert picked out a table near the door and sat by himself. I spotted his silver hair clear from the lobby when he came in and made my way on up to his table, hoping this wasn't going to be the total of my good fortune this day. I am praying to anybody who will listen that he remembered me and wasn't joshing about that earlier job offer.

"Pete," he said, as I came up and before I had a chance to open my own mouth, getting up and sticking out his hand like we was a couple of lawyers. "It's you, isn't it, Pete? I'll be damned! How are you? Sit down, please. Join me."

"Life's great," I said. "I'm at the top of my game, the Saints got another draft pick that might work into a decent water boy, and ain't this a particularly dandy day. Wish we had more of these ninety-eight degreers."

We go on like that, chinning like we was second cousins once removed, for the next five minutes, and I am trying to figure out a way to sneak the topic of jobs into the conversation. He made me sit down and ordered me a Jack and water. The bartender is all smiles now and asks if I want to settle up my bill at this time. Before I can come up with a good excuse why I don't want to do that, Robert chimed up and told him to put it on his account, as we are old friends and it would be his pleasure, and I have a private moment of joy and relief expressed in a physical, though non-sexual way in my glands and I am shooting silent thanks to the Guy Upstairs who is looking after me so well.

You can't just come out and ask for a job, not with a dude like this one, I think. Deal from strength when you deal with strong cats is my philosophy. The minute they think you're desperate they see you as weak and then they got no further use for you. I didn't want to blow my only chance to get out of New Orleans alive.

It all worked out perfect.

"Where's ol' Alonzo?" I said. "You don't usually get too far away from him, do you? He off on his break?" I was trying to act sober and doing a pretty good job, my words coming out straight, even though I am about ready for a nap and the ol' stomach is acting like it thinks we're on the Titanic in heavy seas.

"Oh, yes. Alonzo," he went, and got this moony look on his movie star puss.

"Alonzo is deceased," he said. In this serious Herman Munster voice. "The poor man choked to death on a shrimp. No one was around to aid him in his moment of distress. I blame myself. It was I who suggested that shrimp would make a splendid supper. If only he hadn't ordered the jumbos. If he'd asked, I'd have recommended the medium size. They're more tasty. And smaller. He probably wouldn't have choked on a medium."

Well, that certainly was sad news, and I know *I* was all shook up at the sorrowful tidings and not likely to get over it soon, but this was my lucky day for sure is what else went through my brain, as I see the opportunity presented and went for it.

"Well, sir, could it be you're in the market for a new driver? I would sure hate to see you driving around on these dangerous streets by yourself. There's all kinds of drunks and what-not riff-raff as what you find on the highways nowadays. I've got some appointments coming up, but nothing I couldn't put off for a while, and if nobody else has applied, might I throw my name in the hat for you to consider? Many people have commented on what a fine driver I am, and many times that skill has been bragged on by my friends. I'm hard-working and as loyal as a tick on a basset hound's butt. I would be happy to give you a test spin, show you my smooth style of driving, my grasp of the motor arts. As it happens, those appointments I mentioned aren't all that pressing, and I'm free right at this moment, don't hafta notify hardly nobody I'll be gone for the weekend. I can sign up right away."

That was the longest speech I ever give for a job, even longer than the one I give when I was trying to hook up as the foreman at the car wash when I first got my release and was at loose ends, but I was kinda desperate, what with Deneuvé's boys no doubt already out, searching high and low for me and Tommy. I was sure that by now they had a line on who I was and if not, it wouldn't be long before they did. I wanted to be in a different time zone before that happened. If I could get Robert to take me on, half a plan was already formulating in my skull. If I couldn't get transferred to one of those jobs in Texas he had talked about, then I figured he must have all kinds of valuable things as well as money itself at his house that I could help myself to, and I could just take his limo as well, put some space between me and this burg.

"Let's have some dinner first, let me consider it, Pete. I don't know if that's the job for you. Your talents may be wasted in a menial position as being my chauffeur is, mostly."

Usually, I am as hungry as the thirteenth piglet on a twelve-tit sow, but this time I can hardly choke down the goodies Robert orders for us. They serve us right there in the bar, that's how big a dude he is. They don't even suggest we hike on over to the main restaurant part, but fetch our portions on over, steak for me, some French do-dads for him, and I made like getting this job is the least thing on my mind, only all the time I'm making with the small talk about the stock market and things I don't have a clue about, I'm sweating bullets and wondering if any moves are left to me should Robert default on the employment carrot. The way he's talking, I get the feeling he thinks this job is too good for me, and I try to talk him out of that nonsense in a way that he don't see I'm hot for it to the degree I am. Finally, it's dessert time, at which I pass as I can't hardly wait no longer for the news, good or bad.

He went for it. The good luck surf seems to keep pounding in. Turns out my timing is impeccable, as Alonzo has just bought the farm yesterday and all the guys the agency sends over just won't do, they want their birthdays and Arbor Day off and fringes like that, and besides, he likes the cut of my jib. That's what he says. "I like the cut of your jib, Pete." And I get a tryout, right there on the spot.

He likes my jib, I thought, sure, and he's remembering the hot time we had the night we all had the bash and I called his mama a quarter trick and had all that other fun, but I don't care; this was my back door out of here, at least temporarily, and if he'd wanted to get married, I woulda done it right there. I knew there was going to be a payoff, somewhere down the line probably later on that night, but cross each bridge when you come to it, is my motto, and is especially my motto when things are getting tight.

"Let's go," he said, "You drive me someplace, and we'll see how you handle the car," and out we went, to his limo, which was illegally parked in a loading zone outside the hotel, but there was no ticket on the windshield like you might expect. He give the agency driver waiting there a C-note and told him he was letting him go and the guy started to say something then thought it through and decided not to and hiked off. The cop leaning up against it must have forgot to write one out, and I bet he would smack himself in the forehead later when he realized his oversight. He smiled and waved as I pulled away and I tooted the horn.

This was some machine! You could just feel its power and the dashboard looked like an airplane cockpit. Half the stuff I couldn't figure out, probably assorted toggle switches to run the automatic toaster, condom machine, electronic wonders like that. I was getting sober fast, having so much to figure out in the space craft, and only missed one red light, which Robert didn't seem to notice. These babies are really soundproofed, I thought, and thank God for that 'cause if they weren't he mighta noticed a bunch of cars honking and a tire squeal or two, but he didn't.

I settled back behind the wheel, did chauffeur stuff, drove where he told me to; turn off here, go west there, junk like that, let him play big shot, master of the universe, and before you can unhook a skinny girl's bra, we're out in the country, but not just the sticks, we're in *rich man's country*, with whitewashed fences running for miles in every direction, and horses, thoroughbreds, race horses, all over the place. I even think I see a few nags I lost money on out to Jefferson Downs or the Fairgrounds. There's hardly no shacks around, no cars up on blocks out in front yards, or refrigerators on the porches, so I can see we're in a part of the country I don't usually frequent, and then, after an hour of cruising and listening to the Montovani he favors, he says, pull up that lane, and I do. All the time, he's yapping about what a great weekend this is gonna be, after he gets done with "business." I didn't pay much attention then, but later I wished I would have to that part about his "business." Turns out, we're not going to his usual villa in town, but a place him and his brother own together, way out here in the barefoot part of the state, and he keeps mooning about how nice it is to be out of the rat race and out here in "God's country."

I keep thinking that ain't all rich assholes the same, always talking about how rough life is, trucking around with all the other la-di-das—if he wanted to see how a real rat race was, he oughta come down and hang out with the rodents I usually travel with. Rough! Breaks a nail, he's ready for therapy!

You could tell this was some outta sight place we was heading to, soon's we turned up the drive, which was more like a two-lane highway. There was horses I'm sure I seen run out at Jefferson, and these particular horses is some I seen in the winner's circle, and some kinda cows I ain't never seen before, and the "lane" we're tooling down takes about a half a tank of gas on the first leg, before we even spot the main house. There was some smaller mansions before we get there, only he calls them "servant's quarters." The first one of those we came to before I got this info, I pull into, and he gives a hoot and says you don't think I'd live there now, do you? How the hell do I know? It looked kinda like the place I hoped I'd retire to, after I make my million, but I guess I'm not aiming high enough. After that, I quit slowing down each time we ease up on another of the slave quarters, and then we make a bend and when we came out of the turn I seen the place they musta used in the movie *Gone With The Wind*, only in the flick it looks smaller than it is in real life. You don't get this kinda house less you break a law or two.

I still hadn't caught his last name, and we'd been chatting too long now for me to ask for it, but it turned out I didn't have any need to, as there's a big sign done in Cecil B. DeMille scroll out in the front forty acres in front of the house that tells the name of the place, and I almost put him through the window divider and up with me when I hit the brakes, the instant I spotted what's writ on that sign. I am an instant sober man.

"Sorry, sir," I say, recovering quick, that old shortstop instinct saving my ass. "That was a possum. I hate like hell to hit one of them cute little critters. It's bad luck." I took another gander at the sign, and it hadn't changed.

"Deneuvé Estates," it said. Under, in smaller letters, it read, "Deneuvé Brothers, Proprietors."

The sun was out, and the sky was cloudless, but it felt like rain.

Or maybe more like a hurricane.

Hurricane Deneuvé.

My stomach hurt.

LOAD ME UP ON THE DUMB TRUCK

"Your name's Deneuvé," I said, always a master at grasping the obvious. My stomach was chewing itself up.

"Well, yes, it is. I thought you knew that. Although, I guess perhaps it never did come up, did it? You showed up with Miss Cat and Jackie and we all got along so famously, right from the drop of the hat, I suppose formal introductions were never made. Cat never mentioned who I was? Well, I'm sorry, Pete. I'm pleased to meet you. Formally."

He laughed and shoved his paw over the seat, through the window.

"I'm Robert. I would imagine you've heard of our family. The Deneuvés seem to have some notoriety." He sighed, like it was one heavy burden, being king. "My brother's the one that's really the famous one. Personally, I prefer to shun the limelight. There are drawbacks."

Yeah, like they always make you take the best tables at restaurants, people are always running up, trying to lick your boots, hardships like that. The rich life must be one long series of terrible moments like that. If us poor slobs only knew half the awful difficulties rich folks had to deal with, day in and day out.

The Deneuvé relationship angle was clicking through my brain passages a zillion miles a minute, and it dawned on me that he wasn't onto the special bond between his brother and me. That was the first piece of luck the bird of fortune had shit on me today that didn't smell bad.

Somehow, I got the limo pulled up to the house and stopped without wrecking us, or any more incidents. I flipped off the ignition. I didn't know if I was supposed to leap out and haul him out or what. He seemed to want to stay in the car and gab.

"Pete, I'd like to offer you the job as my chauffeur, if you want it. I think I can judge a man pretty quickly and I can see where you'll fit into our little family quite nicely. The salary is six hundred a week and your room and board. There are quarters for you here in the house that will be yours while you're in my employ. I need my chauffeur to be close by. I never know when I might need you, as I don't keep regular business hours much of the time. You'll be more than just a chauffeur, I can tell you that. There's some other benefits I think you'll enjoy, too, if you get what I mean."

He laughed at that and I got a chill ran down my back *and* a twist in my gut.

"If you say you want the job, we'll get you settled in for the weekend, and first thing Monday morning I'll have my secretary get you the proper forms you'll need to fill out to make it official, but consider yourself hired, as of now. That is, if you want the position." He smiled.

What could I say? No thanks, Cap'n Bob, load my white ass back up and take me back to New Orleans to get killed? Or, save the gas, your brother will be happy to shoot me right here on the old homestead.

"Gee, thanks, Mr. Deneuvé," is what I said, like the smart lad I am. "I sure appreciate this."

"Good," he said, flashing his rich boy perfect teeth grin. "One more thing. Just call me Robert when there's just the two of us. Any other time, it's Mr. Deneuvé. Understood?"

Sure, Robert. And when you find out your brother and I go back a ways together, I know I can come up to you and trade in on this great palship we're establishing.

"One more little thing I almost forgot, Pete."

For a no-rules, comradely kind of deal, there was getting to be an awful lot of by-laws in this man's clubhouse.

"I'm sure I don't really even need to bring this up, but you understand that my little sexual peccadilloes are to remain our little secret. That's understood, of course."

He didn't state it as a question. Ol' Robert was the same as the rest of us unwashed citizens. He didn't want the world to know that between the sheets he was a lopsided jelly bean. I guess he would take a lot of razzing down at the racquetball club from the rest of the players who wear their sweaters draped over their shoulders.

"No way, Mr. Deneuvé. Mum's the word, sir. I'm one guy who knows how to keep his lip zip-locked."

That got him to turn on his high-beams.

"Thank you, Pete. Well, we'd best be going in. The trunk lock is there in the glove compartment. There's just the one suitcase there, if you'd fetch it. I'll show you where to put it."

I hop out, open his highness' door, get his gear and follow him into the Deneuvé digs, and the second we get in there, I get the mainline heebie-jeebies. This could be the mousetrap for ol' Pete. We go in these doors musta been made for ten-foot-tall people, and we're in what I think is the gymnasium, but what he calls the foyer, and I follow along behind him, toting this little bitty bag that woulda really give him a hernia to carry. Four big ants could of done the job. We hike on down the main concourse, and he's filling me in on the weekend schedule. This hallway's so big I keep thinking a plane's gonna land, but I remember there's a roof.

"This is a big weekend coming up, Pete. We've had some trouble. My brother Charles, whom you'll meet later, had a bit of a mishap. I might as well tell you the whole story, since you're working for me now. I know I can trust you to be discreet."

I think I know the story. Discreet? Ha! Sand burrs up my nose wouldn't get me to talk about Deneuvé's "mishap" to a deaf dwarf. Discreet?

"My brother Charles was kidnapped."

"No!" I did an acting job woulda paid big bucks on Broadway. I even set his suitcase down and made my eyes as wide as the hole in my head was gonna be, once they find out my part in this little passion play.

"Yes. It's true. When you're wealthy and famous as we find ourselves, we also find ourselves to be the targets of some very unscrupulous individuals. This is just such a case."

I always wondered how rich people got that way. So that was it. They just wake up one day and "find" they're loaded. Money and problems. Ain't that the way it is, always. I get recovered from the shock of it all, and we proceed to stalk on down the avenue, him gabbing and me working on my Oscar. I kept seeing all these rooms, musta been a hundred of them, and waiting to see some kind of schedule posted tells what time the Roller Derby kicks off. This joint was *big*!

Just then, Robert makes a left turn and I almost miss the hand signal. He woulda lost me for sure, I hadn't kept up. So far, we've marched a good two miles and I haven't laid eyes on another soul. His room's not far now, he says. Good. Much farther and I would have suggested we hail a cab. Golf carts would be a handy item for that house, get around from room to room in.

He has me unpack his ditty bag and help him get squared away, after which he says he's gonna show me where my quarters is. I don't suppose he'd let me bunk in here with him, is what I think when he says that, and then I remember that fun night we had a week or so ago, and I don't care if I gotta walk ten, twelve more miles, but, man, my dogs is barking! I always thought a chauffeur mostly got to ride.

I'm stashing socks and other artifacts as he tells me, nothing that looks like it comes from where I shop or like it has ever been featured on the Blue Light Special, and he tells me all about him and his brother, how they own and oversee this vast conglomerate of businesses, and how some of them might be construed as being on the left of Legal Street by those such as don't have a good sense of humor or as what are sticklers for technicalities. He lets on that a sharp cookie like myself might go far if I kept my shorts dry and my eyes and ears open and maybe not have to stay in the chauffeuring end of things forever, but move on up into the three-piece suit group, proved I was as slick as I seemed to be.

This is all very heart-warming and I'm even beginning to buy the corporate employee pitch a little, when he gets back to discoursing about his brother again, and that jerks me back from the Magical Kingdom.

He says these evil kidnappers had whacked off his brother's hand, at which info I go, oh no! and give out with a couple of little gasps. They held this hand for ransom money, Robert says, which his brother duly remits the proper currency as per instructions, and the hand is now back in his brother's possession, and, if he guesses right, is just about ready to be reattached, as the last he heard the doctor was standing by with all the proper tools and knives and skilled nursing assistants and such, only waiting delivery of the hand, which had been affected. By that, I figure someone has met Wanda and is on his way to the ranch with the mitt.

Not only that, but his poor brother should be, at that very moment, on his way to the spread where we are, in the family helicopter.

This last bit of news gets the blood to zinging around in the old arteries at a pretty good clip. Oh, boy. I could hardly wait to see ol' Deneuvé, reminisce over the good old days, see does he remember me from when. I bet we was gonna have us a high old time, trotting out all the old war stories, drinking tequila shooters and knocking down the lemons. I look around to see if I can figure which is the best way for a person to hike it on outta there, happen such an opportunity presents itself, but I am lost and don't even know where north is.

Then Robert gave out the best news of all.

"This is a kind of rough spot we're in. With these kidnappers.

Not only have they made fools of us, but they have two million of our dollars. That makes us look bad. We'll get it back, of course. They boys have already picked up one of the kidnappers. They're bringing him here in the helicopter with Charles."

There are just some employment opportunities in life a guy shouldn't be too speedy in applying for, and this chauffeur's gig has turned out to fit that bill.

"They got one of 'em?" I hoped Robert didn't note how my voice broke. This might be a good time to point out I thought probably my driver's license had expired, and I was pretty sure I wouldn't be able to pass the chauffeur's physical exam with the hemorrhoids I was cursed with. Maybe he could just have somebody give me a lift back into town, and we could just part friends, admit it just didn't work out.

"Yes. Tommy LeClerc. The irony of it!"

He shook his head and looked sorrowful. I didn't get it, but I didn't ask what this irony was. Keep your lip zipped, I kept telling myself. Don't ask questions, get him curious.

"So far, he hasn't told us anything, but if anyone can get that information out of him, Bruno can."

The picture I got of what Bruno probably looked like wasn't a bit hazy.

Robert was still talking. "This Tommy person has resisted all efforts at persuasion, thus far. It seems he's bright enough to realize that once we know who his partner is and where the money's located, he's expendable. It's just a matter of time before we find out what we want to know. At any rate, I'll be tied up with this matter this weekend, so I shouldn't be needing you to take me anywhere. You just relax and enjoy getting settled in. I'll show you your room."

It was making me dizzy anticipating the good times that were going to break loose around there the coming weekend when the party got to popping, but I'm your basic ingrate, stressing my gray matter trying to work out a way to avoid the gala events.

Maybe I could snatch one of the ten or twenty Rolls-Royces

I seen parked out front, hot-wire it.

Robert finishes up getting all the toes of his socks lined up proper, and takes me on down to where I'm bunking, about two kilometers away. It's in a whole different part of the castle, a section he calls the "West Wing." You could roller skate around here for a month and not meet the same person twice. This is some humongous house, which gave me an idea.

Deneuvé was obviously going to be in a bed with tubes and medical whatsits strapped on, so chances were decent that I'd never run across him. Maybe I could make it through this weekend, get away then. Maybe even get a chance at some of the silverware, help finance my trip out of the continental U.S.A. A plan was starting to percolate.

The room I drew ain't as grand as the boss's by any stretch of the imagination, but it ain't no slouch neither. It's Alonzo's old digs. Since I ain't got my gear, Robert said to go ahead and use Alonzo's razor which is still there with some of his other things, and he'll send one of the other servants over with a toothbrush. Also, a uniform that would fit, socks, underdrawers, junk like that.

The bossman got me all squared away, showed me how to work the remote control on the color unit, and said, "When you hear the buzzer, it means I need you, Pete. Just come on up to the main foyer until you learn the house. I imagine you're tired and could use some rest. I doubt that I'll need you the rest of the evening, so just enjoy yourself. Feel free to explore the place if you want—just be quiet and unobtrusive and you can go wherever you wish."

He stuck his hand out again. He must have got his start selling life insurance.

Just then, we both heard it, the sound of helicopter rotors.

"That'll be Charles," he said. "I'll go and tend to him, get him settled in. Say," he said, and the next words he spoke froze the blood in my veins. "How about you coming along and helping us lift him out? We could use an extra pair of arms."

Oh, shit, I thought. I am supposed to go out there and carry into the house the man whose hand I helped detach from the main part of his body. I am one dead kidnapper unless I can think up a way out of this one. No great plan sprung to mind right off, not unless you could call diving headfirst through a window and making a run for it a great plan, which I didn't, which is why I didn't use it, only went along with Robert like a broke-dick puppy dog who knows he's gonna get swatted for crapping on the La-Z-Boy. I'll think of something, I'll think of something, I'll think of something is what kept going through my head, to the tune of *The Little Caboose Who Thought He Could.*

We come outside and around the corner and I see the helicopter and the old ticker started just throwing the plasma around as I see two heavyweight boxers climb out and they're tugging on a third party who don't seem to be too cooperative at the debarking procedure, and the heart machine's gonna throw a rod the way it's screaming when I saw who the unwilling participant is.

It was Tommy.

I am for sure a dead hunk of ectoplasm.

Tommy don't look none too joyous, got some lumps on his noggin I can make out from this distance even, and his hands are handcuffed behind him.

Why I don't make a break for it right then, I don't know; my brain has froze up and all I could do was follow Robert toward the copter and a sad end. I did a kind of sidle around behind him as we walk, and keep my head down, and I am making some serious promises to the Big Guy, like if He will get me out of this one jam, I will never again own a single blessed thing in my life as He will have claim on it all, besides which I will never do anything illegal or immoral again and will become a man of the cloth and some other odds and ends. It is for sure that if I get out of this, not only will I be one broke son of a gun but can look forward to never having a single bit of fun again, ever, but all that is unimportant right now, and what is important is that

I get out of this fix.

Well, my prayers are answered, as we waltz right around Tommy and the guys what are hustling him away, and he doesn't look up for even a second, but keeps his eyes on the ground, and I am one lucky fella was all I can say.

Except now we are at the whirly-bird and I am going to be on one corner of a stretcher on which will be laying Charles Lacy Deneuvé, and I believe it will probably come up sometime soon in conversation that we know one another.

I am about to soil myself, the part that hasn't melted away with the sweat, and all I can do is step up and grab a corner of the stretcher, and I am talking in tongues just below my breath, working the prayer angle to beat the band and for all it's worth, my eyes closed and my hands shaking like I just been struck with palsy, when I copped a quick peek and I see he's out cold, and I started to go out, faint dead away, right there on the spot, the relief was so great, but I hung on and we toted him into the house and onto this big bed on wheels some guy has brought round.

"Thanks, Pete," Robert said, and I guess I'm off duty so I beat it on down to my digs and collapse on the bed, try and gather my strength so I can do something about the diarrhea that has overcome me, and try to work out a scheme that will get me out of here.

I put my thinking cap on, tried to sort things out. The main thing was I had to beat it out of there and fast. Hanging around the Deneuvé crib was just not harmonious with my desire to keep my vital functions vital. There was another element I kept thinking about though.

Tommy.

Tommy was here and it was pretty clear he hadn't told them where the money was yet, else he'd have been croaked. And if Tommy hadn't told them where'd he'd hid the money, that meant that if I could get him out with me, somehow, I could still get my hands on it.

I didn't see how I could spring him by myself, though. I needed help in that department, but who? I racked my brain, but couldn't come up with anybody, unless...

Of course.

Cat.

Cat might help me. If she thought she could get rich doing so. She had the two things necessary. Guts. And greed.

I got back to my room and picked up the phone, hoping it wasn't tapped. I hesitated a minute, and then went ahead and dialed. I was dead either way.

When she answered, I almost dropped the phone, my hands were so sweaty. I took a deep breath.

"Hi, babe."

"Pete? Is that you?"

"Yeah. Say, you busy?"

"What do you want, Pete? I told you not to call me."

"I know, I know. Listen, how'd you like to make a lot of money? I mean, a *lot* of money! Like a hundred thousand dollars?"

Silence.

"Cat?"

"I'm listening."

Ten minutes after I hung up, I still didn't know if she had agreed to my proposal or not. My hands were just starting to dry a little when the phone rings and my heart does another of those stunts where it tries to get out of my rib cage as I knew good and well it's one of the Deneuvés advising me they're onto me and to kindly stay put until they can send the death squad.

It's Deneuvé, all right, but the one without wrist scars, and he has got what he thinks is gonna be good news for me, and I ain't as sure about that as he is, but I don't say so.

"Some good news. Your girlfriend just called."

Girlfriend? My mind was in park.

I must have said that.

"Yes. Cat."

Oh, Jesus. I started to say something, but he cut in before I got stupid.

"I invited her out for the weekend. She suggested it, soon's she heard you were here, working for me. I'm sending another car for her. Her and Jackie. This will be like old times, won't it? I told them they could bunk down back there next to you. There's a room next to yours they can have. Of course, if Cat wants to slip over to your room, that's fine, eh? That's all right, isn't it? Don't worry about me—it's just a business arrangement with Cat and I. Wonderful girl—but you know that, don't you! You're a lucky man, Pete. Now, isn't that a nice surprise? This couldn't have worked out better, could it! I certainly hope you'll join us later on in the evening. We'll have some fun like before. Isn't this exciting?"

He hung up.

A nice surprise? Life at the edge of this cliff was wearing me out. I hadn't a clue if Cat had bought into my proposal or was coming out for the pleasure of seeing me drawn and quartered. Why was she bringing Jackie, unless she was going to give me up and Jackie was part of the celebration festivities she was going to lay on Robert? One more surprise and they'd be wheeling me in for a triple bypass. These new developments were wearing me down, making me an old man. I was scared to peek in the mirror, afraid I'd see white hair. My next life, I was gonna get into something less complicated, more low-stress, like, say, an astronaut or a bull fighter, volunteer to test parachutes.

Cat.

I need something for my stomach. It hurts something fierce.

Was she going to line up with the Christians or the lions?

CAT

The more I thought about it, the more I was convinced Cat was going to sell me down the river. I never should have trusted a woman, I kept thinking. Conventional bar wisdom always says that.

This was one tight spot I was stuck in. My luck just continues to build and it's all on the debit side. I couldn't even enjoy the shrimp bisque this little chippy in a maid's outfit brought me. She even acted like maybe she wanted me to put a move on her, but she'd be disappointed if I did, as Mr. Happy is stressed out to the max and wouldn't be able to rise to the occasion.

About an hour passed and I'm just beginning to relax and let down my guard for a minute when there's a bam, bam, bam! at the door, and I jumped up and smacked my head on the ceiling which is a good thirty feet above ground level. I don't actually hit it, but I came close.

It was Cat and Jackie.

"We're in the room next door!" they squealed, and they fired off to dump their suitcases, which I bet is full of torture implements, case Robert don't have the right size blacksnake in his whip locker. Cat came back in a few, by herself, and shut the door quietly behind her. I guessed she has told Jackie she wanted to talk to me alone. I am thrilled to no end with this development and I bet my face shows it. I have a good guess that even if she has decided to partner with me, we get to do the high heel waltz with Robert again, and I know I am on pins and needles, can't hardly wait to get this party off the ground. As soon as I laid eyes on Cat again, I knew I had it bad for her, and friendly as she was a second ago, I figured that was for Jackie's benefit, and now she was going to let me know that me and her was on opposite sides. She just didn't want Jackie to know she's snitching me out, although I don't see how she's gonna keep that a state secret.

"Can you believe it!" Cat said, plopping down on my bed.

"Yes, I'm pretty amazed," I agreed. "Who'da thought we'd be seeing each other again like this so soon? It just goes to show you how small a world this really is. So what's it gonna be? You gonna dance on my grave?"

"Shut up, Pete. You always have to be such a smart ass, don't you? You always know the right thing to say at the wrong time. You either say the right thing at the wrong time, the wrong thing at the right time, or you button your lip when you might want to say something a girl might want to hear. It's a talent, isn't it?"

She was right. It *was* a talent. Not a *good* talent, but a talent. No, it wasn't a talent at all. It was a chip. A chip on my shoulder. The same chip that had been there all my life. Something Dusty had said to me came back to me just then. Dusty was the last manager I had in baseball. *Attitude*, he'd said, when he was giving me my walking papers. *It's your attitude, Pete. You've got all the talent in the world, son, but your attitude stinks. Nobody can tell you anything without you get defensive, make some wisecrack. I can't work with a guy like you. Nobody can. That's why we're releasing you. That and the gambling.*

It was wild, all of these thoughts rushing through my head, things I hadn't thought of in years. It was like I was hearing what Dusty had said for the very first time. I could see him now, standing at the top of the dugout, me coming back from giving up six runs, asking me what was the matter, and me saying, *Nothin', Cap. It's just my time of the month.* All this time

I'd blamed the ruination of my career with my inability to throw the slow curve. It suddenly struck me that the ability to throw the slow curve was what got me in professional baseball to begin with. That's all you ever saw in high school and American Legion play. Every other pitch, if it wasn't a fastball, was a curve. That hadn't been my problem at all. I could throw the slow curve like nobody's business. I just needed an excuse was all, so I built this whole thing up in my head, used it for an alibi, when the truth was I was scared shitless the whole time I played ball, and the higher league I found myself in, the more tense I got. And what did I do when things got anxious? Instead of asking for help or even talking about it to someone, I got cocky and cracked wise. That was how I handled pressure. I took a choke. Took a choke, made a joke. That's my style, I realized, and my style sucks. It cost me a big-league baseball career and it probably cost me the girl I coulda been happy with. I was afraid, I realized suddenly. Afraid of her. Afraid of what a relationship with her might mean. Happiness? I was afraid of happiness? I didn't know what to think.

"I kinda blew it, didn't I? You and me, I mean. That why you're turning on me?"

She looked at me and didn't say anything at first.

"You know what your problem is, Pete? Your problem is that you don't want to be close to anybody. You find yourself getting close and you back away. I don't know if it's because you've been hurt by someone, or if you just suspect you might be. Maybe you just imagine it will hurt more than it will, if someone gets to you and then decides to leave or something, dumps you. I don't know what's the matter with you, but I think something is, something that keeps you from responding in the right way, a *serious* way when the right moment is at hand. You know, you remind me of a whore in that respect. When we're with a trick, we withdraw, keep our real emotions under wraps. You do the same thing with *everyone*, I think. Is everyone a whore to you? I know I am, but I'm not, either. I never have been with you. You. You're the whore, here. Not me."

She was crying, but mad, too.

"And, yeah. You really did blow it, big guy." She flounced up and down on the bed like it was a trampoline, snuffled, wiped her eyes on the back of her hand, and then leaned back on her elbows and grinned up at me, a complete change coming over her face.

"But don't lose any sleep over it, asshole. We probably never woulda made it anyway. You don't have enough money for me, anyway. I'm looking for a rich guy. I'm tired of broken-down hustlers. 'Course, that may change, right?" She gave me a little smile, coy-like.

My policy of never saying the right thing at the right time kept me from saying anything at all, losing once again, a golden moment in which if I'd had half a corpuscle in my brain, I could of maybe smoothed things over, sweet-talked Cat, made up some lost ground. Instead, I let the grounder hit to me go between my legs for an error. If I'd done that in a game, I'da blamed it on the sun blinding me momentarily. Even when I had insights, they didn't do me no good. It was like being a Fruit Loop and knowing you were; the knowledge just made you a smarter Fruit Loop. In movies and books, when the nutcase realizes he's a nutcase, that's it; that's the cure, it's all over; he checks out of the Ding-Dong Hotel and goes home to the little woman and kiddies and lives happily ever after, selling life insurance to the neighbors on the quarterly plan.

That's in books. That's not in real life as we know it here on the third planet from the sun. Nosir. Knowing you're a fuckup don't keep you from being a fuckup, it just makes you a fuckup with an extra piece of knowledge than most of your other fuckups don't have. That's what I was, all right. A fuckup with an extra bit of trivia about myself.

Cat didn't appear to be having the same kinds of emotional dialogues going on within herself as I was.

"I ought to let you squirm for a while," she said.

Oh yeah? Wasn't the time between when I'd talked to her on the phone and now, enough?

She quit smiling, turned serious.

"All right. Here's the deal. Let's say I throw in with you, help you on your little scheme. What'd you say my end would be?"

"A hundred—*two* hundred thousand. Tax-free."

"I ought to turn you in. You'd better make me a better deal or I will. I swear I will."

"Half." The heck with haggling.

"Deal." She put her hand out. "Here's what I know. Tell me if I got it right."

She said, "They got Tommy. Right here. I'd hate to be him, time they get done with him we don't get him out. They got him in one of those little houses up the lane. I bet he's tied up by his thumbs."

I was so excited I could just spit a fur ball. When she said that about the thumbs, I made fists around mine.

"How do you know all this, Cat?"

"James told me."

"James?"

"Yeah. Kind of an old friend, it turns out. I'll tell you about it, sometime. James is Deneuvé's chauffeur. Charles' driver. Isn't it sad about Alonzo? I wonder who's next? They say death always happens in threes. James told Jackie and me everything."

"Everything?"

"I guess. About the kidnapping, the hand, all of it. He told us what they're going to do to the kidnappers. This is all so ironic. About Tommy, I mean."

"What's ironic? Robert said something like that about Tommy, too. Whaddya mean? What's goin' on?"

"Tommy's the one hooked me up with Robert. He was kind of a pimp for me at one time."

"Robert!?"

"No, dummy; Tommy. He used to run a phone service. Dates for rich guys. He sent me to Robert the first time."

I'll be damned. It was the goddamndest thing, but I didn't have time to dwell on it. I got back to the business at hand.

"Well, anyway, you got most of it the way it is," I said.

I laid my sales spiel on her.

"Think about this. There's still two million bucks out there, only Tommy knowing where it is."

"So how do we get it?"

"Like this. What if you and I was to cut Tommy loose, get him to take us to the money, and then you and I split it. Half and half. Think—a million bucks each. That's a lot of toot. That's a lot of *anything*."

She was listening and thinking. I could see the gerbil walking the wheel, making it spin.

"Cat, if you rat me out, I'm in the cemetery."

Her eyes got wide.

"Pete, this is too heavy for me. I'm just a simple whore. There's more going on here than you know. I like you, Pete, but I like soft-shelled crabs, too, and I wouldn't die for one of them. No, I'm sorry. They're gonna get it out of Tommy who you are and where the money is before we can get to him probably— and then, my ass is grass. There's things here you don't know about. They're gonna think I'm in on this, too, somehow, 'specially since you been staying with me. If I don't tell them, right this minute, I'm an alligator canape. They'll be walking on *my* back and it won't be with no high heels. I'm sorry, Pete. I got to be going now. I'll ask them not to kill you, maybe just beat you up good. How's that? It's the best I can do. I'm sorry, honey." She was crying again.

She stood up and I grabbed her and pushed her back down on the bed. Her eyes became full moons.

She was scared; I was scared. All God's chillun was scared.

"I'm not gonna hurt you, Cat. Maybe. There's the way out of this. Think about this. There's still two million bucks out there, only Tommy knowing where it is."

"How, Einstein?"

***

I told her my great idea that had sprung up in a half-ass state just before I called her, fine-tuning it as I went along.

"It might work. It just might work." She was breathing heavy, still scared but coming to see things my way. I could tell. I had the hook in her, had her halfway in the boat. They hadn't thrown the dirt on my coffin yet, maybe, even though the hole was dug and the preacher was standing by.

"We'd have to wait till after," she said.

The fish was hooked and in the boat.

"After what?"

"After the party with Robert. You know. You and me and Jackie. It's the best time. It'll be late and everyone'll be asleep."

There was no way. I was two inches from a major nervous setback, electric shock therapy penciled in my future should I still be alive. Another tap dance session with Robert the Freak would send me over the edge, the sensitive state I was in. I just knew it would.

"No way, Cat. We got to do it now. Look, now we got the element of surprise. Tell you what. We'll wait till it gets dark. That won't be long. You go find James, flirt with him, find out what house they're keeping Tommy in. I'll find some wire, some clips, something to hot-wire a car with."

She looked up at me and I could see she wanted to argue, but didn't, only shrugged her head and said, simply, "Okay, let's do it then."

She came around so easy, I almost didn't believe it or trust her. This was one hell of a chance she was taking, especially since all she really had to do was snitch me out and she was home free, maybe even collect a reward from Deneuvé. It couldn't be the money alone, I thought, and my hopes rose a little. Maybe we had a future, after all. And maybe she was just humoring me so I'd let her leave, and she'd run straight to one of the Deneuvé's.

I let her leave the room. I had no choice but to trust her. I'd never make it out without help. If I was wrong about her, my liver was paté on a cracker. I was trusting my life to emotion. Cat's emotion. And I didn't know which emotion was at work. Love or greed.

I hoped it was greed. Greed you could count on.

Thank God for the old-fashioned values.

TOMMY AND ME REESTABLISH THE PARTNERSHIP

Cat came through. In spades. In an hour's time, not only did she cop what house Tommy was being held in, she found out some other goodies as well. Like all the keys to all the cars on the palace grounds were kept in the main kitchen, and tagged, hung on a big board. She'd even drawn me a map to get me there, and other interesting points in the house. It had some fascinating highlights, places I woulda liked to visit if we had more time.

There was one called the "movie room" and she says they don't show *Snow White* in that one. I put that one in so you wouldn't go near it, she said, 'cause there's always somebody watching a flick there. I guess she'd been coming here a long time, way she knew the layout. I didn't like that idea and couldn't figure out why a little thing like that would bother me, and then it hit me: hell, this was what jealousy felt like, I bet. It wasn't a feeling I was familiar with and I wasn't crazy about it. All of a sudden, country western music made sense.

There was more. She'd talked to James, promised to tussle his twinkie, and he'd spilled the whole shebang, all the valuable dope on Tommy. I blocked out the part about her promise to James as best I could, but this jealousy thing was hard on the old blood pressure.

As for Tommy, Cat said the lowdown, according to James, was that he'd hung tough so far, even though they'd give him a pretty good workout. The Deneuvé first string wasn't too happy with the proceedings, as my man Robert had been laying the gaff to 'em, threatening the bejesus out of them, promising to withhold the Christmas bonus checks unless they started getting some answers out of their prisoner. The next day or so's festivities didn't look too promising for Tommy's health and well-being. He hadn't snapped, though, which surprised me. The little snake was proving dodgier than what I woulda ever give him credit for.

They'd left him set up for Dreamland with an interesting mind picture for the next day's schedule. Seems the one called Bruno had this nifty idea to slice off Tommy's fingers, one by one, until he cracked. They left him to ponder that one over. They even had a pool how many fingers it would take before he started singing. Cat said James was sore; he'd drawn the number ten and figured he was out of the serious money unless the whacker got over-anxious and took out four or five digits at once, by mistake. The guy who'd drawn the number one was probably already out spending his winnings.

They'd all cleared out for the night, Cat said, most of them gone into town to catch some action, and the rest had a high-stakes poker game set up. One of them might drop by and invite me, she said; they'd heard I was a new guy in the shop.

Robert had sent a note to Cat via one of the other slaves, saying he wanted her and me and Jackie to meet him at ten o'clock in a room she called "The Playpen." I could see that room in the old mental zoom lens, decked out in Jeffrey Dahmer playthings—chains, whips, nose-hair pullers—fun-stuff like that.

I checked the time. It was already ten till nine. Robert was probably salting his back already, getting ready for the highlights to come.

"We got to move now," I told Cat. "We only got an hour before he buzzes and we got to pack it up and move on down to Robert's Stiff Dick Follies."

"Pete, really, wouldn't it be better to wait till after we see Robert?"

"No," I said. Why was she starting this garbage up again? I tried to explain in a way she'd understand.

"That would be a terrible time. My stars'll all be out of kilter with Jupiter, the moon'll be having a thing with Arbitux 12, and my karma has bad breath. Besides, there's another reason we got to go now. A much better one."

"What?"

"Because I *want* to. No…Cat, I *got* to go now. I can't hack another session watching you do the high heel shuffle on Robert's good side. Truth is, I get a funny feeling when I even think about you doing *anything* with another man. Listen, Cat, I know I never say the right thing at the right time, and this is probably the wrong thing at the wrong time, but I can't stand the thought of another man touching you. It makes me nuts to think of it. I know we ain't got a chance together—you made that clear—but if you want the money, let's go now because I ain't sure what I'll do if I see you naked with another man, even if it isn't regular sex you are performing. It just don't square with my notion of what makes a good time, and I know me, I'll do something stupid."

"Pete," she said, coming over and putting her arms around my neck. "You just said the right thing and it's a miracle—you even said it at the right time. Probably for the first time in your life."

My life kick-started into a different gear the minute I kissed her, and I knew from that point forward I was condemned to a lifetime of sweet misery.

"Let's boogie," I said, in an effort to appear in control, which we both knew to be a lie. Never again would I be in control of anything. "Let's get our asses out of neutral."

I already had on the geek suit they'd sent around earlier, which should help the con look like a regular hired hand. We left my digs, then split up outside the door, so if anyone saw us, it wouldn't look suspicious. I used the map, headed for the kitchen, hoping Cat could mark down directions better'n she could pick out her clientele. Cat was on her way straight out to where the cars was parked.

I made the kitchen with no hitches, only problem was it was another one of them all-day hikes. I shoulda brought my canteen, and my toes were slapping the floor through the holes wore through the shoe leather, and sure enough, it was just like Cat said, there was this big board with about twenty keys on it. I grabbed the set that went to the limo we'd come in, and was halfway out the room when I got this terrific inspiration. I went back and snagged every blessed key on the board and switched them all around, putting the wrong keys on the wrong tag. That would slow them up, case we had to make a run for the border.

This escaping jazz was a breeze, so far. I hadn't even seen anyone yet. Maybe there was a nuclear attack warning and everybody was down in the rec room grabbing a little last tail. I never seen a place that big that didn't have no people in it, not even a museum on a day school kids didn't have to go. Maybe they was all down at the racetrack that was probably in the basement, waiting for the feature race. It was spooky, like the whole world had died and Cat and I were the only ones left. Then I remembered that a lot of the crew had gone into town.

I must of daydreamed, took a wrong turn, 'cause the part I was strolling through didn't have none of the landmarks on the map, I suddenly noticed. I walked by this room all lit up like a whorehouse when the fleet's in, and before I got my brain in gear, I'd poked my head in to see what was the attraction. There wasn't nothing much, just some old geezer sitting up in bed, eating Graham crackers and watching Vanna White on the tube. He looked kinda funny, all wired with a buncha tubes and wires and gizmos, and his whole right arm in bandages, and then an awful realization smacked me in the head.

It was Deneuvé.

In the pink.

Wide awake.

And looking straight at me.

He smiled for a nano-second and then a puzzled look came on his kisser and then he yelled out, "*You!*"

I charged across the room faster'n a sheep let loose after the shearing, and grabbed a handful of the wires he's hooked up to. "Yell again and I yank these," I said.

He gave me an evil grin and picked up a gizmo with his good hand that looked like a remote control to a TV but which I suspected wasn't.

"Yeah?" he said. "Know what I'd suggest, dead man? When you threaten a guy, don't threaten to pull his blood pressure monitor." He pushed the button on the remote control. Instead of the TV popping on, and what sounded like the preamble to the Fourth of July went off—beepers and woofers and tweeters and other kinds of general alarms. Loud. I knew in about ten seconds some football player type was gonna be showing up.

"Oh, fuck," I said. "What'd you have to go and do that for?"

He had a Cheshire Cat grin on now. "I don't think we're gonna amputate your hand, wise guy. I think we're gonna whack something else. I hope sex isn't a major part of your life."

"Oh, fuck," I said for the second time. I stepped over and smacked him with my bolo punch and he went out like a wino after three days on a canned heat binge.

Then I booked. It was time to put the mustard to this plan.

Luck was riding on my shoulder. I ran the right direction, and in only a kilometer or so I reached the foyer and still hadn't seen anybody. I hit the door and the fresh air and there was Cat, out in the front yard.

Talking to some sumo wrestler. Both of them looking at the house and listening to the alarm going off.

There was no help for it. Any second, the whole damn place was going to explode and Cat and I neither one would ever again have the chance to blow out any more birthday candles. I had to do something and pronto. We only had a few minutes leeway before there was going to be a party I didn't want to be at, on the front lawn. I sucked up a big breath and walked right up to them, like I was the new foreman or something.

"I'm Pete," I said, locking eyeballs with King Kong. "Mr. Deneuvé said to tell James he needs him right away. He says that if James ain't there in six seconds, he's dog meat. Maybe you can locate this guy for me as I am new here and don't know who he is. I'd hate to see him get in dutch."

The big fella doesn't say a word, but turns white as my underwear on Mondays, and flies up to the house. The way the ground shakes, I think I'm in California.

Cat rolls her eyes and I grab her hand and we make tracks for the limo. We jump in and I start it up.

"Who was that?" I said, backing up.

"James," she said. "You didn't have to worry. I could have handled him."

"I had to worry," I said, flying out of the drive and onto the access road and back the way I'd come earlier in the day. "Deneuvé spotted me. All hell's bustin' loose. We're in the soup now."

She got a look on her face like I bet the next guy to go on Death Row at Angola wears.

"Which house," I said, cruising at about eighty miles per, on a road meant for speeds in second gear.

"It's the last one going out. I'll show you. Jesus, Pete! Step on it! Forget Tommy, just get the fuck out of here."

"And go where? You got enough for first class to Rio? I got a thousand in a bank account is it, and I can't get to that till Tuesday. Besides, we got a little time. I messed up the car keys. It'll take a while to sort them out."

She moaned almost the same moan she used when we were having sex, but I knew she'd be all right. It wasn't like she had much choice.

It was about a mile to the house. There was just one guy watching him, Cat said, once she saw I was going through with the plan.

I guess they didn't figure Tommy was in any shape to get up

and leave, is why they only left the one guy to watch him. We pulled up in front and jumped out.

It didn't seem no more than two-three hours after I'd begun knocking that the door finally opened and another Godzilla poked his ugly head out and said,

"Who the fuck! What you want? I was sleepin'!"

Charm school graduates ain't what they used to be, I was thinking, but kept that to myself. I didn't want him to lose his good mood, get mad or nothing. Where did Deneuvé get these gorillas? I'd just like to have the steroid concession for his hired hands. The Saints needed to send a scout out.

"I'm Pete," I said. "Mr. Deneuvé's new chauffeur. And bodyguard." I just threw that in, not stopping to think I didn't fit the company profile. I flashed into a karate stance and threw bonehead a smile, let him know I hadn't bulked up as I was into the martial arts instead.

"They want the guy back up at the house. ASAP. I'm supposed to take him up. Fetch him out here, willya?"

"Fuck," he said. "There ain't nothin' left t'beat outta this punk. 'Bout one more head slap and he's gonna require a body bag. Come on in. I'll haul him out." Killer wasn't too happy about being waked up, but he was going along with the program. He didn't even ask Cat why she was with me, which was good, being as I don't believe either one of us had a good reason for why she was.

All the luck that had been heading south, changed direction. The guy guarding Tommy came out, lugging Tommy like a sack of onions and all trussed up, and he was out like draft on tap at a wine-tasting party. I'd been concerned he'd see me and have an airhead attack and say something that would indicate we were acquaintances, but I didn't have to worry. We got all tucked in the car and ready to peel out, when the phone in the house rang. I knew what that was.

"Go get it," I said to plantbrain. "Might be from the big house. They might want something else, want us to pick up his toothbrush or something. I'll wait till you answer it, just in case."

You bet.

As soon as Goofy disappeared inside the house, we burned rubber, flew outta there. We made the main gate with no problems, but just as we were getting there, I seen a set of headlights in the rear-view mirror and guessed I'd missed a set of keys or two or they was just good at hot-wiring. I hit the brakes and jumped out and kicked the taillights out and jumped back in and turned the headlights off and flew through the gate and turned left. I musta went a mile, mile and a half in the pitch black doing a hundred and five, hundred and six, and Cat none too thrilled about this part of the journey, at least I guess she wasn't, by the way she was screaming her lungs out for me to stop one minute and calling me nasty names the next.

"There's the door," I suggested, when I'd had about my limit. It is hard enough to navigate by sonar alone without a banshee screeching in your right ear throwing off your concentration to boot. "You want out, the handle opens to the left. It's a little tricky." She didn't shut up, but a minute later I switched the lights back on, right after we whizzed past a deer standing in the road about an inch from the car, which gave me a urinary problem, and once the lights were on, I really shoveled the coal to the fire. We were going so fast, I half expected the tower to give us clearance to take off.

I was hoping Deneuvé's people had only the one car after us and had guessed wrong and turned right, and they must have since there was nothing behind us I could see, only maybe a deer standing in a foot of deer shit and wishing he was back in the olden days when all a deer had to worry about was a mountain lion or two and Daniel Boone.

We drove fifteen or twenty miles, deeper and deeper into coonass country, and then I spied an abandoned shack back up a lane and I turned around and went down the lane. We had to get Tommy awake and find out where the money was, fast. Time was getting shorter than my grandma's pecker, and she had the shortest one in the entire family.

I drug Tommy out of the car and laid him on the grass and went to work on getting him awake. It took some serious slapping, but Tommy begun to come around. Was he ever surprised, once he seen who it was!

"Pete!" That's about all he could say.

"Yeah. Surprise, surprise. How ya been, asswipe? Run out on any partners, lately?"

He got this sincerely hurt look on his mug.

"Oh, Pete. I'm so glad to see you. That was just a little prank I run on you. You know I was gonna come back and get you, after I had a laugh, don'tcha? Problem was, I got nailed by Deneuvé's people before I could. Ain't that a bitch!"

"You musta been laughing two, three days, that's what you were waiting for, Tommy. That was some good prank, ol' buddy. Now, I got one for you. You're gonna love this one. I bet you won't be able to stop laughing for a month."

I reached over and gave him a little pat in the mouth with my fist to show how much fun this joke was gonna be. Cat pushed him back up from where he'd slipped and fallen backwards. I gave him another little tap to let him get an idea of the situation he was in. And just because it felt good. He fell down again, must of slipped on the wet grass. I let him lay, this time, and hunched down on my knees to talk to him, to be sure he heard me all right. All around us swamp noises were going on: crickets, alligators, big birds from prehistoric times, critters like that making a racket. Inside, I didn't want to stay here any longer than Tommy probably did.

"There's some good news, Tommy. The way I see it, we save a half a million. The half-million Sam's trying to collect. I think we owe it to the Deneuvés. I've done some thinking and it wouldn't be a great surprise to find out that the mobster he works for is our own Mr. Deneuvé. It's the only thing that makes sense to me. So scratch off that debt."

Then I got to the bad news. For Tommy.

"Where's the money, Tommy?"

"Pete, no problem. I'll take you right to it. We're still partners, ain't we? Half and half. Tell you what—you get sixty, I'll take forty percent, 'count of all the trouble you been through. That's fair, huh?" He must have noticed Cat for the first time.

"What's she doin' here?"

I ignored his question. I was the one in charge here.

"You're fucking right you'll take us to it. You know why? Because dumb as you are, you got to figure there's a chance you'll still get some of it, that I'm soft. You can't be sure of that, and I won't even try and run a con on you, except to say that I got more honor than you do, but your only alternative is to tell me. Know why?"

He didn't say anything, but I knew he was dying to know what I had in mind.

"Here's the deal, Tommy. We all go get the money. I might and I might not cut you in. I'm still deciding. Your other choice is not to tell me where it is. Fine. I'll just give Deneuvé a holler and let him know where you are. We'll just leave you here until he can get time out from his hectic schedule and come fetch you. If you're still alive, that is. There's a lotta critters back here in this swamp. Hear 'em? They're all hungry, too, sounds like they missed the Early Bird Special down at the Atchafalaya Buffet. I know you're a cunning, resourceful Indian, and are used to dealing with wild animals like blood-crazed alligators and cougars and such, but you are sort of handicapped, being as you are all tied up, and you're down another strike as you have professed a disbelief in any Great Spirits, so I guess you won't be expectin' any help from that quarter. Plus, you got some blood on you and I figure that's a smell gators just can't pass by without drooling. And you might want to think about this. If Deneuvé gets you back, it's ten little fingers, one by one, until your hands look like catcher's mitts. Remember Bruno? I understand he's a specialist in finger-collecting. They're gonna get it out of you, where you hid the money. We both know they will. Once that happens, you're part of that grand vista we call history, babe.

"Now, me, I just might cut you in on part of the swag. At the worst, I'll let you go and at least you're gonna have some time, maybe get away before Deneuvé finds you again."

I was quiet for a minute, let it all sink in.

"Well, Tommy?" I got up and so did Cat. Tommy just lay there, looking about as woeful as a mouse in a pet store about to be moved to the snake cage.

Behind us, in the swamp, came the roar of a bull alligator. Sounded close.

"What's it gonna be?"

It was on River Road, close by the big grain elevators, buried along the levee. We got lucky, found a shovel in the limo trunk—I wondered what a shovel was doing in Robert's limo, and then I remembered the line of work the family was in and got a chill—and we had the money up in less time than it takes to chuck a woodchuck.

It was all there, just like the last time I seen it in the bale. Cat had a climax, wanted to pull it all out and throw it around, but I talked her out of that.

"Don't go nuts on me now," I said. "We got a lot to do and not much time. This car's getting hot, I got a feeling." The cops might be out looking for us right away, being as the Deneuvé's were connected in city government. Along with their own merry band of madcaps.

"We're gonna trade this pimpmobile in on something a bit less flashy, maybe buy us a little time."

There was this guy I knew lived in Kenner, did a side business in medium-warm to red-hot vehicles, and it was there I made for. He was wagging his tail like a pup at chow time, when I offered to trade him straight up for a Plymouth Valiant that was three-quarter's rusted and the seats rat-chewed. He wouldn'ta been so cheerful and obliging had he known who the real owner of the car was, but that piece of information I kept from giving out. The rubber looked decent and he said the engine wasn't the original but a sweetheart he'd dropped into it, ran like a hitch-hikin' hairdresser dropped off at a hillbilly truck stop, and most important, he had a license plate he slapped on it he said was good as Japanese money as it only just got lifted day before yesterday, off a Pinto owned by a sweet little old lady only drove it to bingo, Wednesday nights and her A.A. meeting on Fridays. I wanted to ask if it was my old landlady, but didn't as we were in somewhat of a hurry. That made the deal, we did the transfer, waved hi-de-ho, and we were on our way. He hadn't even mentioned the guy we had tied up in the backseat, even helped us move him to the new car. He was a pro.

I had something in mind.

"Come over," I said to Cat, and she scooted over by me. Tommy was all trussed up in the back. She got a big grin on her face when I whispered to her what I'd dreamed up and why, and said, sure, she'd do it.

Ten minutes later, we were turning into the NOLA airport road, going by a billboard advertising the New Orleans Jazz Fest.

"Ooooh!" said Cat. "I *love* Jazz Fest."

"Sorry, babe," I said. "Maybe next year. We gotta relocate this year."

I was looking for the long-term parking lot and just then I saw the sign for it and arrow. Just as we were pulling into it, I saw something else over in the short-term lot.

A white Cadillac. Full of Deneuvé's boys.

"Duck down!" I yelled at Cat. She looked at what I was looking at and did what I said. "Gawdamighty!" she said. "It's Bruno and the others!"

Tommy must have heard us as I heard him trying to say something from where he was, trussed up. With the gag in his mouth, all that came out was something sounded like

"Aaaarrghh."

We were on parallel lanes with the Caddy, going the opposite direction. I had no choice other than to pass them. I turned my head as we went by, one row of cars and a fence separating us. We were in luck. They didn't see us.

"You can get up, Cat," I said. "Good thing I ditched the limo."

I wheeled into a parking space and killed the engine.

"Keep your eye on 'em," I told Cat. The Caddy was going down each row in the short-term lot, driving slowly. Looking for the limo, I figured.

"What the fuck are we going to do, Pete?" Cat said. "How'd they figure out we were here?"

"They haven't," I said. "It's just about the only shot they had, I imagine. They know we got to get out of town and quick. This is the logical place for them to go."

"I ask you, again," she said. "What the fuck are we going to do?"

I looked back at Tommy on the floor, his eyes bugged out with terror. I leaned over and whispered to Cat. "Same as we talked about," I said. "Scoot in there and get it. Go now. Bruno's clear down on the other end. Just look out for him when you come out."

She got a huge grin on her face. I had to give it to her. This was some whore. Balls big as coconuts.

"You're evil, Pete," she said. "I love it! Be back in a flash."

She hopped out of the car, took a look to see where the Cadillac was—a long way over in the short-term lot—waved her hand at me and ran to the terminal.

I got to work.

The car next to us was perfect. A ten-year-old Ford station wagon. I tried the doors but they were all locked. No problem. I went back to the Valiant, unlocked the trunk and found a tire iron. I used it to smash the rear window and reached in and unlocked it.

I went back to our car, opened the back door, grabbed Tommy's ankles and jerked his body across the seat. I took one last look, saw the Caddy still way down in the other lot, and grabbed Tommy, flung him over my shoulder and took him over to the station wagon and deposited him in the back seat.

"You're changing rides, partner," I said to him.

Ten minutes later, Cat came back, half running, half walking. The Caddy had come up to our end once while she was gone and turned down a far row and was back down on the far end again. I was sitting in the back seat of the station wagon with Tommy, smoking a tightroll when she came up.

"They're way down there," I said, nodding my head in their direction. "But they'll be here, anon."

"Anon?" said Cat.

I laughed. "Means—"

"I know what it means," she said. "I just never heard you talk like that is all."

"There's lots of things about me you don't know," I said. "What'd you get?"

She grinned and took an envelope out of her pants pocket and handed it to me. I opened it up and took out the airline ticket and looked at the destination.

"Perfect! I said. I turned to Tommy, took the envelop and stuffed it into his shirt pocket. His eyes bulged even wider than they had been and he started making muffled sounds through the tape.

"Yeah, right," I said. "Listen up, pard."

I reached into my pants pocket and took out the Barlow knife I had there. I opened it up and placed it by Tommy's feet.

"Here's the deal, Tommy. That's a one-way ticket to Skagway, Alaska in your pocket. Plane leaves in…" I looked at my watch. "…twenty-six minutes."

I looked up at Cat standing there, watching us. "You got any change? A twenty, maybe?”

She reached into her pocket, took out a handful of bills and handed one to me. I took it and stuffed it in Tommy's pocket along with his ticket.

“There,” I said. “I wouldn't want you to be broke when you arrive.”

I closed the door on him and leaned over inside the broken window so he could see and hear me. “You got about twenty-five minutes, Tommy. I figure you can reach that knife and cut yourself loose in maybe ten. That leaves you fifteen minutes to make your flight. You're gonna hafta steer clear of the bad guys best you can.”

I straightened up, nodded to Cat. Tommy seemed to have a desire to say something to me. “Murph! Scaggalung! Rumph!” was all I could make out.

“I know just how you feel, ol' buddy,” I said. “I had that same feeling down at the 7-Eleven awhile back.”

Cat was walking back to the Valiant and getting in on the passenger side. I opened my door, but couldn't resist a parting shot. I walked back over to the station wagon, and looked in. Tommy's face was all red and contorted and stuff and looked like he was trying to squirm around to get hold of the knife.

“Hey!” I said. He looked up, something like begging in his eyes. “You oughta like Alaska, Tommy. Memory serves, this is the start of the winter solstice. Give you a prime chance to use some'a them survivalist techniques your noble forefathers passed down to you. You got to be one excited Injun!”

I got in the Valiant, backed it out of the space and stopped for a second after I shifted into drive. I turned to Cat. “Babe, this shit is more fun than pitching a no-hitter.”

She leaned over and kissed me on the cheek. I hit the accelerator and we shot past the Cadillac which I'd seen coming up. It didn't matter if they saw us, I thought, since they were on the other side of the fence.

We should have ducked.

They saw us.

I might have made a mistake in not paying more attention to them. It didn't seem to matter to Cat, though. As soon as we saw them shittin' and gittin' and pointing at us, Cat shot them the bird, and began laughing like she'd just inhaled a whole canister of nitrous oxide. I wasn't laughing. I saw Bruno grab the car phone and worse...

He rolled the Caddy right through the fence!

WE GO FOR A SWIM IN THE MIGHTY OIL-SLICK

The Valiant was screaming. I tried to focus as hard as I could on the road, but my eyes drifted up to the rearview mirror to see Bruno and his compatriots not only burst through the fence like it was made out of Cheez Whiz, but knock over a barrier, which didn't seem to slow it down much.

I found myself pounding the steering wheel. "Oh, shit, oh, shit!" I kept saying, over and over.

I screamed out of the airport onto Airline Highway on two wheels. Cat grabbed the armrest to hold on, and the car righted itself, fishtailed and I punched it again. The front end jumped up like a wild horse and leaped forward, leaving shrieking rubber.

"Damn!" I said, in admiration.

Cat looked at me like she was trying to smile but she wasn't making it.

We left Bruno behind in the dust.

"This thing's a Valiant?" Cat said.

"Sort of," I said. "It's got a Police Interceptor under the hood. Don't make those anymore."

I started to ease up on the gas. Then did a double-take.

Here came the Caddy and it was flat-ass moving.

"Oh, shit," I moaned. Cat looked around and saw the Caddy.

"All I ever wanted was to clear up a little debt, get me a pool hall—" I started to say.

"Quit bitchin' and drive!" Cat screamed. "Next, you're gonna tell me you were looking for love in all the wrong places."

In spite of myself and the situation, I had to laugh. "Yeah, that, too," I said. "Up till now…"

We were coming up on a red light, cars crossing.

"Hang on," I said.

"No way," Cat said.

"Yeah, way. You got a better idea?"

At the instant we hit the intersection, I spied the slightest of openings between the two semis that were crossing, cranked the wheel hard left. We made it through, but I don't know how. Now, we're in the wrong lane, but in luck as there were no cars. I tromped on the gas and we were flying down Airline, weaving around cars every two or three seconds, it seemed like.

And the Caddy was still coming. A ways back, but still on our butt. I pulled out in the opposite lane to go around a line of cars.

A school bus pulled out up ahead and turned our way. It was going to be close. I had three more cars to get around. At the last possible instant, I swerved around the last car, just missed getting in the newspapers for killing two dozen kids.

Behind me, for a minute I thought we'd lost the Caddy, but… fuck no…it appeared in the mirror, only it was on our right, driving through yards. These fuckers were serious! Cat was turned around, watching them.

"I think we got more trouble," she said.

"What?"

"They're on the car phone."

"What? Calling a cop to report a speeder?"

"I don't think so…"

I turned right at the first side road, slewing sideways, but making it. River Road and the Mississippi levee appeared, two hundred yards in front of us. A gravel road lay straight ahead, going up and over the levee, unless I turned onto River Road. Behind us, I saw the Caddy make the turn. Jesus! They were close!

"Can you swim?" I asked Cat.

"You're not..." She didn't finish her sentence, just lowered her head, stared at her lap and kept shaking her head back and forth.

I didn't slow for the turn. Instead, I slammed the gas pedal clear to the floor.

We flashed across River Road. The scenery was a blur.

I closed my eyes. I expect Cat did as well.

I felt us hit the gravel road and the wheels catch. I opened my eyes to witness the car slewing sideways, but that didn't slow it down any. We didn't seem to lose any speed at all, and just as we hit the top of the levee, the car straightened out and then we became the remake of the ending of *Thelma & Louise*.

Airborne.

Cat screamed.

I did, too. Even louder.

We were floating!

Damn! This for sure wasn't your daddy's Valiant! Out the back window I saw the Caddy pull up to the top of the levee and everybody pile out. I saw Bruno go over to the front tire and kick it. I bet it was flat. All of them pulled out their guns and began shooting at us.

Luckily, we were floating with the current and headed for the Gulf at a pretty good clip and pretty much out of range. We went around a little outcropping of trees and the last thing I saw was Bruno on his car phone, his arms waving in the air.

Out of sight of Deneuvé's boys, the first thing I did was feel all over my body. It seemed to be intact.

"You okay?" I asked Cat.

"I think," she said. "Unless the devil looks like a guy named Pete and I'm dead. That seems possible."

She craned her neck, looking all around.

"We're floating!" she said.

We were driving into shore which was about twenty yards away. By now we were maybe close to a quarter mile away from Bruno.

"Not for long," I said. It was true. Water was starting to come up. It was ankle-deep already. I guess it wasn't a Volkswagon after all. "We gotta leave," I said.

"I can't swim," Cat said.

"You won't have to," I said. "It's shallow here."

It turned out I was wrong, but we were all right anyway. We just pushed the waterproofed bale of money into the water and held onto it while we paddled to the bank. We reached it, hauled ourselves up and pulled up the bale. Both of us dripping wet.

We sat down next to each other, drip-drying, the bale of moolah in front of us, and gazed out over the Mighty Oil-Slick.

"You sure know how to show a girl a good time," Cat said. She wasn't smiling, so I wasn't sure if she was joking or not.

"I know," I said, agreeing. "This shit's getting old. You suppose we oughta just call Deneuvé, offer to give the money back? We may not even have to call him. I figure they'll have a car there to pick those guys up in twenty minutes or less and then head our way. Won't they be surprised we're so close!"

"And he'll just let us go, huh?" She shook her head as if she couldn't believe what a stoop I was. "We're not giving that bastard Charles a penny. He owes it to me."

"What? What's he owe you? I thought Robert was your client?"

She reached over and dug her nails into my arm. Hard.

"Ouch!" I cried. "What'd you do that for?"

The look she gave me wasn't a good one.

"Charles Lacy Deneuvé is the man who bought me from my mama," she said, her voice barely above a whisper.

"He what? You mean…"

She had honest-to-God tears running down her cheeks.

"You heard me," she said.

I didn't know what to say. I reached for her and brought her to me. At first, she stiffened up, then after a second, melted, and put her own arms around me and began to seriously cry. I kept patting her head like she was a kitten had got a boo-boo from falling off the garage roof. I didn't know what else to do or say.

Finally, I said, "Oh, baby." That was it, the sum total of my understanding words of comfort.

It must have helped. She moved away from me, wiped her eyes on her sleeve.

"Don't you go feeling sorry for me," she said.

"You know what?" I said. "I don't feel sorry for you. I feel sorry for him. What he had and didn't know."

That came out better.

"You're sweet," she said, and leaned back into me again.

"You're beautiful, you know," I went on. "Inside, I mean." I paused. "I just wish I'd known then."

"What?" she said.

"When we were whacking his hand off," I explained. "I wish I'd known this then. I wouldn'ta used so much chloroform. And…I mighta picked another appendage…"

"Shut up," Cat said, her eyes large and shining. "Just kiss me."

In the middle of our liplocking, something occurred to me. "You mean, the whole time you were with Charles you never saw Robert?"

"Not once," she said. "I was kept in another house, one Charles has in town. I don't think he wanted his brother to know how perverted he was. I never saw anybody but James and a couple other guys."

I thought of something else. "Then…you musta figured out what was going on when you saw James. You knew they were brothers before you ever got to the mansion."

She looked at me. I couldn't read her eyes.

"Sure," she said.

"But you didn't tell me any of that. You acted like you were still going to go through with the deal with Robert. You know, the—"

"The sex thing with Jackie and you and him and me? I guess I was just playing with you a little. Once I knew Robert was Charles' brother…"

She flopped back on her back in the grass. I plopped down beside her, on my stomach.

"There was another reason I wouldn't have."

"What?"

Her eyes seemed to soften.

"Because," she said. "I was in love, stupid."

Yeah.

We kissed.

Deeply.

SOME FUN AT JAZZ FEST

It was time to hit the trail. Where we were going, on foot, I didn't have idea one. But we both knew we had to get the hell out of there before Bruno and his boys came along.

We got lucky.

The third vehicle that passed us—a '60s-type psychedelic van passed us sitting on our bale of money with outstretched thumbs, screeched on the brakes, and backed up. Inside, it was filled with long-haired "heads" from another era. All of them looked to be in their fifties, and they all had the "look" from the sixties. A voice I recognized as that of Pete Seeger's was singing *Little Boxes*.

A girl with long, straight, *gray* hair leaned out the passenger window.

"We're going to the Jazz Fest," she said.

Cat climbed in and I handed up the bale to her and then climbed in myself.

At least four people moved to the back to make room for us. A cloud of marijuana smoke rolled out. Just as I shut the door, I glimpsed a limo passing by, headed for where we'd jumped the levee. The windows were tinted, but I had an idea who was in it.

Cat saw the same thing as I did, and both of us watched it drive by and then saw the brake lights go on.

Fuck.

We were going way too slow away from the limo, seemed to

me. The limo sat there a couple of seconds, then started up, turning around on the highway, and whoever was driving it must have hit the gas a little too hard, as it slewed on the gravel and careened into the ditch alongside the road. Looked like it was stuck in the mud. In another minute, we were out of sight and it was long behind us.

I was really getting tired of living on the edge and I get Cat was feeling the same.

This was some van! The gearshift caught my eye immediately. It was a black eightball.

"*Twilight Zone*, am I right?" I said to no one in particular. "You're shooting an episode?"

Cat gave me a hard look and socked her elbow into my ribs. One of the passengers, a long-haired midget, snickered.

"Naw, man," he said. "We're the Drifters. Not the black group."

Everybody but me and Cat laughed uproarously.

"We got a gig at the Fest," he was saying. "You into Odette?"

The girl in the front passenger seat said, "This guy looks like a Peter, Paul and Mary kinda guy. Now, *her*..." She shifted her gaze to Cat. "She looks like she might like Odette."

"I know who Odette is, lady," I said, maybe a little peevishly.

Someone in the back fired up a huge joint and began passing it around. At least they were hospitable. It was really terrific weed.

A few minutes later we were pulling up to the Fairgrounds, huge banners everywhere proclaiming we were at Jazz Fest, in case someone who pulled up by mistake might be confused. There looked like there were six million people in attendance.

We climbed out of the van. I grabbed the bale. I had an idea.

I approached the driver. "I'd like to buy your van," I said.

The woman who'd been sitting in front with him, said, "It's not for sale."

I said, "Not even for..." I reached into the bale and pulled out a couple of stacks of bills and started counting. "...fifty thousand?"

The woman sucked in her breath audibly.

A few minutes later, the hippies had removed all their effects and stacked them in a pile. They left one of their group to stand guard over it while the rest of them left to find the office and find out what sound stage they were supposed to perform on.

I took the keys the woman had handed to me and stuck them in my pocket. "Peace," said, and she shot me the victory sign and walked off to catch up with the others. I hefted the bale and began walking toward the entrance.

"Why don't we just take off?" Cat asked, walking beside me.

"We will," I said. "I just want to get something first."

There were more people here than I'd ever seen in one place before. Thousands and thousands and multitudes. Huge, open-air tents were scattered everywhere, with a different group performing at each. Vendors were hawking everything from alligator sandwiches to daiquiris.

We walked fast. I didn't want to spend too much time here. Finally, I saw what I was looking for. I headed for a large booth that advertised souvenirs. I passed by the bins of trinkets and do-dads and went straight to a stack of large tote bags. I picked out two of the largest and paid for them.

"C'mon," I said.

The first available portajohn I found, I beckoned Cat in with me and as soon as we were inside—drawing a look or two from the tourists as we entered together—I began transferring money from the bale into one of them. Cat caught on instantly and began doing the same. In less than two minutes, we had transferred all of it.

When we came out, we got looks from new people. And then I saw something that made my life pass in front of my eyes.

"Jesus!" I said.

"What?" Cat said and then looked where I was looking.

It was Robert and one of his men. Kim, the mountain.

I grabbed Cat's hand and we began walking fast.

"Keep your cool. I don't think he saw us," I said. "That

must have been the limo that passed us in the van."

"Wrong," Cat said. "They saw us."

Here they came, at a dead run.

We did the same.

We ducked around a tent and fought our way through festival-goers.

"You know when I fell in love with you?" I gasped, as we knocked people down.

"This is a weird time to bring something like that up," she said. She looked as winded as I was.

"I might not get another chance to tell you," I said. "Here!" I turned into a beer tent. We ran, knocking into people, getting dirty looks and a few curses. We got to the other end and ran out into the bright sunlight. Behind us, I could see Robert and Kim just entering the tent. We began to run around and through crowds. I talked as we ran.

"It was when you gave Jackie your money that time. I seen then you weren't some hard-ass chippie. I never knew anybody in my life would do something like that."

Cat looked sideways over at me, and in spite of the mess we were in, grinned. "I wish I was at Jackie's house right now. Having a pina colada, watching *Days of Our Lives*."

I stopped for a second to grab my side where it was hurting from a stitch I'd gotten and cracked up in spite of myself.

"Laughing in the face of danger, eh?" Cat said. "You're a weird one, Pete."

I glanced behind, spotted Robert and Kim maybe a hundred yards away. They had us in their sights, looked like. I grabbed Cat's arm and hustled her into another large tent just ahead.

This one was some kind of souvenir tent, crammed with tables piled high with all kinds of crap. Most of the sellers standing behind the tables were black, while the shoppers were mostly white.

Halfway through, we discovered we had a problem.

There wasn't a back entrance in this tent.

We were fucked.

I could see the top of Kim's head, towering above the crowd. Twenty yards away.

I ran back into the tent and grabbed Cat's arm. "It's over," I said. "I gotta tell you something."

I was watching the tent entrance as I talked. Robert and Kim appeared at the entrance and stepped inside, squinting to accustom their eyes to the relative darkness from the brightness of the sunshine outside.

"I love you, Cat," I said.

She rolled her eyes. She *rolled her eyes*!

"Great timing, Pete. What now?

"Look for Schwarzenegger," I said. "He always shows up about this time."

I'll be damned if she didn't start laughing. What a gal! The problem was she was really laughing—hysterical peals burst from her.

That just helped Robert and Kim locate us. I saw Robert spot us, begin a slow, wide smile. He drew his gun. Kim had the same smile on and did the same as his boss and drew his piece. They both came at us, confident that we had no place to go, sure of their prey.

The shoppers around us seemed to realize something was going on and then a woman screamed and all the activity in the tent just stopped. People started edging toward the entrance. Some just ran out.

We backed up helplessly. I dropped my tote bag and doubled up my fists. "I got 'em, babe," I said to Cat in an aside. "Soon as I drop Robert, then I'll smack the other guy. That's when you make your break."

Granted, it wasn't much of a plan, but I was working on very little rest.

Cat sighed audibly. "Oh, Pete. You watch too many movies."

Both men kept coming, snarky smiles on their kissers.

Cat spoke. "I got to tell you something, too."

"What?"

"I love you, too. See you at the pearly gates, sweetheart."

"I think I'm goin' in another direction," I said.

Robert and Kim were about fifteen feet away and had their guns out and trained on us. The oddest thought went through my head. When was the fat lady gonna start singing?

Then she did.

At least that's what I honestly thought it was for a brief second.

Just behind us, a deep voice boomed out.

"Hey! You the lady with the Tourette's, aintcha? It's me, Henry. You remember me, dontcha?"

I was struck dumb and I think Cat was, too. We both turned around, slowly. There was a beaming black man, standing behind a table loaded down with voodoo dolls. It was the man who gave the beer to Cat outside Claude's.

"Ohmygod!" Cat shrieked.

"Yeah, what's the problem here?" Henry said. Several other brothers, themselves standing behind their tables, began to edge over to where Henry was. I saw razors and guns appear in black hands.

Henry addressed Robert just coming in the front of the tent. "Hey, man. You botherin' this pretty lady?" He was smiling when he spoke, but it wasn't what you'd call a pretty smile. He looked at Cat. "Looks like you need some help, sugar."

It looked to me like Cat needed smelling salts. She looked about ready to faint. I could have used some my own self. We both took a step back and then another.

"Henry," Cat said. "We're in kind of a spot here. Think you could help us out?"

The black man laughed. It was a warm, comforting sound to me, at least, and I bet Cat had the same opinion. The other black men kept coming up to stand behind us in a group. There were at least a dozen guns out now, aimed at Robert and Kim.

"Well, I don't know," Henry said. "This looks like white folks business t'me. What's in it for us?"

Cat reached into her tote bag and drew out a packet of hundred-dollar bills. She hesitated a second, then grabbed another packet. She grabbed my arm and pulled me with her as she stepped around the table to where Henry was standing.

"This is in it for you," she said. She handed him the two packets. "And this," she added, and stretched up on her toes and planted a kiss on his cheek.

Robert took a step forward. "Hey," he said. "You motherfuckers get the hell out of our way. You feel like dying?"

Henry got what I can only describe as a mischievous smile on his face.

"You got an ugly mouth, Mr. Big Shot. And you can't count too good. I only see two of you." He spoke to Cat. "Go on along, sugar. We got things under control here."

Robert's face contorted. "Hey, nigger!" he said. "You're being very stupid."

It was going to get interesting, looked like.

Henry's smile just kind of dissolved. The tent had pretty much cleared out by now. Only a dozen black guys and me and Cat and Robert and Kim were left. Henry made a motion with his hand and one of the brothers went to the tent entrance and dropped the flap.

He pushed the table in front of him aside. "You know what a fool is?" He'd posed the question to Robert.

"Yeah," Robert said. "You."

Four of Henry's friends detached themselves from the group bunched up behind him and approached the two white men. All had guns trained on the pair and their intent was unmistakable.

Neither Robert nor Kim said a word. They just handed over their guns. The black guys appeared to be enjoying themselves. I know I was.

"I got a different definition," Henry was saying. "A fool's a white boy who calls a nigger a nigger."

Robert had some sand. Not much sense, but a lot of sand.

"You're the fool here," he said.

"Well," Henry said. "You know what a dead fool is?" He looked around at the other brothers, most of whom smiled. He turned back to Robert. "A dead fool's a white boy who calls a nigger a nigger…" He paused. "…in front of another nigger."

"Fuck you," Robert said.

Henry looked at him like he just couldn't believe this fool. He said, "And a white boy who calls a nigger a nigger in front of this many niggers…you know what that is?" Neither Robert nor Kim said anything.

"Fucked," Henry said.

The whole tent rocked with laughter. Except two of the participants in this little play.

Henry turned to us. "You folks just mosey along now. We got us some business with a couple of double-dead fools here."

Cat reached into her bag and pulled out two more bundles and laid them on the voodoo table. "Take care of your friends, Henry," she said.

I stepped over and lifted the bottom of the tent for Cat to crawl through. Right before I followed, I grabbed two bundles out of my own bag and threw them to Henry. "Take *good* care of your friends," I said. Just before I ducked out, I asked Henry one last question. "Your name ain't Arnold, is it?"

Just outside the tent, trying to get our bearings to figure out which way it was to the van, we heard Henry say, "I wanna be fair here, boys. Don't neither of you turkeys happen to have Tourette's do you?"

OUT OF THE FRYING PAN...
AND INTO A BIG COW PATTY...

We booked.

Got back to the van in under ten minutes, which was doing something as we had to make our way through what seemed like eight million people.

We jumped in, tossed our bags to the floor and I cranked the engine over.

And heard a voice behind us.

Charles Deneuvé.

"Well, well," he said.

Cat and I both whipped around like we'd been hit with cattle prods.

Deneuvé and James, way in the back. James had a big-ass gun in his hand. Pointed in our general direction. Deneuvé just had a big white bandage on his. I guess he must have been feeling better, to get out of bed.

We were really in the boonies. I just kept following the directions Deneuvé gave me, my brain bouncing between two main threads of thought: One, why me and why does God keep shitting on me? and Two, what kind of plan can I come up with? The first thought kept winning out.

Half an hour into our trip as we approached a side dirt road out in the middle of nowhere, Charles said, "Turn left up there." It looked like it led to a swamp. I did what he said. I could see Charles in the mirror. He just kept mugging on Cat.

"Don't I know you?" he said, at last.

"Yeah," Cat answered. "Think back, asshole."

I could see what I figured was the light bulb going on by Charles' face.

"You're—" he began.

"Yeah," Cat said. "Where you getting your best now, pervert?"

While they were discussing their past history, a half-assed plan began to form in my brain. My hand was on the gearshift knob, that eightball thing. I hoped neither of the guys in back noticed as I began to unscrew it, a revolution at a time.

"You're a fucking slimeball, Deneuvé," I said. I glanced around, caught his eye. "Say, where's your mitt? I kept my part of the bargain, so why isn't it reattached, motherfucker?"

He mumbled something I couldn't catch.

"What?"

"Freezer-burn," he said.

"What?"

James answered for him. "Hand was ruined," he said. "Had freezer-burn. Doc said he couldn't use it."

We couldn't help it. Cat and I started laughing so hard I almost ran the van off the road. I couldn't see for the tears and I was afraid Cat was going to choke to death she was laughing so hard. She was wheezing.

"Oh, Pete," she said, between guffaws. "Don't you know you have to get all the air out when you freeze something!"

"Laugh," Deneuvé said. "Go ahead. You'll be laughing real hard in a minute. Pull over there."

He pointed to a wide spot in the road. I pulled over.

"Now. Get out," he ordered.

I took a deep breath and twisted the last revolution of the eightball off. It was in my hand. For once, I was glad I had hands the size of catcher's mitts. Neither of our captors saw it.

"I ever tell you my nickname for you, Charles?" Cat said. "Neeedle-dick the nose-fucker."

"Walk," is all Deneuvé said. He nodded toward the swamp. There was something that looked like an animal trail I figured he meant us to go on.

Cat and I began to walk. Deneuvé and James followed behind, James holding the gun generally pointing in our direction. They let some space develop between us. I guess they figured we weren't going to make a break for it. Where would we go? We kept walking until we were in sight of a high spot just ahead of us. The two men were maybe fifteen feet behind us.

"Up on the hill and stop," Deneuvé said, behind us. "Don't turn around."

Looked like this was the place he meant to do us.

I kept twisting the eightball around in my hand, just like I used to when I was on the mound. I whispered to Cat, "You know I was a pitcher for the Giants, babe?"

She looked like she was ready to cry but wasn't going to, not in front of Deneuvé. "That's interesting, all right," she said. "Someday I'd like to hear all this fascinating stuff. Right now, though—"

I interrupted her. "You want to listen to what I'm saying. I had a great pick-off move. You know what a pick-off move is?"

She looked at me like I was nuts.

"I know what dead is, baby. That's what we're going to be."

"Maybe," I said. "And maybe not. I want you to do something."

Behind us, Deneuvé yelled. "What the fuck you jabbering about?"

"What?" Cat said, to me.

"I want you to create a diversion," I said. You're good at those."

She looked puzzled, but shook her head okay. "When?" she said.

"Now's good," I said.

She hesitated a split second, then jumped straight up and screamed at the top of her lungs, "Needledick!"

It all unfolded in what felt like slow-motion, but which wasn't. James yanked the slide back to inject a shell, started to bring it up to fire, while at the same time I pivoted and hurled the eightball. Caught him square in the crotch. He folded at the waist and the gun went Kabam! and he shot Charles in the foot.

"Bam, sucka!" I yelled, just for fun, and as I was charging toward them. I got to James before he could bring the gun up again and kicked it out of his hand.

Cat—bless her! Cat wasn't one of those mamas in action movies who stands around while her hero beats up all the bad guys. Or gets beat up. She was in motion almost as quick as I was. She flew over, grabbed the gun, and trained it on the fallen pair. Both of them lay on the ground, moaning and holding their injured parts.

Slowly, she brought the gun to bear on Charles' privates.

"You know how many times I wanted to do this, Charles?"

"Do it," I said.

"You aint got the balls," Charles said. Those Deneuvé brothers might not be the smartest guys in the world, but the both of them sure had sand.

Cat aimed carefully. You could see Deneuvé fighting to stay tough, but he put his hands over his nuts.

She raised the gun, pointed it skyward. "Naw," she said. "Look at him. He's a punk."

You could see Deneuvé openly relax. His lips curled into a sneer.

"You still got them Barbies, girlie?"

Before I could even blink, Cat lowered the gun to aim at his privates, then brought it up, and pulled the trigger. She nailed him smack between the eyes. She scarcely skipped a beat, turning a few degrees and shot James in his foot. He screamed.

Cut that puppy and print it! That's a wrap.

Deneuvé's eyes are round, unseeing, his mouth fixed in a perfect "O."

Cat blew the smoke from the gun muzzle, like a western gunslinger.

She turned to me. "If I hadn't done that, I just plain couldn't have lived with myself."

She turned and began walking up the trail back to the van. I stopped and bent over James. "You might try to get up on the road quick as you can," I said. "I hear there's lots of snakes back here."

"You're dead," he said. "You shoulda killed me, too."

A bull alligator sounded about a hundred yards away. Sounded like the twin to the one we'd heard with Tommy.

"Gators, too," I said. "I wouldn't stick around, I was you." I took some pleasure as I kicked his hurt foot. He screamed which made me feel lots better.

"That's some more incentive for you, scum," I said. "Better take care of that foot, too. It might get infected."

We were hours away. Had just passed the Oklahoma state line. When Cat asked where we were going, I'd just said "west." I had a surprise for her I was saving.

She'd taken over the driving chores.

I looked over at her and just grinned the biggest grin I was capable of. She looked at me and tilted her head in curiosity.

"The badass babe with the heart of—" I began.

"What's that, buster?" she said, not sharing my smile.

"You," I said. "You with the heart of gold."

"How you figure that?"

"You didn't shoot James."

"I was out of bullets," she said, so quickly it was like she was waiting for me to say something and had an answer ready.

"Yeah, well," I said. "What's up with that business about the Barbies?"

"I told you," she said. "He used to give them to me. He wasn't talking about that, though."

"Oh, yeah?"

"Yeah. He was referring to when he kicked me out. He took all of 'em back. Wouldn't let me keep them. My guess is he just give them to the next kid he bought. That's why I shot him."

"Huh?" I said. "I don't get it."

"Somebody needed to stop the Barbie cycle," she said. She kept her eyes straight ahead, concentrating on the road. "Those are classy dolls. Don't belong to trash like that."

Four hours later, somewhere in the middle of Oklahoma, we had us a motel room. I was sitting on the bed, had my shirt off. Bills were all over the bed and floor, scattered everywhere, looked like a green snowstorm had hit. I was watching Cat brush her teeth in the bathroom, in her bra and panties.

She paused brushing for a moment and said, "You think Henry killed Robert?"

I thought about it. "I don't know," I said. "Maybe. I know one thing. The dry cleaners aren't gonna want his pants."

She giggled. "So. What's the plan?"

I stood up and shucked my trousers, stood there in my BVDs.

"Lost Wages," I said.

LOST WAGES

Cat came part-way out of the bathroom, her toothbrush in her mouth. "Vegas?" she said. "That's very intelligent, Pete. You nuts? That's the first place they'll look for us!"

I climbed into bed and pulled the covers up to my chin and reached out and grabbed a handful of the money and dropped it, bill by bill, until my face was covered.

"I got a newsflash for you, sweetmeat," I said. "There ain't no place on earth we can hide from Robert if he's still alive. He's too well-connected. Or James. And don't forget Sam The Bam. What the coonasses won't think of, the Italians will."

Cat rinsed her toothbrush, gargled, spit, and came out of the bathroom, wiping her mouth with a towel. She sat on the corner of the bed.

"You're just suicidal then, is that it?" she said.

I sat up and the bills fell off of my face. I smiled. "With two million bucks and the foxiest chick in the world in my bed? Suicidal? Not hardly. Nope. I got a plan. We're gonna hide right out in the open. And Vegas is perfect for what I got in mind. Vegas is the world-capital for Look-Alikes."

I could tell from the puzzled look on her kisser that Cat didn't understand what I was telling her. "Well," she said. "Don't you have some kind of gambling problem? Is Vegas the right kind of town for your jones?"

"Cat," I said. "I swear to God, Vegas is the safest place on earth for me. No more dumbass bets. You can make book on that."

Three days later, we were sitting in a plush waiting room, sharing a thick book with photos we were scanning. Behind the reception counter was a drop-dead gorgeous blonde who I was having trouble keeping my eyes off of. Behind her was a tasteful sign that read: B.J. Honeycutt, MD. Plastic Surgery. I turned a page and saw the picture I'd been looking for.

"There!" I exclaimed, jabbing my finger at the photo. "That's me!"

It was a picture of Elvis. In his salad days.

"Oh, wow," Cat said. "I think I'm gonna faint. I get to suck the Big El's Dreamsickle."

She turned the page and jabbed her own finger at a picture. She squealed, "Oh, Pete! That's me, that's me!"

It was Cher.

I laughed out loud. "We're not gonna have a kid like she did in that movie, are we?"

She gave me a fake look of being mad, then said, "Pete, this guy is...expensive."

"I know," I said. "But you get what you pay for, babe."

"Yeah, but...I saw this ad...this other guy's a lot cheaper. No waiting, either."

I started to argue, but I had already learned who won the arguments in our house.

I had one of those feelings you get in the pit or your stomach...but what're you gonna do? It's your wife. You gotta do what she wants or else get used to logging in a lot of couch time.

I hate couches. They're okay for sitting on to watch the Super Bowl, but they mostly suck to sleep on.

EPILOGUE: SAFE AND SEMIFAMOUS

It's six months since we hit Vegas and put all that business in New Orleans behind us. If you've been with me so far, you can probably dope out what's gone down since we hit town.

Yeah, we went to the cut-rate guy Cat talked about and the good news was that she was right. The guy really had no waiting. Not like the guy I'd found. Hell, if we'd gone to him we'd just be getting our operations next Thursday. Cat's guy got us in the same day we talked to him.

Talk about service!

Cat took to Las Vegas like a duck takes to giblets and gravy, which I knew she would.

We got married and she gave up the coke habit, which is a good thing. We even talked when we first got there about having a rug rat or two, only I think that was mostly the wine talking. I wish I had known about this marriage thing a long time ago as it is mostly the greatest thing I have ever been around. It is like having a puppy when you're a kid, only better, as you can't hardly take your puppy to bed with you and make love to it, not unless you're one of those perverts, which, of course, I am not, being a healthy, normal kind of guy. Cat still squeals when we hit the sheets and do the horizontal nasty, but I am getting used to it, only she wants to know why I put cotton in my ears and I tell her it is a kinky thing I learned about in which it makes sex better when you can't hear it but can only imagine the noises. She even put cotton in her own ears once, but said she couldn't see the thrill in it and she figured I was just a strange duck, but I was *her* duck and she loved me regardless.

Cat wanted to send her granny some money, incognito, through a lawyer who knew how to keep his mouth shut, which I thought was a grand idea, so we did. A hundred grand. She also sent him a hundred grand for him to give to Cat's mother, who had sold her to Deneuvé. With a stipulation: She wouldn't get the money unless she stayed off smack for a whole year. If she couldn't do it, the money would go to Granny. I wouldn'ta sent the witch one red cent, but Cat was a different breed, had forgiveness and compassion in her soul, which is just one more reason I had to love her.

I got the fever then, too, her giving away money to noble causes like she was, and I made a few calls, mostly to bars up in Skagway, asking which was the scurviest bar in town and found out it was a place called "Gus's." I called and a woman answered, with kind of a gravelly voice and when I asked to speak to Gus she told me I was.

"You got a guy named Tommy comes in there?" I said.

Turned out she did. I got the address of the bar from her and told her I was sending a package and would she give it to him and she said, sure, maybe if it was something he could sell maybe he could pay his bar tab and I said what was it and she told me and I told her I'd send an envelope with the package and take care of that, too.

I told Cat what I had in mind.

"I think that's wonderful of you," she said, "You know, if it wasn't for Tommy, we never would have got the money in the first place and we sure would probably never have met, unless in a professional capacity. We owe him a lot, in a way, even though he is a crud."

What I did was send Tommy a bundle that had a hundred large in it and didn't have a return address on it. That made me kind of nervous, knowing the way the postal service operated, but I didn't want him to get a clue to where we were. I even paid a truck driver a C-note to mail it at the end of his delivery, which was in Chicago, so that if Tommy did decide to try and find us up he'd be looking in all the wrong places. I sent Gus a money order for what Tommy owed her in a separate envelope.

As you might have also guessed, we went to Cat's cut-rate guy. She showed me his ad, and it seemed legit. I mean, it was in the *Yellow Pages*, so it has to be, right? In it, it said this doctor can beat anybody else's price by fifty percent or more, as he has a lower overhead and does not rip people off as other less righteous plastic surgeons do. He claimed he had his overhead cut to the bone, which allowed him to do the work for a less salty figure. On the phone he explained how this is possible and logical to Cat. He works out of his basement, for example, instead of one of those overpriced air-conditioned suites in downtown Vegas, and he cuts back on the frills, such as a nurse with a current license, the higher-priced anesthetics, etc. I said I was against it, anything that sounded that good had to have a flaw in the deal someplace, but Cat don't have the highly-tuned con's instinct that I do, so I let her talk me into going to this guy.

Turns out, he's cheaper, but not quite as good as the first guy who charges the big bucks. We saved about thirty grand each. I wish we'd paid the difference and I haven't asked Cat, but I think she has the same opinion now. The good thing was, the healing part didn't hurt near as bad as I figured it would. Not that it's something I'd want to do every week, but then I've had dental work that kept me up longer at night, after.

Like I say, wouldn't nobody recognize either of us from the old days, and it isn't like you could say we're ugly exactly; we just didn't turn out matching the pictures we brung in.

Me? Well, the best way I can describe my new look is that instead of being a twin for the King, I look sort of like Liberace with yellower teeth and a weaker chin. And Cat? Cat is upset, I believe. She acts like it, at any rate. Cat looks like a famous person all right, just not the one she had in mind, Cher. Cat will remind you of a Bette Midler with black hair. And a bigger nose. Much bigger. A LOT BIGGER. I might as well be honest. For fun, once, I asked her, are you playing the sax or is that your nose? Never again. That is one joke that is not a good idea to ask in her presence. She actually looks good, I think, 'specially when you look at her from the front. Her profile could use some work. Like I don't take verticals when I'm taking her picture from the side.

Looking famous has got its drawbacks, too. I'm always getting these huckleberries from Indiana in town for the slots, what come up and ask for autographs and want to know if I still tickle the old ivories and how's my mother and aren't you supposed to be dead, and Cat, well, Cat don't draw autograph hounds the way I do, but little kids are always staring at her at the grocery store and saying to their mommas, "Momma, is that somebody famous?", and their mommas say, "Shush, child, she can hear you." And then, "See what drugs will do to you? Bet she can't even sing anymore."

But Cat's an upbeat gal for the most part, and don't seem to mind as much as she did right when the bandages first came off, 'cept from time to time she talks about firebombing the good doctor's basement and it's for sure she's not going to be sending him no referrals. It's just talk howsomever; Cat ain't got a mean bone in her body. Soon as we heal up a little more, we're going to go to the plastic surgeon we was going to go to originally and I guess she'll get off my case then and quit whining.

Other than that little setback, things is going well in the main, though we both miss the food from back home. There is not hardly a joint in this town where you can get mud bugs or even a decent plate of red beans and rice, but we got a nice little three-bedroom ranch with central air and a pile of money in a wall safe and cable TV. We're playing it cozy, not showing off our fortune. Cat is sure shaped up, off the coke and all, and she's even talking lately about getting some higher education, maybe go to cosmetology school, and I figure, why not? She's got the brains for it. She says she may do something else, surprise me. Whatever that means.

About a week after I mailed Tommy his package, I made a call back to Gus to see if it had arrived.

"Yes, it did," she said, and she'd gotten the envelope and thanked me for that. "However, there was a bit of a problem with that package," she said.

As it turned out, when Tommy got a package with no address on it, she said he didn't want to open it. He kept mumbling something about "letter bombs" and some guy named "Sam," Gus said. I could see what was going to happen before she finished and I was right.

She said it 'bout drove him nuts. He kept sitting back in the corner, putting down the Turkey shots and staring at the package. Finally, he picked it up and went out the door.

"And?" I said.

"Well," Gus said, "about ten minutes later, there's this big-ass boom—an explosion—and we all went running outside and there was Tommy, sitting in the alley on his ass and green confetti raining down on him."

What she got out of him—mostly from sign language as his hearing seemed to be a bit messed up—was that he was sure it was a bomb so he bought a stick of dynamite from the mining store up the street and blew it up.

When she told me that, I didn't know whether to shit or...to shit. I couldn't help laughing. When I got my funny bone under control, I asked her what happened then.

"Well," she said. "He's sitting at the back table with a box full of Scotch tape and a bushel basket full of green confetti, trying to tape them back together. Got a big-ass pile of green pieces of bills spread out in front of him like the biggest jigsaw puzzle you ever saw."

"How's that going?" I asked.

"I'm not sure," she said. "He does a lot of cussing and I've seen a couple of the bills he's got taped up and I'm not sure they're gonna pass muster down at the bank. He's gonna have to hurry up, I think."

"Why's that?" I said.

"Because we got laws against using dynamite in the city limits, especially by those who ain't got a license. I expect the sheriff will be talking to him soon."

Just before she hung up, she said, "Plus, he's got this bar bill he's running up again. I don't suppose you want to send me another envelope, do you?"

When I told her my answer to that, she sighed. "Maybe they'll let him work on his problem down at the jail," she said, and then we said goodbye and hung up.

I told Cat what had happened and when we both quit laughing I promised her I wasn't going to send another package to him.

"You did the right thing, first time, Pete," she said. "I can live with that. Do it again and I'll cut off your nuts."

I did, though. Only I didn't tell her. And it was for only half what I'd sent before.

I can't help it. I got a soft spot.

Mostly, these days, I hang around the house and watch ESPN when the Giants are playing, catch Barry Bonds work on his homer total, or go downtown once in a while, only not to the glamour places but down on the other end of the Strip where the real people hang out, not where the Bermuda shorts tourist set are apt to be found, shoot some stick, keep my hand in, hustle the hayseeds from out of town. Running a con's somethin' that gets in your blood. You just naturally got to keep doing it, although I was pretty sure I would never again have no interest in a major league scam like when we put the snatch on Deneuvé. Hell, they even got me coaching a Little League team and I kind of like it. Maybe our own kid will play ball someday and make it farther than I did. Maybe end up with Will Clark in the Hall of Fame. 'Course that's pie in the sky thinking seeing as how Cat doesn't even have one in the oven yet, but who knows? This straight and narrow path kinda grows on you. I learned my lesson. I even thought about opening a po-boy shop here, show the high-rollers what good food is all about, but once I checked on the price of shrimp I gave up on that idea. Sixteen bucks a pound! I don't know if people buy shrimp here to eat or put in their safety deposit box. One of these days I may get around to opening a place; after all, that's what I've always kind of wanted, but having money changes your priorities. Although, it would be nice…I just don't have the first idea where to start on such a thing. There's equipment I don't know about and supplies, and how do you know how to pick out a good location? A guy could lose his shirt happen he make the wrong choice, end up in a neighborhood they only eat kosher, something.

The great thing is, I don't go around mooning over a lost baseball career any more, and I don't want any more than what I have, right here, with my little wife and our little home. I have grown up, matured and I owe it all to Cat. A good woman will bring you down to earth, I know now.

No more scams.

No more serious hustling.

Unless, of course, something comes along that is absolutely fool-proof. I'd have to at least take a look at something like that. After all, I'm just retired, not dead, ha, ha!

Just the other day, I'm in a place where you get your beer in a can the way the good Lord intended, and this mook comes in and one thing leads to another, and we find out we're both hustling the other, after the eight ball coincidentally gets put in on the break six consecutive times, three each, and he buys me a beer, I buy him two, like that, and it's like a breath of fresh air to find a compadre. It turns out, he's a serious sharpie, can see I am cut from the same cloth, and we get to talking and damned if he don't lay a scheme on me I got to seriously consider.

There's this joint in town, kind of a low life kind of gambling place what don't have the high-toned security the fancier dumps like Caesars and MGM do, and this guy, whose handle is Slim, thinks a couple of for-real gamers like we are, could go in there and beat their blackjack table. He just happens to be a self-taught electronic whiz that has come up with a way to rig up this gizmo that can tally the cards that's been dealt, in a split second, faster'n the human brain, and Slim shows me how, with two of us working, one placing bets and the other tabulating the odds with his machine which is smaller than a pack of butts and can be easily hidden inside a shirt pocket, we can end up owning the whole spread.

I'd wear this thing that looks like a hearing aid, but is really a tiny, miniature radio, and he'll be firing the moves at me on each card, what move has got the odds behind it. You know: stay, take a hit, bet the ranch, like that.

There is some holes in his basic master plan that we got to work out before it's perfect. For instance, when I went to his garage and we ran through a trial run, put the microphone in my ear, it let out a squeal that brought the fire department running and made me go around saying "Huh?" for the next week or two, but Slim assures me that's just a minor glitch he can fix. I think that's what he said, anyway. He was explaining that part to me while my hearing was laid up. There's some other parts of this scheme I got questions on, but I think I see where they can be straightened out. I didn't promise him nothing as it is absolutely on the level that I am reformed as to the scheming life; I only said that I'd *think* about it, maybe meet him in a couple of days for a brewsky, toss the idea around some more, work out the bugs, go from there, just see. I didn't promise nothing and I for sure ain't said nothing to Cat. No sense in bringing up something that probably will never take place.

The basic idea is there, looks sound, just needs some fine-tuning on the raggedy parts...

I got a talent for that.

POSTSCRIPT TO THE EPILOGUE

Well, forget the blackjack scam. Did I get a shock today! I was just getting ready to go down to the bar to meet my new friend Slim, and see has he fine-tuned the details of our little scheme, when Cat comes in the house and says, "Come on, Pete. I got something to show you."

She didn't care I had a pressing appointment, said forget it Buster, someone else can hold down your end of the bar for a while, I need you to see something. It's important.

Well, knock me down. We get in her Pinto and drive clear to the other side of the Strip and she pulls over and parks in a Handicapped space in this little strip mall. I do as she says, start to get out, when this lady comes out of a store and looks at us and says, "You people ought to be ashamed. You just parked in a handicapped parking space."

I am red all over and about to say something when she says, "Oh, I'm sorry. You obviously *are* handicapped—you can't *read*," and walks away and into a store.

Cat looks at me and grins and shrugs, and I am about to say something, when she says, "Well, what do you think?"

I am not sure what she is talking about as I am not paying attention to my surroundings, and then she points at the sign in the window of the storefront we are parked in front of.

"The Cajun Emporium. Po-Boy Sandwiches," it says in one window. "Red beans and rice our specialty. More Than Twenty

Kinds of Delicious Po-Boy Sandwiches," in the other, and some other stuff, menu items, specials, what-not.

"What?" I say and not much else.

"It's ours," Cat says, beaming like she just spit up a fur ball. "It's your po-boy restaurant you always wanted. It's almost all finished except the snow-ball machine. Twelve flavors of snow-balls it makes, the guy said. Comes next week. We open soon as it's installed and we learn how to use it. Everything else's all set."

"What?" I say again, floored, my vocabulary down to a one-word dictionary.

"This is what I've been working on, the past month. Getting this place ready. I never really wanted to go to beauty school, you know. I just want to work with you. Food service is what got me off the street, you know. I owe a lot to it. And I like it. I really like it." She was flushed, smiling, obviously happy with herself.

"We open next week. This is our future, Pete. This is what you always wanted and what I want to. We're going to be great, working together. And just think when the kids are big enough we can all work in the restaurant together. I'm going to teach you the food service profession. I'm good at it, you know. Whaddya think? Are you as excited as I think you are?"

Excited wasn't the word for it.

Kids? Did she say *kids?*

I was going to ask her about this kids thing, but she didn't give me a chance. Whipped out a set of keys from her purse and opened the door and in we went.

It was nice. More than nice. It was *beautiful.* Had every-thing. Counter, oven, freezer, reefers, counters along the walls, little tables and chairs with red and white checked table-cloths. A roll of butcher paper on the counter. For wrapping the po-boys, New Orleans-style.

Did she say kids?

Kids?

* * *

"…and you're going to love our menu," she was going on. "Of course, we'll have po-boys, but wait till you hear what else I have planned. Snow cones. Just think how many snow cones we can sell in this God-awful heat! We're going to be rich. There's a few other items I want to discuss with you, too, Pete. Some of the menu items. Breakfast. I have some ideas for the breakfast trade."

Snow cones? I have a feeling things are never going to be the same again and that I have just given up the driver's seat and am now being chauffeured to a place I have never been. I don't think I will be seeing my new friend any more, either, as I will be too busy here the next few weeks.

Arguing with Cat about things just don't seem all that smart. I've seen her with a pistol.

Blackjack never was my game anyway.

I'm more of a euchre man, from my baseball days.

I cheat.

You're *supposed* to cheat at euchre, doncha know? If you expect to win.

I found out I like to win.

Like with Cat.

That's like winning the last and deciding game of the World Series with a grand-slam walk-off home run.

Eat your heart out, Barry Bonds.

HISTORY OF
THE GENUINE, IMITATION, PLASTIC KIDNAPPING

This has long been my favorite of all the books I've written. It began as a short story of the same name that *The South Carolina Review* published years ago. Soon after that, I wrote this novel, based on the short story and then I wrote a screenplay of the same title which was named a finalist in both the Writer's Guild and Best of Austin competitions.

I wrote it because I simply went back to my initial roots as a writer. To those days as a kid when I wrote simply to entertain and get a laugh from readers. Some of the books I've written, while fun to write, were drop-dead serious and Kidnapping was simply a return to the joy of writing and watching the reader's face for signs of a smile or a laugh. And, I was fortunate to gain those kinds of responses with this book.

The germ of the idea for it came when I was in perhaps the dullest period of my life. When I was selling life insurance and trying to become what's called "a solid citizen." Yuck...One of the first things I learned from my boss was a term insurance folks call "the million dollars on the kitchen table." It refers to the mindset that most folks have when they're being sold a policy. The million-dollar policy is just an abstract figure and it's a goal for salesmen to move as many of those as possible. The guy sitting across from them usually doesn't have a clue what a million dollars actually is. It's just a number to them.

When you can convey the image of an actual million dollars sitting on the kitchen table to them rather than just an abstract figure, that's when you make the sale.

Well, I started thinking about that in terms of a kidnapping. What I came up with was that when the 'nappers snatch the wife and ask for a million dollars, it's just a number and the husband is fully prepared to pay it and get wifey back. But... and there's the big BUT I came up with that signaled the birth of this novel—when the guy withdraws the million dollars from his bank and it's sitting on the kitchen table just before it gets stuffed into the suitcase or whatever—it suddenly becomes very real to him. It's no longer an abstract number—it's a MILLION FUCKING DOLLARS! And, that's when he calls the cops and the fibbies in on the deal. Suddenly, he realizes just how much a million bucks really is and while he of course dearly loves his snatched loved one...he also realizes how much he also dearly loves his frickin' million dollars. Maybe even a tech more than he really loves his wife...Ask any FBI agent—I think they'll attest to this happening. Of course, hubby denies this to himself. He'll justify calling in the law because he now thinks that they have the best chance of getting the wife back. In his heart of hearts, he knows that if he just paid the dough he'd get the wife back most likely. Only it's his heart of hearts that he studiously avoids going to during this period.

Does this say something about true love? You bet your bippy it does! It says something about our real natures most of us don't ever want to admit. And, it's this realization that my character Tommy LeClerc realizes. Although he's a smarmy little worm, with little redeeming characteristics, Tommy actually has an insight which many people, lots smarter than he is, can never have. And, his insight is that when the million bucks is exposed on the kitchen table, the guy suddenly places its importance up there with retrieving his wife. But...and this is the Big But that's illuminating—if, instead of a wife he's giving the million up for it happened to be his own hand...his outlook changes. If it's his meathook that's at stake—the hand that picks his nose, whacks off his trouser worm, hits his nine-iron with…he ain't gonna dick around and chance losing that appendage by calling in the fibbies…And that's a fairly profound insight…

So, while this is a comic novel, at the heart of it is a very serious truth.

The other reason I had so much fun writing this is that I got to include a character who was very real in my own life. Cat. Cat was a call girl I lived with for a couple of years in New Orleans and I think her character is accurately portrayed on the page. I used her real name in the novel, btw. Like the woman in the novel, Cat was sold by her mother to Carlos Marcello, the Godfather in New Orleans, when she was nine and she made the same poor career changing move—she made the mistake of turning twelve and which was much too old for his tastes and so he kicked her out and she went down to the French Quarters and was a rare survivor. Her history in Kidnapping is precisely her own real-life history with him and with me. Even though Cat tried to kill me several times—shot at me twice, tried to stab me thrice, tried to run over me in Fat City with her car once, sicced her killer brother on me and some other things—she was the most memorable person I've ever been involved with. I didn't love her, but she sure was exciting to be around. And, although she was never involved in a kidnapping—at least not when I was with her—her book counterpart acted pretty much the way I think she would have under the same circumstances. Except for the kidnapping, everything Pete and Cat went through in the novel I went through with the same Cat in real life, including the scene with her, her black friend Jackie, me and the trick in the hotel gig. Who happened to be a real-life person who's very famous and whose real name I couldn't use, alas.

One other note. When I wrote this, I was co-writing a screenplay with Steve Duncan who happens to be a black guy. I ran the scene in the black bar with Cat pretending to have Tourette's and shouting out racial epithets to see if he thought it was racist.

Not in the least, Steve told me. It's just plain funny stuff.

Anyway, there's some of the background stuff about this novel I thought you might find interesting. I'm working on a sequel to it at the moment and hope to finish it by the end of the year. I find I'm laughing out loud at the scenes I'm writing, so I'm pretty sure folks will like this one as well. Hope so!

Blue skies,
Les

LES EDGERTON is an ex-con, matriculating at Pendleton Reformatory in the sixties for burglary. He was an outlaw for many years and was involved in shootouts, knifings, robberies, high-speed car chases, dealt and used drugs, was a pimp, worked for an escort service, starred in porn movies, was a gambler, served four years in the Navy, and had other misadventures. He's since taken a vow of poverty (became a writer) with twenty-one books in print. Work of his has been nominated for or won the Pushcart Prize, O. Henry Award, Edgar Allan Poe Award, Derringer Award, PEN/Faulkner Award, Jesse Jones Book Award, Spinetingler Magazine Award, among others. He holds a B.A. from I.U. and an MFA in Writing from Vermont College. He lives in Ft. Wayne, Indiana, where he immigrated to some years ago from the U.S. and is currently learning the language and customs there. He writes because he hates…a lot…and hard. Injustice and bullying are what he hates the most.

http://lesedgertononwriting.blogspot.com/

On the following pages are a few
more great titles from the
Down & Out Books publishing family.

For a complete list of books and to
sign up for our newsletter,
go to DownAndOutBooks.com.

Adrenaline Junkie: A Memoir
Les Edgerton

Down & Out Books
978-1-948235-41-9

Adrenaline Junkie is more than a renowned, multi-award-winning author entertaining with his life history. Les Edgerton understands that backstory matters. It influences the present. So he journeyed through his past seeking answers for why he was the way he was. Seeking answers for his thrill-seeking, devil-may-care, often self-destructive, behaviors. Seeking a sense of personal peace.

So settle back. Meet a real-life, twenty-first-century Renaissance man. A real-life adrenaline junkie.

Hipster Death Rattle
Richie Narvaez

Down & Out Books
March 2019
978-1-948235-63-1

Murder is trending. Hipsters are getting slashed to pieces in the hippest neighborhood in New York: Williamsburg, Brooklyn.

While Detectives Petrosino and Hadid hound local gangbangers, slacker reporter Tony Moran and his ex Magaly Fernandez get caught up in a missing person's case—one that might just get them hacked to death.

Guillotine
Paul Heatley

All Due Respects, an imprint of
Down & Out Books
February 2019
978-1-64396-009-8

After suffering a lifetime of tyranny under her father's rule, when Lou-Lou sees a chance to make a break with the man she loves, she takes it. Problem is, daddy's also known as Big Bobby Joe, a dangerous and powerful man in the local area—powerful enough to put out a sixty grand bounty on the head of the man she's run off with, who also happens to be one of his ex-employees.

But Big Bobby Joe hasn't counted on his daughter's resolve to distance herself from him. No matter what he throws at her, no matter what he does, she's going to get away—or die trying.

The Furious Way
Aaron Philip Clark

Shotgun Honey, an imprint of
Down & Out Books
May 2019
978-1-64396-003-6

Lucy Ramos is out for blood—she needs to kill a man, but she has no clue how. Lucy calls on the help of aged hit-man, Tito Garza, now in his golden years, living a mundane life in San Pedro.

With a backpack full of cash, Lucy persuades Garza to help her murder her mother's killer, ADA Victor Soto. Together, the forgotten hit-man hungry for a comeback and the girl whose life was shattered as a child, set out to kill the man responsible. But killing Victor Soto may prove to be an impossible task…

www.ingramcontent.com/pod-product-compliance
Lightning Source LLC
Chambersburg PA
CBHW061522210726
48287CB00006B/1783